THE DAY GUARD
THE METAFRAME WAR:
BOOK 4

Graeme Rodaughan

Published by System Zero Productions Pty Ltd, 2018

Copyright © 2018 Graeme Rodaughan

The moral right of the author has been asserted.

Trade Paperback ISBN-13: 978-0-9945952-8-7

EPUB Edition ISBN-13: 978-0-6487843-1-9

Cover art by Huw Jones

For Linda, for her unfailing love and support that always leaves me in awe.

I would like to thank a number of people who have assisted with my progress as an author, including Alex, Tim, Lisa, Lena, Marie, Eldon, Michael, Christopher, Perry, Nick, Andrew, Laura, Daniel, Ginger, Jody, and the regular crew of Beta and ARC readers at the Castle Dracula group and my many friends and followers on Goodreads. You have all contributed more than you know to my craft and your support and encouragement are invaluable for this journey.

Books by Graeme Rodaughan

The Metaframe War Series

A Subtle Agency
A Traitor's War
The Dragon's Den
The Day Guard
The Crane War
The Key of Ahknaton

Omnibus Volumes

A Subtle Agency Omnibus (includes A Subtle Agency, A Traitor's
War, and The Dragon's Den)

Forthcoming Books in the Metaframe War series

The Metaframe Adept

Dramatis Personae

The Ancients

Ahknaton, Ruler of the Southern Realm, High Priest of the Temple of Thoth. Master Architect. Ramp Master.
Hakron, Second prince of the Southern Realm. Master Scribe. Ramp Master. Ahknaton's brother
Mekra, Princess, Ahknaton's wife.

The Vampire Dominion

Cornelius Crane, King of the Vampire Dominion
Chloe Armitage, General, The Americas, ex Order of Thoth and Crane's chief enforcer
Haras Mosule, General, Middle East, ex Red Empire warrior of the 3rd rank
Dieter Franz, General, Western Europe
Clayton Maze, General, Africa
Shen Zhen, General, East Asia

The Order of Thoth

Calvin Woodstock, Interim Head of the Order of Thoth
Bill Shortman, Force Leader, (North West)
Andrew Frick, Force Leader, (South East)
Hayden Brown, Force Leader, Canada
Campbell West, Operative, Shortman force team

The Exiles

Arthur Slayne, (Exiled) Master Strategist, Force Leader, Weapons Grandmaster, Speed Talent.

The Mirovar Force Team

Francis Mirovar, Force Leader, Weapons Master
Jay Creeley, Operative, Weapons Master
Peter Lamb, Operative, Armorer, Strength Talent
Chiara Romano, Operative, Combat Surgeon
Anton Slayne, Order novice
Li Wu, Order novice, Weapons Master

The Independents

Jonathan (Jon) Thunder-Axe, Force Leader (Rank), Metaframe Sorcerer
Prospector, Force Leader (Rank), Alaska
Smith (Smitty), Force Leader, Australia
Mercy Kumar, Operative, Australia
Anita Chang, Operative, Australia

The Blake Force Team

Justin Blake, Force Leader (South West) Weapons Master, Strength talent.
Former student of Gang Wu
Samuel (Coleridge) Taylor, Operative, Weapons Master
Taylor Feury, Operative, Weapons Master

The Red Empire

Shabbah al Ahmar, aka 'The Red Ghost,' aka Dalien Morte. Head of the
Red Empire
Al Ghurab, aka 'The Raven,' Operative inserted into the Order of Thoth
Thueban Kabir, aka 'The Great Serpent,' aka 'Taipan,' Weapons
Grandmaster, warrior of the 3rd rank
Tamsah al Ramil, aka 'The Sand Crocodile,' Fist team leader, warrior of the
2nd rank
Whispering Death, Operative, Speed talent
Steel-Axe, unnamed Operative

Shadowstone

James Haley, Chloe Armitage's aide de comp
Louise Wesson, Head of Operations, United States
Michael Michaelson, Squad Leader (Mike squad), Day Guard

Other Players

Supreme Claw, Head of the Obsidian Claw Ninja Clan
Akimitsu, an elite member of the Obsidian Claw

Kashshak, Chameleon
Gullette, Chameleon, Call of Command

Prologue

North Africa, The Great Forest, approx. 87,000 years ago.

Burnt ocher clouds obscured the sun, shrouding the land in perpetual gloom.

The great forest was sick; great billowing clouds of red-gray ash from the west had wrapped a dusty cloak over it for the last two years. Something had broken across the ocean. The world was still reeling from the wound, every night, a never-ending fire lit the western horizon.

The food animals had died in droves, their dead flesh tainted beyond the possibility of eating. The People had erupted into war – all against all – each attempting to secure the remaining prey for themselves. Into the maelstrom of violence, the People's reproductive cycle had begun, complicating the desire for territory with the desire to mate.

Kashshak carried the consequences of mating within her left hand, a recently laid leathery egg the size of a coconut. She held it close to the armored hide over her chest, the long talons of her left hand extended as if for the killing strike to form an impenetrable cage protecting the egg. Offspring were rare and precious, centuries would pass before the next breeding cycle, and this child was her fourth. The others had grown to maturity and sought territory, contending with others of the People for survival, their fates unknown.

She had killed the father of her child once the mating urge had been satisfied. He was an intruder on her territory, and with prey few and far between, she could not afford to tolerate his presence.

She moved forward, never pausing, there was a cave and an underground river ahead. A place of sanctuary and strength from which she could destroy her pursuers and save her child.

For millions of years, the People had known no equal, passing their oral traditions down from mother to child, but with the breaking of the world some prey animals had changed, suddenly becoming faster, stronger, smarter. Food animals now contested with the People, and some of the prey had killed some of the People.

It was horrific – the world had gone mad – the natural order had turned upside down.

They were perhaps a mile behind her, their soft footfalls on the ashen ground, puff, puff, puff, just within range of her hearing. There were fourteen in the hunting band, all changed, moving with a speed and endurance far above normal for the prey. Against any one of them, it would be no contest, she could win easily against their sticks, sharpened stones, and soft skin, but the prey did something the solitary People never did – they hunted in packs.

Kashshak reached the entrance to the cave and ducked inside. She retracted the talons on her toes, leaving her padded feet to move in near silence over the stones. She backed up to the wall and merged with the dark shadows upon it, her skin tingling with the change, shifting color to match the dark-grays of the rock wall behind her.

She stroked the egg, and it changed too, merging with the color of the cave wall.

The pursuers had closed to within four hundred yards, the leader was slowing down as if he suspected something.

He was within range of her *call*.

Kashshak started singing, a soft melodic murmuring, a haunting sound calling to the male leading the pack of prey. Normally, the People would only use the call to bring a food animal to them. The animal would find their way to the caller, dumbfounded, their eyes glassy and staring, often they would drool – and then they would die. This time she called to send the leader past the cave mouth and into the deeps of the wounded forest beyond. The pack with him would surely follow, and she could escape with her precious egg deeper into the cave system without risk of pursuit.

She waited for the call to take effect, for her mind to connect with his like a snare closing around his throat. She only needed to tug on the connection to send him wherever she wanted him to go. The moment stretched, the sense of entrapment never came – he was resisting – he was coming, and his pack was with him.

Kashshak broke cover, blurring deeper into the cave. She would escape to the underground river. The People were excellent swimmers and could hold their breath for a long time. The hunters were only seconds behind her, carrying fire to light their way, beating the walls with sticks. She kept her skin in match to her surroundings, constantly tingling and all but invisible to her pursuers.

The sticks clicked and clacked against the rock walls behind her, leaving her no space in which to hide. How did they know to do that? It was an obvious tactic to defeat her ability to merge her skin color with her surroundings. This pack knew too much, they were a threat to her egg. A cold fury flared within her. She would have to destroy them all, it was the only way to be certain her egg would survive. She would not hunt them as if they were prey, she reserved her fury for competitors, for intruders upon her territory. She would unleash her fury upon them as if they were People.

The cave opened up into a cavern lit by phosphorescent fungi growing across the ceiling, a softly flowing river disappeared into the far darkness. Kashshak threw her egg into the gloom, a faint splash returning from the darkness beyond the limits of her sight. The egg would float, and she would retrieve it once she'd won the fight, in the meantime, the shadows would hide it and both her hands would be free.

Kashshak grinned without mirth. Serrated triangular teeth gleaming wetly in the blood-pink phosphorescence filled her mouth. They were perfect for shearing slabs of flesh from her prey. She salivated at the thought of feasting, wet drops spilling past her teeth and splatting on the stone at her feet.

She crouched low, balancing with her tail, and leaped thirty feet directly upwards. She retracted her claws as she rose, the surfaces of her hands and feet flattening into soft pads. She landed flat against the ceiling, her hands and feet splaying to maximize her gripping power. She moved gracefully, covering the distance to a point forty-five feet above the ground, a half dozen yards in front of the cave mouth.

She shifted bones and muscles, flattening herself against the cavern's ceiling, her skin tingling with the coloration changes to blend perfectly with the background stone.

Firelight spilled from the cave mouth into the cavern, a restless golden glow bursting into the open space. Secondary membranes closed over her eyes, protecting them from the sudden light while rendering the prey animals below her with perfect clarity.

They had tamed fire, carrying it on top of thick sticks – madness!

The leader was directly beneath her. He was big for a prey animal, filled with blood and flesh, but he smelled wrong – it was the change. He was different, they were all different, heat blooming in scarlet plumes from their bodies. They smelled wrong and looked wrong, running hotter than normal, they would all have to die, they weren't prey – they were foes.

An ice-cold fury swelled within her. Her bones and muscles reverted to their normal shapes. The serrated spines along the outside of her arms and along her spine flared in an ancient response to threat. Kashshak let go of the ceiling, her hands and feet changing as she fell, short, broad talons emerging from her toes, long slim ones from her fingers, all razor sharp and hard enough to cut stone.

She landed on top of the leader, crushing him to the ground. Her left hand scooped his head from his shoulders before her weight crushed the air from his lungs, shooting ribbons of bloody flesh out of the hole where his neck had been.

Kashshak blurred hard to the right, a rippling shadow of grays and shiny blacks in the flickering firelight. The prey lunged, dodged, and shouted, moving around her faster than she had ever seen an animal move. Her attack had surprised them, but they reacted quickly. She rushed the nearest two, her hands blurring left and right, knocking their flint-tipped sticks aside. Passing between them, her hands blurred back, long talons like obsidian shears gutting them in sprays of blood. They fell away behind her, the rich, rank smells of blood and fecal matter filling the air.

The eleven animals left continued to circle her. Two rushed in from behind, her right foot lashed out, crushing the chest of one. He flew backward through the air, striking the wall of the cavern with a satisfying crunch.

The other's flint weapon speared into the back of her left thigh.

She screamed in rage, whirling to the right, the weapon's shaft snapping with a crack. The serrated edge of her left arm passed beneath her attacker's head with a wet slap. His head flew off, blood jetting into the air as the headless body slumped to the sandy shore of the underground river.

The animals called and shouted at each other, coordinating as a team. They were stronger together than they were apart. Their collective power was not lost on Kashshak. They had drawn her blood; this was a fight for life or death. She snarled, her jaw gaping down, her teeth gleaming redly in the phosphorescence and wavering firelight.

Kashshak blurred forward, sand spraying as she kicked away. The ring of nine animals around her moved with her, shouting at each other in their strange language. Her left leg dragged, slowing her down, the flint had cut an important tendon. She rested back on it, and it held, it would still bear her weight.

She sang again, the closer the prey, the stronger the effect of her call. Her melody rang out in haunting notes, rising like an ethereal symphony within the cavern, silencing the animals.

The pack hesitated, some dropped their weapons and flaming sticks to put their hands to their ears, but still, there was no sense of entrapment. She launched herself left, pivoting on her damaged leg, pushing with her right. They were too strong together, she needed to break the circle and regroup, continuing the fight on her own terms, picking them off in ones and twos.

She hit the nearest animal, his spear glancing off her hard chest plate, and ran over him. His blood-soaked entrails looped over her toes, his main bones shattering beneath her stamping feet, his brain splashing in red gobbets onto the sandy ground.

She was through the ring.

A flint tip lanced into her right thigh, tearing through another main ligament. Kashshak screeched in agony, twisting as she fell, landing on her back in a spray of sand.

The first of the animals approached too close for his own good. She smashed her left hand into his chest, her long talons erupting in a row of points out of his back, sending red ribbons of blood over the others circling behind him. She clenched her fist, anchoring his chest, and flicked her wrist. Sending his body across her own to crash into two other animals with a bone shattering crunch – dropping them all to a heap on the sand.

She had a chance to break free of the enclosing ring.

Kashshak pushed back hard with her elbows, her feet and tail lashing for purchase in the sand, she became a dark-gray shadow rising off the subterranean beach.

Three razor-sharp, flint-tipped sticks speared in from different angles, sliding behind her armored chest plate, and piercing her heart.

The pain was excruciating, it was a killing wound. She shrieked in pure rage. They had ended her. She just had the process of dying to complete, and for one of the People – that could take time.

The five animals left held their fires high, cautiously prodding her with their sharpened sticks as she struggled on the sand, growing weaker and weaker.

She croaked and barked in the language of the People, "Death beckons, beset by demons, Kashshak dies!"

She twisted her neck to look out over the underground river. The gloomy shadows advanced toward her, her egg floating somewhere beyond them. Her young remained safe; when hatched, it could and would eat anything. It was only later when it became an adult its diet would fixate on the food animals. Perhaps by then, the world would heal, and the prey would be plentiful again. The shadows crowded in, rolling like dark fog over the mirror-like surface of the river.

My egg floats, darkness claims my song, all alone.

Sensing she was powerless to resist, the food animals struck repeatedly, the flint tips of their long sticks puncturing her deepest flesh, emerging soaked with her dark blood.

Kashshak issued a final plaintive coughing cry. Her breathing slowed, then stopped, endless night washing her life away.

Chapter One

Is the world spiraling into Chaos?

By George Harfinne | Senior Mercury Correspondent AUGUST 23,

We wake up this Wednesday morning to discover an England in flames.

Elite military units of the United Kingdom have been decimated. The RAF airbase at Coningsby all but destroyed. The Yorkshire hamlet of Ogton wiped out by a massive gas explosion. A manor house near Whitby swallowed by the North Sea; torn from its foundations by massive explosions that were heard as far south as Scarborough.

A sober, rational analysis of events will have to wait upon the delivery of full and frank evidence, but surely there will be a far-reaching inquiry into …

— A snippet from a Boston Mercury Newspaper article on the Internet.

ALIENS HAVE LANDED!

August 23 | Permalink | Comments: 123

By **Chief Tinfoiler**

Categories: Secret Government, Aliens, Extra-terrestrials, Signs

Tinfoilers — Aliens have landed in the old dart. The lords and ladies of Westminster will be tucking into their crumpets and tea — just before they're subjected to mass alien probing of every orifice that God gave them.

First Maine, now England, who will be next — well you can bet that we're on their list. The aliens will be swarming all over the good ole U S of A before anything is done by our heads-in-the-sand government.

You know, because I've said it often enough — the aliens can pass for human. Now everyone has to prepare, and this is what you must do …

— Blog post snippet on the Internet

Shadowstone directive #479 August 14th 20[REDACTED]

Incorporating and materially superseding previous directives (#478, #474, #471, and #432)

I hereby direct the commissioning of the second primary Panopticon site on the east coast of the United States (the East Coast Hub (ECH), ref #474, #478). The Technical Directorate of Shadowstone US (SUS-TD), will take responsibility for site security and operation during final commissioning and replication of the artificial intelligence entity from the original site in UTAH (ref #432). The operation of the second Panopticon (2.0) will fall under general Clayton Maze, and the head of Shadowstone US, Louise Wesson.

[REDACTED]

– Partially declassified Shadowstone directive from Cornelius Crane.

* * *

Carpathian Mountains, Central Romania, August 23rd, 05:31

The sun was a pale threat beyond the eastern horizon. The air was pre-dawn cold, misting off the hot carapace of a hypersonic drone squatting like an alien insect in a forest clearing.

Cornelius Crane leaped from the cockpit, wearing his matte-black praetorian combat fatigues and carrying a thick, six-foot long, hexagonal steel bar. Time was short, the sun would soon rise, and he would need to be safely back in his drone before its deadly rays flooded the forest. He lifted his head, his nostrils flaring, his ears twitching, but there were only the wild processes of the natural kingdom. He strode forward, reaching a familiar stone pathway at the edge of the clearing. It rose up along the deeply forested side of the mountain. He set forth upon it, gliding through the deep shadows beneath the ancient trees, his senses alert, but his mind was elsewhere.

He'd done everything he could to assassinate the memory of Mekra, and the cult of her devotion amongst the vampires. He'd propagated the lie of her death for centuries; long enough to almost come to believe it himself. The truth lay elsewhere, in a hidden donjon built into this mountain. A secret prison with a prize beyond measure – Mekra still lived – and no one else knew the truth.

Assassination? He'd imprisoned her in silver for centuries. The white metal slowing her metabolism down to a level of dormancy on the edge of death. He'd turned her from vampire queen into his personal fountainhead of the original vampire blood. Blood untainted by dilution, blood rich with power. A power that belonged to Cornelius and to Cornelius alone.

Mekra was his most closely guarded secret.

The path snaked through the forest, rising up the mountain's side, Cornelius strode along it, reflecting upon the last few hours. He'd refueled his personal drone in New York, feasted upon blood in the feeding halls of his citadel, forcing himself to drink as much as he could carry within himself – he expected he would need it. He'd entered a previsionary state after he'd taken off. His precognitive power provided him with the ability to identify deadly threats and destroy them before they became too dangerous. He needed to understand as much as possible before adapting his strategy. Events were progressing, the probable outcomes becoming clearer as they came closer to manifesting in reality.

One threat had emerged to the fore, clear of all the others. The threat had a name – Anton Smith – but there was a dark shadow over that name, it was clearly fake. Photographs of the young man bore too strong a resemblance to a young Arthur Slayne to be an accident. They had to be related, either son or grandson, and his appearance at the Boston docks, so soon after the death of William and Anna Slayne was too much of a coincidence for him to believe.

Cornelius mentally struck a line through the name 'Smith.' The growing threat on his life was from Anton Slayne, who was almost certainly the son of Anna and William Slayne. The key remaining questions were why had Chloe Armitage, and Ramin Kain agreed that Anna and William Slayne were childless, and why did the records of the Panopticon confirm that fiction?

Had they been honestly mistaken, or had they colluded to present a shared lie? Both options beggared the realm of possibility. They were too competent, especially Armitage to make such a mistake, and too opposed to collaborate on such a scheme.

No. They'd deceived him for their own separate purposes.

Ramin Kain was beyond questioning, his body lost within a small mountain of rubble half-submerged in the North Sea, which left Armitage as the last remaining conspirator.

As for the Panopticon, he could no longer trust it. His enemies had somehow compromised the machine, possibly since its inception. His most recent Shadowstone directive would accelerate its replacement by the next iteration of AI-based surveillance technology.

With two Panopticon systems in operation, he would be able to compare their results, and where they differed, he'd discover his enemies' deceptions.

Cornelius' secure world had vanished into a world of growing chaos. After the events in Boston, he'd acknowledged his complacency, now he faced conspiracy. It was time to leave the comforts of his library, to step up to the front line, and confront his enemies with the flames of war and the cold steel of his blade.

The events of the last forty-eight hours were a mixture of catastrophe and triumph. Evenly balanced, such that the only winner was chaos and the loser was his own position of power. He'd received Gordon Heathmont's full report. The Order of Thoth had nearly destroyed Shadowstone in the UK. Armitage had added a brief, encrypted video report sent from her supersonic jet as she arrived in New York airspace. She'd detailed the destruction of the UK Order of Thoth force team, and the mauling of the Mirovar force team, including the loss of two loremasters. She'd also reported the death of Ramin Kain. His secret alliance with the Order used to stabilize the United States while he readied the Day Guard, was now over.

Cornelius shook his head, this was no accident or coincidence of events, the last two days were not the offspring of bad luck. There must be a flaw in the operation of Allemande's curse, or his prevision, or both, that had blinded him to the true source of the threat to his dominion.

Jean Philippe Allemande hadn't told him everything about the operation of the binding curse and his gift of previsionary power. He'd obviously left something important out. The two powers, both born from the Metaframe, probably canceled each other out. The effectiveness of each power when operating alone had blinded him to what might happen whenever he used his prevision on one of his cursed generals. They had always appeared loyal within his visions, his precognitive power helpless to reveal any action by his cursed generals against his interests.

A blind spot that had come close to killing him.

A cold fury quickened his stride. His knuckles chalk-white on the steel bar in his hands. His mouth set in a hard grim line. His world was spinning out of control. Mastering the information of warfare had been his greatest strength, but his protege, Armitage, had turned it against him. He seethed with icy rage; the cold steel of the bar moaned within his grip. He relaxed his fingers, revealing his fingerprints in the metal. Once he moved against her, he would show no mercy – her fate would become legendary within the history of the Vampire Dominion. However, the most advantageous path lay in using her skills for the most dangerous missions, while he hid his awareness of her betrayal.

Keep your friends close, and your enemies closer. Armitage's nights stood numbered, but first, he would use her up, while he prepared an inescapable trap to bind her to him forever – and if that failed – then only her death awaited his most prized asset. For no matter how valuable a pet may be, if it strove to kill you, then it must die.

He arrived at a landing where the path widened to a dozen feet and faced a sheer rock wall stretching twenty yards upward before it curved away into the forest. Boulders ranging in size from a small car to a ripe watermelon rested in a pile against the base of the rock wall. Cornelius set to work with a will, the stones moved, the iron bar striking bright sparks in the pre-dawn shadows as he dug between the rocks. With the assistance of this lever and the vast resources of his strength, speed, and endurance, he cleared the cover of stones in a handful of minutes.

A twelve-foot-high, flat-faced circular boulder remained. A neat hexagonal hole, the diameter of the steel bar sitting six feet off the ground in the center of the stone monolith. Cornelius rammed the bar into the hole with a crack that echoed across the valley. A hidden lever slammed into position behind the great boulder. Counterweights grumbled and groaned within the rock face. The circular boulder rotated a quarter turn to the right, revealing a nine-feet deep crescent-shaped opening large enough for a tall man to step through.

Cornelius moved smoothly through the opening into the pitch dark beyond. A bare sliver of gray illumination from the outside world cut through the thick darkness in the antechamber, spearing forward across the flagstone floor from the entrance. He moved quickly to his right, pulling down a black-iron lever in the wall, stopping the great stone ejecting the steel bar and rolling back into place. A trap for anyone unwary enough to enter through the doorway without knowledge. No one could open the stone door from the inside without the hexagonal steel bar and the door was the sole entrance to the donjon.

In the antechamber was a single piece of furniture, a wooden table, black with the centuries and parched with age. An ancient ships lantern rested on its top. Cornelius picked it up, oil swishing to and fro within its base, and lit it with a single swift application of a modern gas lighter. He lifted the lantern high, the shadows fleeing to the corners of the room. Opposite the main entrance was a wide descending hallway, Cornelius strode down it, his booted feet making soft footfalls upon the flagstones, the darkness flowing like water behind him until the antechamber returned to a gloomy silence fit for a grave.

Deep inside the mountain, the hallway opened up into a second chamber – the donjon itself. On the back wall leaned a great rectangular box enclosed within a black-iron frame. The sarcophagus of Mekra; it was nine feet long, four feet wide and three feet deep, composed of solid silver, gleaming in the lamplight.

Cornelius sighed, the sharp tang of the shining metal filling the chamber with a repulsive reek. His senses screamed 'flee,' but he ignored their warning, advancing on the sarcophagus. A metal web of pulleys, levers, and chains descended from the dark shadows above the iron frame.

He pulled down upon a lever, a set of locks opened with loud clanks of ancient machinery. He pulled down on a second lever setting in motion a set of counterweights, whirring pulleys and creaking chains. The lid of the sarcophagus separated from the rest of the casket, ascending into the shadows above. He lifted the third lever, and the iron frame began to rise and tilt forward, lifting the sarcophagus into a vertical position.

Cornelius moved forward, Mekra stood revealed within her silver prison, her bare ebony skin laced in fine chains of gleaming metal. He pulled a pair of thick gauntlets from hooks on the black-iron frame and fitted them over his hands. Protected; he lifted the silver net away from Mekra, hanging it on the iron frame surrounding the sarcophagus.

He turned back to her, standing three feet in front of her motionless form and waited, the lantern resting on the iron frame near his left shoulder casting a buttery glow over the chamber.

Her dark skin glimmered beneath the soft lantern light. She rested in silent, immaculate beauty. Her skin was flawless, her body sleek and vital, her long dark hair hanging thick and lustrous down to the small of her back. She took a breath and then another. She moved slightly, her hips swaying, thick steel chains forged in Damascus rattling against the silver walls of her prison, heavy manacles around her ankles, wrists, and throat, flat and dull in the soft light, binding her within the confines of the sarcophagus. Her eyelids flickered open, her eyes charcoal pits consuming the lantern light, giving nothing back. She stared at Cornelius, an innocent beauty blooming within her face, her full lips curving into a smile of delight.

He had to hold himself back from sighing with deep regret.

A sly awareness shadowed her gaze, stealing the innocence and joy away. Her voice whispered, soft and dreamlike, "How long has it been my lover … my betrayer … my usurper."

"Four hundred and eighty-seven nights," he answered almost haphazardly, pushing the sleeve on his right arm to above the elbow.

Her gaze fell on his bare arm, her ripe breasts lifted with a sharp intake of breath. Her hunger had arrived.

"You have kept me here too long, I feed on nothing but your blood – I am changing," her lips pulled back, her canines descending, ivory scimitars curving down toward her chin, gleaming wetly in the lamplight, "into something else."

Cornelius' arm dropped. His eyes widened with surprise. This was new – Mekra's fangs had changed since his last visit, becoming longer and slimmer than any he'd seen. He peered into her eyes. They had always been dark, but now all trace of humanity had disappeared beneath a uniform patina the color of midnight.

"Your eyes betray you," Mekra observed, her voice cold and penetrating. "I have become repulsive. I am monstrous in your sight."

He glowered suspiciously at her for a long moment, a troubled frown creasing his forehead. *What has she become?*

"What do you expect after centuries of imprisonment?" she snapped with sudden anger. "Something pleasing to your ideals?"

Cornelius muttered, "I expect only that you'll feed – as you have always done," and thrust his bare forearm in front of her face. His veins were ripe with fresh blood, he'd fed to more than his fill at the citadel.

Mekra's eyes widened with bloodlust. She hesitated for a moment, a sinister glower overtaking her hunger, and promised, "There will come a day when you will wish our positions reversed, my forsaken lover. The world is changing … I can feel it."

What does she know? Cornelius thought furiously.

Mekra lunged forward to the limit of her chains, her fangs sinking into his arm, his veins bulged as blood surged along them to her voracious mouth. Her tongue lanced into his flesh, its tip sharp as a barb spearing his bones, anchoring her mouth around the gaping wound her elongated fangs had made.

A dreadful warning screamed at the back of his mind. The veins in his arm bulged and darkened. The excess blood he'd consumed scant hours earlier flooded through the tear in his arm. His own reserves began disappearing down her throat. In moments, he would lose consciousness, and in seconds she would drain him dry. Cornelius pushed hard against her, his left-hand blurring against her forehead. It was like striking stone, her head barely moved backward.

Mekra growled deep in her chest, a ravenous, demonic sound.

Agony ripped in waves along his arm. In a single desperate movement, he threw himself backward, his arm coming free, a loud crack of snapping bones resounding through the chamber.

Mekra's mouth yawned unnaturally wide, her long dark tongue awash with gore retreating into her bloodied maw before it closed.

A terrible lacerated wound gaped in Cornelius' forearm, blood splashing to the floor. With his left hand he stripped off his belt and made a tourniquet – he could ill afford to lose more blood. Weakened by the attack, he staggered back and slumped against the wall opposite Mekra.

Mekra laughed once, a dreadful clashing sound like broken bells. She regarded him with half-lidded eyes, a knowing smile on her bloodstained lips.

He gulped air, two, three, five breaths, his hands trembling with shock. He rose and staggered over to the sarcophagus, knelt down before her, grabbed her hips and savagely bit into her left thigh.

She writhed above him in agony, cursing his name, her words retreating back to the ancient Egyptian of her youth. The Damascan steel of her chains and manacles groaned and screeched, but stood firm before her strength.

He drank hungrily, her blood pouring down his throat. He counted seconds, one, two, three, he wanted to go on drinking until she was dry. She was the original source; the experience of feeding upon her was as close to divinity as Cornelius could reach.

Five seconds; he ripped his mouth away and stepped back. The wound in Mekra's thigh vanished in seconds even though she was resting against silver.

Her powers were accelerating – where would they end?

Cornelius opened a wide pocket over his left thigh and extracted a transparent flask with a short, thick needle attached to the top. He plunged the needle between Mekra's ribs, filling the flask with her heart's blood. Pulling the flask away, he closed it with a twist of a short lever. Mekra's wound healed in seconds, leaving her skin once again a marvel of flawless perfection.

He shook his head, he couldn't heal that fast, although his right arm was returning to full strength with the genius of Mekra's blood flowing through his veins.

He donned the protective gauntlets and restored the silver net.

Her eyes remained open, watching him avidly. "Do it," she whispered harshly. "Encase me in perpetual darkness. I can wait. I'm good at waiting, but do not make me wait too long."

"Why?" he spat.

Mekra smiled, her long fangs descending over her bottom lip again. "My hunger … it grows and grows … one day I must be released."

"Never!" he vowed.

She stared at him, purring with absolute conviction, "My time will come. You can imprison my body, but beware my old lover, my mind has grown wings."

Without hesitation, Cornelius pulled and pushed on the levers above his head. The ancient machinery cranked and whirred. Moments later, the sarcophagus lay on a diagonal against the back wall as if he'd never disturbed it.

Mekra's transformation left his heart hammering, for centuries she'd been the same from visit to visit – now it was all different. What had happened? Had she passed some critical threshold triggering this horrific metamorphosis? As dangerous as she'd become, he still needed access to her blood, to her power, but in future he would do it differently. He would bring her a warm body, someone to feast on, while he waited at a safe distance.

Could he safely drink from her? Would he become the same as her? He hadn't noticed any change within himself. He felt his jaw, probing his teeth with his fingers – they remained unchanged.

He sighed with relief and restored his composure. Her blood was essential for maintaining himself at the peak of his powers, giving him an edge over all other vampires, except Armitage, who was born from the same blood source. He patted his thigh pocket where the flask of Mekra's blood remained hidden, an essential ingredient in the next step in his new and decisive strategy – a strategy that must succeed.

Mekra had become immune to silver, the gods only knew what else may have happened to her. Heaven forbid she was ever set free – she may well be too powerful to capture again – let alone destroy.

Cornelius fled the donjon, only pausing long enough to seal the great doorway and restore the concealing stones at the base of the rock wall. With the steel bar in hand, he blurred along the path back to the glade, and his hypersonic drone.

Sunlight tore through the treetops as he took off, reflecting off the gleaming surface of his craft. The ascent to cruising altitude was uneventful, except for images invading his thoughts of Mekra. Images of her triumphantly free, and unleashing a plague of unstoppable uber-vampires upon the world.

Cornelius set course for Tokyo. His world was beset by dangerous women, and he vowed to take steps to secure his rule.

Else, they'd kill him.

* * *

Harsh overhead lights eliminated the shadows in a large underground chamber within the Red Empire citadel.

A dozen men stood at ease around a great marble table, dressed in simple gray robes with blood-red waist sashes, the aroma of excellent espresso coffee dominating the air – it was still too early for breakfast.

Taipan stood opposite his master, the only man who ranked higher than himself within the Red Empire – Shabbah al Ahmar, the Red Ghost. Flanking the two men were another dozen senior fist leaders, the inner core of the Red Empire leadership cadre.

A twenty-foot-wide circular polished stone disc, resting four feet off the floor on top of a dozen stout stone pillars served as a high-council table. In its center stood six large backpacks, the prize cargo of a Russian special forces submarine captured beneath the Arctic ice by a Red Empire fist team two months earlier. Each backpack disguised a special atomic demolition munition weighing a hundred and fifty pounds each, with an explosive yield of twenty kilotons, similar in capacity to the weapon used to destroy

Hiroshima. When triggered, nuclear fire would obliterate everything within two miles of each device.

"Thueban Kabir, attend to my words," the Red Ghost ordered calmly.

"Yes, Sir?" Taipan replied.

"The time has come to execute a great strike against our enemy," the Red Ghost said, his voice rising in volume with growing animation. "The mission to acquire these weapons from the hapless Russians has given us the means to act upon the intelligence provided by the traitorous vampire general, Chloe Armitage."

The Red Ghost smiled triumphantly, pausing to glance around the assembled men.

Taipan waited for him to continue; one didn't lightly interrupt the Red Ghost.

"Thueban Kabir," the Red Ghost declared, his gaze focused on Taipan. "You will assemble a hand-picked force from our fist teams. This mission is our highest priority, and none here will brook the sacrifice of their best team members to it."

The assembled fist leaders nodded their assent.

"You will select twelve men, including three team leaders of the second rank. All will be initiates of the test of the Olgoi Khorkhoi."

Taipan nodded, the Red Ghost, his best student the Raven, and himself were the only initiates of the third level within the Red Empire. They'd navigated the secret maze of the Olgoi Khorkhoi, and survived the presence of three ravenous adult worms within it. He already knew who the premier warriors within the Red Empire fist teams were, he would take them all, his team would be the most powerful concentration of combat experienced talent ever assembled by the Red Empire.

The Red Ghost pulled a black data stick from a fold within his robe, and with a flick of his wrist, tossed it over the table.

Taipan caught it without comment, placing it within a pouch at his belt. He'd personally led the scout team of four operatives who'd verified the location of Crane's citadel in New York. That part of Armitage's information had been correct, but she may have lied about the location of the famous artifacts. They would only find out the truth of her words once they penetrated Crane's personal quarters and accessed his secret chamber of Metaframe lore.

"All the details of your mission are on the stick," the Red Ghost instructed. "Bring me Crane's head and the Metaframe artifacts. Use the nuclear weapons to erase the citadel and the mark of the vampire from that accursed island."

"Yes, Red Ghost," Taipan vowed. "Your will be done."

The Red Ghost planted his hands on the marble tabletop and leaned forward, his dark eyes focused hard on Taipan. "One last thing, your entire mission will occur in silence, no one will speak of it, no one will communicate with you. Your mission is a spear thrown at the heart of our enemy; it must succeed."

"Yes, Red Ghost, communications silence will be enforced."

"See that it is," the Red Ghost directed his best operative, stepping away from the table and departing the room.

The room cleared, Taipan remained with the weapons, his mind alive with plans. He would annihilate Manhattan Island. New York would cease to exist as a functioning city, and if the wind were blowing in the wrong direction, much of New England would become an uninhabitable wasteland. It was a price the Red Empire was willing to pay to acquire the Metaframe artifacts, kill Cornelius Crane, slaughter his praetorians, and destroy the heart of the Vampire Dominion.

He tapped the marble table top with the index finger of his right hand. Once, then twice, then thrice, it was a habit he only displayed when alone, when something was troubling him. Armitage knew the Red Empire had this information. She would expect them to attempt a mission on Crane's citadel.

Is Armitage drawing us into a trap, or are we her willing cat's paw — expected to do her dirty work, while she swoops in to retrieve the artifacts at the last moment?

Taipan turned from the table, despite his misgivings, it was time to assemble his team.

* * *

All bar one of the hi-def screens lining the walls of the ultra-secure war room of Crane's citadel were alive with Panopticon feeds. The main screen displayed a single image, a blue crane over a silver field, the personal shield of Baron de Grue, aka Cornelius Crane.

Chloe Armitage sat at the end of the long boardroom table, opposite the main screen. She'd taken the opportunity on the flight over from the United Kingdom to change her clothes, and now wore a bespoke black pants suit, a crimson shirt, slim red belt with a fine gold buckle, and matching red shoes. She rested her chin on her left hand, her elbow on the table, quietly staring at the main screen.

Crane's standard will have to go ... replaced by a red dragon rampant, facing sinister on a sable field ... yes, that will do perfectly.

Her mind was drifting, she'd been running hard for several days, and while her reserves of vampire-based endurance were far above those of a human, even vampires needed to rest. She lifted her head off her hand, leaned back in the chair, unconsciously gripping her right forearm and rubbing it.

Beneath Chloe's sleeve was a white scar, twinned on the other side of her forearm where Juliette Mirovar's silver dagger had erupted from her flesh. Normally vampires healed seamlessly without scars of any sort, except when injured by silver. The scar would fade with time, but she would be wearing long sleeves for months. Losing a knife fight to a loremaster was not a story she cared to relate to anyone.

Juliette Mirovar's attack was the second time this year she'd caressed Death's scythe. Was she doing something wrong? Was there a flaw in her strategy or tactical approach? Chloe leaned back in the chair, her fingers steepling over her nose, her index fingers pressing into the point directly between her eyes.

Risk was unavoidable, the best she could hope for was to minimize it. Keep the pressure on Crane, keep moving forward with her plans, be always ready to adapt to changing circumstances. If anything, she needed to accelerate events as much as possible, to close the window of opportunity for failure and ensure success.

And yet I must be patient, and careful, ever so careful not to snatch defeat from the jaws of victory.

The time was coming when Anton Slayne would be ready to meet Cornelius Crane and put an end to her imprisonment by Allemande's curse.

The main screen flicked to a new view with a ping. Crane sat in the cockpit of his personal hypersonic drone, a closeup of his face framed by the dark-gray headrest of his seat. His voice came through the speakers in the war room with perfect clarity and natural volume, as if he was in the room.

Crane's gaze flicked over her, and he remarked with measured sarcasm, "I see you're looking very relaxed after your 'adventures,' in England … some of us are still working."

Chloe digested the veiled rebuke, sat straight and declared, "Sir, the Order has lost two of their loremasters, including Juliette Mirovar, and the UK force team has met its end. Shadowstone in the UK have taken heavy losses, but those are only men you can replace with Phase V day guards in the near future. Yes, Ramin Kain, who you asked me to keep safe has died, but the stability you seek to complete the Day Guard program remains in place, as the Order of Thoth is now on the verge of destruction."

Crane stared at her incredulously for a long moment, and snapped, "On the verge of destruction? You're not one for hyperbole, explain yourself."

"With Ramin Kain dead, the Order will be forced to call a conclave."

"And? … What does that mean? They've called conclaves for centuries without our knowledge. Whatever techniques they use to call a conclave have always been beyond our abilities to discover."

"I have some ideas, hints that have become apparent over the last few days. I will pass this new information to James Haley and Shadowstone,"

Chloe smiled confidently. "I've a 'feeling,' we're close to discovering when and where the next conclave will be held."

Crane's lip curled sardonically and he stated skeptically, "Well, if you can deliver such a coup I will be impressed." He frowned. "In the meantime, I have a critical mission for you."

"Yes, Sir?"

"The Red Ghost is taunting us with a video of Haras Mosule. Morte has chained him in silver, and threatens to behead him. Haras still lives. I will send you a copy of the video. You have one mission now – find him and rescue him, I would have him back in our ranks. You will find the Red Empire prison, free Haras, and bring him back alive."

Chloe's eyes narrowed, her mind leaping into high gear. *Crane is sending me on what he must believe is a suicide mission. Why would he do that? He must suspect me of betrayal and now seeks to test my loyalty – I must either win a great victory or die.*

Their recently achieved closeness and trust had evaporated, as short-lived as morning dew on a sunny day. Chloe weighed her options, compliance was the only choice this time, but what Crane didn't know would leave open a thin window of opportunity to survive.

"Yes, Sir, I will see it done. However, I have a request."

"Yes?"

"This mission will require the utmost stealth. I will act alone, except for daylight cover by James Haley, and I need to rest for the next twenty-four hours."

Crane nodded. "So be it."

The main screen returned to Crane's standard.

Mosule's prison was near the real Red Empire citadel, and Chloe knew exactly where the real citadel was. She remembered her footsteps perfectly from early May when she'd traded information for a viewing of the Interpretive Codex. Even while hooded by the Red Empire, the ambient noise had given her much of the layout of the citadel. In the following weeks, while pretending to look for the Red Empire citadel, she'd secretly mapped its location and perimeter defenses. All her information stored away in her perfect memory and now available for use.

Chloe nodded her head, she could rescue Mosule, but only a fool would imagine that infiltrating the Red Empire citadel was anything other than the most dangerous possible mission.

She hadn't lied to Crane; she would require the utmost in stealth to succeed. Her eyes hardened, and hard-hitting violence to deal with the inevitable contact with Red Empire fighters.

She'd need a distraction, a damn good one. Chloe smiled; James would be perfect to assist her with that.

Chloe rose from her seat and left the war room. It was time to burn her alliance with the Red Ghost to the ground. Once the Red Ghost realized who had stolen his prize prisoner, she would lose access to the Raven. She cast any possibility of concern aside. She would have to make sacrifices to secure her position with Crane.

* * *

Someone was knocking on James Haley's front door.

He glanced at his alarm clock, it read 05:30. "Damn it," he cursed and rolled out of bed. He dragged on a pair of shorts, grabbed his Glock 9mm off the bedside table and strode down the hall toward his front door. He kept well to the left side of the corridor in case someone fired shots through the door.

"James," Chloe Armitage whispered from the other side of the door. "I know you're awake, I can hear you sneaking along the left side of the hall. Please let me in."

James unlocked the door, Chloe pushed it open and slipped inside. She caught his gaze, smiled and said, "We did this two weeks ago, I might be making a habit of visiting your apartment."

James arched an eyebrow as Chloe swept past him, a long black duffel bag in her left hand. She dropped the bag on the floor of the hall with a solid clunk before striding into the living room.

"I'd love to chitchat, but there isn't time," she said over her shoulder as she sat down on James' sofa and patted the cushion next to her. "Come here, we must talk."

"Sure," James agreed. He put his 9mm automatic down on the coffee table in front of the sofa and sat down next to her. Two weeks ago, Chloe had given him a head massage and a shave in his kitchen. The experience had been surreal, but she'd shared her plans with him, and she'd switched him on to her vision for the future. Vampires would be the immortal protectors of humanity, as strange as that had sounded at first, in the end, it had made perfect sense. He was now her man, her ace in the hole inside Shadowstone. She'd formalized his position as her personal assistant with an appointment as her aide-de-camp. A role that superseded his previous role, while preserving his enhanced privileges with the Panopticon.

In every way, he was her daylight guardian. He'd thrown his lot in with her, his fate now bound up with hers. They would succeed or fail together, and James would do all he could with his considerable skills to ensure it was success rather than failure.

James studied her face, she really was mesmerizing up close, not in some sort of stupid 1930s vampire movie way, she was an extraordinary beauty, capturing his gaze and keeping it fixed upon her. Her presence radiated a dominating power impossible to escape.

A mischievous smile lit her face, he'd never seen her in this mood before, she seethed with secrets bursting to reveal themselves.

"What is it?" he asked.

"Three things, firstly the Order of Thoth will be calling a conclave, a meeting of the leadership of the Order."

James' heart leaped. "You know when and where it's happening?"

Chloe laughed, putting her right hand casually on his left knee, an electric thrill sparked along his thigh into his groin, James was suddenly more awake than he'd been for weeks.

"No, not yet," Chloe conceded. "This is where you come in. The Order will broadcast an advertisement, it will be entirely innocuous, the words will have special meanings established at the last conclave and known only to the force leaders and loremasters. It will tell them the exact time and date of the conclave; the location is already known."

"And you already know what to expect."

Chloe smiled broadly. "Yes!"

"So, what are we looking for exactly?"

Chloe leaned toward him. "The trick is ..." she whispered in his ear.

"You're kidding?"

"No."

James laughed. "We have them."

"Yes – it is also Order protocol to attend a conclave unarmed – as equals. Early conclaves were often messy, bloody affairs."

"They'll be sitting ducks."

"Indeed. The leadership of the Order, the loremasters, and their best warriors will be in attendance, we can expect to kill them all with a single stroke."

James shook his head with wonder. "How did you come by this information."

Chloe tilted her head slightly and remarked sardonically, "Ramin Kain was quite effusive in the end ..."

"He's dead?"

Chloe nodded; her eyes fierce with triumph.

"So, the Crane – Kain detente is—"

"Over."

James stared at Chloe for a long moment, digesting the changes. So much had happened in a very short time. The situation was fluid, bordering on chaos, but Chloe remained relaxed, in control, self-possessed. She exuded confidence. Her positive mood, allied with her stunning physical presence set his soul spinning.

Old disciplines re-asserted themselves, her plan was clear, it didn't need further explanation. James said, "I'll start a standing search for the advertisement. Once it shows up, we'll know about it. I'll do it quietly – off the books."

"Excellent," Chloe said. "I knew I could rely on you."

"You mentioned three things, the second is?" James asked, shrugging his broad shoulders and spreading his big hands wide.

Chloe clapped her hands once and said enthusiastically, "I need you to find me a lizard. At least one, two or three would be better."

James rubbed his right eyebrow, perplexed. "A lizard?"

"A big lizard."

What is she talking about?

"Okay, a little history, long before the vampires, humanity was not the apex predator on the planet – you were the prey. The lords and rulers of this world were a species of oversized chameleons that looked a lot like a velociraptor mixed with a bald wolverine having a bad day."

James suppressed a derisive laugh. No, she was entirely serious under her bantering exterior, and besides, she was not someone he could ever safely laugh at.

"Okay, what am I really looking for?"

Chloe produced a data stick from a pocket, and instructed him. "Everything you need is on here. Look for a cluster of killings and disappearances. Look for grotesquely murdered victims who appear to be torn apart, with most of their flesh missing, and the marrow sucked from their bones."

"I'll keep this off the books too."

Chloe nodded. "Good. Send me the coordinates at the center of a cluster, and I'll do the rest."

"Copy that," James affirmed, "and the third thing?"

"I need to permanently requisition a Shadowstone safe-house, slash, rendition facility. I need a safe place I can store up to half a dozen high-value prisoners."

James stroked his chin. "Most of those sorts of facilities are outside the US and operated by sub-Shadowstone organizations like the CIA, or MI6. I can only think of one facility in Arizona that will meet your needs."

"I only need one."

"Who do you want to put on ice?"

Chloe smiled, a mischievous gleam in her eyes. "It's better you don't know."

James shrugged his heavy shoulders, and said knowingly, "Sure, no problem, I'll get it set up ASAP. Who do you want to staff it?"

"Nasr al Dam, and the rest of the Red Empire fist team that we have sitting on their thumbs in New England."

James lifted both eyebrows and nodded. "Consider it done."

Chloe ran her fingers through her hair, and stated, "I'm taking your spare room today. Get off to work – you have a lot to do, and when you get back tonight be ready to fly out – we have a new mission in the middle east."

"Jerusalem?"

Chloe nodded, a half-smile curling her lips. "We have to rescue Haras Mosule from the Red Empire."

Chloe moved, collected her duffel bag from the corridor and disappeared into James' spare bedroom.

Wheels within wheels – does she ever stop scheming?

James shook his head, there was work to do.

* * *

Chloe shut the bedroom door behind her.

She'd used James' spare room two weeks before, and it suited her needs perfectly. It butted up against an internal wall of the apartment building and was without windows. Even with the door wide open, there was no way for direct sunlight to enter.

Her eyes hardened, her face shedding the enthusiasm she'd shared moments before with James like a serpent's excess skin. She threw the long-black duffel bag onto the floor and unpacked it, lining the items up on the bed. Brand new upgraded praetorian combat armor and tactical helmet in standard Shadowstone matte black, with matching gauntlets, and stealthy combat boots. The Red Dragon katana in its scabbard. A pair of custom-made .50 caliber auto-pistols fitted with twenty-shot magazines of hypervelocity caseless depleted uranium penetrators. A single augmented round could shoot through a concrete wall or make a wet mess of a human being. She hefted the guns, her hands blurred forward, and she sighted along them toward an imaginary target. The weight and recoil of the weapons made them unsuitable for human use, but a vampire was strong enough to handle both effects, making the guns a deadly part of her arsenal.

She usually didn't carry handguns, but the objective of single-handedly infiltrating and then escaping the Red Empire citadel required every resource she could muster. She put the auto-pistols into their black-leather thigh holsters and set them aside.

She checked the tactical helmet; it was an advanced prototype built to her own specifications. The full-face mask was proof against aerosols, including vaporized silver. It provided a minimal reflective surface, appearing as a smooth dark sheen on the front of the helmet. While her scouting of the Red Empire citadel hadn't revealed a hint of silver usage in their defenses, she'd be very surprised if they weren't using silver somewhere on the boundaries and approaches to their main base of operations. The lack of detectable silver simply meant the Red Empire had hidden it perfectly.

Chloe checked her combat harness and webbing next. The webbing carried four anti-personal fragmentation grenades and four spare clips of ammunition for the auto-pistols. She smiled wryly at the spare ammunition. If she needed more than a hundred and twenty shots on this mission, she'd have to wear the consequences. If the Red Empire captured her, no one could save her from their specific brand of 'justice.'

Next to the webbing was a bandolier. It would stretch diagonally across her chest plates from her right hip, over her left shoulder, and back to her right buttock. It carried a dozen powerful shaped charges, perfect for cutting through walls or fortified doors. She expected to use all of them to enter and escape the Red Empire citadel.

She nodded at her equipment, she was prepared, she had everything she needed. There was no room left for failure.

She paused for a moment, visualizing a three-dimensional model of the citadel, the prison wing was to the south of the main complex. The vampire prison was of recent construction, perhaps less than twenty years old. It was in conflict with the 'Way,' of the Red Empire. What use a vampire prisoner to the Red Empire who viewed the killing of vampires as a holy duty. Clearly, Dalien Morte, the current Red Ghost, was not a fundamentalist in his interpretation of the Red Empire's sacred text.

This was an important point, his lack of personal investment in the beliefs of the Red Empire opened up a range of exploitable points of contact on his personality. Dalien Morte was a key target for Chloe, one day she would need to co-opt or kill him. There was no future for the Red Empire in the world she would create.

Perhaps she would do both, first co-opt Morte, then almost kill him – then recruit him into her forces as a vampire. He would make a useful servant. He had skills and undoubted abilities, and his courage was not in question. Against Morte, she could not use fear as a lever for control, but desire and pride were available to exploit, perhaps an opportunity would arise to bring him into the fold.

Chloe smiled grimly. Whatever happened with regards to the Red Ghost would have to overcome her part in the loss of their current citadel. It was a foregone conclusion Dalien Morte would realize who had freed his prize prisoner. The capabilities she would use would mark her identity as certainly as if she'd walked into the Red Empire citadel in nothing but combat fatigues and wielding the Red Dragon.

The Red Ghost would know, and he would fear her.

Crane was using her in what could easily be a suicide mission. With the non-strategic goal of rescuing another general, it indicated just how expendable she was to him. He'd issued his order nearly five hours before, giving her plenty of time to adapt her plans.

Crane doesn't know, and it's highly unlikely that Haras Mosule knows how close his prison is to the actual Red Empire citadel. If Crane knew that I know where the Interpretive Codex was and was able to get it – that would be the primary mission and rescuing general Mosule would just be a casual afterthought, a nice to have, but certainly not essential.

Of course, there was no way that Chloe would willingly bring the Codex to Crane, or worse, destroy it. If Crane acquired or lost all hope of acquiring the Codex, it would signal the end of her necessary usefulness to him and would begin the countdown to her own assassination.

The Red Empire citadel would fall, but the Codex must remain in possession of the Red Ghost, anything else would be a disaster.

Chloe repacked her duffel bag, it was time to get some sleep.

Even hard-working vampire generals must rest.

* * *

Rain sleeted upon the dark windows lining the walls of the boardroom, running down the panes in silent waves.

The chamber stood decorated in a sparse, modern style, befitting an international Japanese technology company. Through a series of holding companies, Cornelius Crane was the majority and controlling shareholder of Control Systems Incorporated. A multi-billion-dollar corporation supplying the world with the latest in industrial, scientific and medical robotics, however, it was not robots that interested Cornelius, it was an obscure part of the R&D arm of the corporation named 'Medical Control Systems,' but known to Cornelius as research facility number seven.

Cornelius, freshly dressed in an expertly tailored, dark-gray bespoke suit, sat at the head of the boardroom table. The company's CEO, and the Head of Research from the Medical Control Systems unit flanked him on the left and right. Both men registered undercurrents of fear and distress beneath their calm and professional exteriors. Cornelius well knew the effect he had on people, often triggering their instinctive sense of him as an apex predator. He leaned forward slightly, turning to the right to regard the lead researcher, and inquired, "Are the prototypes ready?"

"Yes, Sir. My assistant is bringing them now."

"My apologies," the CEO offered meekly on Cornelius' left, bowing his head low toward the table top. "We were surprised by your sudden arrival this late in the evening, nearly everyone has gone home."

Cornelius arched an eyebrow and stated, "A small delay matters not, if," he turned back to the Head of Research who visibly paled under his gaze, "the implants work as specified in my requirements."

The man's Adam's apple bobbed up and down in his throat, and while visibly frightened, a flash of curiosity lit his eyes. "To the extent that we could test them they work perfectly. However, the external bio-polymer sheath remains rejected by human tissue, and a payload of powdered silver," he shook his head, "makes no sense."

Cornelius smiled wolfishly at the man. The scientist was completely unconscious that his curiosity could easily get him killed. Cornelius allowed the implied question to go unanswered, and demanded, "And what of the black and gold implants?"

"A matched pair, should the gold implant cease to monitor a life sign, the black will fire."

Cornelius nodded.

An intercom came online, a soft feminine voice announced, "Sir, your package has arrived."

The door opened, and an impeccably dressed young woman entered the room, she bowed, and walked toward Cornelius, placing a black, leather briefcase on the table in front of him. She passed her thumbs simultaneously over a pair of biometric scanners on either side of the case, and a faint whirr emanated from the middle of the case. A seam appeared around the outside of the case. The top lifted an inch and slid backward revealing the contents. A carefully packed gray plastic mold held an injection gun, fourteen inch-long implants, twelve color-coded red, and a separated pair, one gold, and one black. A nearly transparent loading cartridge encapsulated each implant, enabling easy insertion into the injection gun.

She glanced once at Cornelius, an almost imperceptible shiver traveling up her spine, and stepped away. With her head slightly bowed and not making eye contact, she instructed him quietly. "Sir, when you close the case, if you pass your thumbs over the biometric scanners, only you will be able to open it."

"Thank you," Cornelius said politely. "You're dismissed."

The young woman bowed deeply, walked backward to the door, and was gone a moment later.

Cornelius addressed the Head of Research, "How long will it take to manufacture a thousand red implants?"

"The bio-polymer sheaths are the limiting factor," he shrugged his shoulders, "six months at least."

Cornelius stared at him for a moment. "And the worst case?"

"Twelve months."

"What's the name of your best scientist?"

"Tanaka, she's very talented. She was just here. She brought us the briefcase."

"Indeed. She seems quite self-possessed and competent. Is she fully across the program?"

"Yes, she knows all parts."

Cornelius' arm blurred, his hand appearing around the researcher's throat. He squeezed, there was a sharp snap as the man's neck broke like a twig.

The CEO leaped to his feet with a horrified gasp, his chair falling over to the carpet. Cornelius rushed him, lifting him up and pinning him against the wall. Cornelius' head tilted to the side, struck forward, the man squealed for half a second and then fell silent, apart from momentary twitches of his shoes floating a foot off the floor.

Cornelius stepped back, allowing the CEO's body to fall to the blood speckled carpet. After his encounter with Mekra, he'd been almost drained of blood. He turned to the head researcher slumped over the boardroom table, he would need even more blood before leaving here.

He paused long enough to open his smartphone and dial the local head of Shadowstone. The Japanese organization would clean the boardroom and quell the Tokyo police investigation. They were a loyal and efficient organization and he could trust they would complete their tasks without issue.

Five minutes later, standing in pelting rain on the building's helipad, Cornelius stowed the secured briefcase into the small hold of his personal drone. His next destination was within Japan, a short hop to wilderness and mountains, and the secret stronghold of the Obsidian Claw ninja clan.

His lip curled at the thought of drenching the interior of the drone, but it was unavoidable. Grim-faced, he stroked his right index finger along a line at the edge of the drone's cockpit. A seam split open at his touch, the top half of the front of the drone lifting up and back. As soon as there was room, he blurred to his seat in the cockpit.

He fired up the engines. The fuel counter registered twenty-three percent capacity. He'd have to refuel before the flight back to New York. The nearest available hydrogen-based fuel for his specialized scramjets was available at Tokyo airport. Cornelius set the course, better to fuel up now then come back to Tokyo a second time tonight.

Ten seconds later the drone was airborne.

Chapter Two

"You can only lead from the front." – Francis Mirovar, Senior Force Leader of the Order of Thoth

* * *

Scotland, northeast coast, August 23rd, 13:00

The sky stretched in bright blue from horizon to horizon, the sun standing high overhead.

A crisp, cold breeze nipped at the Raven's cheeks. They smeared a tear away with a swipe of their right arm and sniffled quietly, staring at the freshly turned soil covering the graves of Juliette and Yvette Mirovar. Next to their graves were three more for Mary Turner, David Wilkinson, and Joan Lewis. The only Walker force team members they could recover from the nightmare of Armitage Manor.

The Order helpers had led the team to a remote village on the northeast Scottish coastline. The local cemetery provided the tools and space for new graves. One of the helpers from the trawler had negotiated a deal with the local sexton, ensuring the identity of the newly interred would remain hidden forever.

Everyone in the team had helped to dig the graves, and lay the bodies to rest. Jay and Francis had taken sole responsibility for filling the graves of Yvette and Juliette respectively.

Jay threw the last shovel load of dirt onto Yvette's grave and slammed the shovel down. He bristled with thinly controlled anger, striding away from the grave to an ancient, stonewalled church. He sank down to the ground, his back against the dark-gray-blue wall, his knees up, burying his face in his arms.

Francis fell to his knees at the head of Juliette's grave, the shovel forgotten next to him, a low moan escaping his lips before he bowed his head in awful silence. He knelt there unmoving, still, as if he was as dead as Juliette.

Perhaps he wished he was.

The Raven could relate to seeking final release. The scene at the exfiltration point had been too much for them, the overwhelming guilt sending them into the darkness beyond the cliff edge. Anton had saved them, pulling them back from certain death on the black rocks below. They glanced across at him. Anton's face was tight, his jaw set like stone, his right hand rubbing over his good eye, the rest of his face still wrapped in bandages.

The Raven slowly shook their head, their eyes closed. The world was too dreadful to look upon.

Could Juliette and Yvette still be alive? What if they had done things differently? What if they had lied to Armitage and sent her in the opposite direction, away from the exfil site? What if … what if … what if?

The Raven uttered a single, long-drawn-out sigh. The death of everyone buried in this churchyard was on them. How could they ever tell the other team members, and especially Jay and Francis, who they really were? They should never have put attempting to manage Armitage ahead of the team. From now on, the team would come first.

A dark sea of guilt lapped at their soul; its cold depths frigid beyond all despair.

The Raven wondered if they would ever be free of it. They shivered in the bright sunlight, cold goosebumps rippling over their skin beneath their clothes.

Francis was so alone, they moved toward him and then faltered. What did they have to offer him? They glanced about, the churchyard sat on top of a low hill, the North Sea stretched across half the horizon. Its slate-like surface was just as merciless as the dark ocean of guilt dragging at the Raven's soul.

They staggered forward toward Francis and put their hand on his stiff shoulder in a gesture of comfort.

It was all they could do.

* * *

Anton closed his good eye and shuddered within.

Jay and Francis were suffering terribly. He understood their pain, which was so like his own. The team needed them to be healthy, strong, and capable. There was no way they could defeat Armitage, Crane, and the Vampire Dominion without these men at their best. The sooner they emerged from this storm of grief the better. He resolved to do all he could to help them through it.

Anton strode over to where Jay sat alone against the church wall, his head bowed over his arms and knees. He stopped in front of Jay, his feet to either side of Jay's boots. He thrust out his open hand and declared, "What would Yvette want?"

Jay lifted his head from his arms, stared at Anton with tear-filled eyes, growled, and said, "You're an asshole Slayne." His hand snapped up, taking Anton's in a powerful grip. "But, you're my kind of asshole."

Anton leaned back, and Jay rose to his feet, his eyes hardening in the bright sunlight as he looked past Anton's shoulder. "Francis," he whispered. "He's a mess."

Anton turned. The rest of the team had crowded around Francis. He was on his knees in front of Juliette's grave. Anton whispered, "He loved more strongly than anyone else here." He glanced at Jay, who stared back and sighed in silent agreement. "It can hardly be called a flaw ... we'll need to protect him while he recovers."

Jay nodded. "Agreed," and grasped Anton's shoulder with a grip of iron. "But no more stunts like leaving the team and stealing a commander tank." He lifted an eyebrow. "Yes?"

"No ... no more stunts," Anton promised. It was an easy promise to make, as he would only do what was necessary to save the team and destroy the Vampire Dominion.

There would be no stunts; Anton was certain of that.

* * *

It took a long moment for Chiara, Peter and Li's presence to reach him.

Francis stared at the fresh soil in front of his knees. With one hand he crumbled a handful of clay, the dirt breaking easily, falling apart and slipping through his fingers.

Like his life.

His mind drifted, random snatches of the past flitting through him. Juliette's smile ... her eyes filled with trust looking into his own ... her serene belief in him and their team.

Her face still and pale, her eyes staring at nothing, her lips flecked with her own blood.

He'd betrayed her with his failure to keep her safe. Her blood was as much on his hands as it was on Armitage's.

Someone must have told Armitage where the exfil site was. It was possible the trap in the manor house was little more than a distraction used to keep the force teams busy while she hunted down and slaughtered the loremasters.

The loremasters were strategically the most valuable assets in the Order, and targeting them made sense. There remained a single small silver lining; they'd recovered both loremaster implants intact, as well as Joan Lewis's laptop loaded with Order software and linked to her implant.

But someone had betrayed the team, one of his own was a spy.

A horrible sick feeling filled his stomach. Francis blurred to his feet and away from Chiara, Peter and Li. He whirled at the other end of Juliette's grave, the White Dragon hissing free of its scabbard, the gleaming blade hovering in the air before him.

Jay and Anton pulled to a halt on his left, the rest of the team stood in shock at the other end of the grave.

Francis swept the sword left and right, snarled once, and said, "One of you is a traitor!"

Everyone stared at him in shocked silence.

Francis beckoned with his left hand; his right holding the White Dragon resolutely before him. "Jay, Anton, Li – come to me."

Jay, Anton, and Li stepped forward, taking positions to his left and right, leaving Peter and Chiara standing together at the other end of Juliette's grave.

"I should have done this before we came here," he slashed the air over the graves with the White Dragon. "My lack of vigilance has caused this."

Francis glowered at Peter and Chiara, and demanded, "Handover your smartphones to Li."

Peter pulled his phone from a pocket on his shirt and looped it over the grave to Li, and averred, "Hey Boss, it's not me."

"I'm not a spy," Chiara declared hotly, tossing her phone to Li. "My allegiance is with everyone here."

Francis ignored them, turned to Li and commanded, "I want a full forensic analysis of both phones. I want to know if there is anything on those phones that shouldn't be there."

Francis focused on the pair opposite the remnants of his team, and ordered, "Peter, Chiara, you will watch each other. One of you is a spy, the other is not. The rest of us will watch you both."

He paused for a moment, his gaze boring into Peter and Chiara. "I promise here, and now, my sword will taste the heart's blood of whoever is the traitor, and nothing and no one will stop me from killing the one who has betrayed us all."

Francis turned and strode away from the churchyard, and down to the docks. The rest of the team fell in behind him, Jay and Anton, bringing up the rear.

* * *

The rest of the team followed Francis away.

Li paused for a moment, dropping to her knees at the feet of Juliette's grave. Tears spilled down her cheeks. She lifted a small clod of clay and crushed it into fragments, scattering them over the grave.

"Goodbye Sensei," she said softly.

The words didn't do justice to the loss she felt. In a little over two months Juliette had come to fill some of the space that Li's mother Tatsu had occupied, but the relationship was beyond that of a daughter with her mother. Juliette had always treated her as an equal, as a gifted apprentice she could guide into her mature powers. Juliette had been the wise woman of the small tribe of the Mirovar force team, and the true power behind the visible leadership of Francis. She was ever the far-sighted strategist behind Francis' courage and tactical flair.

Francis would always run decisions past Juliette, she was the one who had the final say on the direction the team had taken. She was the team's heart and soul. She was the fulcrum on which the team turned, both foundation stone and sunlit goal.

And now she was gone.

Li stared into the abyss in front of her. A vast space; once filled with the potent powers of the most gifted and capable loremaster in the history of the Order of Thoth. In the center of the darkness was a single ghostly light, a golden flame, the final legacy of Juliette Mirovar.

A light that staggered within the gloom, assailed, and guttering like a candle in a storm.

Li's chest was tight, her eyes blurred with tears. There was no one else who could accept the burden.

Her hand raised from her side, reaching out over the cold earth of Juliette's grave.

The fiery mote leaped forward.

Li gently closed her hand into a fist, the light disappearing within.

She rocked back onto her feet. She wiped her left arm across her eyes, sniffed once, and looked down the stony path leading away from the churchyard. The team was a hundred yards away, walking down to the docks.

Anton looked over his shoulder, paused and waved her forward.

She sniffled a final time, thrust her hands in the pockets of her jacket and strode after the team. In half a minute she caught up with Anton and Jay, slipping in between them. Just for a moment, perhaps a long moment, it comforted her to have Jay and Anton beside her.

The world had darkened, creeping shadows, mirror to the distant storm clouds gathering on the eastern horizon, beset her soul. Juliette's legacy had carried with it a terrifying request. An invitation she couldn't refuse; to confront the horrors of the world, to be a true servant of the flame, to be a bearer of the light. Her hand had closed around the flame, it was cool to the touch, she was unharmed as she answered its call. But would she succeed or would she fail, when all she wanted at that moment was to be safe? There were fates worse than death waiting to claim her. Would she be able to withstand them?

Her father's voice filled with warmth, trust and love whispered within her, 'You are strong my beloved daughter, you have what is necessary within you. You are the Doragonzu no musume.'

'The daughter of dragons,' she hoped he was right.

* * *

"I don't believe Peter's a spy," Anton whispered.

Jay leaned toward him and replied, "So it's Chiara? I don't see how she could have fooled us for all these years."

"If this was the Red Empire rather than the Order," Li said quietly, "they'd both be dead."

Anton shook his head. "If it was Peter, I don't think I could kill him."

"I could," Jay uttered. "I could do either of them – if it was proven." He looked at Li and asked, "How long to test the phones?"

"I'll have answers by tomorrow, but the phones might not tell us anything conclusive. If I were a Red Empire spy – any software on my phone would mimic empty space, or something else equally innocuous, or be self-obliterating if anyone ran forensic diagnostics. I'll do my best and see what I can find out."

Jay walked stiffly next to Li, and declared, his voice filled with murder, "Someone's going to pay for 'Vette."

Anton and Li glanced across at Jay, his eyes stared straight ahead, hard with intense emotion, glistening beneath the bright sky, and as cold as the North Sea stretching away to a storm-darkened horizon.

Anton reached out behind Li, clasping Jay on the right shoulder. "We're with you brother. Let's take this war to the Vampire Dominion. With Kain dead, it's time we unleashed the Order force teams."

Li nudged Anton in the side. "What's with the royal 'we,' kemosabe?"

Anton glanced down at Li. "I'm being serious."

"I know, but you can't speak for me." Li leaned forward and caught Jay's gaze. "Of course, I'll stand with you too. We have to destroy the vampires, but it's easier said than done. Whatever the Order or even the Red Empire have done in the past hasn't been enough. The vampires are in the dominant position, and we're desperately in need of new strategies, or else we'll all end up dead."

Jay nodded and said, his voice dripping with venom, "Kain turned out to be a fucking prick. He got off easy when I took his head. Who knows what damage he's done to the Order or the extent of his lies?"

"Perhaps he lied about my grandfather," Anton suggested. "After all, he's the one who benefited from Madison's and your mother's deaths, and my grandfather was his chief rival for the position of the Head of the Order."

Jay was silent for a moment. "You could be right, but we'll never know for sure. One thing we can be certain of is that Kain was the most corrupt and evil traitor the Order has ever known, and I'm glad he's dead. Too bad he didn't die back in Maine, then we'd never have made this cursed trip."

The hillside flattened out. The cobblestone path they were walking on leveled out as it circled around a modest-sized fishing village. The docks were in front of them, a sea-worthy trawler waiting for them to board.

Li ducked to the other side of Jay, taking his left arm in a soft grip. "We've all lost people we love, and most likely will again."

Jay sucked in a big breath and sighed deeply. "I know, I know all about that stuff. Yeah, noble advice but I just don't feel it." He looked across at Anton, and then back at Li. "The trawler captain has a case of excellent whiskey. He offered it last night, and I need some buddies around me." He glanced back and forth again, the offer mixed with desperation and sadness. "Help me forget what happened and help me remember her."

"Sure," Anton agreed, his strong hand tightening on Jay's shoulder.

"Of course," Li offered, firming her grip on his left arm.

They walked up the gangplank side by side and boarded the trawler. It was time to leave the United Kingdom and make their way back to the United States.

* * *

The tavern doors pushed open, warm yellow light spilling into the laneway. A raucous laugh filled the cold night air. Two burly fishermen, leaning on each other for support pushed out into the night.

A young man with sallow complexion and dark, lank hair, half hidden beneath a rolled up, black balaclava, leaned against the shadowed brickwork wall at the end of the laneway. He fingered a six-inch blade with his thumb. He watched the pair of drunks stagger out of the bar and set off down the deserted laneway toward the docks.

The young man's head lifted up, his expression shifted to keen alertness and a sly grin crept over his mouth. He pushed himself away from the brick wall, heading toward the pair of men weaving their way along the laneway. His free hand flicked up, and dragged the balaclava down over his face, leaving only his dark eyes visible.

He didn't reach the yellow glow pooling in front of the tavern door.

Tamsah al Ramil fell upon him from the tavern roof, pushing him back to the end of the laneway. Tamsah's left hand closed over the young man's right wrist with a crushing grip, the knife spinning away to the cobblestones. His right hand clapped over the young man's mouth before he could scream with agony. With the knife out of the way, Tamsah shifted his left hand to the young man's trousers, established an unbreakable grip on the contents of his groin and leaped up to the tavern roof.

A moment later, Tamsah stood balanced on the top of the tavern's roof next to a chimney. He held the man close, both facing the trawler crowded docks less than a hundred yards distant. The man was ripe with fear, hot urine soaked the front of his trousers, and he writhed helplessly within Tamsah's iron grip.

Tamsah whispered harshly into his ear, "You know these boats? Nod if you do."

Tamsah relaxed his grip over the young man's mouth enough to allow him to move and his head nodded forward.

"I'm going to allow you to speak, if you make too much noise, I'll snap your neck. Do you understand?"

The young man's head nodded forward again.

Tamsah grinned, his fangs had descended into attack position, and hunger was tearing at him. Hardening his will, he pushed his vampiric needs aside, he needed information more than he needed blood.

"One of the trawlers is missing. What's its name?"

"Aye, the Orion. It left early yesterday, and came back early this morning."

"When did it leave?"

"About two o'clock."

"Where did it go?"

"I don't know."

Tamsah clamped his right hand hard over the young man's mouth, his other hand snaked around to grip his wet groin. His hand cupped the young fellow's manhood and started to squeeze.

The young man's body went rigid with agony, and he screamed silently into Tamsah's right hand.

Tamsah squeezed harder, listening to the young man's heart rate accelerate toward two hundred beats per minute. He held for another ten seconds and then relaxed his grip just short of causing permanent injury.

"Where did it go?" Tamsah asked again.

"Oh, my God ... oh my God ... I don't know ... I don't know," the young man gasped out. "They could go anywhere."

Tamsah knew the truth speaker was a member of the Mirovar force team and based in the United States, but not more than that. He asked, "How far could the Orion go? Could it reach the United States?"

"No. It's too far. They'd run out of fuel first."

"Then where?" Tamsah asked, gripping the man's groin again, but without squeezing.

The young man went rigid again in terrified anticipation. "I don't know, how am I supposed to know?"

"You live here, you must know what these boats would do. Where would you refuel?" Tamsah asked, and began to lightly squeeze the young man's testicles.

"Wait! Oh, my God, please no."

Tamsah relaxed his grip. "Where?"

"Iceland. Iceland, oh my God, it's gotta be Iceland."

Tamsah held the young man still and considered his words. It seemed reasonable to expect the Mirovar force team to return to the United States, they would need to do so while avoiding the Vampire Dominion, Shadowstone, and the civilian authorities who would be hunting them after the battles in England. It made sense for the Mirovar force team to stop and refuel in Iceland, and perhaps to find another boat or even a plane to return to the US or even Canada. At this time of year, with the long days and short nights of the northern summer, there was little risk of vampire contact in Iceland. There was minimal Shadowstone activity on the island. Iceland was too small and out of the way for Shadowstone to pay much attention to it.

Tamsah had the information he needed and gave way to his hunger. He tilted the young man's head to the right and bit hard into the left side of his throat. The young man screamed again into Tamsah's right hand.

Tamsah drew upon his internal muscles, creating a vacuum effect that accelerated the flow of blood, in a handful of seconds he drained the young man dry. His heart continued quivering with nothing to pump and then fell silent.

Tamsah's arm muscles bunched and he tore the young man's head from his shoulders, a handful of stray blood drops flew through the air. He examined the stump; the tear line obliterated his bite mark. He positioned the corpse over the top of the roof, directly behind the chimney, and out of sight from the lanes and streets below. Due to the lack of blood, the local authorities would naturally assume the killer had struck elsewhere and then positioned the corpse here. With a little luck, it would take longer than a week for anyone to discover the body.

The last thing Tamsah needed was for the Vampire Dominion to identify the existence of a rogue vampire. He needed to keep his existence secret from everyone, the Vampire Dominion, the Order of Thoth and the Red Empire.

He drew in a long deep breath and let it go, there was a hint of weather change on the night air. A storm was coming, and there was nothing he could do to aid the truth speaker in her travels back to the United States.

It was time to leave the United Kingdom, he would make his way to an airport and find a freight aircraft to the United States. He should be able to find a way to remain hidden on such a flight.

He would wait in the United States until the truth speaker arrived, then he would find her and protect her.

Tamsah turned, his dark coat whirling, he leaped to the laneway below and disappeared into the shadows.

* * *

Anton's hair littered the floor of the cabin.

Chiara had shorn it off for him to even up his appearance. The heat in the destroyed commander tank had burnt more than half of his hair into a frazzled mass. With that simple task out of the way, she lifted the set of bandages away from his face. They were alone together in a crew cabin within the body of the trawler. Anton sat on a wooden bench while she tended to his wounds.

Anton watched her face as she worked. She'd pulled her long dark hair clear of its usual plait, letting it fall past her shoulders and down to the small of her back. Her fingers glided over his skin with a sure and confident touch. She'd occasionally lift her eyes from her work and glance into his surviving eye, warmth and honesty filling her gaze.

Her careful hands told the truth about her professional and committed approach to her work as the last surviving combat surgeon in the team, and the way she kept looking at him hinted of something more.

Francis had accused her of being a spy for the Red Empire and the Vampire Dominion. His hand stayed from executing her by the absence of definitive proof. If she was concerned by the accusation and its attendant death sentence, it didn't show in her actions. Anton relaxed and allowed Chiara to get on with patching him up after his battle with Marcus Drake.

Two days before, Drake's whip-like chain had ripped through the upper left side of his face, taking out his left eye. Conversations he'd had with Peter, Francis and the rest of the team since the battle had indicated it was possible to regrow the eye, but it was a tricky, touchy business fraught with failure. Even with the benefit of the accelerated healing of Ramp genetics, it was all too easy for an eye to scar over resulting in permanent blindness.

Peter had explained that even with a lost eye, a Ramp master could learn to adjust to the loss of depth perception by relying more on all the other sensory systems operating at peak human capacity.

Much as he'd learned to fight hand to hand blindfolded, he could learn to operate at a distance with a single eye.

Chiara opened a jar of healing balm. The same herbal mixture Gang Wu had used to assist Anton to heal bruises and cuts sustained during his early training. It was an ancient Order recipe of medicinal plants that dovetailed with the Ramp genetics, producing miraculous healing results. She ran a pair of fingers through the surface of the balm and picked up a dollop of goop, and then smeared it liberally within the wound on Anton's face.

He winced at her touch and forced himself to stay still. His nerves were still raw from the injury.

"I know it hurts. It's a good sign, Anton," Chiara asserted. "If it stops hurting, you won't heal past whatever point you have reached at that time."

"So, keep it hurting."

Chiara smiled wryly. "I'll do my best." She reached for a padded patch and fitted it over his left eye with a black strap around his head. "We can dispense with the bandages now. The patch and the balm will keep your eye socket moist while you heal. We'll need to change it every day."

"I'll make sure I do."

She looked at him intently. "So, will I. You deserve to heal."

Anton's hand flashed up, taking hold of her wrist. "Is there someone who doesn't deserve to heal?"

Chiara blinked and retorted, "I'm not a spy for anyone."

Her words rang true. To the best of Anton's ability, he couldn't detect any deception in her voice or manner, she seemed sincere. If she was working secretly for someone else, it was beyond his abilities to detect. Anton knew he had no special capacity to determine if someone was lying, and surely a spy who had hidden within the Mirovar force team for a decade could hide from his meager detection skills.

Knowing that either Chiara or Peter was a spy left him unsure of how to work with either of them. He'd been trusting both of them with his life for months now, and trust was essential in combat. A lack of trust between teammates would destroy the team faster than a platoon of praetorians.

Trust was essential, or else the team was lost. Without the team, he'd lose everything that mattered to him.

The team had to survive.

Whoever the spy was, the team needed both Chiara and Peter. Chiara was a damn good fighter, brave, skilled and fast, and Peter was Peter – the sort of bad-ass warrior you'd always pick first to go into battle with.

He'd finished reading Francis' copy of Sun Tzu. They could turn a spy, flip them, and reorientate them to a new commitment. From the ashes of tragedy and defeat, they could forge a new opportunity for victory. Anton briefly imagined the team breaking a guard line of praetorians around Crane and Armitage, Chiara and Peter's weapons were red with vampire gore as they stood beside him. The imagined scene faded away. He'd need both of them to have any hope of defeating those who had destroyed his family.

But this would place him against the rampant vengeance fueling Jay and Francis' pursuit of the spy. They wanted blood, and they wanted it soon. Anton could relate to their feelings. Juliette had saved his life on the operating table and had stood by him when few others had, and Yvette was a great girl who had been a staunch member of the team. He felt for their deaths like he felt for the loss of a family member.

And yet … Anton made his decision in a moment. A deep wave of certainty flowing through him. He let go of Chiara's wrist and declared with absolute sincerity, "Trust me with who you really are. Trust me and stand with me against the vampires, and I'll trust you, and stand with you against anyone."

* * *

The cabin fell into silence.

Chiara stood frozen on the spot, staring into Anton's eye. Echoes of the cliff edge swam within his intense regard. She'd been willing to kill herself then, and Anton had saved her life, dragging her back from the darkness.

Now he offered her this new lifeline.

A shiver fled up her back, her eyes widened, her mouth suddenly dry. The cabin door remained shut, they were truly alone. But what if Anton was lying to her? What if he turned her over to Francis and Jay? A wave of fatalistic calm washed through her, if the next few moments led to her death, at least the nightmare of her guilt for Juliette and Yvette's deaths would have an end.

She wet her lips with the tip of her tongue, took a deep breath, stared into his face and admitted, "I am Chiara Morte, true daughter of Dalien Morte – the Red Ghost. I'm a princess of the Red Empire, initiate of the third rank, known as al Ghurab, the Raven, I am the—"

Anton put his finger on her lips, and whispered gently, "Enough."

The gentleness of his touch and the soft tone of his voice tore through every wall within her. His acceptance, so at odds with her expectation of harsh and trenchant rejection left her giddy. A warmth surged upward from deep within, a golden fountain extinguishing all shadows as it flowered feet above her head.

To trust another human being, to truly trust them with everything, and have them trust her in return. She blinked with amazement. It was a universal key unlocking all the doors in her soul.

She lost all sensation of standing on the floor of the cabin, there was only the golden fountain coursing through her, and the aura-limed man standing before her.

She breathed.

Everything was beautiful.

There was beauty everywhere.

* * *

Light filled the cabin.

Insight flooded Anton. A spy had died on the cliff edge. The Raven had leaped to their death, now only Chiara remained. Anton's heart thudded in his chest. He gripped her shoulders tightly, staring into her face. "Whatever was in your past has to stay there. It is only the future that matters now."

Chiara nodded, her eyes shining. Her hands lifted to cradle Anton's head, and she leaned in close, kissing him once on the lips, her mouth lingering on his.

Time fell away as space evaporated between them.

She pulled back half a dozen inches, searched his face for a long moment, and then promised with utter certainty, "Anton, I'll always be with you."

Energy bloomed around them, rushing in hot currents between them. Its power surprised him, there was something immeasurably rich moving between them, a deep sense of connection beyond anything he'd ever felt before. Her soul mirrored his own. Her secret was his to keep, revealing it would get her killed by Jay or Francis – and he wouldn't do that, he couldn't do that. He must protect her.

He pushed her gently back.

Her face was bright, tears welling in her eyes.

He drank in the vision of her and said quietly, "And I thought I had it tough."

She leaned forward into his embrace, and he held her tight against him. She started to shake and began weeping into his chest. The currents flowed harder through them. His heart tore, and he waited until her tears passed, gently stroking her hair and her back.

Everything she was feeling resonated through his bones to his deepest being. There could be no deception in such a place. The honesty was overwhelming, filling him with a deep sense of presence to something beyond words.

She grew still, her head turned to his left, resting against his chest. She whispered, "I'm not sad, don't … please don't think I weep because I'm sad." She pulled back and looked up at him, her mouth spread into a luminous smile. "I'm free. For the first time in my life, I'm free."

Anton nodded and instructed her. "Say nothing of this … to anyone."

She opened her mouth to speak; he put a finger gently against her lips and shook his head. "Say nothing more. There is nothing we can do about the past. You might still survive Francis and Jay's efforts to discover you. We have a shared purpose. Stick with me, and we'll get it done, and every *sacrifice* we have all made will be worth it."

Anton emphasized the word sacrifice, filling it with everyone they'd recently lost as well as anyone they might lose in the future. His words offered her redemption for everything that had happened.

Anton leaned forward, his forehead brushing against hers and whispered, "No one else can know."

"Yes," Chiara replied softly.

Anton paused for a moment, watching her face – she was completely genuine – no one could fake the feelings they'd just shared. He blinked, breathed, and hugged her again.

Somewhere deep within his soul, beyond the light, and the euphoric rush of what he was sharing with Chiara, a splinter of ice emerged from a deep well of unresolved pain. Shifting gears, he leaned back, touching his black eye patch gingerly, and asked softly, "Are we done?"

Chiara nodded, her face betraying her confusion at his sudden withdrawal.

"Good," he said, and squeezed her hands once, and made his way to the door, paused and looked back briefly. Chiara stood in the middle of the cabin, just a young woman looking very much alone.

He opened the door and mounted the stairs to the deck. He needed some fresh air to come to terms with what he was willing to do to reach his goals. His own growing ruthlessness surprised him. Francis and Jay's loss tore at his heart, and yet … if their grief stood in the way of what he must do, he would sweep it aside with barely a second thought.

And Li, Peter, and … Chiara, he would keep them safe. The last thing he wanted to do was see them in danger, and yet, *'The end and aim of spying in all its five varieties is knowledge of the enemy; and this knowledge can only be derived, in the first instance, from the converted spy. Hence it is essential that the converted spy be treated with the utmost liberality.'*

Sun Tzu's quote came to mind. Chiara was a window into the world of the Red Empire, and the Red Empire was a part of the puzzle of the world of the vampires. She was not someone he could waste as an object of Francis and Jay's need for vengeance.

Anton shook his head, shocked at the stone-cold utility of the thought coming hard off the thoroughgoing emotional intimacy he'd just shared with her. There was a cold logic within him, marching forward with relentless inevitability to its conclusion. A frozen berg of fearsome vengeance at the core of his soul. The warm currents of Chiara's love had washed over it, and eddied around it, but it remained untouched, a glacial force within his life and just as irresistible.

"But what price am I willing to pay?" he whispered. *Any price, any price,* whispered back, and he couldn't rule the truth of that out. How could he reconcile the feelings he had for those close to him with the implacable need for justice against Crane and Armitage? Where he was going would lead Li, Peter, and Chiara into the utmost danger, and how could he do that to people he'd come to love?

Anton took a deep breath and stared at the vast, cold horizon.

Life had just got complicated. Horribly complicated.

He leaned back, closed his eyes and sighed deeply.

* * *

The atmosphere in the long cabin was thick with tension.

Francis had marshaled the team into the trawler's mess room. They sat around a wooden table bolted to the floor. Jay and Anton stood at the ends of the table, naked swords in hand. Everyone else remained unarmed.

Francis sat with Li, opposite Chiara and Peter. He stared at the two suspect team members, his eyes hard and flinty. They both looked back, Chiara could have been playing a masterful hand of poker, while Peter appeared to be struggling to hold back a quip or a joke.

Despite the impromptu inquisition, they remained themselves.

Without taking his eyes off them, Francis slipped into a partial Ramp, time slowed, his senses expanded, taking in every minute action in front of him. He commanded quietly, "Li, please give us your report." His words sounding slow and drawn out to his ears.

He'd already spoken with Li and knew the details of her report. The theater he was conducting now was the last chance to shake the spy into a mistake. As much as he wanted to discover who the spy was and kill them for their betrayal, he couldn't condemn either Chiara or Peter to death while innocent. It would be like killing his own child on suspicion alone, and he couldn't do that. He had to know for certain who the spy was before he could act.

Li looked at Chiara and Peter, and declared confidently, "The phones are clean. If there was anything on either of them, its evaporated without a trace."

Francis studied his team members like a hawk watching for a mouse to twitch its tail. He dropped out of his Ramp, he'd discovered nothing new. A disappointed frown creased his forehead, and he said flatly, "The evidence is inconclusive. We're back to square one."

"What now boss?" Peter asked.

"You're both on probation," Francis ordered. "We will not share tactical information with you until the last moment. Li, keep their phones for now. Anton, Li, you are set to watch Chiara at all times. Jay and I will watch Peter. The only exceptions are for briefings when Chiara and Peter will watch each other. Also," and Francis dropped a pair of small notepads in front of Chiara and Peter, "you will keep a daily diary of what you are doing on an hourly basis. We will do a diary reading every day, directly after dinner. I expect both of you to be able to account for your time with a witness in agreement. Is that clear?"

Everyone agreed that it was.

Francis nodded. It was a start, he needed to make sure that neither of them was attempting to contact anyone outside the team, or doing anything the least bit suspicious. He expected the spy would go to ground, but there was always a chance they would make a mistake. He still had an ace up his sleeve, an Order traveler, and Truther, but that would have to wait for the Order conclave. There were no travelers he could reach where they were going, and he needed someone sane, not a fanatic like Deon Lamar. There was a traveler he could trust, Patrick Wichowski from Justin Blake's force team. He would discuss the matter with Justin when he got the chance, but for now, he would keep the option of Truther to himself.

Francis glared at Peter and Chiara. "We start now. You two can go up on deck and admire the view from the bow of the ship. The rest of us have work to do."

Chiara and Peter picked up their notepads, got up in silence, and left the cabin. Jay pushed the door shut behind them, and returned to the table where everyone now sat. Jay and Anton returned their swords to their scabbards and propped them against the table.

"We need to be clear about what we're doing next," Francis declared. "We're heading for Reykjavík in Iceland. We'll leave the trawler, and it will stay for the remainder of the summer fishing season and then return back to Scotland. We'll pick up a flight with a private aircraft, a smuggler of sorts I happen to know, and fly to Canada. From there, we'll make our way as best we can back to the northern United States."

"What of the Order?" Anton asked, "Li's inquisition is still open, and neither of us are full members."

"With Kain dead, the Order will call a conclave immediately. As for Li's inquiry, given the evident corruption of Kain, the new Head of the Order will have no option but to drop it. She's in the clear, we just need to formalize it. As for your status as novices, I will sponsor you into this team. Within a couple of weeks, three at most, you will both be full members of the Order of Thoth and we will have cleared Li's name from Lamar's ridiculous charge."

Li nodded, a look of relief flitting across her face. Anton leaned forward and asked, "And what of my grandfather?"

"What about him?" Francis replied.

"Everything about Kain must be suspect, including his rise to the Head of the Order. He's a proven liar, a traitor, and a likely murderer. My grandfather could well be innocent and at the very least worthy of the benefit of the doubt. Why should he have a death warrant on him given it was Kain who issued it, and Kain obviously benefited from my grandfather's exile, and if the Order ever caught my grandfather – his death?"

Francis sat back. "It would be for the next Head of the Order to make that call. It is possible, he'll rescind the exile and death warrant."

Li asked, "Who will be the next Head?" she looked expectantly at Francis. "Are you in the running?"

"Force leaders nominate the candidates, and another force leader has to second the nomination. The candidates can be any full member of the Order. Only the force leaders vote for the head of the Order. I could be in the running, more to the point, I will help select who is the next head of the Order."

Anton nodded, and Li asked. "Do you want the job?"

Francis smiled wanly. "It would mean retiring from this team, and handing it over to Jay. The Mirovar force team would end, and the Creeley force team would begin." He shrugged. "I'll see what happens. Any other questions?"

The silence stretched without response. Francis glanced around the table and directed his team. "It's not long till dinner time. Sort it out amongst yourselves who's on kitchen duty and start cooking." He sighed. "And break out a couple of bottles of wine and some whisky from the stores. We need to depressurize."

"Yes, Sir," the team members chorused.

Francis left them to their work and ascended the stairs leading to the deck. Peter and Chiara were waiting at the bow of the ship. He signaled them over with a wave of his hand and sent them downstairs to assist the others.

Francis stood alone on the deck before the guardrail. The Atlantic Ocean surrounded the trawler as far as the eye could see. He pulled his coat closer around his shoulders, shoved his hands in his pockets, and leaned against the guardrail.

Despite the gathering storm clouds in the east, the vista was peaceful, filled with natural beauty, but he couldn't feel it – peace remained denied to him, hidden away behind a locked door – the key to which he couldn't find.

Juliette…

* * *

Perspiration lathered the man's body, his muscles rippling, the veins in his arms popping underneath his tanned skin.

Louise Wesson glanced at the wall clock, it had just clicked over to 21:30 on Thursday night, the 24th of August. It had been three days since she'd ran the first batch of subjects through the Day Guard implant and serum process. Twenty young men, all under thirty years of age drawn from the special force's elite of the US military, eight were dead, and twelve had survived – a better result than she'd expected.

She'd told the survivors the dead had washed out of the program. In reality, Shadowstone had cremated their bodies in the bio-hazard waste facility at Rikers Island while the PSYOPS directorate of Shadowstone constructed elaborate lies to cover their disappearances from their families and friends.

A white label glued to the man's chest on the low cot in front of her read, '0040.' He was the last of the second batch of twenty men to pass through the process. Louise stood at the end of his cot, a pair of med-techs dressed in white fatigues monitoring him, adjusting restraint straps and drip lines. Subject forty had intravenously consumed two gallons of fluids in the last three hours while under the thrall of the serum; gaining about twenty-five pounds of high-density bone, tendon and muscle tissue. Most of the changes were beneath the skin, the subject had gained some extra muscle definition on his already elite body, but the visible changes hid the rewiring of his nervous system, the hijacking of his blood, and the density packing of existing muscle and bone.

Two days before, her staff had led the first subject cleared of side-effects into a room with four of the Phase IV prototypes. They'd given the Phase IVs knives and ordered them to kill the first subject. He'd walked out of the room fifteen seconds later. A pair of med-techs had spent the next half hour cleaning up the mess with mops and buckets.

Louise had watched the video of the fight, and it reminded her of the events in the Noodle House back in June when the triads had taken on Gang and Li Wu, and Anton Smith. The Phase Vs were approaching the capabilities of the Order of Thoth.

She closed her eyes, rubbing the right side of her forehead with her hand. She'd slept for about six hours in the last three days. When not shepherding young men through the Day Guard 'onboarding,' process she'd been dedicating herself to her new mission – subverting the Day Guard and using it to overthrow the Vampire Dominion.

A secret cabal of vampires had destroyed the Republic of the United States from within. Cornelius Crane, the mysterious head of the Shadowstone organization ruled her homeland in secret. It was intolerable; Louise considered herself a cast-iron realist, but the last two months had forced her to realize how deeply the vampires had duped her. The vampire's lies were ubiquitous, the common tenets of society were real enough as far as they went, but when she scratched beneath the surface with an ounce of honest inquiry, those same tenets revealed themselves to be paper thin. The world was a living breathing Potemkin village, a facade hiding a horrific secret reality.

The vast majority of people lived their lives, secure in their ignorance, righteously believing in the primacy of the human race. They were oblivious to the fact vampires ran the world for their own benefit and that humans were little more than food.

A government/private contractor agreement established decades in the past had enabled the construction of the hidden base surrounding her.

Shadowstone listed the secret site as research facility number nineteen – implying there were other sites whose function and location she knew nothing of.

The president who had authorized the Fort Dix secret site must've known more than he'd ever revealed. How deep did the lies go? Whose will did the president bow to when he signed the base's framework documents into law with an executive order bypassing the oversight of Congress?

Presumably, Crane, the current head of Shadowstone in some previous disguise. He was the one who the generals reported to, and there seemed to be no others above him. He ruled the Vampire Dominion, Shadowstone, and by extension and proxy, the rest of the world.

Louise opened her eyes, cameras were everywhere, it wouldn't serve her interests to show any weakness. She glanced around the large medical chamber where all the Day Guard transformations occurred. General Clayton Maze had appeared in the observation suite behind her. Louise handed her checklist to one of the med-techs, and commanded, "Fill this in Jones, and wrap this subject up, then begin setup for the next batch."

The med-tech nodded; his face drawn with exhaustion. "Yes, Ma'am."

Louise turned away, strode to the nearest exit, making her way into the observation suite. She closed the door behind her, faced the General and inquired, "Good evening, Sir. What can I do for you?"

Maze stood in near perfect stillness, his big hands clasped behind his back, breathing quietly as he stared through the observation window at subject forty. He ignored Louise for a handful of seconds. He always did, whenever she initiated a conversation.

Twelve days ago, Louise had accepted the combined role of head of Shadowstone US and the Day Guard Development program, reporting directly to general Maze. She was the human point of contact between the Vampire Dominion and their human organizations. James Haley, still entrusted with a high position within Shadowstone, had moved sideways to personal assistant to General Armitage.

Maze's ambitions had quickly become visible. He sought to use her and the Day Guard to advance his standing amongst Crane's generals, oblivious that she would groom him in return. Louise had formulated a strategy around exploiting his desire for primacy amongst the generals. She would exceed his expectations and give him a force worthy of an ambitious vampire general.

Maze turned to face Louise; he flicked an imaginary fleck of dust from the left arm of his impeccably tailored, dark-blue suit. His black shoes reflected the strip lights in the ceiling, and a gold watch gleamed at his left wrist. He regarded her with dark-brown eyes and declared in precise tones, "We have to accelerate the Day Guard program. We must deliver a combat-ready force of sixty guards within two weeks."

Louise hid her disgust of Maze and his orders behind a facade of determined professionalism. She'd spent the last two months recruiting elite special forces soldiers into Shadowstone US to replenish the spectrum teams after the debacle in Boston. Many of those men were now in the Day Guard program. It was an ugly fact that nearly half of them would die within three days of receiving the serum, and they had no idea of the real risks of the program. She'd even had to tell them the implant inserted next to their brain stem was there to monitor their bio-signs, not that it held a deadly poison so that Shadowstone and the vampires could terminate their lives by remote command.

Louise was a past master of deception, but that particular lie – to these men – it was a rank poison in her guts, and she loathed the necessity of telling it.

She returned her attention to matters of immediate concern. "Sir, we'll need training resources to assist with teaching the men to use their new abilities."

"I will provide staff to assist with that. I will take personal control of the training, and conduct it from within Fort Dix."

Staff? He means vampires, fighters like the ones on the Boston docks. "Sir, there is a problem … I've tasked a technical team to assess the standard issue TAC helmets. They'll need an upgrade."

Maze's eyes tightened, and his lip curled derisively. "What's the issue?"

Louise approached a table in the middle of the room, a brand-new tactical helmet sat on its stainless-steel surface. She tapped the helmet and instructed the vampire general. "The standard electromagnetic shielding in the helmets will block the signal to fire the TEF-4 neurotoxin implant."

Maze frowned, baring his teeth in a grimace and snarled. "Then they'll be out of control with their helmets on." His eyes went flat and cold. "How long will it take to fix."

"I've already initiated a software update of the EM shielding system, but I need your authorization to deploy the update to the field."

Maze stared at Louise for a long moment, assessing her. "Granted," he replied in clipped tones. "Email me the details, and I will deal with it tonight."

"Yes, Sir. Will do."

"Is there anything else?" Maze inquired, his tone suggesting he'd not tolerate another issue.

Louise had saved the best until last. "A software and hardware update, already prepared. The Phase IVs complained about the heads-up display on their helmets – it was crowding their vision with too much useless data. One of my Shadowstone technical teams has developed a new design for an ergonomic HUD and integrated weapon sight populated with direct feeds from the Panopticon. The Phase Vs will have direct target identification and tracking from the Panopticon overlaid upon whatever they're looking at. The feeds connect wirelessly to a new digital weapon sight on their assault rifles to automate the detect, identify, engage and kill process."

Maze grunted. "The Panopticon will be connected to every assault rifle?"

"Yes, Sir. In real time. It's an augmented target and shoot capability."

Maze's face filled with surprise. "I'm impressed, Wesson. Send me the details, and I'll approve the update tonight."

Louise suppressed her autonomic and parasympathetic responses, hiding all hints of deception; general Maze had just approved the first step in her strategy. The conversation continued for another twenty minutes, Maze drilling her on the results of the first two batches of Day Guard subjects and her preparations for the next four batches to meet the requirement for sixty men. In the end, the general was sufficiently satisfied with the rate of progress to leave the observation suite.

Louise took a cup of cold water from a drinking fountain and returned to face the transformation chamber. The med-techs had transferred subject forty to the test section, his cot taken away and replaced with a fresh one. She appeared to be watching her staff prepare for the third batch of subjects, but her mind was far away.

Five hundred doses of the serum would produce at least two hundred and fifty enhanced super-soldiers. The new weapons system integrating a guard's assault rifle with their tactical helmet, automating target acquisition, tracking and shot release would be effective against any fast-moving targets, including vampires.

Louise aimed to wrest control of the Day Guard away from the vampires and destroy the main Panopticon hub in Utah. That would cause the vampires to accelerate the commissioning of the second Panopticon on the East coast. Shadowstone would seed the surveillance system with a brand-new AI, not a copy replicated from the first Panopticon. She could ensure the new AI would be under her control. She could blind the Vampire Dominion while delivering a knock-out blow against their leadership during daylight hours when they were at their most vulnerable. With Crane, Armitage and the rest of the generals out of the way, she could turn the new Panopticon and the Day Guard against the rest of the vampires.

And then, she would tear down their tyranny and restore the republic, and humanity would finally be free to chart their own destiny.

General Maze ascended to the Fort Dix base above, departing the facility via a nightfalcon helicopter. Louise tracked his progress with the monitors on the wall of the observation suite. Once the helicopter had taken off, she returned to the main chamber where half a dozen med-techs had prepared twenty fresh cots.

She frowned slightly, yes there would be sacrifices, terrible sacrifices, *but the tree of liberty must be refreshed from time to time with the blood of patriots and tyrants.*

Jefferson's words and hers too, now she needed the Order of Thoth to prove they really were smart enough to be useful. She would throw the biggest clue she could in front of them. She hoped they had the wit to see it and the courage to act upon it. She'd equipped each helmet with a direct feed from the Panopticon and a GPS link. All she needed to do was ensure one of the new TAC helmets fell into the hands of a tech-savvy Order of Thoth operative and let them do the rest. She considered her plan, a slight smile on her lips. The upgraded TAC helmets were the key to harnessing the Order of Thoth to her strategy without anyone realizing it.

If her plan worked, the Order would destroy the Panopticon site in Utah, enabling her strategy to move closer to her end game – the unleashing of the Day Guard against the Vampire Dominion.

She blinked her eyes once slowly, the desire to sleep clawing at the inside of her skull. *If my plan works, it'd be a miracle.*

A damn miracle.

Chapter Three

"Deflect, co-opt, absorb or annihilate. It doesn't matter if you're in a sword fight or conducting a worldwide military campaign, these are the options for dealing with your opposition." – General Chloe Armitage

* * *

Jerusalem, August 24th, 22:00

Chloe pushed back against the concrete of the access pipe and pulled the manhole cover back into place above her.

The pipe plunged into darkness. Chloe extended her senses to their vampire maximums. The pitch-dark gloom around her evaporated away, replaced with a twilight realm of sharply delineated shadows. The fathomless quiet retreated, new sounds blooming into her awareness, the steady drip of water, the dull thrum of distant traffic, and the scurrying of rats moving away from her position.

The rats were wiser in their instinctive awareness of her presence than humans typically were.

Chloe shifted her position, letting go of the ladder and dropping thirty feet down to the sewer below. She landed lithely on the dry access pathway. The concrete stretched for two yards from the curving brickwork walls to the drop off into the sewer proper.

She paused for a long moment, listening, sniffing, watching – filtering everything around her. The stench of the sewer she put aside, able to ignore that useless signal and focus on what she needed.

She was alone, she turned to her left and began walking silently along the walkway. She wore advanced combat boots providing a perfect combination of grip, stealth, and protection. She'd donned her praetorian combat armor and tactical helmet in standard Shadowstone matte black. She'd strapped the Red Dragon to her left hip, and a pair of long holsters to her thighs. Her custom built, .50 caliber auto-pistols resting within them. Dark combat webbing covered her chest, sporting four anti-personnel grenades, and spare twenty-round magazines for the auto-pistols positioned for quick loading. A bandolier with a dozen coke-can sized shaped charges snaked from the front of her right hip over her left shoulder, and back to the top of her right buttock.

In her custom-built matte-black armor and tactical helmet, Chloe was a moving shadow when she wanted to be. In the pitch black of the sewers, she was a veil of silence moving through space. Her vampire senses rendered her world into a fey twilight. She moved forward with lithe, effortless surety. She paused at a 'T' intersection, leaped over the sewer to the far side, and headed along to the right. She didn't need to consult a map or GPS signal; she was retracing her steps to the entrance of the Red Empire citadel. The last time she was here, she'd worn a thick black hood, and a team of Red Empire assassins had escorted her.

She paused for a moment; lay down on the concrete pathway and squirmed along for twenty feet, then leaped a dozen more. The movements seemed nonsensical but were perfect renditions of the precise actions she'd performed on her first passage of the pathway to and from the citadel.

Chloe turned and examined the path she'd leaped over. Pressure plates secreted beneath the concrete path? A hidden laser sensor? Something guarded the area she'd just passed through. The Red Empire would monitor all possible approaches to their citadel to detect humans, vampires or drones, and once they detected a threat, they would take active measures to neutralize the intruder. She'd not encountered any yet, no sentry guns or prowling drones.

She frowned slightly. Were the Red Empire expecting her, allowing her to approach before triggering a deadly trap, or was the path she was on a secret route through the citadel's defenses? She suspected the latter. She was betting her life on it. The vampires had long maintained the belief the Red Empire habitually placed a secret path for their own use through any defensive system. They always built a concealed 'back door.' Her experience with the Raven and the destruction of the Order safe house in Maine had confirmed the practice. Her forces had exploited the Raven's secret path to cut through the Order's defensive sensor arrays and disarm the whole system before obliterating the safe house.

After another ten minutes of careful navigation of the convoluted pathway, Chloe stopped again. She was a hundred and three steps from the entrance to the citadel. The citadel's front doors remained hidden behind three corners. She'd left the sewers behind, now she stood in a purpose-built Red Empire access tunnel twelve feet across and the same high, made of smooth pale concrete and ocher brickwork walls. Two yards in front of her the tunnel turned to the right, and no doubt, into the line of fire of a sentry weapon.

When the Red Empire operatives had escorted Chloe to and from the citadel, the final path required no special maneuvers. There were no hidden sensors or traps before the citadel entrance – no, instead there would be powerful weapons designed to target and kill vampires and Ramp masters. The three turns in the remaining tunnel were simply there to create three kill zones where remote weapon systems could target intruders from multiple angles.

It was a death trap.

She drew her .50 caliber auto-pistols, flipped the safeties off, and held them ready in front of her chest. The magazines of caseless hypervelocity ammunition fitted neatly into the pistol-grip, giving her a combined total of forty shots before she'd have to reload. Each round would travel at twice the speed of regular ammunition, and the depleted uranium penetrators would slice through anything they hit.

Her immediate targets would be the nearby sentry weapons, but first, she'd need a distraction, a big distraction to keep the Red Empire from reinforcing the front door with additional troops. She activated an encrypted point to point tactical network with James Haley, and whispered, "James, are you in position?"

"Yes, Ma'am," James replied.

"I'm ready. Initiate the plan."

"Firing now, ETA in three seconds."

Chloe reached deep into silence, as a former Ramp master she could combine Ramp capabilities with her native vampire powers to produce a superior effect. She prepared herself to ramp hard, time slowed, seconds dragging past, three … two … one.

Explosions reverberated through the yards of concrete, rock, and masonry above her, fine dust falling from the ceiling in a gray mist.

She blurred around the right-hand corner into the tunnel, both hands extended forward, the auto-pistols level at shoulder height.

It was time to kick in the front door.

* * *

Four air-launched hypersonic cruise missiles speared into the corners of the Mount Scopus Museum campus. Their ground penetrating five-hundred-pound warheads lighting up the night sky, demolishing four of the museum's gardens and parking lots.

The violent thunder of the detonations cracked against James Haley's earpieces, setting his ears ringing. He grimaced in pain, tightening his grip on the side of a ventilation tower. He perched on a maintenance platform fifty feet above the roof of the museum, next to the main air shaft providing fresh air to the Red Empire citadel hidden beneath it.

The museum was a multi-building site spread across a large campus. The cruise missiles fired from a shadowstar drone loitering two miles overhead had targeted the Red Empire citadel beneath the museum campus and not the museum itself.

Chloe had provided the coordinates and James had set up the shots. She intended the attack to force a fast evacuation by the Red Empire. The Vampire Dominion could obliterate the site with heavy weapons and a sustained bombardment, but that would also destroy the Interpretive

Codex. Chloe and James could not allow anyone to destroy the Codex on their watch. Crane would kill them both for losing it.

The shots had been surgical, cutting the main power and water lines servicing the citadel. The museum above the citadel had only suffered minor damage to windows and facades.

James' ears stopped ringing in a second or two. He pulled aside a foot-wide metal square cut from the side of the tower. It fell at his feet with a clang. An open military-style lock box sat next to him on the platform. He reached inside and drew forth an aerial mini-drone. It sported a pair of rings surrounding propellers and a smoke grenade payload. It started automatically and flew through the hole in the tower, another thirty-nine identical fliers lifted out of the lock box and flew after it.

James wasted no time fleeing the tower, descending a set of metal ramps toward the ground. The shadowstar drone would land at the exfiltration site in ten minutes. He needed to be there to meet Chloe and General Mosule. Soon the museum campus would be swarming with outraged Red Empire warriors spoiling for a fight, and James was fully aware of just how long he would survive against them. If he met just one of them, he could measure his lifespan in seconds.

How was Chloe going? The mission's success or failure hinged on her abilities.

* * *

Time stretched, dilating to the extreme.

Chloe's ramp embraced the supreme edges of her powers. Her mind descended into stone-cold silence. She eliminated thoughts and words, operating on her deadly, predatory instincts alone.

The gray powder falling from the ceiling after the cruise missile attacks arrested, floating slowly in the air, seemingly resisting the powers of gravity. At the highest levels of the Ramp, her senses amplified to beyond vampire maximums. She accessed capabilities transcending anything she'd experienced before, her vision extending deep into the infra-red and ultra-violet spectrums.

The twilight realm of her vampire senses, conditioned by the absolute absence of light, slipped away. A low-power, infra-red sensor net, crisscrossed the first hall. Invisible to mortal eyes, it stretched dark red threads throughout the thirty-yard length of the corridor. Chloe leaped and rolled through the first gap in the net, buying herself a dozen feet. The infra-red net reconfigured instantly, a new lattice appearing around her. She leaped, landed, flipped and rolled, gaining another twenty feet. The net reconfigured again, random strands spearing through the hallway at crazed angles. She ran along the nearest wall for eight feet, then dived through another gap, twisting mid-air and landing on her feet in a tight crouch.

The net shifted again, each cast coming closer to catching her. She spun toward the middle of the corridor. The net transformed again, a stray beam catching her left ankle, the dark red threads vanishing back into the darkness.

The sensors had tagged her.

Chloe surged forward, accelerating toward the left-hand corner into the second hall. Brickwork and mortar bloomed silently toward her from the far wall. An instant later the sound arrived, reverberating explosive cracks thundering around her. A 7.62mm minigun, mounted on steel rails burst through the gaping hole in the far wall and began firing. The twilight world of her senses snapped suddenly into vivid color, lit by the golden-white muzzle flashes. The individual bullets resolved, lancing toward her chest, gleaming strobes of golden fire from each bullet painting brilliant zebra stripes on the ocher brick walls.

She pivoted to her left, leaning backward. The first of the bullets tore past her chest, crossing two feet above a second stream of fire coming from her left. A second minigun had burst through the rear wall. Chloe's hands snapped out, hard left and right, her auto-pistols erupting with jets of azure fire in opposite directions along the corridor.

The augmented ammunition raced away, striking white-hot sparks off the bodies of the miniguns, sharp cracks resounding along the corridors. The miniguns spinning barrels continued to fire. Two streams of golden light swung toward her, one at chest height, the other at mid-thigh.

If they hit, they'd tear her apart.

Chloe pivoted in mid-air around her center of mass, squeezing herself between the two streams, which passed above and beneath her. Her guns stuttered and roared, her second fusillade striking the spinning engine at the heart of each minigun. Metal screeched and tore, electrical sparks jagged wildly, pale-blue smoke rising in a plume around each weapon.

Chloe came to a halt just inside the left-hand corner to the second hall. Her back rested against the wall, her auto-pistols held in front of her chest, wisps of grayish-blue smoke curling from their hot throats. To her left, the wrecked minigun's barrels ground to a halt, the stench of burnt metal filling the air. The second hall beckoned. She couldn't waste her strongest ramp, in seconds it would fade, she had to act now. With a downward jerk of her hands, she released the magazines from her auto-pistols, and they floated slowly downward. An instant later she'd reloaded from her webbing, blurring around the corner and into the second corridor.

The second hallway was just like the first, twelve feet across and the same high, made of smooth pale concrete floors and ceiling, and ocher brickwork walls. It ran another thirty yards, before disappearing around a right-hand corner. Beyond that corner was the third and final corridor leading to the front doors of the Red Empire Citadel.

Chloe lined up on the left side of the second corridor and sprinted forward. If a human had been in a position to watch, it would seem she'd simply vanished into thin air. Her hearing was practically useless in this place, everything dangerous was happening faster than sound could travel. Whatever sensor system was in place in the second hall, it was beyond her ability to detect; even her advanced, custom-built tactical helmet provided no clues. The wall directly in front of her path erupted into a cloud of gray and ocher dust. A third minigun appeared, its barrels spinning into motion before the body of the gun came to a halt on its rail. Bright silver tipped bullets streamed toward her chest, muzzle flash from the minigun strobing along the corridor.

She instinctively ran toward the fire, rising up the left-hand wall, the bullets passing beneath her. To her right, a second stream of 7.62mm minigun fire passed by her, tearing the brickwork apart on the far wall. Chloe's fist, still holding one of her auto-pistols, pushed off the ceiling, changing her momentum, and sending her over the second stream of silvery fire coming from behind her. She landed flat on her back, skidding over the floor, her right arm flung above her head, her left hand beside her thigh.

Both auto-pistols stammered, spitting blue fire. Depleted uranium penetrators wreathed in bright-blue flame, shredded the air of the corridor, spearing toward the opposing miniguns.

The minigun's moved on their cradles, their spinning barrels describing figure eights from side to side, and from top to bottom of the hallway. There was nowhere to hide. Chloe's eyes widened, she grimaced, her fingers tightened on the triggers of her auto-pistols, the hypervelocity rounds thundering away at the automated weapons.

Sparks erupted in showers, and the minigun beyond her feet fell silent. Chloe was already on the move, rising off the floor like a dark shadow. The auto-pistol in her right hand fired once more – then clicked on empty.

The remaining minigun from the front of the corridor continued to track her, its bright silvery rounds closing in. She brought her left hand up, the auto-pistol barking like a mad dog, the final rounds in the magazine ripping through the air.

She turned violently aside. Silvery fire scored the nano-ceramic plates of her chest armor, missing the shaped charges on her bandolier by a miracle. The rounds ricocheting off her combat armor, spraying into the walls in wild anarchy. The deflected impacts pushing her back a step.

The last round of her auto-pistol took out the engine driving the remaining minigun. The weapon blew apart in a cloud of gray-blue smoke and crackling electrical sparks.

Still ramped, Chloe blurred forward to the inner wall of the right-hand corner. Her movement triggered another defense. A silvery cloud jetted down from above, blooming around her, and obscuring her vision for a moment as she slammed up against the wall next to the corner. Behind her, dozens of foot-long blades speared down from the ceiling. If she'd been caught by the silver cloud, the blades would have cut her to ribbons. Her custom-built tactical helmet, recently proofed against silver aerosols, had saved her life.

Chloe dumped the empty magazines of her auto-pistols and loaded her last pair. She had forty rounds of hypervelocity ammunition left – it would have to be enough. Whatever was in the third and final corridor would be the worst of what she would face this side of the entrance to the citadel.

The supreme ramp was tearing at her from within, drawing upon her reserves of vampire strength and endurance. In the past, she'd only ever used the supreme ramp as a momentary burst of great power. To defeat the draw stroke of an Order weapons grandmaster, or tear the armored nose off a nightfalcon gunship, or slaughter a pair of Order blademasters attacking her at the same time.

But if she dropped out now, it would be at least a minute before she could peak again – and she didn't have a minute to spare outside the front doors of the Red Empire citadel.

Time was draining away – there would be no second chance.

Chloe strained against the rising agony flooding through her, blurring around the final corner. Thirty yards in front of her were a pair of large mirrored rectangular steel doors. There was no obvious way to open them. The hallway was empty. Her heart thudded once in her chest. Something would defend the corridor – something must be about to happen. She made it halfway to the doors before the trap closed shut.

There was just enough time for the tiny hairs at the nape of her skull to tingle and rise. Before they completed their movements, her predatory instincts drove her violently aside. Her hands blurred to the left and right, her loaded auto-pistols rising to cover the main angles of attack on her position.

A crimson laser beam cut through the space where she'd just been. The hard light passed through the barrels of the auto-pistols in her hands, hot metal expanding into bright-gray clouds as her guns fell apart.

The Red Empire's weapon was on her left, opposite the main doors. The laser scored a chest high, horizontal streak of red-hot metal upon the citadel's entrance. Chloe had no hope of defeating the potent cutting beam – it was impossibly fast, but the mount on which the weapon moved was another thing entirely. If she could move faster than the mount could track her, she could beat the laser. The Red Dragon hissed free of its scabbard. She turned toward the laser, a two-foot-long, six-inch-wide white tube, resembling a hobbyist's telescope mounted on a powered cradle. A sensor array surmounted the weapon and began tracking her movement.

Agony warred with her will, and she almost faltered. The supreme ramp had been running far too long. She dug deeper, power and energy surging within her, coruscating along her limbs. She scaled the left wall, defying gravity with her speed, racing across the ceiling. The weapon tracked her every movement, a bright crimson beam of light ripping through the concrete and brickwork behind her. She jerked away from the beam, dropping through growing clouds of pale-gray and ocher dust to the floor. The beam sparkled overhead, the reek of burning stone flooding her nostrils.

Chloe closed on the weapon, rolling underneath its searching beam, rising suddenly beside it, safe from its deadly ray. The Red Dragon flashed down, gleaming wetly in the scarlet light, plunging into the laser's electrical heart.

The crimson beam winked out.

Her supreme ramp faded. Chloe took a deep breath and sighed deeply, the agony of the extended Ramp retreating from her bones and sinews. The Red Dragon disappeared back into its scabbard. She moved hard, appearing thirty yards away in front of the main doors. She blurred, two of her shaped charges appeared in her hands, and she slammed them into the right-hand seam of the door. Moments later, she'd planted another four on the middle seam and left edge of the doors. She armed them all and stepped back.

The Red Dragon swished free of its scabbard.

A grim smile graced Chloe's full lips, and she counted softly, "Three … two … one."

* * *

A klaxon wailed in the distance. Red emergency lighting lit the hallway, rendering the front doors of the citadel the color of clotted blood.

Steel-Axe was proud to have earned the honor of guarding the main entrance to the Red Empire citadel. The Red Empire fighter was too young to have earned a proper name. His fellow door guards had given him the nick-name to make up for his lack.

A series of massive explosions had cut the external power lines, and the emergency lighting had been on for less than five seconds. He watched a screen displaying the scenes in the halls leading to the entrance. Cameras showed a dark figure blurring through the death traps. Whoever they were, their movement was mesmerizing and frightening in its exemplary display of raw power and skill. The intruder had somehow navigated their way through the approaches to the citadel, managing to avoid the many sensors and traps designed to detect and destroy the unwary before they got to the final halls.

Were they one of their own, possessed of secret knowledge? A rogue Red Empire operative of the third rank? A mighty warrior turned by the vampires and sent against the heart of the Red Empire?

Steel-Axe put his questions aside. No one should be able to survive the three halls, and yet, the dark figure still lived. Muted minigun-fire reached into the guardhouse and filled the air.

Gray and ocher clouds bloomed, and azure and golden lights flared in the monitor displays. Amongst the chaos, the black figure blurred like an unstoppable wraith.

Steel-Axe took a deep breath and stilled his mind. His emotions retreated and his years of training came to the fore. The Red Empire had inducted his cousin, Iron-Hero, and himself into their community as young children. Lifted from the outskirts of Ulan-Bator, they had found a new home within the Red Empire citadel. Still unblooded by combat with vampires, they stood shoulder to shoulder and faced the approaching nightmare.

"Where are the others?" whispered Iron-Hero. His hands gripped his bared swords, thickly muscled forearms disappearing into the voluminous sleeves of his dark-gray Red Empire robe.

A red light flashed across the monitors; the laser had fired. Surely it would have sliced the attacker in two.

"No one's coming," Steel-Axe observed quietly, his eyes hard as black river stones. There would be no time for reinforcements to arrive. The attack was as sudden as it was violent. The two cousins stood alone. He glanced at Iron-Hero. A bead of perspiration appeared on his cousin's right temple and started rolling down it. Steel-Axe drew his blades, squared his shoulders, and prepared to Ramp.

Whatever was going to happen – it was upon them now.

Silence reigned in the outer halls, and then came a series of staccato thuds.

Iron-Hero shouted, "What the—"

Blinding light ripped through the doors. They blew off their massive hinges, crumpled like tinfoil, and flew along the hallway.

Both young men ramped hard, leaping out of the way of the reeking, flaming slabs of metal. A wave of searing heat washed over Steel-Axe. He landed on his feet, his twin blades snapping into high and low guard positions. Iron-Hero landed a half a dozen feet away, mirroring his pose.

Smoke, fire, and gray-ocher dust eddied in the doorway. A slim, athletic, feminine figure, as tall as Steel-Axe, and clad in matte-black praetorian armor emerged into the entrance hall of the gatehouse. Everyone paused for the briefest of moments. The three of them, all assessing the options of battle. The vampire carried a katana, its immaculate blade snapping into attack position over the vampire's right shoulder. In the handle of the sword, a ruby gleamed like a swollen eye in the emergency lighting.

The vampire was faster than anyone Steel-Axe had seen. She was above the third rank. Even Taipan, the premier warrior of the Red Empire, would struggle to survive the death traps of the three halls.

A name out of legend ripped through his thoughts, *Armitage*. His guts went to water, his heart thudded. *The two of us against her?*

He stilled his mind, dropping into silence as deep as he could go. There was no space for thoughts of retreat or the dishonor of flight. He would stand with his brother-in-arms, Iron-Hero, and they would prevail over the demon who'd entered their realm or die together defending their home.

Time slowed; the vampire rushed forward.

Iron-Hero stepped to his right. Steel-Axe moved to his left, hiding behind his cousin's body. It was a classic surprise attack against a single opponent perfected through thousands of repetitions against skilled Red Empire warriors. The maneuver would allow the two cousins to bring four blades against the vampire at the same time.

Steel-Axe blurred to his left, his cousin blurring in front of him. Armitage hidden beyond Iron-Hero's robed body. In another moment they would take position to strike her down.

The tip of the vampire's katana erupted between Iron-Hero's shoulders, a slim rope of blood splashing across Steel-Axe's chest. Iron-Hero's body jerked backward as if struck by a giant's fist, a two-hundred-pound missile barbed with a foot-and-a-half long length of gore-splashed metal flying toward Steel-Axe.

Iron-Hero's body slammed into him, Armitage's razor-sharp blade still skewering his cousin, ripped into his chest. His feet skidded on the stone floor, the momentum of the attack pushing him over onto his back. Armitage flew overhead, the red emergency lighting seeming to fill her helmet visor with blood. The vicious katana drew down and out, in a reverse cut to the vampire's forward momentum, unzipping both men from the heart to the groin.

Half smothered beneath his cousin's corpse, his body in disarray, Steel-Axe's ramp faded. His courage spent, his swords rolled free from limp fingers, the release of infinite darkness claiming him a moment later.

* * *

The readouts on two of his warriors flatlined.

"The main entrance has been breached," one of his aides announced.

"Tai—" *no, Taipan is already gone.* Dalien Morte, aka the Red Ghost, surveyed the wall of monitors in his command center. A dozen Red Empire operatives manned the consoles around him. Damage reports were already coming in from remote sensors. The missile strikes had cut the main power cables and water conduits, and fatally compromised the citadel's secrecy. There was only one option.

"Signal all our forces," Dalien commanded, his voice thundering throughout the chamber. "Evacuate the citadel. Initiate the immolation protocol."

"Yes, Red Ghost," his men chorused, their hands blurring over touchscreens. One of the monitors started a five-minute countdown. It would be all the time his forces would have to fully evacuate the citadel before pre-set explosives destroyed all traces of the secret base.

A single monitor covered the hall leading from the front doors into the citadel. A dark figure wearing praetorian armor blurred along the corridor and ran into a squad of four of his own warriors. Blades crashed against each other and sparks flew. A spray of blood jetted over the camera lens, obscuring half the screen. The lone vampire cut through his men in a handful of seconds. They had barely slowed her down, his regular troops were no match for her – and it was definitely her.

"Armitage," he whispered in cold fury. She must have found a way to retrace her steps back to the citadel. Her betrayal had finished their secret alliance. He would contact his daughter in the Mirovar force team at the earliest opportunity, he must warn her about the 'other operative.' However, He wouldn't share with Chiara that Armitage was the other operative. He would need to carefully explain to his daughter that he'd entered into an alliance with a vampire, lest she misunderstood and rejected the wisdom of his choices, and with that, his rule.

"Sir, the cruise missiles came from a shadowstar drone two miles above us. We have it on our scopes."

Dalian snapped a rapid command, "Kill it."

"Sir, our surface to air missile battery has been engaged against the drone."

Dalien directed his staff. "Contact the prison complex. Issue a command to kill all the vampires and then evacuate."

Dalien surveyed the room. His men were well trained and understood exactly what to do. They would fight bravely and well, but they'd lost the citadel with its discovery by the Vampire Dominion. It was a pointless waste of good men to spend any more lives defending a doomed base. He clicked his fingers and signaled four men in full combat gear to his side. The warriors blurred into position next to him; they were all of the second rank, and equivalent to fist team leaders. They were his personal guards, dedicated to the protection of his life and the Interpretive Codex. He turned on his heel, the hem of his simple dark-gray robes swishing around his booted ankles and strode from the chamber.

Dalien stepped into the hallway outside the command center. A loud hissing came from the nearest air-vent, a moment later a cloud of gray smoke billowed through the grate.

Dalien's lip curled in dismay, what else could go wrong?

"To the Codex vault," he snapped, and blurred away, his four guards vanishing after him.

* * *

Four fiery streaks erupted out of the ground and speared into the sky, converging on a hovering shadow riding high against a sea of stars.

James Haley sprinted across the deserted parking lot. Above him, blue fire appeared from the rear of the shadowstar drone. It bucked hard, pulling tens of gees of acceleration. The forces involved would have turned a human occupant into wet sludge. The empty drone was able to use its full maneuvering capability to evade the threats rising like vengeful spirits from deep beneath the museum's extensive grounds.

Multi-spectral countermeasures blossomed like fireworks in the sky, the drone became a bright blue star streaking toward the horizon. One of the missiles diverged into the hundred-yard flowers blooming above James' head, detonating in a blinding glare.

James threw his left arm up to shield his eyes. The air cracked and thundered for a few seconds after the explosion. The other three missiles curved away, accelerating after the fleeing shadowstar drone.

A second volley of countermeasures lit up the night sky. A second surface-to-air missile diverted away, dying short of its target in a thunderous fireball. The blue light of the shadowstar's exhaust, the only marker of its passage visible to the human eye, streaked like a meteor across the sky.

A sonic boom shattered the night.

"Go, baby go!" James shouted. The drone had to survive; it was their only ticket out of here.

The last two missiles closed in.

The shadowstar drone's close in laser weapon system activated, a flash of scarlet light illuminating the lead missile which evaporated in a cloud of brilliant fragments.

The final missile flashed past its sibling's destruction and reached its target. The shadowstar drone vanished in a blinding fireball, its hydrogen fuel adding to the explosive detonations.

James pulled to a halt, his jaw dropping open. "Holy shit!"

Somewhere beyond the edges of Jerusalem, a cloud of high-tech confetti descended to the ground in hurtling streamers of flaming debris.

He grabbed his chin with his right hand, drawing his fingers down it, then sighed and rubbed the back of his neck. "Oh, fucking hell."

James clicked the throat mike for his tactical link to Chloe. She needed to know that shit was officially hitting the fan. The earbud hummed and gave a faint chirp of futility. She was out of contact. The Red Empire was blanketing the area with electromagnetic jamming for anything but their own equipment.

They were both on their own. He still needed to get to the exfil site to meet up with her, but now there wouldn't be a drone to pick them up and spirit them away before the Red Empire could overtake them.

James ran through the parking lot, looking around for options. There had to be something here they could use to get away with, or a Red Empire army would overwhelm them.

A shape loomed out of the darkness.

James grinned wryly, *it just might work*, he thought, *after all, beggars can't be choosers*.

* * *

"Kill all the vampires!"

The command was as concise as it was expected. There was nowhere to take the prisoners, and no easy way to keep them constrained in an emergency evacuation. With a flick of his hand across his throat and a hard stare, Whispering Death sent two of his men into the prison complex to deal with their captives.

Most of the monitors in the prison guardhouse displayed the cells where they kept the vampires. Two additional screens showed the four-hundred-yard access tunnel leading from the main base to the prison complex, each taking a feed from a camera at the end of the long corridor. Gray smoke began billowing out of the main base and into the far end of the access corridor. All his men carried a breather mask in their kit; it would be sufficient to allow them to escape through the smoke.

One of the monitors counted down the seconds before pre-set explosives immolated the base. It read, '4:40,' then ticked over to 4:39. The sudden crack of a white-phosphorous grenade going off in one of the prison cells signaled the beginning of the end for the vampires. One of the monitors lit up with bright fire, a living human-shaped torch began bouncing around at the bottom of a ninety-foot-deep reinforced glass cylinder. Five seconds later another pair of grenades lit up two more monitors.

Whispering Death watched the displays implacably. All vampires deserved death. Once he was certain the task was complete, he would lead his men from the prison complex to the emergency egress points in the main citadel.

In another minute, ninety seconds at most, his men would terminate all the vampire prisoners, and his team would still have three minutes to evacuate the citadel.

Perhaps it would have been better if they'd mined prison as the rest of the citadel was. They'd designed the immolation explosives to eliminate evidence and leave nothing useful for the Vampire Dominion, but the Red Ghost had insisted on manual methods for the prison complex. He hadn't trusted the loyalty of all members of the Red Empire. The Red Ghost had carefully selected the prison guards and trained them to maximize personal loyalty to himself. To even place his orders above the words in the Book of the Way. It was why all the guards were young. Whispering Death himself, had only earned his true name three weeks earlier, after completing the first level of the test of the Olgoi Khorkhoi.

A flicker of movement on one of the displays caught his eye. A vampire in praetorian armor blurred into the long access hall. His team would have to go through the enemy to evacuate – there was no other pathway of escape. A moment of regret flew through his soul on shadowy wings. He was wearing the traditional gray robes of peace with a narrow red waist sash of his rank, worn as a reflection of the hearthstone of the Red Empire, not the fierce dark-red robes of war.

Whispering Death sighed, it would have been more fitting to enter battle wreathed in red, but there was no time to change. Still, they all wore their body armor beneath their robes, only a fool would allow an enemy to catch him naked – even at home. He glanced once more at the monitors. The vampire was female, it was the general, the Red Empire's most formidable foe.

They were about to win great honor. He called on the remainder of the guards, drew his thick-bladed swords, and blurred toward the corridor.

It was time to fight.

* * *

Gray smoke flooded the halls.

Chloe blurred to her right into a four-hundred-yard-long corridor. The smoke thinned rapidly. James had concentrated the mini-drones on the main air ducts, and this hallway was new and distant from the main base of the citadel. The corridor led to a prison complex, constructed in the last couple of decades. The capture and imprisonment of vampires represented a shift in Red Empire policy by Dalien Morte. For what ultimate purpose, she didn't know, perhaps she would discover the Red Ghost's intentions by the end of her mission.

The strip lighting in the ceiling glowed a dull red, klaxons ululating in the distance. The concrete floor and ceiling, and dark-gray brick walls stretching into the distance. The long hall ended at a double pair of barred gates. Directly behind the gates were a pair of archways to the left and right, and beyond them was a wide-open single steel door.

Half a dozen Red Empire warriors, dressed in their traditional gray robes, blurred into the corridor. Glimpses of black and tan body armor showed at the edges of their robes. Each wielded a pair of short heavy swords – there were no other visible weapons. Flashes of light lit up the chamber beyond the open steel door, the sharp crack of exploding grenades echoing along the corridor.

They're killing the prisoners. How many have they got back there? I'd best hurry – Crane won't be satisfied with the delivery of a corpse.

Chloe blurred forward, covering the distance to the gates in an even eight seconds. She pulled to a halt ten yards short, slipping one of her anti-personnel grenades off her combat webbing and holding it behind her left hip. She flourished the Red Dragon, and shouted, "Are you going to hide behind steel bars for the rest of your lives? I thought brave warriors filled the Red Empire … perhaps I'm mistaken."

A lean young man, built like a greyhound, all sinew and bone beneath his body armor, robes and red sash of the first rank, curled his lip and snapped, "Ho, general Armitage, you'll find our blades are sharp enough to cut the hide from your bones."

"I certainly hope for your sake, they're sharper than your wit."

The young warrior snarled, his fingers keying a control panel to his right on the wall. The steel bars retreated into holes in the walls, ceiling, and floor, leaving the corridor clear of all obstacles.

Chloe's eyes widened as she assessed the kill zone in front of her. There were six warriors in front of her, and at least one more in the chamber beyond, perhaps as many as three more. She armed the grenade and let it fall as she blurred forward, the Red Dragon arcing down toward the Red Empire team leader's head.

His blades flashed up, deflecting the Red Dragon away. He surged forward, running past her on the right.

The man to Chloe's left, swung his blades low, aiming to disembowel her. She rolled over the top of them, and he ran past her, positioning behind her with his team leader.

There was a wild shout from the team leader behind her, "Grenade!"

Chloe blurred forward, the Red Dragon capturing and lifting the blades of the nearest fighter on her left. Her free hand grasped his tunic, and she flung him behind her.

The grenade detonated with a thunderclap, the flash delineating everyone in the corridor into stark relief. Hot, steel fragments filled the air, pinging off Chloe's armor. Someone screamed behind her, and a heavy body crashed to the floor, swords clanging against brickwork and concrete.

The ramped warriors in front of her lifted arms to protect their faces, their body armor taking the brunt of the grenade's force.

An instant later, they'd all recovered, launching immediate attacks.

Chloe flicked her blade high and low, then left and right. Sparks flew as her blade ground against half a dozen Red Empire swords. Her right foot lashed out, one of the warriors crumpled around her boot, and flew twenty feet away to crash into the wall.

She blurred through the gap created by her kick. The Red Empire warriors swirled around her. Ramping, blurring, their swords flashing beneath the blood-colored lighting of the emergency system.

The grenade had claimed the warrior she'd thrown behind her, his body lying against the left wall in a spreading pool of blood. A second warrior was slumped against the opposite wall, but he was still breathing. The team leader was unharmed, he must've moved very fast to escape the grenade.

The young team leader blurred back to about five yards short of the battle and paused.

Chloe's blade danced. What was the young team leader up to? One of her opponents leaned forward, attacking one of her feints.

The Red Dragon blurred in a horizontal slash.

* * *

The vampire's katana lashed out, drawing a line through the throat of one of his Red Empire guards.

There was a visible pause before blood sluiced forth from the major arteries. The head slumped backward, barely attached to the man's shoulders as the body collapsed forward. The guard's swords clattered to the concrete floor, his corpse following them down, spraying blood as it fell. The vampire blurred forward another two yards, engaging the remaining two guards in front of her with her glimmering blade.

Whispering Death dropped out of his Ramp. He activated his tactical communications link, opened a direct line to the Red Ghost, and called out, "Sir, we're under attack! Send reinforcements!"

The Red Ghost responded, "You have a single opponent?"

"Yes, Sir."

"Kill her. That is your only duty."

"Yes, Sir," Whispering Death replied, but the link had already disconnected, and if the Red Ghost heard his words, he didn't know. There would be no reinforcements. Suddenly feeling desperately alone, he shouted, "Mountain Hawk, Storm Shield, to us, to us!"

Slaughtering the trapped vampire prisoners could wait. There was a deadly opponent to defeat, and the young team leader needed every blade he could muster. Stilling his mind, Whispering Death dropped deeply into silence, time slowed, and he rushed forward to attack. The vampire's back was toward him, perhaps in this one moment, the famous vampire general was vulnerable.

His blades flashed down in the red light.

* * *

Chloe spun in a half circle, the Red Dragon blurring through the air in a sweeping arc.

The gleaming katana collected a pair of Red Empire blades at just the right angle, shattering them into clouds of hot metal droplets and shards of spinning metal. The young fist leader blurred defensively, his amazing speed once again saving his life. He recovered his poise, scooping up a pair of fallen swords from the limp hands of one of his dead comrades.

The tips of the fist leader's blades blurred into invisibility as he snapped his new weapons into high and low guard positions.

No doubt a talent, Chloe thought, drawing on her deepest reserves, this battle was taking longer than anticipated. The last thing she needed was for the Red Ghost to realize he had a single vampire attacking his citadel and reverse his evacuation. She could end up having to fight a hundred or more Red Empire assassins.

And one of them could get lucky.

She dueled the team leader, while two warriors, a half-dozen feet away from her back kept probing her defenses. She constantly moved between them, deflecting attacks, setting up traps, and searching for weaknesses.

The team leader was unnaturally fast, a true speed talent and he fought like two opponents. A spark of covetousness flared within her, she'd prefer to collect him one day, rather than kill him here and now.

The warrior slumped against the wall woke up, shook off the effects of her grenade, growled and leaped to his feet. Two more warriors blurred through the steel doorway from the prison complex.

It was getting crowded, were her reserves restored enough for another supreme Ramp after defeating the machines before the main entrance?

Chloe reached into silence, her mind stilling to a single point of utmost concentration. Time slowed beyond the normal boundaries of the Ramp. Power exploded from deep within her being, flooding her limbs. She broke through a gap between the Red Empire warriors, wall running half a dozen yards toward the entrance to the prison complex, landing between the two new oncoming warriors and the three she'd been dueling.

The supreme ramp flowered into full bloom. The Red Dragon lanced forward past one assassins' weapons, and through his chest. The draw stroke opened his lungs to the outside air before her gore-soaked blade arced a hundred and eighty degrees overhead to strike down through the skull of the warrior opposite. His weapons floated free of his nerveless hands, the mighty katana ripping through helmet, skull, body armor and chest, painting a broad swathe of blood on the wall behind him.

Chloe pivoted at right angles. The four warriors around her described an 'X' centered on her, two were already falling away. The other two were reacting, their blades arcing toward her in a race against time to beat the immaculate majesty of the Red Dragon's voracious edge.

Chloe brought her katana down through a diagonal slash against her third opponent. His left sword evaporated in a bright cloud of super-heated metal as the Red Dragon passed through it like it wasn't there. Her blade continued on its inevitable journey through his left shoulder, bisecting his heart and lungs, and exiting halfway down his right-side ribs in a spray of bright blood. The top half of his body slid away to the floor. The lower half collapsed, intestines, and other organs slopping out onto the cold concrete.

Chloe pivoted again, thrusting behind her with the Red Dragon, the fourth warrior rushing onto its blade in his efforts to land his own attacks. Her draw stroke spilled his heart's blood onto the floor, he fell forward, his life fleeing before he hit the blood-slick concrete.

Chloe stepped out of the way of his falling body, her supreme ramp fading away.

The team leader remained, and the recovered warrior stunned earlier by her dropped grenade.

Chloe blurred to her right, her fingers flashing over the control panel.

The wounded warrior surged forward, then halted suddenly, his progress barred by the stiff right arm of the team leader.

The bars slammed back into position, separating the two Red Empire warriors from Chloe.

Chloe's lips curled wryly. "Looks like you get to live to fight another day."

"You'll not escape us demon," the young team leader snapped furiously.

"You know," Chloe declared airily, turning away from the two men. "Many have said that, and yet, I'm still here."

Two pairs of boots turned and thudded away into the distance behind her.

* * *

The strip lighting in the ceiling began to flicker.

"Emergency power is about to fail," Chloe whispered to herself. She glanced through the two archways, taking in an array of monitors. One was counting down, it clicked past 04:00 as she watched. She spun away through the open steel doorway and into the prison complex. She wanted to be long gone from here before the counter hit zero, and the Red Empire erased the citadel.

The cells comprised rows of long cylinders in the floor, forty in all. Their top hatches stood open, random voices calling out for help from their depths. The air hung thick with greasy smoke, and Chloe's nose twitched from the stench of severely burned flesh. A pair of bandoliers of white-phosphorous grenades lay halfway along the prison floor. The guards had been wiping out the prisoners. Whatever was going to take out the citadel probably wasn't going to take out the prison complex.

Chloe sighed with relief; it had always been a possibility the Red Empire would use a low-yield nuclear weapon to cleanse their citadel upon discovery. That seemed to be off the cards, but still, there was no time to waste. A pair of secure doors marked with the bio-hazard symbol occupied the left-hand wall. They stood protected by a security access handprint reader and looked too solid to take down with a kick.

She mused to herself, "A biological research center, and vampire holding cells. Just what has the Red Empire been up to here? If only I'd more time."

Chloe picked up the first bandolier and got to work. She checked each cell, and if general Mosule didn't occupy it, she dropped a grenade into it. Flames roared up each cylinder, and the vampires within howled and shrieked. She blurred over the prison floor, methodically removing any potential witnesses who could attest that the prison complex was next to the Red Empire citadel, and hence the Interpretive Codex.

She didn't need that piece of information getting back to Crane.

The only remaining conduit would be Haras Mosule, and what did he know, and more importantly, what could he prove on his own?

It would be his word against hers.

* * *

The cell door in the ceiling of Haras Mosule's cell stood open. The usual green background light replaced with red emergency lighting. Distant klaxons had warred for supremacy with the clash of blades and exploding grenades.

But who was attacking the Red Empire? Would he find an escape in the safe hands of the Vampire Dominion, or would the implacable agents of the Order of Thoth deal him a quick death? In nearby cells, the other vampires had shrieked and screamed in utter agony, their burning flesh sloughing from their bones. Haras' nostrils had twitched at the stench of their melting flesh and boiling body fluids. His throat had become parched as he'd waited for the inevitable white-phosphorous grenade.

The swords had fallen silent, and he'd recognized a feminine voice despite the screams of dying vampires. He'd whispered in dismay, "Armitage."

He stared longingly at the open cell door, but without a rope, the sheer thirty yards to the lip was too high to cover with a leap. The violent crack of grenades began anew. The remaining vampires howled their torment, their body fluids turning to steam and bursting their flesh apart.

Haras concluded somberly; it was to be destruction rather than salvation. Chloe Armitage had betrayed him to the Red Empire. Now she sought to eliminate him, and with his death, any evidence of her betrayal.

What the hell was she really doing? Did she believe that she could outwit Cornelius? A natural born leader who'd torn down Mekra and her cult of blood. Who'd united the vampires under a single banner and established effective and secret rulership of the world. Who'd lived and fought for eight centuries longer than Armitage had existed. Haras shook his head, perhaps madness lurked behind her cool facade, he had no other explanation. In moments, Armitage would toss a grenade into his cell and eliminate him. Haras backed up against the wall. Perhaps if he leaped high at the right time, he could escape the effects of the explosion.

The seconds dragged, the wails of tortured despair died, extinguished with the lives of the other vampire prisoners.

Armitage appeared at the top of his prison cell, a long rope in her hands. She threw one end down to him, holding the other end with a grip of steel.

What trickery was this? But, if she were going to release him from this place, he'd be a fool to refuse her. Haras grasped the rope with both hands and scaled it quickly. A handful of seconds later, he was clawing his way free of the cell. He couldn't help grinning as he landed on the floor of the prison complex. He was free. He was a general of the Vampire Dominion, and whatever game Armitage was playing, he would stand with his king against her.

But for now, she was his ticket out of the heart of the Red Empire, and he would do everything he could to ensure his escape from their clutches. Greasy black smoke filled the air of the prison complex, the particulate remains of nearly two score of vampires, some of them destroyed by Armitage.

Haras accused, "Why did you kill them?"

"I can't exfil a horde," Armitage declared, her eyes flashing in the red gloom. "I only have room for one prisoner – you. Do you want freedom or not?"

Haras nodded. He would keep his suspicions hidden until he could share them with Cornelius. He followed Armitage to a wall at the back of the prison. She took all of her remaining shaped charges from her bandolier, and stabbed them into the wall, outlining a circular hole three feet across.

Armitage looked over her shoulder at Haras, her eyes glimmering with a trace of mirth, and suggested, "You'll want to get back for this." She flicked a master switch on the rear of one of the charges. The other five charges began blinking with a small red light, and she stated calmly, "Five seconds."

She blurred back to the other side of the chamber, Haras followed her, crouched at her side, his right arm lifting to shield his face. The small red lights blinked another four times, counting down the seconds. The shaped charges detonated with a thunderous roar. Gray and ocher dust bloomed in a great cloud. Haras followed Chloe to the blast site. The wall had been torn apart, in the distance, water dripped faintly. They had breached the wall into the sewers.

The way was clear. Armitage clambered confidently into the hole, and in moments was through to the ancient chambers beyond.

Haras glanced one last time around the prison; what a tale of betrayal he had to tell Cornelius. The king would finish Armitage and Drake for good, there was no way she'd be able to slip out of this one.

He moved forward and exited the prison.

* * *

The sewer grate popped a dozen feet up into the air, before clanging away into the shadows.

Chloe and Haras blurred out of the sewer and into an alleyway opening up onto a children's playground. Chloe ran between the play equipment, twisting around, and scanning the night sky. "Where the hell is the drone?" she asked, consternation filling her voice. "It should be here."

They'd run at speed through the sewers, heading southeast, the seconds ticking away in her mind. They'd covered three miles in three and a half minutes. She looked to the northwest. A dozen narrow fountains of flame lit the heights of Mount Scopus, the rolling thunder of the underground explosions reaching her fourteen seconds later.

Her earbud came back online with a chirp, a second later James Haley's voice called out over the tactical link, "I'm almost there."

A minibus turned into the street and pulled to a halt next to the playground. The window wound down, and James shouted, "I've got a way out."

The livery of 'Mount Scopus Museum – Sentinels of Wisdom,' emblazoned the side of the minibus. Chloe remarked acidly, "It's a little obvious isn't it."

"They shot down the drone, it was the best I could do on short notice."

Chloe blinked once, then rushed to the side door. Haras followed at her shoulder. Once inside, James hit the accelerator, and the minibus lurched away from the curb in a cloud of blue exhaust smoke.

"Shadowstone still has an asset in Jerusalem," James offered.

"Really?" Chloe asked.

"Yes, Ma'am. Gareth Nightingale. He's got a business jet on a private runway well out of the city. We'll be there in thirty minutes or so. It's fully fueled and ready to roll."

"Flight plans?"

"Sorted. All the way back to New York, and considering sunrise and sunset as well."

Chloe arched an eyebrow and smiled. "Well done. It looks like this mission will end well."

She turned to Haras, sitting next to her and remarked sardonically, "You can thank me now."

He looked back at her for a long moment and then said sarcastically, "Of course, how remiss of me. Thank you, general Armitage for freeing me from the enemies of the Vampire Dominion. I am forever in your debt."

Chloe smiled and leaned back in her seat.

What an asshole.

* * *

The might of the Red Empire assembled in loose ranks on a soccer pitch. More than a hundred and twenty fighters, their body armor and weapons hidden beneath voluminous gray robes, waited for orders.

Vertical jets of flame lit the horizon to the south, a deep-throated rumble washed over them five seconds later. The immolation protocol had sanitized the citadel. There was nothing left that could be of use to the Vampire Dominion or the Order of Thoth. All their computer hardware and networks now melted into scrap metal. While the data was safe in quantum encrypted vaults in the cloud and his staff could easily restore it to fresh networks, the loss of the citadel was a heavy blow.

"Armitage! That bitch!" Dalien growled past clenched teeth.

One of his personal guards inquired, "My Lord?"

Dalien waved him away with a short chop of his right hand. The distant flames, starved of fuel, faded rapidly away. Sirens wailed across the city, the local authorities rushing emergency and police services to Mount Scopus, and the location of the fallen shadowstar drone. They would only find mystery piled upon mystery. Their own systems hijacked by Shadowstone and the Panopticon. Secret agents would alter and lose critical evidence. Those who pushed too hard to discover the truth would find themselves assigned to other roles, fired, or even disappeared.

The Vampire Dominion and Shadowstone would keep the existence of the Red Empire secret even as they sought to destroy them.

Images of Chloe Armitage slaughtering his warriors swam before his mind. He'd always understood their 'alliance,' was an attempt by her to play him, but he'd sought to play her in return. An attempt that was now ashes in his mouth. Dalien spat with disgust. Losing was a rare experience, but instead of burning with barely constrained rage, he was a tumult of conflicting emotions.

She'd bested his automated defenses and killed his men with ease. A brief thrill of awe shivered over his skin, such speed and power – she was extraordinary. The shiver faded, replaced by heart-thudding desire. A hot lust blew through him like a hurricane. He clenched his fists. He'd have her, he'd possess her, he'd own her. What an ornament at his side she would be. With all the Metaframe artifacts within his possession, he would usher in a new reality. He'd eliminate vampires in a single stroke, and return Armitage to her human form. He would rule the world at the head of an immortal dynasty, his lost wife returned, his daughter at his side.

The Red Empire would transcend the vampire's false godhood with something made whole and true.

He took a deep breath and let it out slowly. A convoy of dark SUVs entered the stadium and began pulling up before his men, enough to carry them all to safety. He'd ensured each vehicle was equipped with the latest Red Empire technologies, designed to temporarily blind the Panopticon as they passed any camera, drone or satellite surveillance. The seat of power of the Red Ghost would return to Matahat al Diydan, a secret fortress that rested over the maze of the Olgoi Khorkhoi. The fortress had been in possession of the Red Empire from the beginning of their sacred Way.

It was time to go east of the Caucasus' and return to the Red Empire's most ancient home.

A charcoal-gray Chevrolet Suburban with deeply tinted windows pulled to a stop in front of him. His personal guard leaped forward and opened the door. He stepped forward, taking a seat by himself in the back of the vehicle. A moment later the SUV pulled away. With smooth efficiency, the rest of the Red Empire army boarded their vehicles and left the stadium by as many routes as possible. There would be no tell-tale convoy to Matahat al Diydan witnessed by hungry eyes. Stealth was second nature for the Red Empire and the fleet of cars dispersed into the night.

Dalien replayed in his mind what he'd witnessed on the command center monitors. He needed to know how Armitage had done it. What were the flaws in his defenses, and in his operations that had allowed her to succeed in her mission?

She'd infiltrated his outer defenses. Did she simply retrace her steps from the one time he'd granted her access to the citadel? She must have done so, and if she could do that, could she remember a complex statement in a dead language with a single glance?

Dalien's guts froze, he'd greatly underestimated her. Armitage had a copy of the Interpretive Codex in her mind. She must have a photographic memory. The other two artifacts were in Crane's possession. Of all the players, she was closest to seizing all three, and with them, mastery over reality.

But what was stopping her? Surely Crane was unaware of their secret alliance. Her actions had always been her own. Something Dalien had learned painfully in the last hour – she was no one's puppet. She had to be playing her own game. For some unknown reason, Armitage could not seize the Key of Ahknaton and the Papyrus of Hakron the Scribe from Crane. She was waiting for something. Was she waiting for Taipan's mission? Was she waiting for a strike by the Red Empire to create chaos in the Vampire Dominion's heartland? Did she need chaos to mask her strike from Crane and to hide her hand if she failed?

Dalien stroked his darkly bearded chin. His eyes were hard, black stones, focused on the streets passing outside his car window without seeing them, his mind twisting deep within his plans.

Armitage had given Dalien the location of the other Metaframe artifacts. Taipan had validated the location of Crane's citadel and now led a mission against it, but what if she'd lied? What if she was setting a trap? Given her remarkable skills, could she ambush Taipan's team after he'd retrieved the artifacts, and seize them for herself?

By sending Taipan and his team to Manhattan Island, was Dalien playing to her tune? He stared out the window at the passing streets. It was impossible to recall Taipan. His team had already dropped out of sight and contact. Their mission would have to proceed as planned. Dalien would have to trust in the skills of the premier warrior of the Red Empire and his elite team to win through whatever challenges Armitage put in their way.

Armitage swam into the middle of his mind's eye. Her armor melted away, revealing the perfection of her naked form. Dalien remembered the night of the viewing of the Codex, and the revelation of Crane's citadel. Her beauty had stolen his breath away, and she'd haunted his dreams every night thereafter. Of course, he'd told no one of his thoughts and nightly visitations. To have such feelings for a vampire was an obscenity.

But she would not remain a vampire forever. For the last sixteen years, his scientists and technicians had researched a cure for vampirism. He'd constructed the prison complex to provide the researchers with test subjects. There were several promising lines of inquiry that may yet bear fruit. Of course, there were many of the older Red Empire warriors who believed the only way to cure a vampire was to kill them. While he'd maneuvered around the older members by co-opting the best and brightest of the newest recruits of the Red Empire, his strategy of finding a cure and ending the war had become personal.

There was one vampire Dalien had long sought to save. A young woman, his wife, and the mother of his daughter Chiara. Crane had snatched her from the battlefield, converted her into a vampire, and no one had seen her again.

He would have her back if he could and punish Crane severely for his theft of her. As for Armitage, be it via an application of a curative serum for the disease of vampirism, or by the transformation of reality via the Metaframe, Dalien would see her at his feet – an ever-willing concubine of the highest rank.

His tongue wet his lips, and he instinctively swallowed, then whispered to himself, "To the victor – the spoils."

* * *

The full moon was an hour above the western horizon, it's light illuminating the four guard towers reaching into the night sky.

Lanterns on stands lit the courtyard of the Obsidian Claw fortress with a buttery glow, a dozen men and women huddled in chains in the middle of the courtyard. Around them stood twelve ninjas in a loose formation, the hand-picked elite of the clan of the Obsidian Claw.

Cornelius Crane stood opposite the 'Supreme Claw,' the titular head of the ninja clan. The two men regarded each other with a measure of respect. Cornelius had saved the clan from obliteration by vampire blood cultists in the seventeenth century, a debt the clan had never forgotten.

The Supreme Claw was the first to speak, "This sacrifice repays our debt in full."

"Indeed, it does," Cornelius replied, his gaze flicking over the assembled ninjas.

Ten minutes earlier he'd administered one of the red implants to each of the selected men. The implants carried a payload of powdered silver and would fire directly into the brain stem on his verbal command. He'd coded the system to his voice print, and no one else could fire it. However, any attempt to remove the implant would cause it to fire. Injecting a sufficient dose of powdered silver into the brain stem of a vampire had proven to be lethal in all test cases.

The implants were a fail-safe system to guarantee the ninjas would remain loyal after they became vampires, and if they were disloyal, he could easily eliminate them with a word. All that remained was to administer a dose of Mekra's blood. During the flight from the Carpathian Mountains to Japan, he'd split the flask of Mekra's blood into a dozen small syringes arranged inside a leather folio. Mekra's blood didn't coagulate outside her body, remaining potent indefinitely.

Cornelius lifted the leather folio. "It is time to proceed to the final step."

The Supreme Claw nodded, then called to his men, "Form a circle around the prisoners."

The twelve ninjas moved quickly, forming a circle ten feet back from the moaning men and women in the middle of the courtyard. The lantern light reflected off the captives blanched faces. They trembled with terror. The clan had stolen them from their homes only hours before, and it was clear a dreadful fate awaited them.

Cornelius opened the folio and extracted the first syringe. He approached the first of the ninjas and plunged the syringe into the base of his throat. A second later, the man's eyes widened, his face paled, and he fell to a writhing heap on the dark-gray flagstones.

The stance of the man next to him tightened.

Cornelius caught his gaze, and he selected the second syringe. "Courage, the agony passes, and you will bring great honor to your clan."

The man stared back at him. Cornelius' hand snapped forward, the syringe injecting Mekra's blood directly into his jugular. He dropped to the ground a moment later.

The first man began shrieking.

Cornelius completed the rest of the doses in a blur, the men falling like a row of dominoes. He returned to the Supreme Claw's side. There was nothing left to do but wait, the transformations would complete in a handful of minutes. He relegated the screams to background noise. The prisoners were attempting to break their chains, their efforts were as futile as the remaining moments of their lives.

He glanced down at the Supreme Claw and swept his left hand backward. "It would be best to step back and make sure the prisoners are closer to the new vampires than you are."

The man nodded, and moved back half a dozen yards, positioning himself well behind Cornelius.

The minutes slipped past. The moonlight gave a luster to the black stones of the fortress towers. The pale-yellow glow of the lanterns left deep shadows along the base of the walls. Thirty-seven other ninjas occupied the fortress, many of them watching the initiation unfolding in the middle of the courtyard. Cornelius mapped their locations from the sound of their heartbeats and used the time to reflect upon his past experiences with the clan.

He'd saved them from a posse of vampires holding to the ancient blood cult of Mekra. Over the subsequent centuries he'd visited from time to time to train with their best warriors, occasionally he would learn something new, and the Obsidian Claw had become the ultimate exponents of the art of Ninjitsu. From this night on, that relationship was over. They'd repaid the debt they owed him, and he would not come to this place again.

The first ninja injected suddenly blurred toward the prisoners, ripping one away from his chains and burying his face in the helpless man's throat. Blood splashed to the flagstones from the man's right wrist, the hand amputated by the iron manacle. The flow stopped almost immediately, the man's blood rushing away from his limbs and into the maw of the new vampire.

"Mekra's blood," Cornelius whispered. Only Chloe and himself had been born from it. They were the two most powerful vampires in the world, and now he'd created another twelve of equal strength. Twelve great servants bound to obey his will or die. Hunters who could track down and capture Chloe Armitage, and war effectively against the Ramp masters. A way to ensure he had a secret edge against any who threatened his rule.

The other eleven ninjas joined the first in feasting upon the prisoners. The men and women howled their despair, their shrieks of terror cut mercifully short.

The first vampire dropped his bloodless victim, his body falling limply to the flagstones. He turned to face Cornelius, his eyes were midnight orbs, and long scimitar fangs jutted over his bottom lip.

Cornelius' heart froze, something had gone horribly wrong.

A look of recognition flitted across the ninja vampire's face as if he was really seeing Cornelius for the first time. A wave of focused hatred followed on the heels of the recognition. The ninja's hands blurred, a pair of ninjatos whirling from their scabbards on his back. The two-foot-long straight blades gleamed in the yellow lantern light. The ninja, his face filled with loathing, blurred toward Cornelius.

Cornelius's blade hissed from its scabbard, a three-and-a-half-foot long bastard sword he normally wielded with a single hand. With skills honed over nearly a thousand years of warfare, and having trained with the previous masters of the Obsidian Claw, Cornelius deflected the first attack. The ninja whirled lightning quick, his second attack stopped a hairsbreadth from Cornelius's throat, sparks blooming around his head as his bastard sword ground against the ninjatos.

Cornelius snapped the command word for this ninja's red implant to fire its load of powdered silver. The ninja's head rocked backward, and he slumped to the flagstones like a stringless puppet.

"What has happened?" the Supreme Claw shouted. "You have birthed demons!"

Cornelius ignored the man, his gaze fixing on the rest of the ninja vampires. They were dropping bodies onto the cold flagstones and turning toward him, like moths attracted by a single flame. A low murmur swept through them. Blades sprang from their scabbards, held in deathly stillness by pale hands. Eyes darker than night focused upon him.

A rare shiver of fear flashed up Cornelius' back, he uttered the master command word to kill them all. The red implants all fired at once, dropping the eleven ninjas to the stones.

There was a sudden intake of breath behind him. Cornelius whirled around. The Supreme Claw was backing away, the first ninja vampire was rising off the ground.

Silver didn't kill them. Mekra had passed her growing immunity onto the new vampires with her blood.

Cornelius blurred forward, the ninja's blades arced upward, his bastard sword slashed down, its Damascan steel blade shattered the first ninjato and continued on, severing the ninja's head. The body flopped to the ground and lay still, the head rolling away to land near the Supreme Claw's feet.

Cornelius grunted, plucking the second ninjato from where it jutted from his gut. He dropped the bloody blade on the ground. His recent feeding in the corporate towers of Tokyo healed him quickly, but it had been a very long time since someone had got a blade past his defenses. These ninja vampires born of Mekra's blood were deadly fast with a sword.

He turned on the rest, blurring toward them. His blade slashed down, separating the closest ninja's head from his shoulders. Blood jetted over the flagstones. His gore-streaked blade blurred again and again, as he sent the nearest ninjas to their final death.

The eighth died, as the final four began to rise.

Cornelius' blade snapped down, taking the first, who dropped immediately back to the flagstones. The second rose to his knees before Cornelius' horizontal slash sprang his head into the air on a fountain of blood. The third rushed him, his blades striking sparks from Cornelius' sword as he gave ground defensively.

Cornelius drew upon his ancient Order of Thoth training and dropped deep into silence. Already blurring at maximum vampire speed, his ramp took him a notch faster. The ninja's blades appeared to slow slightly, the advantage shifting to Cornelius. His blade flashed out, thrusting through the ninja's throat, with a flick of his wrist, it cut through flesh and bone as if they were made of air. The third ninja joined the rest on the flagstones, his blood pooling around him.

A shadow blurred over the fortress wall. The last ninja had fled. Cornelius chased after him, his leap carrying him to the top of the fortress battlements. Beyond the fortress walls, forest rose on all sides.

Cornelius paused, he could see perfectly in the full moonlight, but there was neither sight nor sound of the ninja vampire. The sole survivor had escaped. Cornelius had let loose a brand-new type of vampire into the world.

"Catastrophe," he whispered hoarsely. "This changes everything."

Armitage – I still need her, but I must bind her to my life.

He turned back to the interior of the fortress. There could be no witnesses to what had happened this night. He must destroy the Obsidian Claw and erase every witness in the fortress, he must kill them all.

Cornelius blurred to the nearest tower and the two ninjas within it.

The rest of the Obsidian Claw clan mostly died in silence.

* * *

Chloe's smartphone pinged, indicating an incoming video call from Crane.

She answered the call. Crane's face resolved in ultra-high definition on the screen, behind him was the interior of his drone. Shadows haunted his eyes. A look she'd not seen before. Something had happened, something momentous.

His eyes tightened, and he inquired, "What of your mission?"

"Success. I have freed Haras and he rides safely on this flight back to New York."

"Good. The Vampire Dominion needs him for a mission of the utmost importance. I see you're traveling by private jet. Once you are in New York, come to my citadel immediately – there are new arrangements that must be made."

"Yes, Sir."

Crane nodded, and then said matter-of-factly, "Chloe, perhaps I chose too well when I chose you. Your ambitions have come to the fore over the last few months, and if I am correct, it begins with the recovery of the Papyrus of Hakron the Scribe, and the elimination of Anna and William Slayne." He paused for a moment; his gaze locked on her eyes. "However, you have overstepped the mark by lying to me about the existence of Anna and William's son – Anton Slayne."

A cold shiver rose up Chloe's spine. Her worst nightmare had just become real.

She almost began shaking her head in dismay, but froze into stillness, her mind shifting into high gear.

How did Crane find out? How much does he know?

"The story about Anton Smith, the orphan who was taken in by Gang Wu and switched on to the reality of the Ramp is your concoction, isn't it? Don't bother denying it. I'm sure it's a clever mix of truths, half-truths, and outright fabrications, and would have worked on most people, but not me." Crane frowned. "Really Chloe, I'm insulted that you thought me so vulnerable, so stupid, and so easily gulled."

Chloe stared at her phone in silence.

"… Your only hope of survival is utter truthfulness and complete loyalty. You've created Anton Slayne as a weapon, and you're somehow exploiting a flaw in Allemande's curse. What is it … the flaw?"

The silence dragged out.

Crane's eyes flashed with sudden insight. "Slayne doesn't know he's your creature? That's it isn't it. That's the trick. No aware intent that he is working to your purpose."

Shadows of pain writhed behind Chloe's eyes.

Crane grinned wolfishly. "It's amazing how well I think when my life is at risk. I've remained cloistered in my library for far too long. But what should I do now?"

Chloe stared at him in silent dismay, he would tell her soon enough.

"Maybe I should tell young Slayne the truth, and if he pursues his course, he destroys you by attacking me. But no, why should I suffer an attack? There is a better solution," Crane paused for a long moment, his face giving nothing away, waiting, dragging the moment out.

Chloe could see it coming, the order was obvious.

Crane's eyes hardened, his voice replete with dreadful certainty, he commanded, "You will find the young Slayne, and you will kill him."

Her plan for Anton was in tatters.

Crane stared, raising a quizzical eyebrow. "You have nothing to say?"

"Sir?" Chloe asked softly.

"Your mission?"

"Sir." Chloe nodded. "Yes, Sir."

Crane nodded. "Yes, that is the best solution. Now, bring me the head of Anton Slayne. That is your only concern now. It should not take long. I'm sure you've been keeping tabs on where your weapon is."

Chloe nodded again, her heart sinking.

"I will expect detailed progress reports every night."

"Yes, Sir."

"Yes, indeed," Crane snapped imperiously and closed the video call.

Chloe leaned back and closed her eyes, her mind whirling. When she opened them again, Haras was watching her from the other side of the cabin, a half-filled whiskey glass in his hand, and a smirk on his face.

"You should have stayed loyal. If I were king, you'd be dead by now."

"If you were king, I'd want to be dead," Chloe snapped.

"Well, you'll never be queen," Mosule asserted, snorting derisively before taking a sip of his whiskey.

Chloe looked away, the sky outside the window was full night. The plane was chasing the night to New York, they'd arrive in darkness. Something Haras had just said tweaked her mind, why had Crane stayed his hand. He must be furious with her. His justice had always been swift and certain in the past, but instead of hunting her down and killing her, or worse imprisoning her forever – Crane knew all too well how to hurt her – he'd given her a mission. He'd even stated that she could survive with truthfulness and loyalty.

What was his motivation?

Fear? He's not frightened of me; he can kill me anytime he wants to. No, something else has got him frightened. The target of Haras Mosule's mission of 'utmost importance?' He needs me if Mosule fails, and he must think that is a real possibility. What the hell has just happened to him? And how on Earth did he find out about my plans for Anton Slayne?

Crane was a highly intelligent polymath; many would consider him a genius, but he was not a mind reader. How had he found out? Chloe's mind cut through the problem. Crane had spent a lot of time with Jean Philippe Allemande. He'd obviously acquired more than the binding curses. Allemande had gifted him with some power of information, a special secret edge.

If only she could question Allemande, but that was impossible, she'd purged him on Christmas Eve, 1899. Her mind searched back through her perfect memory, what were Allemande's final words? She remembered him kneeling before her, rows of pale candles lining the walls of his temple, wringing his hands and pleading with her, *'Don't kill me! Please, don't kill me?'*

She frowned. Before the pleading, Allemande had bargained and talked openly about many things. After providing her with a binding curse on Marcus Drake, he'd suggested with a sly smile. *'Crane knows more than you'll ever understand.'*

At the time, she'd considered it a throwaway line by a man desperate to buy more time. But now her actions seemed precipitous. Perhaps she should have lingered and questioned him more thoroughly, for Crane really did know more as if he possessed a true sorcerous power. She pursed her lips; she could not undo the reckless actions of youth.

Chloe's mind returned to the present. Crane's world was shifting beneath his feet. Perhaps her opportunity was drawing near, and she could exploit the imbalances in his world to tip him over entirely.

How can I draw out the finding of Anton Slayne? And what of my plan B, surely the Red Empire must be acting on the knowledge of the location of Crane's citadel?

Chloe shook her head gently and stared into the night sky. There were many moving parts, and the configurations had changed greatly, but the game remained the same. She was still alive, and still in play. It would be up to her to find new levers to bring Crane, Anton and the Key of Ahknaton to the same place at the same time, or wait for the Red Empire to strike at Crane's citadel and take advantage of the ensuing chaos to seize the Key for herself.

Whatever happened would need to happen quickly before Crane lost patience with her. For the moment, his own need for her powers stayed his hand. As soon as he didn't need her, his hand would fall.

She needed to ensure she stayed indispensable to Crane, and … well, there was more than one way to do that.

'Let your plans be dark and impenetrable as night, and when you move, fall like a thunderbolt,' Sun Tzu was right, regardless of this setback, she was still a player in the game.

* * *

Chloe and Haras Mosule walked into the ultra-secret war room at the heart of Crane's citadel. Six praetorians in full combat array were waiting with Cornelius Crane and general Clayton Maze.

Crane smiled warmly, strode over to Mosule and gave him a fierce hug. He stepped back, his hands on Mosule's shoulders, and declared, "Haras, my friend, it's wonderful to have you back. Unfortunately, there is no time to discuss your experiences at the hands of the Red Empire, such dreadful tales will have to wait until we have a quiet moment. However, I've read your report in full," he threw a sharp look at Chloe standing five feet away, "and I understand your concerns. Rest assured, I have the solution at hand." He sighed deeply, his gaze intensifying. "Our world rests on a precipice, the slightest misstep will send it over into chaos. To you goes the most important mission. Leave now, and assemble a team of twelve praetorians. Gather our best, none will brook you. Once you have your team, report back to me, and I will detail the full parameters of your mission."

Crane dropped his hands from Mosule's shoulders and stepped back.

General Mosule thumped his left chest with his right fist and vowed, "Your will, my king." He stepped back a step, turned on his heel, and left the war room without another word.

Chloe stilled her expressions. She could not let her face reveal what she was really feeling. *My god! This boy's club sucks.*

Crane frowned at Chloe, and stated, "You have come armed. Hand over your sword—"

"We came directly from the airport," Chloe asserted, her eyes widening.

"... now don't look like that, you'll get it back presently."

After the faintest of hesitations, Chloe unstrapped her katana and passed it to Crane.

Crane received the Red Dragon in its scabbard, arched an eyebrow, and began handing the famous sword to Clayton Maze. He stopped suddenly, raised both his eyebrows, and said with a sardonic grin, "Perhaps we should keep this sword."

"What?!" Chloe snapped, her eyes flashing.

"Ah... but who would Chloe Armitage be without the Red Dragon?"

Chloe's eyes narrowed, a dangerous fury building within her.

Crane answered his own question, "Diminished I would think."

The praetorians watched impassively, and Maze openly smirked behind Crane's left shoulder. Chloe tamped down on her rising fury, and it flattened out, turning to ice within her veins.

"You'd need a new enforcer," she suggested candidly.

"Indeed," Crane agreed casually, handing the katana to Maze. "I do need a new enforcer." He swept his right hand toward the middle of the boardroom table dominating the war room. A slim, black leather briefcase rested within Crane's long reach. He leaned forward, flicked the lid open, and spun the case a half turn, revealing its contents to Chloe. "And I propose to make one."

He looked at her, his eyes narrowing beneath a serious frown.

Inside the case was an injection gun, and a pair of implant cartridges color-coded gold and black. Another dozen cartridge slots in the grey mold sat empty. Crane had already used the injection gun.

But for what purpose? Chloe asked, "What's this?"

Crane replied coolly, "An insurance policy against any more attempts to kill me."

Chloe glanced at the implants; her gut tightened with a dreadful realization. The walls of the room seemed to close in. Crane's will flooded around her, a suffocating force dragging the air from her lungs. There must be a way to escape. She couldn't fight Crane; Allemande's curse made that impossible. She breathed hard for a moment. She'd just have to accept it for now and find a way through it. She reassured herself. *Every system has a flaw.*

Chloe tilted her head, and remarked sardonically, "A matching pair, how intimate."

Crane raised an eyebrow, a slight smile passing across his lips. "Indeed, it has come to this. Let me explain how this will work."

"I'm all ears," Chloe offered, sardonically.

Crane snorted dismissively and loaded the gold coded cartridge into the injection gun. He opened his shirt revealing his pale, finely-muscled chest. He placed the barrel of the injection gun to the left of his sternum and fired.

He blinked, and instructed her. "The gold implant now rests against my heart, nano-fiber tendrils are embedding themselves within the outer wall of my left ventricle." He retrieved the black cartridge from the briefcase and loaded it into the injection gun.

Crane beckoned Chloe forward with his left hand. "Come here my dear and please turn around."

Chloe's eyes narrowed with suspicion, but she complied.

"The pain is trivial," Crane asserted. He rested the cold barrel of the injection gun on the back of Chloe's neck, an inch below the base of her skull, positioned slightly to the left of her spine. There was a brief concussive blow and a sharp momentary sting. She blurred forward and whirled around.

Crane watched her with cold eyes. "Your implant is already positioning itself next to your brain stem. It carries a payload of powdered silver, and will fire if my implant registers the failure of my heartbeat or you make any attempt to remove it." He paused and grinned wolfishly. "You now have a vested interest in keeping me alive."

Chloe's face hardened into inscrutability. Now was not the time to give anything away. While Crane lived, Allemande's curse forbade her to touch the Key of Ahknaton or harm him. She'd have to protect him against Anton Slayne, and the Red Empire's strike against the Citadel.

Damn this implant, she thought furiously. *I'm trapped until I'm free of it.*

Crane put the injection gun down on the table and spread his long-fingered hands expansively, his eyes glistening with hidden meanings. "I understand you chafe beneath Allemande's curse. I can see the elliptical thrust of your weapon ... Anton Slayne. I applaud the cleverness of your stratagem, but I have found you out." He looked at her with cold admiration. "Had I discovered this as recently as two days ago. I would kill you where you stand, but instead of death, I must leave you alive – and why – because I need you. Now, more than ever."

"Why?" Chloe asked.

"There is a new and powerful type of vampire loose in the world. Haras and his hand-picked force of praetorians will soon be hunting it. They will join generals, Dieter Franz and Shen Zhen, our praetorian forces in the East, and as many Shadowstone and Panopticon resources as I can allocate to this most important mission."

"How did this happen?"

Crane's eyes became hard as flint. "That's not important now. The only objective is to kill it before it starts to produce more vampires like it."

"What do you want of me?"

"General Haras and his forces will be scouring Asia and Eastern Europe. You are needed here, to deal with the mess you have created."

"Anton Slayne?"

"Indeed. Nothing has changed, I want his head brought to me as proof of his death."

Chloe's eyes widened with dismay.

"Is that clear?" Crane asked.

"Yes, Sir."

Crane glanced at Clayton Maze, who was still holding the Red Dragon in his left hand and flicked his eyes back to Chloe.

Maze moved forward and handed the katana back to her.

Crane stiffened and ordered, "You have your weapon and your mission. You're dismissed."

Chloe bowed her head, took the regulation three steps backward, turned and left the war room. She entered the Vampire Dominion command center, a dozen vampires working at consoles registered her presence and just as quickly returned to their duties. She strode to the elevators. She'd have to learn everything there was to know about the implant technology. Surely there was a way to thwart it. She had to get it out of her head, or Crane would hold her trapped to his will forever.

This was the last straw, she burned with a furious need to be free of Crane.

When will I know liberty again?

Chapter Four

Iranians Probe Israel's Defenses

At 10:02 PM local time, an Iranian military drone was shot down in spectacular fashion by the IDF over Jerusalem in another attempt by the rogue theocratic state to test Israel's defenses …

Tragedy Narrowly Averted!

Authorities have confirmed that a massive gas explosion underneath the Mount Scopus Museum has caused substantial damage to the museum's buildings and grounds. Fortunately, no one was hurt as the museum was closed at the time. Earlier the same day hundreds of visitors were enjoying the many exhibits showcasing the last five thousand years of cultural history of the middle east.

– News articles on the Internet.

* * *

Reykjavík, Iceland, August 26th, 17:30

A light fog wreathed the port of Reykjavík. The gray sky threatened to turn mist into rain. Iron-clad storm clouds dissipated their fury on the eastern horizon, a flock of white seagulls squawking and wheeling in stark contrast to the darkness in the east.

Peter leaped from the trawler's deck to the pier, crouched down on hands and knees, and kissed the sodden wood. He rose to his feet, shouldering a large kit bag. He looked at Anton, Li, and Chiara with wide eyes and half-pleaded, "Don't ask me to travel by boat across the Atlantic again."

"You and me both," Anton offered, pulling his gray hood tighter over his crew-cut scalp. His gear was in a dark backpack across his shoulders, the Blue Dragon sheathed and masked by a carry case strapped to the backpack. Neither man had shaved for three days. They sported the beginnings of short beards, Anton's dark, and Peter's a dark-fiery red to match his thick head of hair.

"C'mon boys," Li said, brusquely clapping their shoulders. "What's a little storm to worry about, we got through it."

"Was it thirty hours straight?" Peter asked.

Anton moved in front of his friend and clasped his broad shoulders. "Thirty-four at least."

"Storm tossed."

"Twenty-foot waves."

"More like thirty."

Anton glowered with mock intensity. "Staring death in the face."

"A watery grave for sure," Peter said, grinning.

Anton's right hand waved in query. "Such a storm could summon a Kraken."

Peter frowned with mock fear. "Giant tentacles of death."

"Dragging us to our doom," Anton asserted fervently, his eye sparkling.

Li slipped between them and faced Anton, tapping him on the chest with her right forefinger, and asserted, "We need to get off this pier. I need a shower."

"The same here," added Chiara, wringing seawater from her long, dark plait.

"And this is my problem to solve?" Anton inquired, leaning toward Li, his face half a dozen inches from hers.

Well, if he wanted to play it that way. She crinkled her nose and sniffed loudly. "Absolutely!"

Anton lifted his left arm, sniffing his shoulder. He winced, rolled his eyes and shook his head. "Right." He looked over Li's head at Peter. "When she's right she's right."

Sometimes Anton could be so annoying – especially lately. Li elbowed him painfully in the ribs, stepping past him and Peter. "Have it your way, we'll find our own showers," she called over her shoulder.

Chiara slipped past the two men, wrapped her arm around Li's shoulders. "You and me, Sis."

"You'll need to do that together," Peter called after them. "Shower that is, Chiara can't be left on her own."

Li turned back, her eyes sparkling. "Well, you could watch us both, and make sure we don't get up to any … mischief."

Peter grinned broadly. "I have a sudden vision of hot springs, steam rising over snow, the four of us—"

"Team!" Francis declared firmly from the gangplank.

They whirled as one.

Francis and Jay descended to the pier and approached them. Francis lifted a house key and addressed his team, "We have a safe house or at least a place to stay overnight. Jay and I will be organizing transport out of here. Stay at the safe house until we collect you."

Francis pulled Li aside, gave her the key, and requested quietly, "Keep an eye on the rest. Make sure they don't get into any trouble. I know you've the wisest head amongst this lot."

Li nodded. "Sure, Francis."

"The address is on the key ring. We'll see you later tonight."

Li noted the address and pocketed the key. She'd check the address with her smartphone and GPS, finding it would be easy enough. She pulled out her smartphone and caught up with the rest of the team, who were waiting a handful of yards away.

"Hot showers," Chiara murmured, rubbing her hand down her face.

"A fresh change of clothes," Anton remarked.

"Food," Peter declared with gusto.

Li caught Peter's gaze and shrugged. "Does fermented shark, and sour ram's testicles take your fancy."

"Damn it – I'll eat anything," Peter replied.

Li lifted the key and said, "Then it's time to move."

The team followed her from the pier, heading toward the safe house.

* * *

The final rays of the setting sun gleamed off the sleek Gulfstream G500 private jet as it descended toward Keflavík International Airport.

Boris Hartman lifted a glass of one-hundred-year-old single-malt scotch to his full, sensual lips and sipped the amber liquid. The taste was exquisite, but it didn't satisfy him. He drank in the vision of the woman sitting opposite him. She was five-feet-seven-inches tall, a true blonde, big blue eyes, long eyelashes and a curvaceous body best described as ultra-high-class escort. He'd converted her ninety-seven years earlier, capturing her at twenty-three years of age, her name was Helena.

Sitting across the aisle, and sipping drinks of their own, were his private mountain of muscle, Charles, and his business partner, Zeke.

The sunlight faded from the world, and true twilight took ownership of the sky. The Gulfstream's wheels touched down. The pilot executed a perfect, silky landing. He'd learned many years before to never disappoint his employer.

Boris was not above sharing his true nature with selected humans; the laws of the Vampire Dominion be damned. He'd do whatever he wanted to do and saw no reason to change the habits of three centuries. His original family's business had been banking and finance. He'd left after his own transformation into a vampire, but had returned in the early twentieth century – with a startling vengeance for the descendants of his long-dead mortal brothers. He considered himself the true originator of the term, 'hostile takeover.'

He'd taken the business further, assisting with the financing of the rise of the Nazi party in Germany, and the rebuilding of the Wehrmacht into a war machine capable of conquering Europe. After the second world war, business had boomed, he'd help fund half a dozen wars, insurgencies, gun-running, terrorists, drug cartels, human trafficking, and slavery. Along the way, he'd co-opted governments from London to Washington, countless NGOs, and the United Nations. Criminal syndicates from the Sicilian and Russian Mafias, through to the Triads, Yakuza, and the Mexican and Colombian cartels, all exclusively used his banking services.

Boris would do anything for a profit. It was amazing what one could achieve when one had centuries to execute a business plan.

His number one customer eclipsed all others, the secret wealth of the Vampire Dominion exceeded eight percent of the world's economic output. His banks managed trillions of dollars for Crane, the vast majority of it entirely legitimate. Crane had a penchant for legitimacy, for laws, for due process. Boris sighed. If he were in charge, he'd run the world completely differently, but he didn't have a weapon of the caliber of Chloe Armitage at his beck and call. There was no question of a direct confrontation with Crane – that would be suicide.

No, he would bide his time, all he needed to do was outlive Crane, Armitage and the Vampire Dominion – and his time would come.

The Gulfstream pulled to a halt within his own private hangar. He'd been here before; more than a dozen times in the last three decades. A long charcoal limousine waited for his party. It was thirty miles to the center of Reykjavík by car; with the sun beneath the horizon, they could relish the delicious experience of long hours of harmless twilight. They would hit the bars in Laugavegur street, and party into the night. Later, the screams would begin, and the blood would flow.

He grinned mercilessly; it would be a blast.

Helena leaned forward, her superb cleavage drawing his eyes, she never failed to excite him. She said with a mischievous grin, "I do hope we will have time to play."

"Of course, my dear," Boris answered, gesturing expansively with his whiskey glass. "There will be plenty of time to indulge every desire."

"Every desire?" Helena asked, her eyes widening with excitement.

"Everything," Boris crinkled his nose, his dark gray eyes sparkling. "There will be no constraints."

Charles and Zeke chuckled; they so enjoyed their fun. Iceland was perfect for a getaway from London, so few cameras, so little interference from Crane, his uptight praetorians, and his lackeys in the Shadowstone organization.

Iceland, a vampire could get away with anything in Iceland.

Boris loved the place.

* * *

An open wood fire warmed the lounge room.

The television displayed a popular news network on mute. A story about the Iranians sending a hypersonic drone into Israeli airspace two days earlier. A handsome host and a panel of experts appeared to dissect the story; their faces filled with certainty. Everyone in the room ignored the television.

"It's after ten, when do you think Francis and Jay will come back?" Peter asked the room.

Anton lifted his gaze from the fire, frowned slightly, and stated, "Li should know. She's Francis' gatekeeper now."

Li's head snapped around. *Where did that come from? What's he doing? We're not at war with each other.*

Chiara looked up from where she was sharpening her katana with an oiled whetstone and glanced at Li.

Li frowned and declared, "Yes. Francis put me in charge of you lot, and he said to wait here until they returned."

Peter frowned at Anton, as if surprised by his words, then shook his head. "I'm feeling cooped up. We could hit the local nightlife and blow off some steam."

Li was lounging in an overstuffed chair, her legs curled beneath her, nursing a green tea that had already lost most of its heat. She swung herself upright in the chair and put her mug of tea aside.

There was a brittleness in Peter's voice, his usual deadpan humor had died on arrival at the safe house. He'd recently lost a mother and a sister, sure not blood relatives, but they might as well have been, and relationships forged under the stress of shared conflict were stronger than most people had in their everyday lives.

Li had lost both her parents and her brother; she could relate to how Peter was feeling. Chiara wasn't faring much better, but she was keeping it inside. Anton seemed to be spending a lot of time by himself lost in his own thoughts. Everyone dealt with grief in their own way.

She sighed. Either Peter or Chiara was a spy. She had her own suspicions, but given her recent experiences of false accusations, she was loathe to voice them. If either one of them was a spy for the Red Empire or the Vampire Dominion then whatever loyalty they had for those organizations was dying on the rocks of grief for lost loved ones.

Li didn't believe that anyone could fake the feelings that she felt flooding throughout the team. The grief for the loss of Juliette and Yvette was universal and real. It affected everyone in the team, Francis and Jay the most, but recent loss had torn everyone apart in their own way. The only one who seemed least affected was Anton, protected behind his seeking of retribution against Armitage and Crane.

With the accusation of spying and the loss of Juliette and Yvette, Peter and Chiara were taking it hard. While she didn't think it was likely, the prospect of either one losing it and taking out their frustrations on the locals didn't bear thinking about. Li couldn't allow something like that to happen, but by the same token, she couldn't leave them hurting. She needed to do something about the team's pain.

She could see where Peter and Chiara were coming from, but there were some very real practicalities to deal with if they were going to travel underneath Shadowstone's radar. She asked Peter, "You want to hit a bar?"

"More a pub crawl," Peter explained, an intense need shadowing his eyes.

Chiara wiped her katana dry, sheathed it, and looked at Li. "I would like to go dancing. Can we do that?"

Peter said, "I'm up for that. It's time we had some fun."

Anton smiled wryly and suggested, "Perhaps we could get some real food. The long-life rations they have here taste like left-overs from the last zombie apocalypse."

Chiara looked up at Anton, and declared, "I want to have some fun and forget about vampires for a while."

Li nodded once. "We need to ensure we keep a low profile."

"We all know how to do that," Anton observed with a nonchalant shrug.

"I wasn't suggesting otherwise," Li replied, nettled by his suggestion that she was stating the obvious. "There's the little problem of currency, no one can use a credit card here. Even with our pseudo-accounts, it's too much of a risk without the cover of a loremaster."

Anton nodded and strode into the kitchen. He rustled about for a moment or two, then called back over his shoulder, "There's a stash of cash here. No doubt for exactly this situation." He returned to the lounge room with a small metal case. He flipped the lid. The local currency, the krona, filled the container. "I've checked the current exchange rates; it looks like we have about three thousand US dollars."

Peter grinned. "Enough for meals and drinks."

"That's the Order's money," Li declared, leaping to her feet. "It's meant for Order purposes."

"Oh, we have a purpose," Anton stated, glancing around the room. A notepad and a pencil rested on the coffee table in the middle of the room. He scribbled a quick message, tore off the sheet and stuffed it into the metal case. He took out half the bills and declared, "Back pay for the last three months for all of us. If there's an issue, they'll know who to contact."

Li blinked; the team really needed some time off. "We'll need to leave our weapons here. Carrying around katanas and battle-axes is going to get us noticed, even in Reykjavík."

"Sure," Peter agreed. "What's the chance of vampires lurking around here in late summer?"

"Don't be so certain," Li warned. "We shouldn't make assumptions."

"We'll all keep our eyes open and blend in," Anton promised. He headed for the front door, picking up his gray hoody from the arm of a chair on the way, and pulling it over the top of his body. His nearly bald head emerged from the cloth, and he grinned at Li. "We'll be as ghosts."

Li watched Peter and Chiara troop after him, sighed and shook her head. She regarded Peter and Anton. With Anton's crew cut and black eye patch, and Peter's burn scars, and their mutual physicality, the chances of those two being 'ghosts,' together was about as close to zero as anything could get.

She followed after them, locking the door as she left. At the very least she could ensure they didn't make a mess. Francis would be okay as long as they stayed out of trouble.

She caught up with Chiara and looped her arm in with hers, and said, "Hey, Sis."

Chiara tightened for a moment and then relaxed, leaning in toward Li.

Li kept her eyes open; she'd keep an eye on everyone. It's what a loremaster would do.

Even if she was only an apprentice.

* * *

The clouds had cleared away, the open skies bringing forth the first chill whisper of autumn. Twilight had deepened with the approach of midnight, darkening toward full night and the folk of Reykjavík had come to the bright lights of Laugavegur street to party. With late summer, the tourists were still in abundance, joining with the locals to crowd restaurants, bars, and nightclubs. On a Saturday night, the true nightlife didn't begin until midnight.

Peter pushed the restaurant's doors open and exited into the street. He lifted his face up to the sky, took a deep breath, and let it out in an exaggerated sigh. "What a meal."

Anton slapped him on the back and remarked dryly, "It was unforgettable."

Chiara and Li walked out into the street. Chiara asked innocently, "So how were the 'Sour Ram's Balls?'"

Peter looked at her and declared with a half-shout, "Mighty!"

"What was better," Li asked with a wry smile, "the balls or the fermented shark?"

Peter shrugged his shoulders. "I can't pick between them."

Anton shook his head, and said with wide eyes, "I don't know how you're keeping it down. I couldn't swallow a mouthful, I had to put it back on the plate."

"You should have picked the fish soup," Li remarked with a knowing smile. "Mine was creamy, subtle and delicious."

Peter turned back to his friends, and declared, "All that salted fish has given me a thirst." He flicked his head at a nightclub opposite. "Does anyone want to do some shots?"

Anton nodded; it was an easy decision to make. "I'm in!"

"Same here!" Chiara declared, the lights from the dance floor on the first floor of the building reflecting off her upturned face.

Anton looked at her. Chiara was the happiest he'd seen her since he'd met her at the safe house in Maine. She smiled at the dancers visible beyond the glass, her face lit with innocent joy.

It struck Anton then, what she must have had to give up, living as a double agent for half of her life. She'd never had a childhood. He suddenly felt incredibly privileged and sad for her. His own childhood and youth had been easy, the only real challenges he'd faced he'd created for himself, and they were nothing to what Chiara must have gone through. How did the Red Empire train a gifted child for deep insertion into the Order of Thoth? The amount of discipline required ... how much did she suffer, and for what?

His mind jumped. Were there others? Why would the Red Empire stop at one?

Anton turned away, the rest of the team flowing around him like a river around a boulder, following Peter's temporary lead to the nightclub's doors. The world within stilled, each breath washing through him. The people around him on the streets smiled and chatted, oozing relaxed happy vibes, everyone was just looking for a good time.

Then the sky darkened. The lights became brighter, sharper, the shadows deeper, a shiver stole up Anton's spine. The fine hairs on the back of his neck lifted, and goosebumps rippled in waves over the skin of his shoulders and arms. He turned full circle, scanning the rooftops, peering hard into the shadows between buildings, but there was nothing there.

Paranoia? Am I missing something because I only have one eye?

Anton took a handful of quick steps, crossing the street to join his friends at the entrance to the nightclub, the sense of threat hovering right behind him.

Li turned as Anton approached, her smile dropping instantly from her face. Her eyes looked past him, becoming flat and hard. A look of puzzlement stole across her face, and she whispered, "What's got you spooked?"

"Damned if I know."

"You sure?"

Anton pressed his lips together, then said in a half-convinced voice, "I'm just jumping at shadows."

Li scanned the street, revelers were everywhere, soaking up the last weekend of summer. She turned back to him and said sardonically, "You're a terrible liar. Better not try and go professional on that effort."

Four people left the nightclub. Peter got the go-ahead from the doorman and moved forward, Chiara a step behind him. Anton and Li moved forward after them. The nightclub was near capacity, a long bar to the left, lots of small, chest-high tables you could stand and drink at, a dance floor toward the back of a large, long rectangular room. A set of stairs spiraled upwards to the right of the stage, leading to the first floor. The crowd on the ground floor were getting drunk, high, or just having fun.

Peter called back over his shoulder to Anton, "Find us a table, I'll get us the first round of drinks."

There were some unoccupied tables. The nightclub's patrons were a fluid group, coming and going between the bar, the tables, and the dance floor. Anton picked a table, Li and Chiara circling around it. Chiara was already moving to the music, she grinned and looked hard at Anton.

Her eyes were huge, dark, and filled with mystery that drew him forward. Anton found himself falling into them.

Li's phone pinged, breaking the spell. She scanned the text message and reported to the rest of the team, "Francis wrote, 'We've found our pilot. Still negotiating. Will be back later.'"

"Pilot, huh. So, we're flying out. Well, that's a relief!" Peter remarked, returning from the bar. He placed a tray with a dozen shot glasses filled with a clear liquid, lines of salt and wedges of lemon on the table. "Tequila shots!"

Li laughed, seemingly reassured by Francis' text message. "Is any of that for us?"

Peter looked hurt, but his eyes were shining. "It's a smorgasbord."

"The night is still young. We can sleep on the plane," Chiara suggested, her eyes wide, drinking in the nightclub's ground floor, trance music playing loudly from a DJ on a stage against the back wall.

Peter was the first to lift a glass. The rest followed him. He suddenly looked nonplussed and asked, "What do they say here?"

Li looked hard at his red hair and said, "You don't know?"

Peter shrugged, picked up a wedge of lemon with his free hand and dabbed it in the salt, and declared, "Cheers." Upending the glass down his throat, and following by sucking on the salted lemon wedge.

Anton grinned and downed his first shot of tequila, following immediately with the salt and wedge of lemon. By the end of the third shot, the shadow of threat had retreated into the distance. Chiara leaned into him, and his hand went around her waist.

She looked up at him, her dark-brown eyes capturing him again. "Hey big guy, time to dance."

Anton smiled and followed her lithe form onto the dance floor.

The shadow vanished.

* * *

Li turned her head to the side, her eyes narrowing in disbelief.

Could Chiara grind herself any closer to Anton's groin? She turned away from the dance floor and looked at Peter.

He shrugged. "Looks like sparks are flying between those two."

"Yes," Li agreed, a trace of astonishment in her voice, "and all of a sudden too."

Peter stared at the ceiling for a second, his gaze becoming distant, musing quietly he remarked wistfully, "I miss my girlfriends."

"You had girlfriends?" Li asked.

Peter faced her and grinned wryly. "'Have girlfriends,' back in Maine. A pair of sweet girls too. Willing ... and able."

Li tilted her head. "Strange names for girls, don't you think?"

"No, no, ah... Hanna and Gillian."

"You had to think about that for a second, you're not making this up, are you?"

"Well, I wouldn't be carrying a photograph around with me – it would be dangerous for them."

"How come I didn't see these girls when we were in Maine?"

"What do you think? I couldn't invite them to the safe house."

"So how did it work? How did you hook up with each other?"

"Did you ever wonder why supply trips into town took three hours when the town was four miles away?" Peter lifted a large glass mug of foaming larger and downed a third of it. "I was never gonna chase Chiara, she's too much like a sister, the same with Yvette." His face fell, and he took another slug of beer.

"What about Jay, he obviously felt differently about Yvette?"

"He joined the team about four years ago. Transferred in at a conclave. He wanted out of Seattle and wanted Francis as a mentor. Yvette and Jay got serious about two years ago." Peter took another long swallow and observed sadly. "That's all past and gone now."

"I'm sorry. I shouldn't have pushed."

"It's no problem. What about you Li, anyone special?"

Li half-smiled for a moment then shrugged her shoulders. "Only a teenage infatuation."

"All blades and no boyfriends, eh?" Peter asked, nonchalantly. "It's an occupational hazard." He shrugged his heavy shoulders, briefly resembling a moving wall, and observed quietly. "The force teams end up feeling like family, it's hard to find someone special." He glanced at his nearly drained mug of beer, finished it off and asked, "Another round?"

"Sure, get four – the lovebirds are returning to the nest."

Peter sauntered off to the bar, carving a gap through the crowd like a killer whale through a pack of seals, everyone intimidated by his sheer physicality. Li overheard a couple of mentions of the name 'Thor.' Did they really think a god walked amongst them?

She scanned the crowd, all the girls and most of the guys watched Peter walk all the way to the bar. She sighed, perhaps they were right. He was extremely strong, and capable. She snorted suddenly behind her hand, a smile curling her lips. They hadn't seen Peter half-naked; he was more bear than man. Perhaps the gods were hairy, who would know?

The girls in the nightclub continued to cast admiring glances at Peter as he stood at the bar. The fading burn scars on his face just made him look rugged and heroic, like a man who'd seen real danger and lived to tell the tale. Li doubted they would care about the thick, curly, dark-auburn hair over his broad, deep chest, or the way it thinned out over his massive shoulders and down his powerful arms. No, they would be staring into a pair of wide-set blue eyes, more often filled with laughter than not, and too busy trying to get their thighs around his muscular hips to notice anything else.

She shook her head and asked softly, "What am I doing?"

Li looked around, Anton and Chiara were just leaving the dance floor, her hand in his. Loneliness tugged at her heart with cold claws. She sucked in a breath of air, her lips curling wryly, *I don't have to be alone, I can do something about that.*

Tonight, was for fun. Tomorrow the team would leave, it was time to make the most of every moment.

She vowed to enjoy herself.

* * *

Anton let go of Chiara's hand as he reached the drinks table.

Li looked at him blankly, and then slowly arched a quizzical eyebrow.

Anton shrugged, was Li attempting a little subtle ownership? He gently bit his lower lip, and ever so slightly shook his head, an 'it's never been the right time,' look passing between them. In his heart of hearts, the time had never been right for Li and him to become an item. If anyone asked him who was the most important person in his life, who had the deepest emotional connection with him, it was Li, with Peter running a close second. After her revelations, Chiara was moving strongly into the mix, but she wasn't Li.

Li was amazingly capable, whip-smart, beautiful, honest with her emotions, deeply committed to the team, and the fight against the vampires. And yet, things didn't quite jell between them, not enough to take their relationship to the next level. For some time now, there always seemed to be an abrasive edge between them, and it had gotten worse since Maine.

The events in Whitby had broken the soul of the Mirovar force team. There was another team forming amongst Li, Peter, Chiara and himself, but who would lead it?

And that was the rub. Peter and Chiara weren't competitors for leadership, but Li was.

Anton rubbed his three-day growth with his left hand and looked at Li anew. So, that was the problem between them. Well, there was no sense fighting that fight when so much else was going on. He'd take a step back, and give a temporary respite until things got better. But one day, sure as sunrise, they'd have to have it out and determine once and for all who was boss.

Peter returned from the bar, supporting four large mugs of the local beer in his big hands. He deposited the foaming glasses in the middle of the table and said, "There you go. Get this into you, it's delicious."

"Excellent," Anton said, letting his thoughts about Li go. It was starting to feel like a post-game celebration. His memory reached back, just over four months ago he'd been playing college ice hockey on a scholarship.

His mind backflipped over a chasm of horrific events. In another two days, it would be the four-month anniversary of his mother's murder and his father's abduction.

Anton hid his face behind a long swig of beer and then burped into his fist. The anniversary had crept up on him. A wave of shame knotted his guts – he'd forgotten all about it.

Li made a joke about the beer, and he barely heard her words. Chiara said something about never having a beer before and tried her first taste, screwing up her face in dismay, and exclaiming in wonder how anyone could actually like it. Peter retorted something about beer being liquid ambrosia, food of the gods.

The nightclub swam, there was too much light and noise to allow him to get his bearings.

Reality jarred back into sharp relief and Anton's mood with it. He put the half-empty mug of beer back on the table. "Now here's a question for all you long-timers," he declared, a dark light shadowing his eyes. "Legend has it that Hakron had the Key of Ahknaton just after Mekra became a vampire. Why didn't he simply reset the Metaframe at that point? He'd every fucking chance to do so. Why the hell didn't he solve the problem there and then?"

Li shook her head, her face filled with surprise at the sudden turn in the conversation. "He didn't know how. Only Ahknaton really understood the Key."

"He tried, but it didn't work," Chiara offered, she glanced at Li, her voice uncertain. "At least, that's what I was taught."

Li looked hard at Chiara for a moment, a question began to dawn on her face, then vanished as quickly as it had arrived.

Peter weighed in; his face serious. "No records survived. No one knows why. He must've had a good reason for not doing it because he was a really smart guy."

Anton paused for a moment. *What was Li about to ask?* Something in what Chiara had just said must've clued her in. Then he asserted, "In any event, he let a golden opportunity go begging." He lifted and drained his mug, slapped it back down on the table, looked around for the toilets and declared, "I'll be back in five."

Peter said, "Yeah, me too," and followed after him.

Anton pushed through the crowd. It looked like Li had just decided Chiara's guilt. He hoped she'd keep her suspicions to herself. The last thing he needed was Li pushing Chiara's secret out into the open.

The fun had gone out of the evening, the brief illusion of normality had evaporated. He'd been foolish to indulge … no, not foolish, just naive. They all needed to regroup and tonight had helped that. The team needed the rest. They needed to recover, rebuild and refocus upon the war against the vampires. The rest tonight was just that – rest – a brief respite to recharge before the war flashed back into hot life. Of course, one night wouldn't be enough. How could it be? The team lay deeply wounded, riven with suspicion and lust for vengeance.

One of those topics he had to admit knowing a thing or two about. He'd always been a quick study; the last four months had thrown him into the deep end of life, forcing him to learn quickly or die. Gang Wu's words came to mind, *'The man who walks in the shadow of vengeance is a different man from the man who walks in the light of justice.'*

"Gang was right," he whispered to himself. His words drowned out by the noise in the nightclub. Anton grinned mirthlessly, a fell light behind his blue eye, a dark and certain purpose surging through his heart. He'd made his choice.

I will write the justice I deliver in the blood of my enemies.

They'd taken blood and blood he would have in return – nothing less would do.

* * *

The nightclub was Boris' favorite.

He detested the decor, the ridiculous-modern music, the heaving mass of sweaty humanity drunk on alcohol and endorphins, but he loved the easy opportunity to pick up fresh meatsacks, filled with delicious blood. He had an old strategy, tried and true, Helena, Zeke and himself would make acquaintances, invite them back to a pre-booked hotel room for a private party, and then the real fun would begin.

Boris slipped the doorman a pair of hundred-dollar US bills, and the doors into the nightclub opened before him. With Helena on his arm and Zeke and Charles behind him, he strode into the bar as if he owned the place. They always attracted attention when they were together. Boris, stood six-foot-one-inch tall, blessed with thick dark hair, and male-model good looks, and Helena was the epitome of a Hollywood blonde bombshell, attention was inevitable. He smiled at the crowd around him, if only they knew what they were really looking at, they would be running in panic, not displaying admiration, lust or envy.

Charles peeled off behind him and headed for the bar. It was important to buy some drinks, something top-notch, and impressive to share. It was the first step in the process of blending in with the meatsacks and earning the minimum of trust necessary to get them away from the rest of the herd.

Boris scanned the crowd; he wanted the best-looking ones. Any vampire could attack someone ugly or common, but what was the fun in that? It was the seduction of the beautiful that added the extra frisson of excitement to the night. A pair of delicious brunettes caught his eye. They were alone at one of the stand-up tables, apparently deep in conversation while nursing a pair of barely-touched beers. One was Asian, the other Mediterranean; they possessed a rare poise and athletic presence. Boris despised athletic women. The only reason a woman, a real woman, someone worthy of his notice had to sweat, was when she was working with rapt enthusiasm on his rigid member.

His gaze moved on.

Boris' lip curled with delight. Across the room was a young couple, tall, lean, exquisite. The flower of youth from the island. He was three inches taller than Boris, blond, beautiful, a face that Michelangelo would've immortalized in marble. His partner outshone him; pale, flawless skin, eyes the color of the sea at dawn, a river of dark-auburn hair running down to her hips, and a body shaped to fulfill any ardent desire.

Boris squeezed Helena's hand. She zeroed in on the pair, a slight smile gracing her full lips. She knew what to do, she'd had decades of practice. Within minutes they would be interested, their desires inflamed, within an hour they would be back at the hotel – and moaning in ecstasy – the agonized screams would come later.

Food was so interesting – there was so much you could do with it.

Boris never tired of his games, even after three centuries, each night was fresh and filled with new opportunities.

He considered himself blessed to be a vampire, freed of the narrow restrictions of humanity. Their ephemeral lives, growing old in what seemed a moment, beset on all sides by urgent, yet trivial needs, barely satisfied before a few brief decades consigned them to the grave and eternity as dust.

Boris breathed deeply, extending his senses. The world was rich, luminous, a grand and compelling sensual reality. There was no end to the resonate need to live, to feel, to experience the act of living to the outer limits of possibility. That the couple he was walking slowly toward was destined to die tonight in horrific agony was just another moment in the rich tapestry of his life. Their life's purpose fulfilled in the extremity of his pleasure.

Boris and Helena reached the table at the same time as Charles arrived with four flutes of Krug champagne. Charles left the tray and joined Zeke to find the others they would need for a proper party back at the hotel.

The local children looked at Boris and Helena with a measure of curiosity.

Perfect, Boris thought. *I can always work with curiosity.*

* * *

The nightclub thumped to a heavy beat.

The floor above was as busy as the ground floor. An attitude filled with relaxed fun and excitement ruled the atmosphere. It was one of those nights when everyone had the right attitude, and no one wanted to make trouble.

Peter exited the toilets, Anton a step behind him. He lifted his right fist to his mouth and burped into it. The mix of fermented shark, sour ram's balls, and salted fish he'd filled up on at dinner half rising up his throat. He grimaced, it wasn't 'mighty,' after all, but he wasn't going to tell his friends that. Another couple of pints of larger would fix what ailed him – one way or another.

Perhaps he'd be staring down a toilet bowl later on, but if he did, at least traditional Icelandic cuisine would be off his bucket list.

He moved through the crowd, heading back to the table where Li and Chiara had their heads together deep in conversation. Their beers remained untouched, obviously not to their taste. Anton grabbed his elbow, shouting over the noise, "I'll get the next round."

Peter nodded. "Get something for the girls."

"Sure," Anton agreed, veering away toward the bar.

Peter scanned the crowd, it may be a party, but an ingrained vigilance never left him. There was plenty of distracting natural talent in the nightclub, a young man could do very well in this place. His gaze moved on, completing a security scan coming to rest on a big lump of muscle with no neck, but very well dressed, and exuding a sense of utter indifference to everyone there. He was clearly someone's personal security, his gaze kept moving from a high-class foursome at one of the tables and a pale, fashionably well-dressed, slimly built man half a dozen feet in front of Peter. The pale man's face suddenly twisted into an angry leer, the young blonde he was talking to, took a shocked step back. His left hand flashed forward, grabbing her right wrist. She winced with pain, her mouth opening into a shocked 'O.'

"No one turns me down, you stupid little bitch!" the pale man snarled, his whole face working its way into an epic sneer.

Peter automatically closed the distance between them, his deep voice cutting through the noise in the room, "I think the young lady said no."

The big lump of security closed in behind him – fast. The pale man half turned to him without letting go of the girl's wrist, his gray eyes flashing beneath the half-lights, and warned menacingly, "Back off meatsack! Mind your own business before someone hurts you!"

Alarm bells went off in Peter's head, no one but a vampire would call him a 'meatsack,' and a vampire wouldn't have a human security guard. The heavy guy standing two feet behind him was a vampire too, and he'd been watching another table – that meant at least three vampires were on this floor of the nightclub. The place was swarming with filth.

Peter stood his ground, leaned forward slightly, shifting his considerable mass onto the balls of his feet. He summoned the Ramp to the edges of manifestation, no need to signal who he was with a heat plume. He could feel the guard stiffening behind him, an attack would come from that direction without fail. The girl started to draw breath to scream. The pale man, apparently having lost interest in her, let her go. She took another step back, swore in angry Icelandic for half a dozen seconds before turning away.

The pale man stepped in front of Peter and grinned up at him, his head not quite reaching Peter's chin, but he exuded total confidence, certain nothing bad could possibly happen to him. He called to his bodyguard and ordered, "Charles make sure this fool doesn't disturb us again – ever."

Peter pivoted to the right, bringing the security guard, Charles, into view. The pale man watched Peter, cruel mirth filling his eyes. Peter assessed where everyone in the nightclub was, it was important to ensure no bystanders were hurt, and there was the third vampire to deal with as well. He wondered for the briefest of moments if Anton, Chiara, and Li had noticed the vampires in the nightclub. There was no real way of warning them without tipping his hand to the two vampires confronting him.

He would have preferred to have his weapons in hand. Vampires were pound for pound, twice as strong as a Ramp master. He didn't know who these vampires were, what they knew, what they might have studied. Against that, he had his strength talent, which would allow him to match it with their security guard, and he'd trained with some of the best hand to hand fighters the world had to offer. Plus, they obviously had no idea who they were trying to intimidate, surprise would be on his side.

Peter waited, he wanted the vamps to make the first move, and demonstrate what they were capable of. It would allow his trained instincts to give the best response.

The security guard's left hand shot out to grab the back of Peter's neck. A simple move that would have worked perfectly on a regular human.

Peter ramped hard, diving deep into silence. The lights flashed overhead, dropping into a slow strobe under the impact of his accelerated senses. He blurred a foot backward, the guard's hand flying past his throat. He trapped the guard's wrist with his left hand, his right forearm exploding forward against the back of the guard's elbow. The vampire's arm folded in two, the elbow joint separating, the bones splitting the skin on the inside of his arm, blood spurting in a thin spray across the nightclub floor.

The vampire shrieked.

Peter lifted his right elbow, sliding it up and over the guard's trapped left arm. His whole body blurred right, his elbow flashing through a short arc into the vampire's nose. The nose imploded like a ripe tomato struck with a sledgehammer, blood splattering in a rosette across the vampire's face.

To Peter's left, the pale man snarled, his fangs emerging into attack position. The pale man's right hand flashed forward, a gleaming switch-blade knife appearing from nowhere in his grip.

Peter released the guard's left arm. His left hand swept down against the pale man's wrist, his whole body pushing hard right against the guard to give him space against the knife attack.

The guard took a step back, pivoting to the left. His left arm retreated out of harm's way, his right fist thundering in toward Peter's face.

Something snagged Peter's shirt, and he felt the thin bite of steel caress his ribs. Peter's right foot stamped down against the guard's left knee, the joint cracking like a dry log. The guard's bloody face became a mask of agony. Peter's right forearm, held vertical, swept past his face to the left, catching the guard's incoming right wrist. His right hand snapped backward, wrapping around the base of the guard's skull. Pivoting on his right foot, his left foot slammed down on the floor like an immovable anchor, his right hand whipped forward, launching the guard through the air into the pale man. The pair smashed through a vacant table, crashing to the floor in a cloud of splinters and fluttering drink coasters.

Someone screamed, her shrill voice cutting through the nightclub.

The crowd started to surge, backing away from the fight as quickly as possible. Peter glanced back at the high-class foursome, at least one of them was a vampire, and most likely two were. Halfway across the room from them, Chiara and Li, their faces alight and focused for battle, were moving toward him. Anton was striding from the bar, straight down the middle of the nightclub. His face dark with thunder, his head flicked left toward the high-class couple. They both stood out, looking calm, despite the mayhem.

Anton's spotted them; there are another two vampires over there.

The vampires in front of him were rising from the floor, and blurring forward. The guard hobbled toward Peter, lagging the knife-wielding pale man. The vampires were still reacting blindly to his resistance, they didn't seem to realize there were another three Order of Thoth closing in, and even without weapons, things were going to get messy fast.

It was time to finish this damn fight.

Peter snarled. He'd had enough. He held his position, his right foot snapping out, catching the pale man just below his ribs. He folded over Peter's boot and flew across the nightclub, slamming into the wall next to the stage, plaster dust blooming into a cloud around him.

The big security guard lunged at Peter, his right fist coming down for a hammer blow. Peter ducked underneath the attack, deflecting the strike to his left. Coming in close to the guard, he took him by both ears, head-butting him furiously.

The vampire groaned.

Peter's hands blurred, shifting his grip to the vampire's throat and groin. He whirled around one hundred and eighty degrees, throwing the guard through a brick wall into the street in front of the nightclub.

Masonry, shattered glass and brick dust burgeoned around the ragged opening, swirling in a sudden gust of chill air from the street.

Peter turned, scanning the crowd for more vampires.

* * *

The big, red-headed, meatsack blurred, his heavy fists clenching against Charles' flesh.

Boris sharpened his vision, the motion slowed. Charles, his limbs flailing helplessly, flew through the air like he'd been shot from a cannon, smashing through the external wall and disappearing into the street outside the nightclub.

Boris half-shouted, "The Order!"

Heat plumes were running high on the red-head and three others. The two girls he'd noticed earlier and dismissed as targets were moving to aid the red-head. Unnecessarily it seemed, with Charles in the street, and Zeke dragging himself painfully off the floor next to the stage.

The last Order member was heading straight for him. His face filled with a deadly lust that Boris recognized all too well.

This one's a natural-born killer.

He pushed Helena away, his hands blurring, an instant later, he held the dark-auburn-haired Icelandic beauty trapped in his embrace, his right hand around her slender throat, ready to tear it open at a moment's notice. Her oh-so-beautiful boyfriend smashed aside, his head dented by the brickwork wall.

"Back off," Boris shouted, his head flicking left and right. "Or I'll rip her pretty little throat out."

* * *

Anton's blood boiled, a red mist descending before his vision. Was there nowhere safe from vampires?

The male-model vampire had snatched a young woman, holding her tight against his chest, his fangs bared. He growled a second warning at Anton, and said, "Take another step, and I'll pour her blood on the floor."

Everyone stopped for a moment. One of the waitresses began screaming. She silenced herself, backing away from the vampire with her hands over her mouth, her eyes wide above them.

Anton snorted in grim mirth. His right fist pummeled the top of one of the drinks tables. The top sprayed into fragments, the four hardwood legs popping free. He grasped two of the wooden legs, swinging them in his fists as the others crashed to the floor.

His lip curled. "Rip her fucking head off for all I care." He advanced toward the vampire, flipping the table legs like a pair of Arnis fighting sticks. Their swirling movements, a blatant promise to beat the vampire into a quivering pile of bloodied meat within the next few seconds.

The vampire snarled, hurling the woman head first over Anton's head, far across the room toward the bar.

Anton ramped hard, blurring in a single leap through the air, the chair legs falling from his hands. He twisted mid-air, catching the young woman as she descended, cradling her in his arms. He hit the wall over the bar feet first. Bottles shattered beneath his boots, fine alcohol painting the wall. Anton dropped into a deep crouch, washing off his speed, twisting down to the floor behind the bar.

He rose to his feet, the dark-auburn-haired beauty still in his arms, her long pale arms around his neck, her head buried against his shoulder.

Anton's eye was blue glacial ice scanning the room.

The vampires had vanished.

* * *

The buildings blurred past, street lights strobing overhead, shadows flickering past like a bad 1930s movie reel. They'd left the comfortable lights of Laugavegur street far behind.

It was a long time since Boris Hartman had known real fear, and he felt it now. A cloying urgency curdling his guts. A shiver rippling up his back and concentrating at a point between his shoulder blades. A constant need to look over his shoulder that could not be satisfied filled his soul.

Was he hunted? Where the hell were they? What the hell was the Order of Thoth doing in Reykjavík? They needed to get back to their plane and off this accursed island as soon as possible. Even if they had to run the whole distance to the airport.

He could sacrifice Charles in a heartbeat. Zeke too. Everyone in his entourage was replaceable, even Helena. Anything to ensure his own survival.

Boris glanced over his shoulder. Zeke and Helena were about ten yards behind him, Charles was lagging back another thirty yards, snorting great breaths through the remains of his destroyed nose, his left leg barely holding his weight, his face white with pain. His vampire healing would be kicking in, but given he'd not yet fed, not fast enough to speed his escape.

Damn him to hell, the devil take the hindmost.

Something blurred from the shadows between two buildings. Boris couldn't see it properly, which was shocking, how could a vampire not see something moving.

It collected Charles, transitioning him from a full, albeit limping, vampire sprint, to moving sideways in an instant. Charles weighed more than three hundred pounds and disappeared into an alleyway opposite from where his attacker had come from. What the hell could break his momentum like that?

Against his better judgment, Boris paused and turned. Zeke and Helena pulled to a halt next to him. They all looked back at the alley mouth that Charles had vanished into.

There was a single low, inhuman grunt. Suddenly, a ghastly rope of guts flew out of the alleyway and into the street. A still beating heart, one and a half lungs, more than half a liver and yards of intestines littered the flagstones in a broad splatter of blood.

"Charles?" Helena uttered in shocked dismay.

She'd always been one to attach herself to familiar things.

Whatever had taken Charles — it wasn't the Order. Best to put 'it,' between the Order and himself. Maybe it would slow the Order down.

Movement in the distance caught his eye. Four humans were blurring toward them. The Order was in pursuit. It was time to leave. Boris had studiously avoided Ramp masters all his long life, it was one of the reasons he was still alive. Leave the Order and the Red Empire to Crane, Armitage, and their professional soldiers – that was his motto.

He was a businessman, the last thing he wanted was to put his own life at risk. His guts clenched into a tight knot, lending speed to his feet. The streets blurred past. If he found the time, he would call his chauffeur and get the car to meet them on the road to the airport. Anything to speed his escape from the Order and whatever had just taken Charles.

Boris faced forward and fled for his life.

* * *

Anton pulled to a halt; vampire guts lay strewn all over the street.

"Who the hell did this?" he asked incredulously. He turned and darted down the left-hand alleyway. Within half a dozen yards he came across the dismembered, gutted corpse of the big vampire security guard.

Whoever had taken him out had been extreme. The largest remaining part of the vampire was the upper part of his barrel-like torso still attached to a shoulder, arm, and the head. A nearby streetlight cut the alley in two, a wide swarth of light bathing the vampire's face in cold illumination, freezing a look of complete shock and horror upon it. The rest of his body was a Rorschach blot on the street. The body parts were still steaming in the cold night air. The blood and gobbets of flesh growing tacky, adhering to the soles of Anton's boots like obscene gum.

"Anton!" Li called out from the street. "They're getting away."

"Well damn that all to hell," Anton uttered, blurring back into the street and joining his friends in the chase. There was no way the other vampires were getting off the island, even without the Blue Dragon in his hands he was ready to take them on. A vampire with a broken neck was only a moment away from an open-hand beheading. Peter had taken a vampire's head off with his bare hands, and if they could spill vampire blood tonight, he'd be there for the kill.

But who was getting in the way? Whoever had taken out the security guard was bad-ass. Was it one of his grandfather's lone wolves, operating up here, out of sight of everyone else? But then again, the wounds were not smooth cuts. They were ragged tears like someone had fed the vampire through an industrial machine and torn it to pieces.

Anton's skin shivered with goosebumps. They weren't alone on this island. Someone was out there who could tear a vampire apart better than anyone he knew, and they were nearby.

Anton put on a burst of speed, catching up with Peter, Li, and Chiara. He called out to them, "Eyes open, we're not alone."

The three remaining vampires blurred around a distant corner and out of sight.

He ran harder. He was adamant, he wouldn't allow any of the vampires to escape.

Not on my watch.

* * *

Boris, Helena, and Zeke blurred around the corner.

Charles had bought it a half mile back. The meat-head, he'd really been little more than a glorified thug whose winning feature had been his willingness to do anything that Boris had told him to do.

Boris never respected stupidity, especially when it got people killed. Charles had died because he'd let himself get too injured to run properly. It was his own idiotic fault that he was dead.

Good riddance to bad rubbish, that was another of Boris' mottoes. He really considered that he should write a book one day; a list of insightful aphorisms to record his accumulated wisdom. However, the vast majority of humanity could never appreciate his razor-sharp intellect. They rooted like pigs in their own swill, lost within the miasma of their witless ignorance. There was no saving them and why should he care – after all was said and done – they were only livestock.

He shook his head briefly. *Pearls before swine ... nothing but pearls before swine.*

A breeze ruffled his hair. His gorgeous locks, the envy of anyone with an ounce of fashion sense, swished over his scalp.

Zeke grunted beside him. "Huh—"

Boris whirled around. Zeke's head flew through the air. His body still running forward another dozen steps like a headless chicken, blood jetting out of his open neck like a pair of garden hoses had escaped from within his chest.

Zeke's body flopped over onto the bitumen, slid forward a couple of feet and lay still, blood pooling around his headless torso. Boris didn't see where Zeke's head landed. His gaze transfixed by the thing that had just ripped Helena's heart out.

It stood in front of her, seven and a half feet tall, it's scaled arm thrust through Helena's chest, her still beating heart held in its black-taloned fist half a foot outside her back. Her body lifted off the street, her feet dangling and twitching above the dark roadway. The arm blurred with a disgusted flick of a hugely thick wrist; her body flying like so much detritus into the nearest wall with a sickening crunch.

The thing appeared in front of Boris. Its breath bloomed before it, rancid, foul, stinking of three-day-old carrion. It loomed above him, blocking out the streetlights on the far side of the street.

"Wait, wait!" Boris pleaded. "I'm innocent—"

Long, razor-sharp talons clawed into both his shoulders, ripping through meat and bone. Agony flared. The creature grinned, white teeth gleaming in the streetlight. Boris' hands gripped the thing's arms, he pulled with every ounce of his vampire strength. The creature began to push with his left hand, and pull with his right.

Boris' efforts meant nothing. He wasn't even slowing it down, then like a zipper coming undone, his body tore down the midline beginning just to the right of his neck.

The pain was far beyond anything he'd ever imagined could exist. His left lung remained connected to his vocal cords, and a thin whistling screech came out of his mouth. He couldn't recognize the sound coming from his throat – surely someone else had made it.

In his final extremity, Boris' eyes focused on one salient feature of his assailant. Its great lamp-like orbs, clearly non-human, lizard-like with a vertical yellow iris, and filled with a dreadful enmity. The creature's jaws parted. Rows of triangular teeth like a shark's gleamed beneath the streetlights. The jaws gaped open, wide enough to encompass his skull, enveloping his face in the rancid stench of long dead meat.

The creature tearing his body apart bowed forward, obscuring the street lights completely. Boris' head vanished into the creature's foul gaping maw.

The great jaws snapped shut.

Boris' world vanished into the eternal dark.

* * *

Anton, Li, Peter, and Chiara rounded the street corner together.

The corpses of three vampires lay where they'd fallen. The female sat slumped against a shop front; her chest evacuated as if someone had shot an eighteenth-century cannonball through it. Her blond hair in disarray, a startled look of surprise frozen on her blood-splattered face.

The slim one was headless in a pool of his own blood, his head lying face down in the gutter about twenty feet from his body.

Anton paused next to the last one. He'd been torn vertically from the right shoulder down to the hip. It looked like someone had taken to him with a blunt chainsaw. The top half of his head above the mouth was also missing. He glanced around, then realized the remains of the vampire's head lay splattered across the nearest gutter.

Li called out, "Hey, look at this, a blood trail leading away."

Anton strode over to where Li was standing, pointing at bloody smudges and tacky splatter on the street. Peter and Chiara walked over together. Li pointed to the nearest stormwater drain entrance and stated, "The trail leads in there."

They approached the drain in a wary line. Anton declared in disbelieving tones, "That gap is six inches high. None of us could fit in there."

"We don't have to," Li asserted quietly.

"Who could do all this, and get down through a narrow space like that?" Anton asked, incredulously.

"Not a 'who,'" Li declared, her eyes wide with sudden insight, "but a 'what.'"

"Pop quiz folks," Peter asked dead-pan. "What lives in a drain, can fit through narrow gaps, is invisible, and can tear vampires apart with its bare hands?"

They looked at each other in silence.

"Something out of legend," Francis declared softly from behind them.

Anton jumped and whirled around. Francis and Jay were standing side by side a dozen feet away. Li took a step forward and apologized, "I'm sorry Francis, I couldn't keep them at the safe house."

Francis shook his head. "That doesn't matter now." Without taking his gaze off the drain mouth, he put his hand on Jay's elbow and said, "Take Li and the car. Pick up all our gear at the safe house, plus any spare weapons we could use, and meet us at McCoy's hangar at the private airfield."

Jay replied, "Will do, Francis." He flagged Li with a 'come on,' flick of his fingers, and the two of them disappeared back around the corner into the next street.

Francis lifted his gaze from the drain, his eyes narrowed as he looked at Anton, Peter, and Chiara. He sighed, backed away from the drain and commanded, "Follow me, we have to leave immediately."

"Now?" Anton asked.

"Yes, Anton. Now. It may already be too late."

Francis turned and blurred away, heading toward the edge of the city. Anton glanced once more at the remains of the three vampires. It stung that someone else had got to them before he did.

Chiara called out to him. He looked up, she was standing next to Peter about fifty yards away, and waving him over. He ran toward them, and they turned and blurred off after Francis.

A question nagged at him, what had escaped into the stormwater drains? No, 'not escaped,' no one was hunting it. It was the one doing the hunting. It had simply decided it wanted to be somewhere else. A shiver rippled over his skin. There was something else out there, something that could kill vampires with ease, and worse – it was invisible.

Was it watching me as we entered the nightclub?

Another shiver stole over his shoulders. Fighting vampires was one thing, attempting to fight an invisible monster that could come and go through a drain mouth was something else.

Anton decided he wanted off this island in a hurry and focused on his running. How far away was this private airfield anyway, and who was McCoy?

* * *

Anton, Peter, Chiara, and Francis reached the hangar's entrance, revealing what lay inside it.

Peter groaned and declared loudly, "What a piece of junk."

A voice called out from the other side of a Douglas DC-3 aircraft standing by itself in the middle of the hangar, "Ahh... laddie, I'd not have you speaking badly about my 'Mary Sue.' She might not look like much, but she's as reliable a lass as you could hope for."

The owner of the voice limped around the front of the plane, his left hand caressed the nose, where someone had welded a rusty metal plate on, a weathered patch for some nameless damage incurred years in the past.

"Reliable?" Peter asked, his astonishment written in bold letters in the tone of his voice. "Where do you go for spare parts – a museum?"

The pilot whipped a lit cigarette from his mouth and thrust it at Peter. "I'll tell you, laddie, you can flap those great big arms of yours and fly to Canada on your lonesome for all I care."

Francis stepped forward, striding over to the old pilot. "Hey McCoy, don't mind him, he's too young to know any better."

"Well, when I was his age, I had manners, and knew how to keep my great flapping gob shut."

Peter rubbed the bridge of his nose and remarked quietly, "He's smoking next to avgas."

McCoy looked at Peter, took a desultory drag of his cigarette and blew a cloud of blue smoke toward him. "I might be old, but there's nothing wrong with my ears. She's already fully fueled. She's got extra long-range tanks, installed by the yanks back in the war. She's a real sweet stepper, great long legs," he winked at Peter, "she could take you anywhere you wanted to go."

Old but effective fluorescent strip lighting lit the hangar. Peter ran his eyes over the DC-3. He walked around the right wing. It had been heavily patched in a pattern that suggested machine gun strafing. More patches littered the main body of the craft. He found three more pieces of evidence the DC-3 had survived machine gun fire.

"This is one tough old bird," he whispered to himself. *At least it's not a freaking boat.*

A dark-green Volvo station wagon pulled into the hangar. Li and Jay stepped out of the car.

Francis called out, "Okay everyone, come over here and listen up."

The team formed a loose half circle in front of him, McCoy standing to the side, puffing on his cigarette.

"We're leaving in ten minutes," Francis declared. "Transfer your gear from the car to the plane, but before you do that – McCoy, please explain our itinerary."

"Aye laddie," McCoy said enthusiastically, moving in front of the team. "We'll fly from here to a little town called Clarenville, on Newfoundland. We'll be flying not more than three hundred feet above sea level. It's a bit over sixteen-hundred miles, and at one hundred and eighty miles per hour, it's a nine-hour flight. I'll be dropping you off just after sunrise, around oh-six-hundred local time."

Francis said, "From there, we'll travel by cars provided by Order helpers to Port aux Basques. We'll lie low and catch a ferry late on Sunday night. We'll be in North Sydney, Nova Scotia, early on Monday morning."

"Newfoundland sounds like the middle of nowhere," Anton observed with a sigh.

"That's a good thing," Li suggested, "fewer cameras."

Jay looked around the team and recommended, "Unlike tonight, we need to keep a low profile in Canada."

Anton snorted. "Vampires, Jay," he threw up his hands, "what would anyone do?"

"Maybe stay undercover."

Peter leaned forward; his face suddenly serious. "Jay, the filth were all over the place. Frankly, we saved … what? Two, three, four people from ending up dead tomorrow morning, and countless numbers going forward." He shrugged his heavy shoulders and winced. "We did what was necessary."

"Peter, you're bleeding," Chiara noted with a frown, looking at his left ribs where blood soaked his slashed shirt.

"Just a damn scratch."

"Lift your shirt, and I'll check," Chiara said forthrightly, moving over next to Peter. Peter did as Chiara asked, revealing a four-inch slice across his ribs. She looked up at his face and said, "I'll need to stitch that."

Francis commanded, "See to it now. The rest of you, load our gear. McCoy, ready to roll?"

"Just waiting for your team to get their shite sorted."

Francis nodded, and addressed his team, "You heard the man, time to get moving."

The team set to work, ten minutes later the DC-3 took off from the private airfield and slipped into the night.

* * *

McCoy had pointed to piles of dark-grey blankets, then grinned and told them there was no 'sissified,' in-flight heating, before heading up into the cockpit.

Anton watched as the other's grabbed armfuls of blankets. Peter nudged his elbow on the way to the pile and whispered, "At least it's not a boat."

The aircraft had previously been a freighter. There were no seats for passengers, just a long open space with curved walls. With only six passengers in a cabin that could hold thirty, or forty at a pinch, there was plenty of room. Minimal strip lighting on ad-hoc power lines taped to the main cabin's ceiling ran the length of the hold, providing just enough illumination not to deem conditions 'pitch black.'

Anton picked up a thick wad of blankets and moved to the back of the plane. He wanted some space; he was still digesting the impact of Chiara's revelation. Where did he want to go with this? His immediate reaction had been to support her, she'd needed it, and he'd given it, and yet – she'd betrayed everyone.

The war between the Ramp masters and the Vampire Dominion didn't matter that much to Anton. They'd been waging it for five millennia, and what difference had it made? His goals were personal. Chloe Armitage had tortured and beheaded his mother before his eyes. Then abducted his father, turned him into a vampire and hidden him somewhere. Somewhere he was suffering horribly without hope of release. Marcus Drake had paid the price, slain by Anton's hand. Only Chloe Armitage and her commander, Cornelius Crane remained for him to deal with. He vowed to do whatever was necessary to kill them both, only then, would justice be satisfied.

And one day he'd find his father too and end his torment. He didn't like to think about it, but the only way he could ever deal with his father's situation was to kill him. It was just another terrible thing Chloe Armitage had forced him into doing. He would lay his father's death at Armitage's feet too.

A shadow separated from the gloom; an armful of blankets held against her chest. She whispered, "It's too cold up front, have you got some room back here."

Anton had made a cocoon of blankets, half underneath to shield from the cold deck of the DC-3, and the rest above. He moved aside, lifting the top blankets back to create space.

A dark-haired beauty slipped in next to him, her own blankets adding to the base and the covers. She whispered into his ear, "You don't mind how close I get?"

Anton shook his head, his arm going around her shoulders.

She pushed up close to his body, leaning into his chest, and asked, "Would you really have seen her throat ripped open?"

Anton's mind flashed back to the nightclub and the vampire who'd grabbed the auburn-haired Icelandic girl. "No, not really. But I had to convince him that I didn't care."

"You were bluffing?" she observed quietly, her right hand sweeping over his chest.

"The important thing was he believed me and threw her away. I forced him to use her as a distraction to allow their escape, instead of a shield, and it worked."

"I watched. You sold it really well. I was convinced you'd just wade in there and pound him into the floor with those table legs you picked up."

"I did, didn't I."

"You acted like a Red Empire operative."

"And would you like that, Chiara?"

"Very much."

Anton was silent for a long moment, listening to the rest of the cabin. The roar of the engines drowned out any other noise. No one could hear them. In the near darkness, no one could see them. Was Chiara, right? Was he more aligned to the Red Empire than the Order of Thoth?

She leaned in against him, her hand sliding down across his hard stomach, and whispered, "Have you considered where your true spiritual home might be?"

Anton's heart jumped. He turned to face her and asked, "Does it matter?"

She suddenly moved above him, her hands appearing on the sides of his head. She kissed him urgently on the lips, then broke away, breathing hard. "No, it doesn't matter."

Chiara's hands whipped down, finding the base of his shirt, and sliding up underneath it over his smooth, naked skin.

Anton crunched forward, lifting his arms, allowing his shirt and hoody to come off over his head. His hands blurred, slipping a line of buttons down the front of Chiara's shirt. She arched backward, sliding it off her shoulders. She was naked underneath. She'd undone her plait, her long dark hair flowing like a river down the smooth skin of her back.

She pushed forward, her mouth enveloping his.

Desire flooded through Anton's being, his hands rose up over her breasts.

Chiara's hands gripped his broad shoulders, and she ground her groin slowly back against his.

Anton turned her aside, stripping off his trousers and the rest of his clothes. She did the same. Seconds later, they lay entwined together, with her on top, pressing him back against the blanketed hull of the DC-3.

Her skin shivered with desire, and she whispered urgently between short, tight gasps, "Ramp with me, Anton. Make this last forever."

Anton held her tightly to his chest, every inch of his skin alive to her presence. Deeply within her, he let go, falling into silence.

Time slowed to a crawl.

Heat surged between them, like a swollen river breaking its banks.

Somewhere in the depths of his soul, his voice called out.

OH MY GOD.

OH MY GOD!

OH ... MY ... GOD!

All possibility of thought vanished.

* * *

The Order of Thoth called the conclave as the ferry docked at North Sydney, Nova Scotia.

The call arrived as a public advertisement. An innocuous invitation on the Internet for a corporate breakfast at a specific location in Minneapolis at ten am on Sunday morning the tenth of September. Francis was confident he could get the team there a week before the conclave, which would allow plenty of time to assess the political dimensions of the event.

Francis directed the team to a gas station half a mile from the dock. They filled up their vehicles with fuel and had a quick, 'greasy spoon,' breakfast. He paid cash for their expenses, and pulled his team together for a tight conversation in one corner of the gas station's cafe, away from any cameras or microphones. They were all wearing hoodies of various colors and common street clothes designed to blend in, limiting the visibility of their faces.

"Listen up," he ordered quietly. "We have two cars, so we're not all exposed at the same time. Jay and Li will travel with me, Peter, Anton, and Chiara will take the other car. Keep about ten to twenty miles between us at all times to minimize risk to the team. We will go via Montreal, and then north of the great lakes and cross south of Thunder Bay into the US. We'll have to dump our cars before the border, then cross on foot, pick up new cars in the US, and proceed through Duluth to Minneapolis. I have contacts organized along the route to assist with car changes, fuel, food and rest stops. It's going to take a day and a night to cross the US-Canadian border in secret; a delay we can't avoid. Any questions?"

Anton looked up from checking his smartphone. "A direct course by cars is a two-day trip at most. Could we do this a little faster?"

"We have to be careful Anton," Francis warned, his gaze intense. "We have no ... loremasters." He glanced at Li. "At least not yet."

Anton nodded, and conceded the point. "No problem, I'm sure we'll cope."

"And so, you should," Jay interjected. "Treat it as an exercise for practicing stealthy travel in hostile territory. The Vampire Dominion thoroughly control North America. It is their heartland and has been since the early twentieth century. It is the epitome of hostile territory for the Order of Thoth, but it is our base of operations too, and we will not give it up."

"An exercise? Sure, we'll be quiet," Peter promised.

Anton added. "And sneaky."

"We won't complain."

"For a whole week – even though hiding is boring."

"We won't talk about this ever again."

The rest of the team looked askance at Anton and Peter.

Francis sighed. "You two are incorrigible, make sure you stay out of trouble on this trip."

"Will do boss!" Peter agreed.

"Yes, Francis," Anton promised.

Francis pointed his finger at Chiara and Peter, and commanded, "Daily logbooks you two. Nothing has changed."

They both nodded.

"Then let's go," Francis said and watched his team leave the table. He followed them to the cars. He regarded the team with cautious eyes. He doubted he could provide them with the leadership they needed against the challenges rising against them.

He couldn't pick between Chiara or Peter, one of them was guilty, and the other was innocent. He was having trouble waiting for the opportunity to use a traveler and the drug Truther. The uncertainty was killing him inside. The spy could go quiet for years, or for the rest of their life. How could the team stay together and operate effectively without trust? The team had lost its center. Juliette had been the spiritual center of the team, and he couldn't replace her, and now the lack of trust was eating away at the foundation of the team like a ravenous cancer.

He took a deep breath and let out a slow sigh. He frowned, his eyes hardening with determination. He would practice patience and calm. The spy's day of judgment would come, and he would be the willing agent of execution.

In the meantime, and despite his doubt, he would provide the best leadership he could. He would always do his best; anything less would betray the memory of Juliette and everything they'd stood for together.

The barely scarred-over wounds in his heart tore. *They would never be together again – Juliette was gone – forever.*

He vowed to get his team safely to the conclave in Minneapolis. Then he would find the resources necessary to get to the truth.

Chapter Five

Thor Returns!

Thor sighted in Reykjavík nightclub. Ancient Norse god cleans up thugs in Iceland.

— News article on the Internet.

Icelandic Girl @ IcelandicGirl012 – 2m

'Thor threw this guy through a brick wall!!! Watch the video. #Amazing #Badass #ThorReturns'

— Twitter post.

* * *

Shadowstone HQ, New York City, August 28th, 20:00

Shadowstone had sourced the high-definition video from a smartphone at the scene. It showed Peter Lamb taking two vampires to the cleaners with his bare hands.

James Haley studied the video's timestamp; it was almost two days old. The Panopticon had not alerted on this video. He'd made sure the members of the Mirovar force team were 'flying beneath the radar.' However, there was little he could do about the virality of the video on social media – it had gone too far, too quickly. The whole notion of vampires and the great secret of their existence was beginning to unravel in real time. If events continued to progress as they were, the existence of vampires would not remain hidden.

A revelation that Chloe Armitage didn't seem opposed to, and so, he would not be as well.

"It's a strange world," he whispered to himself. Alone in his office on the top floor of the Shadowstone HQ building, he leaned back in his chair, rubbed his fingers over his scalp, pulling them down hard against his tight neck muscles.

There were so many wheels within wheels that they could provide assistance to former enemies when it was advantageous to do so. The UK arm of Shadowstone had abundant, full-face video of half the Mirovar force team, and especially Peter Lamb, who they'd held captive for a number of hours. He'd ensured that any searches initiated by Shadowstone UK fell into a black hole, courtesy of his Panopticon privileges as aide-de-camp to general Chloe Armitage.

James was fully aware that his use of full access to the Panopticon was an ability with a limited lifespan. The timer was already counting down to the day where the highest level of the Vampire Dominion discovered his contrary actions. No matter how hard he worked to hide his efforts supporting Chloe, sooner or later Crane would find out the truth.

They must complete Chloe's plans before that fell day, or else Crane would execute them both without fanfare.

Earlier that morning, the search for the Order conclave had borne fruit. James had waited until nightfall to pass the information onto Chloe, there was no sense in waking her. There was no one else to tell, the search itself was secret. The conclave would occur in thirteen days' time, on the tenth of September, in Minneapolis.

A successful attack on the conclave would destroy the Order, bar the mopping up of a few lower-level operatives. No secret organization could survive the loss of its senior leadership. He'd prepared the encrypted text and sent it to Chloe. She would know what to do next.

She always did.

James leaned forward, his fingers flashing over the keyboard, putting the finishing touches to a formal report on the communications blackout of August the twenty-second between Crane and Shadowstone UK. The official finding was the UK force team had successfully hacked Shadowstone communications for a day. Now that the UK force team lay beneath the rubble off the cliffs at Whitby, there was no one to argue otherwise.

Dead men don't tell tales, but he could make them tell lies.

James emailed the report to Cornelius Crane, and cc'ed Louise Wesson, Gordon Heathmont and Chloe Armitage. He logged out and headed down the building to the basement gym and the firing range. A couple of hours of working out and practicing with a variety of weapons would round the day out nicely.

He needed to be the best he could be if he were going to help Chloe achieve her noble goals.

* * *

Cornelius Crane sat at the head of the boardroom table in his war room and looked across the fine dark wood of the table top at Chloe.

His face clouded with an inscrutable mask as he digested the revelation of the date, time and location of the Order conclave. He conceded. "I must admit that I doubted your ability to provide this information." He nodded. "It's a triumph," his voice sharpened, "provided it pans out."

Chloe had just revealed to him the details she'd received from James Haley. She watched him closely. He was evaluating her, no doubt wondering precisely what was involved in this new intelligence. She expected the opportunity would be too strong for him to refuse. He would react, and he would react decisively.

"In accordance with ancient protocol, the Order will be unarmed," Crane asserted, he leaned forward slightly, his face hardening. "This will be the perfect opportunity to test the Day Guard. The Order will never recover from this blow."

"A daylight attack when they least expect it," Chloe suggested.

Crane paused for a long moment, and then grinned wolfishly. "Indeed, general Maze reports that a force of sixty day guards will be available for the assault on the Order Conclave. He has equipped them with the latest tactical helmets integrated with the Panopticon, and an augmented target and shoot capability for their rifles."

"Augmented?" Chloe asked, this was the first she'd heard of this advance.

"The Panopticon will overlay the Heads-Up-Display in the tactical helmets with target information linked directly with systems on their close-quarter carbines. Each guard's rifle will automatically adjust to the target's movements, improving accuracy and first chance to kill. We are deploying systems to optimize the Day Guard for combat against the Ramp masters."

Chloe kept still, revealing nothing. Such a system could just as easily be used against vampires. The Day Guard was on the path to becoming an effective weapon against the Vampire Dominion. Was the development of that capability a deliberate move against the Vampire Dominion, or simply a misunderstood side-effect of attacking the Ramp masters. Crane was putting a lot of faith in his implant technology to maintain control of the weapons he was creating, but was his faith justified? Given the implant sitting next to her brain stem, she hoped not, and she would do everything possible to find out for sure. Regardless of the Day Guard's capabilities, she'd destroy them when the time came to do so. Augmented humans had no place in the world she would create.

Chloe asked, "What role do you want me to play, Sir?"

Crane's eyes tightened. He stared hard at her. "Your mission is unchanged. Your discovery of the location and date of the next Order of Thoth conclave is a once in a lifetime event. Anton Slayne is new, he will need to be confirmed as a member of the Order, he is certain to be there. You will work with general Maze, Shadowstone, and the Day Guard to ensure Anton Slayne is eliminated and the Order of Thoth is smashed beyond all recovery. I want his head brought to me as proof of his death."

He remains obsessed with Anton Slayne. How he found out is still a mystery. A Metaframe spawned sorcerous power is the most likely possibility, but how do I confirm that? Even if I can't confirm it, if there is a shadow, there is something that casts the shadow. I will proceed on the principle that Crane can 'see,' things beyond anyone else, and can anticipate threats. The Red Empire must soon pass over a threshold and loom into his secret awareness if they haven't already done so.

She smiled slightly, and replied, "Of course, Sir. This is advantageous. We don't need to wait for a random hit by a Panopticon search. We can predict where he'll be and make our strike certain beyond all doubt."

Crane frowned. "You seem untroubled by the loss of your weapon against me?"

The unspoken question hung between them – were there others poised to attack Crane? There was no way Chloe would willingly reveal her recent and now defunct alliance with Dalien Morte and the Red Empire. James Haley had spirited the Red Empire fist team, led by Nasr al Dam, aka the Blood Eagle, to a remote safe house in Arizona. The four high-level Red Empire operatives would be out of contact with the Red Empire and completely unaware of the collapse of the secret alliance. Beyond her pet Fist team, the Red Empire loomed as a disruptive force. They almost certainly had a plan to destroy the building Crane and Chloe were sitting in now, but not without first stealing the Metaframe artifacts. She would bide her time, holding the advantage of knowing an attack would come, while Crane still believed his citadel was secret.

Chloe stroked her right index finger up the final few vertebrae of her spine, flicking her finger forward through her hair in a dismissive gesture, and said, "All possible attacks are out in the open. Your implant has seen to that."

"Good!" Crane's palm slammed against the boardroom table. "The world is as it should be."

Chloe shrugged, no longer monitoring her body language in front of Crane. She'd worn the implant for nearly three days. Crane had sourced it from one of his secret research facilities, but which one, she didn't know. He'd kept his research network private to himself, only sharing what he had to with his generals on a 'need to know' basis. Despite his stratagems, she would never give up attempting to find a way out of Crane's latest trap.

She leaned forward to emphasize her words. "With regard to Slayne, there is little for me to do. We know where he will be on the tenth of September, all we have to do is wait."

Crane paused for a long moment, and then instructed her. "All I require is for you to be ready in Minneapolis. General Maze, Shadowstone, and the Day Guard will take the lead on the operation. All you have to do is ensure that Anton Slayne does not escape. That is your one and only objective."

Chloe nodded and affirmed quietly, "Yes, Sir."

Crane leaned forward. "Make sure there are no rat holes for Slayne to bolt down."

Chloe smiled ironically. "Of course, Sir."

Crane frowned. "You're dismissed."

"Indeed, I am."

She got up and left the boardroom without the usual displays of obeisance.

Crane made no objections over her absence of protocol.

Her plans were in flux. The goals remained the same, they always did. Kill Crane, free herself from Allemande's curse, seize the Key of Ahknaton and bring forth a new reality – one that spoke of truth.

And before the truth, she would reveal – all would tremble.

But first, she needed to find a way to save Anton Slayne's life. Well, at least that would be preferable, she had fewer strategic options if he died.

Yes – Anton's death would be regrettable – after all, he has talents that should not go to waste.

Chloe struck the elevator button. A Shadowstone transport chopper waited on the helipad to transfer her to her Manhattan penthouse. As the elevator ascended, she devoted her mind to pursuing pathways that would put Anton Slayne next to Cornelius Crane, the Key of Ahknaton, and herself without the damned silver-loaded implant next to her brain.

It was time well spent.

* * *

Cornelius watched the door close behind Armitage.

He sat alone in his war room, closed his eyes and silenced his mind to a still point of concentration. His memory unfurled before his mind's eye, beginning the process of accessing his Metaframe inspired precognitive powers. The past flowed like a silvery river through him, he stood tall within it, apparently untouched by its passage, but emotions, dark and powerful surged within the river's depths.

Cornelius sharpened his mind to a diamond-like focus. The power of prevision bloomed within him. The near future came into view, as the momentum of past events spread out into a multi-dimensional matrix of possible events aligned with his own life. Bright lines anchored in the certainty of the past, whipped through the nodes of the matrix, linking the most probable future paths.

The three brightest lines converged on a single dark node – the node of his own death.

Cornelius emerged suddenly from the grip of his previsionary experience. He drew his hands down his face and looked at them in shock, his palms and fingers were clammy with perspiration.

"Slayne," he whispered, "and now Mekra, and the Red Empire."

Anton Slayne was still the brightest thread, the closest to realization. Chloe Armitage was the primary defense against this line of attack. The second was Mekra, but how could she kill him unless she was freed. The escaped Obsidian Claw ninja must be the agent of her release – but how would he know where she was? He was of her 'new,' blood, was there a psychic connection between them? The early reports from generals Haras Mosule and Shen Zhen indicated the ninja vampire was leaving a trail of death through Japan as he headed south and east. The last report placed him within the port city of Nagoya.

It was a festering disaster, as Nagoya was a gateway to the world. The one piece of good news – the death rates around this vampire had not doubled, or diverged on a different path – he remained alone.

General Dieter Franz was marshaling forces in eastern Europe. His force would guard the approaches to Mekra's donjon in the Carpathian Mountains, even though Franz's men had no comprehension of the prize they protected or the true nature of the threat approaching them from the east.

If worst came to worst, he could move Mekra, but that would entail revealing her existence to a select few. He could subsequently eliminate them, but preparing a new ultra-secret donjon to hold her would take time, time he didn't possess. He could kill her, it would remove the threat, but if she was drawing the ninja vampire to her, it was better to leave her alive – as bait. At least that way, they knew where the ninja vampire was going. Cornelius could arrive at Mekra's prison and guard the final passage. When the ninja vampire arrived, he could kill it, and then either destroy Mekra, or retain her for future use.

With the vampire ninja removed, keeping Mekra alive still made sense, her blood had no unexpected impacts on an already established vampire. He would see what tale his prevision told once he'd destroyed the ninja vampire, and Mekra no longer had an offspring to champion her.

The third threat remained nameless. A Red Empire operative surrounded by many shadows. It was a Fist team, an elite force, and there was a sense of something serpentine writhing through them.

Slayne and Mekra he understood. He knew how those threats had come into being. But the presence of a Red Empire operative was infuriating. That meant a breach of his personal security. Someone had revealed his carefully protected identity to his arch enemies. Somehow the Red Empire had managed to find him and target him.

Cornelius leaped to his feet and shouted, "Damn it all to hell!" his right hand flashed down, striking the boardroom table. The wood cracked and splintered along its length, collapsing to form a 'V' of two halves. He surveyed the damage for a long moment, his face livid with fury.

Let them attempt an attack, he would cut them down like wheat before a scythe.

He took a deep breath, turned away from the sundered table, and stormed from the war room.

* * *

Louise Wesson rocked back in her office chair and looked at the clock again, it was 20:05 on Tuesday evening, August the twenty-ninth.

Her days and nights had blurred together. There was only the mission and her subterfuge against the vampires. The first sixty day guards had arrived at the training barracks in the secret Shadowstone facility beneath Fort Dix. They'd passed the tests by surviving the Day Guard serum process. Another fifty-seven candidates had died. They'd fallen victim to berserk rage, followed by progeria, and catatonic depression. The firing of the TEF-4 neurotoxin implant next to their brainstems had been a final necessary mercy.

The rows of trolleys filled with previously fit, healthy, vital young men, shrouded with white sheets haunted her dreams. The presence of death in this factory of super-soldiers was like nothing she'd ever experienced before.

It revolted her. It was one thing to put a 9mm bullet into the brainpan of a known spy as she'd done more than a dozen times. Each time, they'd been a traitor to her country or an agent of a foreign power. These young men had all volunteered to serve. They'd given everything to reach the highest levels within the special forces of the United States. She'd recruited them from the Green Berets, Delta Force, Navy Seals, Marine Recon, and half a dozen other elite services.

Her staff had shipped their bodies to Rikers Island, a bio-hazard facility for eliminating waste, which was all they were to the Vampire Dominion. Whereas their hopes, dreams, and personal visions for their lives, and whatever they'd imagined they could achieve had vanished into oblivion.

The Vampire Dominion saw them as nothing. Louise saw them as heroes who'd laid down their lives in a false cause. She vowed with a terrible will to redeem their hidden sacrifice. The day would come when their brothers in arms would strike at the heart of the Vampire Dominion and rip it out, and that bloodstained day could not come soon enough.

Louise forced herself to be patient; she was alone in her quest, no one could help her. She closed her eyes for a long moment. Later that night, she'd soak in a long hot bath laced with essential oils. She'd submerge herself and forget about the world as her lungs slowly ran out of oxygen. Then she'd emerge and breathe again.

It was the only time she could let her defenses down.

The rest of her time she spent on the mission.

The phone rang; a rare landline call. Louise picked it up, the caller ID displayed on her computer screen, and she asked, "General Maze, what can I do for you?"

"Ms. Wesson. We need another sixty day guards as quickly as possible. How long will that take?"

Louise paused for a long moment. "A month, or even longer. We don't have candidates ready for induction into the Day Guard program."

"A month is unacceptable. We need another sixty men ready for combat deployment within two weeks."

Louise took a deep breath, there was only one way that could happen. "We can pull men from the current US Shadowstone spectrum teams and bring them straight into the program. They have the combat skills and will adapt quickly."

"Then do it."

"The spectrum teams will be decimated, US Shadowstone will be radically undermanned for tactical operations."

"It doesn't matter, start rebuilding the spectrum teams as you go."

"Yes, Sir. I'll make it happen."

"See that you do."

Another sixty men would enter training by the fifth of September and be ready for deployment on the twelfth. By the same date, there would be an equal number of dead young men, and there wasn't a damn thing she could do about it.

At least not yet.

* * *

Louise Wesson lifted the new F91 close quarters carbine and fired three short bursts from the hip in rapid succession.

The three human-shaped targets stood four hundred, five hundred, and six hundred yards distant, spread across an arc fifty yards wide. The heads-up-display in her tactical helmet marked the targets. Each burst of five 5.56mm rounds hit the designated target in the center of their body mass in a cluster the width of her hand.

Had the targets been real human beings – they would all be dead.

She turned away from the open-air target range and faced her men. The first sixty survivors of the Day Guard serum stood in a long line in front of her, dressed in full Shadowstone combat armor, with the new enhanced tactical helmets and augmented carbines. They all stood at one end of a long rectangular combat-shooting range surrounded by a high earthen berm. Floodlights the envy of any NFL training ground lit the field. She'd ordered the Fort Dix regular forces away from this part of the base – this was a purely Shadowstone training facility for the next week.

To her immediate right, general Maze stood with four praetorians. The vampires wore and carried their standard praetorian armor and weapons.

Louise lifted her visor and addressed her men, "Your new carbines are good out to six hundred yards, but you should expect to be using them at much shorter ranges." She pumped the under-barrel grenade launcher. "There's a standard grenade launcher you should all be familiar with." She ejected the magazine and held it up. "An eighty-round mag. The standard load is 5.56mm caseless, high-velocity, armor-piercing ammunition. A standard burst is five rounds. Sixteen trigger pulls, and you've got an empty magazine. If you're not sure, there's an ammo counter on the main body of the weapon, just forward of the stock."

She reloaded the magazine, set her gun's safety, and scanned her men. They all had their visors lifted, and she made eye contact where she could. She'd memorized all their names and personal details, and organized them into squads based on mutually supporting characteristics. She declared, "As enhanced as you are, your opponents are stronger and faster, but you will have a decisive edge in technology and tactics that will tip the battlefield in our favor. We have organized you into four-man squads for a reason. The first rule of combat is to get numbers on your targets. Single one target out, and bring all four guns to bear on that target at the same time. Let the Panopticon guide your target selection for you. Trust the system and get the results. The second rule is also simple, avoid hand-to-hand combat with your opponents. They will bring edged weapons to bear and at hand-to-hand ranges they will kill you before you can react … trust me in this, I've seen them fight – they are blindingly fast."

Louise paused for a moment to allow her warning to sink in. "We have a mission. Our opponents are meeting at a known location in eleven days' time. We will bring all of you to bear on the targets with full Shadowstone and Panopticon support. Your training begins tonight, and you need to be ready within a week. I have no doubt you are up to the challenges in front of you, and you will defeat our opponents and bring honor to our unit."

Louise scanned her men again, an approving smile on her lips and stepped back. She swept her hand to her right and declared, "General Maze will now address you."

General Maze moved forward a couple of yards and faced the men. His visor was up, the lights over the training field mirroring the surface of the visor and gleaming off his smooth, ebony complexion. He looked up and down the line of men, assessing them, and while not finding specific fault, his expression could not hide an inherent belief in his own superiority.

He kept them waiting for close to a minute, and then said, "My squad of four praetorians are superior to our enemies and all of you. They will provide you with an opposing force to train with. This is a necessary privilege to ensure you have the correct capabilities to survive against our enemies. You will not waste our time with weakness, stupidity or cowardice. Anyone not demonstrating the necessary levels of capability will be removed permanently from the program."

Louise's eyes widened momentarily at Maze's words, then she suppressed her responses. She was thankful she was wearing her full armor and tactical helmet, even with her visor lifted, personal responses were more or less invisible beneath her gear. As for her men, they stiffened beneath their armor, but thankfully, they remained disciplined enough to keep their mouths shut. However, their body language spoke volumes, general Maze was not someone to inspire their loyalty.

Louise smiled within, her face remaining dead-pan. General Maze was making her mission easier. When the day came to re-direct the Day Guard against the vampires, these men would not have forgotten his words.

General Maze, frowned at the men. Then glanced over at Louise and inquired, "Are they ready?"

"Yes, Sir. We have training ammunition, rubber bullets that can't penetrate armor. The men are ready and eager to start."

"Call up your first four squads."

Louise nodded, turned and called out, "Squads Alpha through Delta, advance to the line and maintain five yards between each squad. Squad leaders, organize your teams and confirm training loads."

The designated squads moved forward, taking up positions at the head of the firing range. Each team faced downrange, their squad leaders holding up magazines with a broad red stripe down their length indicating a load of rubber bullets. The squad leaders handed out the magazines to their men, slapped one home into their own carbine, and moved in close to stand with their teammates.

General Maze nodded once. His praetorians blurred downrange to the end of the open field, taking up positions hard up against the far berm, eight hundred yards in front of the squads.

There were several sharp intakes of breath from the assembled guards. They were much faster than normal, but this was their first contact with vampires, and the praetorians had covered the eight hundred yards in under thirty seconds.

Louise called out to her men, "Close visors, activate your links with the Panopticon, allow the system to select your targets. Fire when the praetorians come within effective range."

Louise was close enough to hear general Maze say quietly, just for his praetorians to hear, "Begin."

Louise stared down range. The praetorians blurred forward; within six seconds they'd passed the six-hundred-yard line. Closing fast, they started zig-zagging across each other, confusing the shooters. The squads started firing, short disciplined bursts. Their experience of special-forces training and warfare serving them well. She was sure they would adapt quickly to the new circumstances.

The vampires crossed the four-hundred-yard line.

Her eyes flicked back to her men; they were beginning to stiffen up. The praetorians were closing, they'd never seen anyone move that fast. Her head flicked back. The praetorians crossed the two-hundred-yard line. The squads shifted to auto-fire, the praetorians leaped or darted left and right. She flicked down her visor, the Panopticon fed heads-up-display immediately filling her view. Most of the rounds were missing their targets.

The praetorians hit the squads, barreling through them. Fists slamming against armored chests, sending all the squad leaders flying.

General Maze shouted, "Reset for the next run. Reload and reform."

The praetorians blurred away toward the other end of the range. The squad leaders picked themselves up and staggered back into position. The men reloaded their carbines with fresh magazines filled with rubber bullets.

Louise consulted the Panopticon directly from her tactical helmet. Only twelve percent of the bullets fired had struck a target. The teams had hit only three of the praetorians. One of the teams had missed everything.

"Your men will have to get better," general Maze asserted, his voice dripping with derision.

"Yes, Sir. They will." *They must get better, or all is lost.*

General Maze turned away from her, and she heard him whisper, "Again."

The praetorians blurred forward.

They had a week of training; this group would learn quickly, and the next group would follow. They would master what they needed to learn. Louise would ensure it, and when the time was right, she would destroy the vampires.

* * *

Louise sat alone in her office at the Shadowstone facility beneath Fort Dix, reviewing the training data from the previous evening.

The first attack by the praetorians had met with a twelve percent hit rate from bullets fired. By the end of the training session that had doubled to twenty-four percent and all the praetorians had taken hits on the final attack run.

General Maze had harrumphed his displeasure at the results, but he couldn't deny the improvement. With nearly a week of training to go before preparations for deployment to Minneapolis would begin, Louise was quietly confident the Day Guard was destined to become a finely-honed weapon.

To her immediate left sat a brand-new tactical helmet. She'd powered it on, and wirelessly connected it to an augmented carbine resting behind it. Both pieces of equipment had the latest GPS systems to enable the Panopticon to understand precisely where they were, a level of precision Louise was relying on for her strategy.

Some might have considered it an undiscovered bug, for Louise it was a desirable feature. She connected wirelessly to the tactical helmet with her laptop and fired up a set of specialized Shadowstone network sniffer programs to track the GPS data from the helmet, and the carbine, back to their integrating source.

A map of North America displayed on her screen. Two little red flags showed up on top of each other at Fort Dix, and a third in the middle of Utah.

Louise sighed with relief, gently biting her bottom lip – it worked.

She disconnected the carbine, and re-ran the sniffer programs, producing the same result from the helmet alone.

Louise frowned slightly, she had all the advantages of a laboratory setting, running Shadowstone software against Shadowstone equipment where all the network protocols and encryption aligned perfectly. The Order of Thoth would require an exceptional hacker bordering on genius to break through the tactical helmet's outer defenses in the middle of a combat environment. She mentally reviewed the list of people associated with Anton Slayne. Li Wu was the standout candidate; she'd graduated from the Massachusetts Institute of Technology with a double major in mathematics and computer science at eighteen.

Yes, Li Wu could do it, all she needed was the opportunity.

Louise swapped screens, and digitally signed off on the functional testing of the tactical helmet's augmented target/kill system. She was always careful to provide a rational context for every action she took. She'd hidden the verification that the helmets were an open door to the location of the Panopticon in Utah within the suite of functional tests of the broader augmented weapons system.

Have your tracks out in the open, but ensure they are misinterpreted. It was spycraft one-oh-one, and something she'd become a master at long before she joined Shadowstone.

She glanced back at the helmet. Now all she needed to do, was make sure that at least one helmet came into the possession of the Order of Thoth and specifically Li Wu. The Order of Thoth was a key risk in her plan, but there was nothing else she could do to help them work it out. They would have to seize the opportunity for themselves.

She was depending on the capabilities of an eighteen-year-old girl. Li Wu was her only hope for the success of her plan.

If worst came to worst, and the vampires discovered the bug, at least general Maze had signed off on the deployment of the technology and would suffer some blowback if all this failed.

Louise stared at the little red flag in the middle of Utah. A nowhere place, surrounded by nothing, and holding the most strategically valuable asset of the vampires. Its loss would blind them and allow her to progress to the second step in her plan. The co-option of the developmental second Panopticon at the East Coast Hub, and with that under her control – take over the Day Guard, turning the most powerful elements of Shadowstone against the vampires and destroying them with their own weapons.

It was a day that had to come.

She'd dedicated her life to that goal.

It would be victory or death – there were no other options.

* * *

Harold P. Slaughter dealt in illicit drugs.

The local district attorney had called him a high-level drug dealer to his face at a swanky charity function. Harold had laughed it off – that time. He never referred to himself that way. No, he was an entrepreneur, a businessman who was simply meeting people's needs, providing a fine set of products for which there was an ever-present demand. After all was said and done, if he weren't helping people have a good time someone else would.

His mother had insisted on calling him after his uncle Percival. Fortunately, his father had convinced his mother that she should honor her beloved older brother by using his name for their first born's middle name. Harold was happy with that, anyone calling him 'Percy,' was likely to get a cap up their ass if he didn't beat them to death with his bare fists first. Percy was a name for faggots, just like his ass-bandit nephew-abusing uncle. Harold reached up to the lapels of his jacket and adjusted the fit of his finely tailored navy-blue pin-striped suit. He hated waiting, but the current shipment demanded his personal attention.

People being late was an unforgivable display of bad-manners, but the Colombian cartels were notorious for their lack of manners. If they didn't have a lock on the supply of cocaine into New York, he wouldn't deal with them. But the lock was in place, and he didn't have a choice.

Harold adjusted his jacket a second time, flicking a barely visible dust mote from his left cuff.

A long black limousine with dark, tinted windows rolled into the warehouse. A pair of dark SUVs followed it. The cars pulled to a stop, their headlights adding to the pool of light supplied by his own SUVs in the otherwise unlit warehouse.

The Colombians had finally arrived. Their leader, a slim, dapper man, with an olive complexion, dark brown eyes like a pair of river pebbles, and a puckered scar on his right cheek, emerged from the rear of the limo. A second man, built like a short refrigerator and carrying a pair of duffel bags, exited from the other side of the limo.

Harold's half-lidded eyes tracked the duffel bags. They carried the product. Supposedly forty kilograms of the finest Colombian cocaine provided the cartel rat-fuckers weren't about to try and rip him off.

The SUVs disgorged eight guards, little more than hired muscle, high on the idea of working for the cartels like that was a privilege. They carried AK-47s, and MAC-10s, the usual assorted rubbish that ignorant, dumb-fuckers liked to use. He could easily imagine them holding their weapons sideways like they'd seen in some fucking movie, happily sending spent shell casings into their stupid, dumb faces before someone smarter put a fucking cap in their ass.

God, he despised who he had to work with to get a simple transaction done.

He'd arrived with six men, perfectly well armed with FN P90s, and with the training and experience to use them to effect. Under his suit, he wore a bulletproof vest and carried a pearl-handled .45 pistol. The pearl-handled automatic was a family heirloom. He'd picked the gun up from his uncle Percival's personal collection after he'd given his uncle a second grin with a cut-throat razor. His uncle's taste in guns had been the only feature of his uncle's personality Harold had liked. With the .45 and his well-armed team, he could guarantee his safety for this particular job.

Harold frowned at the man with the scar, tapped his own left wrist with his right forefinger three times, and stated brusquely, "Enrico, you're late."

Enrico shrugged and declared, "New York traffic, what can I say?"

"You could've made allowances for that and got here on time."

Enrico's lip curled into a lopsided, derisive grin, his puckered scar stretching tight on the other side of his face. "I thought we were here to do business, not discuss the time?" The Colombian crime boss nodded at his colleague with the bags. He stepped forward to a spot halfway between the two men. He placed the duffel bags down on the cold concrete of the warehouse floor, unzipped them, and spread the openings wide. Plastic-wrapped bricks of white powder filled the bags.

Harold harrumphed, and nodded at the man to his right, who slung his sub-machine gun, approached the bags, and made a small slit in the topmost one with a flick knife. He licked his finger, dabbed it in the powder, and rubbed a trace amount over his gums. After a few seconds, he spat on the floor, stood up and nodded.

The product was good. Harold nodded to the man on his left, who carried a slim briefcase. He placed it down on the floor next to the duffel bags, flicked it open and spun it one hundred and eighty degrees to face the Colombians. Inside was a single sheet of white A4 paper, covered with a typewritten list of codes.

"Two million in traceless cryptocurrency spread across forty wallets," Harold declared.

The scarred man stared hard at Harold and said, "Thank you amigo, but there is a problem." The Colombians stiffened behind Enrico, their hands tightening on their weapons.

Harold frowned and declared, "And what would that be?"

"The price has gone up."

Harold's face flushed red. He clicked his neck from side to side. His men spread out in pairs to his left and right, their sub-machine guns ready to fire. He snapped, "Gone up! My ass it has!"

Enrico stared hard at Harold, his grin evaporating and he stated in a voice filled with menace, "That can be arranged."

What did he just say?! "What the hell!" Harold shouted. His hand reached behind his back for his .45 automatic. "I'll tear you a new one!" his fingers curled around the pistol's grip.

"I'll tear you a new one!" an inhumanly loud voice called out from the shadows behind the Colombians. It was a perfect rendition of Harold's voice, cutting through the warehouse like an icy whip.

Everyone froze.

A second disembodied voice, opposite the first one called out in identical tones from the shadows behind Harold's team, "I'll tear you a new one!"

Harold's head turned to the left and right. His eyes darting, trying to see everything at once.

Enrico snarled, and asked savagely, "What is this? A trick?"

A third disembodied voice called out from the left wing of the warehouse, and stated in perfect mimicry of Enrico, "What is this? A trick?"

A second later the exact same phrase rang out from the right wing, the words thrumming through the warehouse with a power and resonance no human voice could match.

One of the Colombians, his face pale, took a step backward. His AK-47 swung left and right, hunting for a target he couldn't find. He whispered hoarsely, "El Diablo."

One of the shadows lifted away from the darkness, rising up behind the man.

He took another step backward, his lips slightly parted, his teeth clenched tight.

The shadow blurred forward, gray hands with black talons ripping into the man's shoulders. His head arched backward, his mouth gaped open, his machine gun dropping uselessly to the floor. He rose into the air, his arms and legs spasming, uttering a high-pitched shriek – and then fell apart in a shower of blood and gore.

Harold turned and dashed for his car. His driver was already gunning the engine, the passenger side door was only a couple of yards away. Machine guns started firing. Men shouted, cursed, and screamed. A pair of his men stood back-to-back, their sub-machine guns firing on full auto, their faces pale, jaws clenched with desperation. They didn't seem to be hitting anything.

Harold pulled the door open, diving into the passenger seat, the wheels spun in a pale cloud of smoke on the smooth concrete, then the SUV lurched forward toward the exit.

The guns fell into silence behind them.

The SUV picked up speed. Harold could see the big warehouse doors leading out into the street. They were wide open, looming toward him, brightly lit by the SUV's headlights.

The rear of the car lifted off the warehouse floor. The SUV must've weighed two tons; it flipped over onto its roof, sliding along the concrete in a shower of sparks. Harold slammed into the ceiling of the car, just managing to put his arms up and stop his head hitting first. His driver was dangling from his seatbelt, a startled look on his face. A gray hand, the size of a dinner plate, tipped with razor-sharp, black, six-inch talons smashed through the side window and into the driver's chest. Thick ropes of blood splattered over Harold. The driver gasped, the half-slashed seat belts snapping as he ripped through them, vanishing out of the car's window.

Something shimmered into view next to Harold's window. A pair of heavy reptilian feet, attached to thick ankles and massive calves, all sheathed in a gray, pebbly hide. Behind the legs, a thick, powerful tail lashed through the air.

Harold gibbered. "Huhhnn—"

A gray, black-taloned hand smashed through his side window, ripped through his bulletproof vest, and into his chest. The world twisted and blurred. Agony flared, scorching his soul. There was a strange staccato snapping noise, which might have been his ribcage being torn in half.

Darkness engulfed Harold P. Slaughter before he could find out for sure.

* * *

Shadowstone marshaled forces in the east.

State authorities were on alert from Tokyo to Budapest. The situational displays across the monitors in James Haley's office told a story of vast resources applied to solve a single problem. Someone was evading a tightly-woven net, that much was obvious, but it wasn't a Ramp master – it was a rogue vampire.

A trail of death led from the hinterlands of the island of Honshu in Japan, southward to the metropolis of Nagoya. From there the trail disappeared, until it began again at a small fishing village on the Korean peninsula, before cutting northwest into China.

General Mosule and his hand-picked team of praetorians hadn't made contact with the rogue vampire yet, but they must be closing in. General Shen Zhen was also bringing more praetorians to bear, along with the Chinese arm of Shadowstone masquerading within Chinese military intelligence.

James' laptop pinged. It was a Panopticon hit for one of his specialized, secret searches. A new set of windows opened up on his screen. The NYPD had an active crime scene at a New York warehouse. Apparently, a drug deal had gone badly wrong. He delved into the available data on the police servers; it was all immediately accessible to the Panopticon. The crime scene photographs were extensive, documenting a gruesome and violent end to eighteen men. All of them armed with automatic weapons, or at very least a hand gun, and yet none had died from gunfire.

They'd been torn apart, ripped to shreds and feasted upon.

The NYPD was sitting on the evidence. Their internal analysis assumed someone had let loose wild animals within the warehouse. An assessment kept from the public to avoid a panic. The NYPD assumed that there was a new player in the drug market who was getting rid of the opposition and was using methods designed to instill terror in their competition.

James knew otherwise. He categorized, and summarized the data, sending it by a quantum-encrypted self-deleting email to Chloe's smartphone. Once she'd seen the information in the email, it would disappear along with all evidence of its existence.

James' phone rang thirty seconds later, the displayed caller ID was Chloe. He picked it up and asked, "Yes, Ma'am. What can I do for you?"

"Hi James, thanks for the data, precisely what I'm looking for. I have new tasks for you. I need information on corporates or quasi-government bodies with leading capabilities for medical implants. I want them cross-referenced with nano-technology and manufacturing of exotic bio-polymer implant sheaths. Then, I need you to match that against Crane's movements between the twenty-second and twenty-fifth of August."

"Crane isn't tracked by—"

"The Panopticon, I know. I want you to consider the specialized hydrogen-based fuel used for scramjets. There are not many outlets in the world where it's available. Look for sales at night in the three-night window I've provided to you. We should be able to narrow down where Crane went and who is supplying him with exotic biomedical implant technology."

James frowned. "By exotic, you mean designed for use on vampires?"

Chloe paused for a moment before replying. *She's evaluating how much to share with me, how much she can trust me.* "Crane put an implant next to my brain stem eight days ago. It will kill me if he dies. You're the only person I can count on to assist me with this problem."

James took a deep breath and let it out. "Yes, Ma'am ... yes, Chloe, you can count on me."

Without Chloe, her whole agenda of protecting humanity would fall apart. He couldn't allow that to happen. James would make sure he found a solution, and found it quickly.

"Thanks, James. I knew I could trust you with this. Now I have one more thing for you tonight. I need you to reinforce the defenses around New York City and especially Manhattan Island. Do this with full visibility to Crane and anyone else in the Vampire Dominion leadership group, the generals, praetorians, senior Shadowstone – make this seem to be your primary task, and make sure it's visible that I have requested it of you."

"Yes, Chloe, are we looking for anything in particular."

"A Red Empire fist team. They're bound to send one sooner or later against Crane's citadel on Manhattan Island."

"They know the location of the citadel! How did that happen?"

"Indeed James, they do. As to how that doesn't matter, what matters is being prepared. We need to ensure we can detect any team coming into New York, and do so in a timely fashion. Can you do this too?"

"Of course," James replied. "Consider it done."

"What about our tame Fist team, are they safe and well in Arizona?"

James' fingers flashed over his keyboard; a screen came up displaying a dozen video feeds from the Shadowstone safe house in Arizona. The four Red Empire Fist team members under the command of Nasr al Dam were all accounted for. "Yes, Chloe, They're fine."

"Excellent. Good work James, keep it up."

"Copy that."

Chloe hung up the call.

James' eyes returned to the feeds from the safe house. A quarter of the displays were a set of cells buried deep beneath the main building. They were all empty. The bars on the cells were reinforced to hold prisoners with extraordinary strength, such as vampires or Ramp masters.

"Who is Chloe expecting to hold in those cells and guard with a Fist team?"

James shook his head and put the question aside. He set to work on finding the source of Crane's exotic implant technology. Within minutes, he'd narrowed down sales of the specialized scramjet fuel within the three-night window, to London, Berlin, Moscow, Los Angeles, and Tokyo.

"Well that narrows the search a bit," James whispered to himself. "Let's see what turns up next?"

* * *

A crescent of diffuse streetlight illuminated the drains beneath a partially open manhole cover.

It had been two hours since the hunt in the warehouse. Gullette and his three companions had fed ravenously on the gangsters and then made off into the stormwater drains with a few choice snacks for later. Gullette clawed at the remains of one of the humans. He snapped the femur's ends off with his fingers. He'd gnawed the long bone clear of flesh, only the juicy marrow remained. He took an end in his mouth and sucked heartily, a few seconds later the bone whistled as air flew within its length.

A smirk passed over his face as he smacked his lips and declared, "Snap bone tips, suck juicy marrow, what whistles?"

A second large male's head rose. Kavanne's mouth was slimy with blood; tendrils and gobbets of flesh dangling between his shark-like teeth. He snorted, his hands fluttering like wings, and said, "Human souls, flying by starlight, forever gone."

A third male loomed out of the darkness, standing on the edge of the wan light, his tail lashing angrily in the gloom. "No starlight, live in shadows forever, hate drains." He lifted his nose toward the manhole cover yards above his head and sniffed with poignant longing. "Dancing skies, soft breezes through trees, lilting songs."

Faroke's words cut through Gullette's soul like a blade of ice. The stormwater drains were not a fit place for the People to live, but only a temporary necessity born of desperate need. One by one, their enemies had hunted them down and killed them. His mother's songs had told the terrible tale well. The population of the People had fallen to a low ebb, and then the world had taken a turn for the worse – vampires had arrived. A nocturnal competitor, easily destroyed on their own, but like the enhanced humans, they soon organized themselves in packs.

Between the enhanced humans, who now called themselves the Order of Thoth, or the Red Empire, and the vampires, the People had approached the edge of extinction. Gullette surveyed his companions. Faroke had been born from the same reproductive cycle as himself and was of a similar age. Older than the vampires, they both remembered a time when northern Africa lay covered with dense forests rather than deserts.

The younger pair were both born from the most recent reproductive cycle. Kavanne had seen two thousand summers, recently passing into full-grown adulthood and the narrowing of his diet to human flesh. Shemina had also reached adulthood and was ready for the next reproductive cycle to begin.

Faroke and Kavanne would challenge the moment Shemina entered her breeding cycle. He dismissed Kavanne, he would best him easily in combat, he was still too young. Faroke was older, wily and dangerous. Perhaps he should strike first and not take any chances.

He held back; that was the voice of instinct, of the old ways – ways that had brought his species to the verge of extinction. There had to be a way forward, to avoid dying out, to avoid annihilation. He shook his head slowly. Individually one of the People was more than a match for any human or vampire, but it was rarely one on one. More often than not, it had been five to one, or ten to one, or twenty or more to one. With the slow cycle of reproduction, the People could not replace their losses. They were dying out. He estimated there were less than thirty still alive, and if nothing happened soon, they would vanish from the world.

Gullette responded to Faroke's words and declared, "Time consumes us all, eternal night creeps forward, fear will destroy all."

Faroke, Kavanne, and Shemina all stared at him, their spines bristling with fighting rage.

Gullette hummed low in his throat, a complex musical cadence that ran for about ten seconds, and the others quieted. He wanted more than a long life and progeny, he wanted true immortality and the restoration of the People to supremacy. He'd learned the prey animals' dominant language, easy to reproduce perfectly, but difficult to think in. When talking amongst themselves … they struggled with it, but Gullette had insisted they persist and learn. The old language of the people was a defeated language. It was no longer fit to survive, and it must die along with the instincts of the past.

It had been difficult to forge others into a group, but Gullette had found a way. He could use his call to calm one of the People. He'd learned a new and very different song. It could calm the others to the point of insensitivity to themselves. A sort of hypnosis, yes, that was the word, one he'd learned from a human book. He could quell their instincts long enough and often enough to prevent them from destroying the group.

As for his own instincts, those were a different matter entirely. Sometimes a dark rage would sweep through him, he'd leave the group, and sequester himself away in the darkness for days. Then after he'd calmed down, he would call, and they would come.

His head drooped a little, swinging left and right in a posture of classic wariness. The others cued off his behavior and followed suit. It was dangerous to move in a group, but the instincts of solitary hunting and defense had become a weakness against foes that hunted in packs. Gullette would make it all different if he could, and he'd discovered a way over the last five millennia. He'd heard the story of the Divine Engine of Thoth and the power of changing reality that lay within it. If only Gullette could reach the Engine, he would become master of all, he would raise his people out of hiding and bring them once again to primacy within this world, and he'd extinguish the usurpers and the vermin like bugs beneath his feet.

Gullette threw his nose into the air, sniffing heavily. His eyes narrowed, his shoulders sank, his gaze rising up to the manhole cover. He turned to Kavanne and Faroke, and whispered urgently, "Vermin lurks, sharp claws from shadows, kill it quick."

They nodded, their heads bobbing forward and back. They turned as one, blended into their surroundings, vanishing into the darkness.

They could safely eliminate a lone vampire, but they would have to move, for more would come.

There was nothing new in that.

Gullette waited a dozen slow breaths, then leaped up, closing the manhole cover with a single swipe of his hand. The cover dragged noisily over the concrete, before slamming home. The noise would distract the vampire, and help Faroke and Kavanne to attack.

His skin rippled with reaction as he landed, helping another member of the People to hunt was always hard.

One day the struggle would no longer be necessary.

* * *

For the first time in her life, Chloe was hunting chameleons.

A species long thought to be extinct, but she'd always doubted that. No, they'd simply retreated into the fringes of the world, remaining hidden, and biding their time until they could rise again.

She stood still, a sleek praetorian-armored statue on the parapet of a warehouse roof. She lifted her visor, extending her senses to their maximum capacity, allowing the world to flood into her. She breathed in through her nose, her ears twitched, her eyes scanned the derelict buildings around her position. The night stood revealed in all its vibrant glory; a rich, multi-layered tapestry of sensation. The stars lay in a sparkling wreath over her head. Strands of dark hair escaped the edges of her tactical helmet, a slight breeze ruffling through them. A dog barked hysterically in the distance, and then suddenly fell silent. Traffic droned on distant highways, the occasional truck or van driving down local streets.

Concrete rasped across concrete on the street beneath her. The distinctive scent of blood struck her nostrils like a slap, her teeth descending into attack position on instinct.

She'd denied herself blood all of the previous day, her senses were always sharpest when she was hungry. However, nothing came without a cost, a lack of recent blood would reduce her healing capabilities. She'd weighed the advantages, detection capability outweighed healing capability when hunting a creature that could become almost invisible.

The chameleons were nearby, somewhere beneath her on the street. She couldn't see them, but she could smell what they'd been eating. They'd recently killed and fed, the distinctive metallic tang of blood filling her nostrils. She sighed, tilting her head to the right, blinking slowly, pressing down on her vampiric hunger. She'd have to wait. She needed to find these chameleons if she could, and bring them to her cause. No one else would have an asset like them, and at the right time, they could prove decisive.

She silenced her mind, making herself ready to activate a supreme ramp on reflex. Her prey remained notoriously dangerous, normally a match for any vampire in a one-on-one fight, and tonight she was hunting three, or even four of them. A pack, something no one had ever seen before. They were adapting, as they must to the survival pressures first applied by the rise of humanity, and then by the rise of vampires.

Chloe rotated gracefully where she stood, checking her environment one last time before descending to investigate the blood trail leading into the drains. Jutting access ramps and air-conditioning towers covered the roof. A patch of shadow muttered a secret threat; she let her eyes pass over it without reaction, noting the position perfectly. She continued rotating and a second shadow whispered the same wrongness.

The shadows were too still to be real.

Her right hand slipped to the handle of the Red Dragon.

The hunter had become the hunted.

* * *

The air stilled.

The fine hairs on the back of Chloe's neck began to rise. Before they'd moved more than a fraction of their width, her mind speared into the depths of a supreme Ramp. She was taking no chances with these chameleons; her first attack would be her strongest.

Chloe whirled on the parapet of the warehouse. The Red Dragon appearing in her hands as if it had teleported there. Her senses rushed beyond normal vampire maximums, her sight expanding deep into the ultra-violet and infra-red spectrums. A pair of large shapes moved toward her, launching out of the shadows, one to the left, the second to the right. Under the impetus of the supreme Ramp, they almost resolved into full and detailed view. The outlines of their bodies couldn't adapt fast enough to their own movements to hide them from her. What might have worked against a regular vampire or a Ramp master failed before her supreme Ramp.

The Red Dragon flashed to her right, the katana glimmering in the wash of the streetlights. The chameleon blurred further to Chloe's right away from the blade. Her wrist flicked. The tip of the blade appeared in front of the chameleon's face. He rushed upon it, the Red Dragon erupting from the base of his skull, sending a thin ribbon of blood into the darkness behind him.

The other chameleon spun on Chloe's left, his right foot lashing out, catching Chloe across her armored torso. She flew off the parapet in a flat arc, agony ripping through her body, her breath bursting from her lungs. She slammed into the side of the building on the opposite side of the street.

Ocher brick dust bloomed around her.

Chloe's world went dark.

* * *

A soft choking cry came from above.

The street muffled the sound, but Gullette's ears picked up the cry's meaning perfectly. He barked a brief response, sighed and declared, "Faroke falls, our people vanish, all song dies."

Shemina looked at him, her eyes black pools in the shadows. "Vermin lives, breathing on cold stones, snap neck quick."

They raised their heads as one. Gullette blurred first, clambering up the walls of the stormwater drain and back out through the manhole, the cover fragmenting in a cloud of gray dust as he passed through it. Shemina followed after him.

They landed in the street, heads swiveling, tails lashing.

Kavanne coughed, climbing face-first down the brick wall. He leaped the last handful of yards, landing lithely on his feet next to Gullette and Shemina. He snapped angrily, "She sees us, bright blade speared Faroke, he is gone."

Gullette peered along the street. He lifted his right hand, opening it up like a gray flower, a finger unfolded, a single talon extending out to point along the street. "No vermin? Flight, fight, or waiting? No answers?"

Gullette turned his head from Kavanne to Shemina and back to the street. He tilted his head slightly, looking, listening, he lifted his face sniffing the night air. The vermin had struck the building opposite where they stood, leaving a scar in the brickwork three stories above the street. She'd fallen to the pavement, a dusting of orange brick fragments littering the gutter where she'd landed, along with the cracked remains of a helmet, but now she was gone.

She'd killed Faroke and survived Kavanne's attack. She was tough and dangerous, but where was she? She knew they were here. They couldn't leave her alive. They had to hunt her down and destroy her. He stared into an alleyway next to the building. Had she disappeared in there? Kavanne and Shemina were scanning their surrounds, their predatory senses on high alert.

Gullette turned away from the alleyway, facing his companions.

Kavanne blurred, his right arm lashing out sideways, razor-sharp spines along its length erupting into attack position, creating a cutting-edge as sharp and hard as tempered steel.

Gullette whirled on instinct alone, trusting Kavanne had seen something he hadn't. His attack was low, his left arm sweeping beneath Kavanne's attack.

Something dark, blurred between them, rolling over his strike, and passing beneath Kavanne's attack. It rose before Shemina, hitting her hard from the side, toppling her over, and dragging her back half a dozen yards.

The wan streetlights gleamed off bright metal.

Gullette stared. Kavanne and himself stood reflected in the mirror-like surface of a sword. The vermin held the bright blade, a female of their kind, her dark hair slick with her own blood. She held Shemina tight, her cutting edge resting across Shemina's throat.

Faroke's blood still dripped from the end of her weapon. Gullette's talons sprang out to their full fighting length. The spines along his arms and back flared with blood lust. To his left, Kavanne responded in the same way. They could not bear such a challenge, in a moment they would charge, either they would kill the vermin or they would die.

The edge of the blade moved against Shemina's throat. The razor-sharp steel bit into her gray-white hide and she uttered a rasping cough of distress.

Gullette and Kavanne froze, then waddled backward a step. The distress cry of a female was the only thing that could stop a male from fighting. It was why the females always had the best territories and were the most dangerous fighters for a male to confront.

The vermin stared at Gullette and Kavanne, her eyes flicking between them, and demanded, "Who's in charge?"

Gullette snarled, and Kavanne growled low in his throat.

The vermin pulled the sword tighter against Shemina's throat, her eyes hard as stone, and demanded a second time in a louder voice, "Who's in charge?"

Gullette grimaced, Kavanne was watching him closely, waiting for his cue. He would follow Gullette's lead.

The lids over Gullette's eyes lowered halfway, and he said, "Let her go. No use to you dead. Or to us."

"I'll let her go," the vermin declared, the edge of steel in her voice as sharp as the blade in her hands, "but first you must promise."

"What promise? Why ask for promise? A sly trick?"

"To talk instead of kill."

Gullette snorted. "Talk of what? Sunrises and sunsets?" he pointed a long black talon at Shemina and demanded, "Give her back."

"We can talk about how I can make you powerful," the vermin insisted. "Promise to talk, and I'll let her go."

Gullette stared at her. She'd killed Faroke and captured Shemina. Kavanne had reported she could see them, even when they moved hidden to the world. She was faster and stronger than any vermin or human he'd ever seen. She was special; this singular vampire was different from the rest.

Gullette was three and a half thousand years old when vampires first walked the Earth. He'd never bargained with one before, but then again, he'd never had to. But times change, even the People now walked together in groups. What did he have to lose by talking with her? He would gain Shemina's freedom, and that was important. Shemina was the only female he'd seen in more than a hundred years. She might even be the last one. If the vampire proved to be false, he could always kill her.

Gullette leaned forward slightly, his head bobbing forward and back, and said, "We will talk, all truths and no lies, I promise."

The deadly blade swished aside. Shemina leaped forward and whirled around.

The vampire stood in front of them and said without fear, "Now I see if you are creatures of your word."

Gullette's eyes widened, and his nostrils flared.

Yes, they were creatures of their word, while it suited them to be. He would ensure she would never find out the truth, until it was too late.

* * *

"You promised, now speak of power, we listen."

Chloe looked at the three chameleons standing half a dozen feet in front of her. The Red Dragon was resting naked within her left hand, only a fool would've put it away. She stood at an even six feet in her boots, the blood in her hair congealing into a tacky mess. The bleeding had stopped, and the wound was knitting back together. The chameleons loomed over her, anywhere between seven and eight-foot-tall depending on how they stood, big through the chest, long arms and legs, powerfully muscled, elegant frames superbly equipped for killing.

Time was ticking; within another half minute she'd have recovered enough to attempt another supreme ramp. One she would use to escape if the chameleons attacked.

She'd struggled with two of them, taking on three at the same time would be suicide. By the same token, having three creatures who were all but invisible and were also deadly killers as allies was exactly the edge she was looking for. A secret force that only James and herself would know about. James would be their handler. He would move them about and keep them secret while they did the things that needed doing that, she couldn't do herself. But first, she needed to convince them to join forces with her. She'd anticipated correctly that they were interested in power. They were on the verge of extinction and must know it. They had a strange way of talking, always in patterns of three, five and three syllables, but nothing indicated that they were stupid.

Far from it; they were highly intelligent, just different.

She pointed to her chest with her right hand. "My name is Chloe, what are your names?" *Assuming they have them.*

The largest one to her left responded, "I Gullette," he pointed at the other two, the smallest in the middle and another big one of similar size on the other side and stated, "Shemina and Kavanne, the People."

Everyone's name for their own tribe always translates as 'The People.' *Truly, there is nothing new in the world.*

"You've heard of the Metaframe?"

They shook their heads.

"The Divine Engine of Thoth?"

Gullette's eyes opened wide, and he hissed as he said, "I know this, the engine shapes everything, true power."

"With your help, I will have access, and I will share it."

Gullette took a step back his head lowering, his eyes narrowing. "You so close. What need of us three? You trick us!"

Chloe shook her head. "No tricks. I have a difficult ... adversary. It will take time to reach our goal, I promise you will be there at the end and will be well rewarded."

Kavanne barked three times.

Shemina made a dry, coughing cry.

Gullette looked at his companions for a long moment, then his head swung back toward Chloe, and he declared, "We agree. We will help you win," his mouth opened in what she guessed was a lizard grin, and he uttered hungrily, "Share power!"

Chloe nodded.

The chameleon's heads bobbed forward and back. They turned as one and blurred away, in moments they'd vanished.

Chloe sighed. The night had progressed better than she'd expected, but she could trust them about as far as she could throw them. Which wasn't far enough.

She turned for home; she was ravenous, and she needed to feed. James hadn't discovered the source of her implant, and she still didn't have a plan for saving Anton from Maze, Shadowstone and the Day Guard.

Scratch that, she thought. She could throw the chameleons into the mix during the attack on the conclave and guarantee an escape route for Anton and his friends through the stormwater drains. But with so many Shadowstone assets in play, and Panopticon-linked cameras on helmets and guns, the last thing she needed was for Shadowstone and Crane to discover her new pets.

No, it looked like Anton would be on his own for this one. In any event, she had to get rid of the implant beneath her skull before she could use him properly. If he were as worthy as he appeared to be, he would find a way to survive the impending attack on the Order conclave. On the other hand, she could be wrong about him.

Chloe frowned, pursed her lips and retrieved her broken helmet from the sidewalk.

She set off down the street toward home, it had already been a long night.

* * *

Shadows like oil slicks swam along the edges of pools of sickly, pale-yellow street lighting.

It was surprising how quickly a vampire will talk once it's in pain. The coward had given Tamsah the location of the Shadowstone site before he'd taken the creature's head from its shoulders. It had been the third vampire he'd interrogated in New York. Of course, it'd only known about the system, Crane's system, not the specifics of Shadowstone operations. For that, he would need an operative.

The one named Rose, heading for his car parked in an alleyway next to a nondescript Shadowstone building. His colleague had said his name five minutes before as Rose was leaving his office on the third floor. Now he was reaching for his car keys, oblivious to the hidden presence in the darkness opposite his vehicle.

Tamsah blurred forward, colliding with Rose, crushing the air from his lungs. Rose grunted loudly. He pushed Rose up against a brick wall next to a dumpster. His right hand speared under the man's ribs, reaching up into his chest cavity to cradle his beating heart. His left hand flew to the man's mouth, a steel-like clamp blocking the scream building in Rose's throat.

Tamsah pushed up against the taller man, looked him hard in the eyes and stated calmly, "We need to have a talk."

The man's eyes bulged. He squirmed in a vain attempt to get himself off Tamsah's forearm which had disappeared up to the elbow into his body. Rose's blood ran in dark rivulets down Tamsah's arm, dripping off his elbow in fat drops onto the ground.

"What's your relationship with God like?" Tamsah asked, his voice filled with a dreadful calm. "Are you a man of faith? Are you a servant of justice?"

Rose's face blanched, his eyes darting left and right. He whimpered behind Tamsah's steel clamp of a hand. No matter how hard he searched, there was no one else around to help him.

"Do you feel that your life is tightly bound by rules and regulations?" Tamsah inquired, tilting his head quizzically. "That's the thing about faith ... that's the thing about justice ... they have no boundaries. There is no such thing as too much faith or too much justice. Rules and regulations are no substitute for the real thing ... let me ask you this Mr. Rose, how strong is your faith?"

Tamsah lifted his left hand an inch away from Rose's mouth to allow him to speak.

Rose panted between low moans, his body rigid against the cold bricks of the wall.

Tamsah's fingers caressed the beating curve of Rose's heart. His hand was deep within Rose's body. As deep as it could go without killing him instantly. His touch was a loveless intimacy that was driving toward an inevitable goal. Rose's heart jumped within his hand. Tamsah leaned in close and whispered, "If I weighed this heart, would I find guilt in it? Would I find acts worthy of retribution?"

Rose gasped, his face pale, streaming with sweat. His eyes stared into Tamsah's face, he uttered hoarsely, "No ... no ... no."

Tamsah closed his hand slightly, he could feel the cardiac muscle straining under his fingers.

Rose clenched his eyes shut, shaking his head.

"You have a big hole in your chest," Tamsah said without a hint of irony, "but all your major blood vessels are still intact; you could still survive. Tell me about the operation against the Mirovar force team, and I will free you from this torment."

Rose's eyes flickered open. "Mirovar?"

"Yes, Mirovar. There must be an operation."

"Minneapolis. They're in Minneapolis."

"When?" Tamsah growled, tightening his grip.

"A week. It's a week from tomorrow, at an old converted chapel."

"What's the address?"

Rose whimpered and whispered the address.

Tamsah grinned briefly. His arm blurred from Rose's chest, ripping his heart free from his body and tossing it down the alleyway.

The Shadowstone operative dropped limply to the pavement beside the dumpster, his white business shirt darkening in a flood beneath the ghastly pale-yellow street lights, a tormented grimace writhing on his sweat-drenched face.

Tamsah looked down at the dying man, watching the light flee from his eyes and explained with dreadful finality. "I promised you freedom Mr. Rose, you shouldn't have expected mercy."

He turned on his heel and left the alleyway, it was time to get to Minneapolis. The truth speaker would be there, and she would need his protection.

It was good to have a purpose; everyone needed a purpose.

Chapter Six

"The idea that there is a species of intelligent lizards living and hiding amongst humanity is pure hokum." – Jeremy H. K. Smithers, Ph.D. Director of the National Museum.

"People just up and disappear. I blame the alligators that people let loose in the sewers." – Unknown.

* * *

Minneapolis, September 2nd, 22:30

The house was a rental in an upmarket suburb of Minneapolis.

The four Order operatives had cut the power at the fuse box, and then cleared the site of electronic surveillance. They now stood guard, keeping watch by street light in the grounds of the two-story building.

Flickering shadows shrouded the ground floor lounge room. An even dozen candles rested in the middle of a low coffee table providing the only illumination. Four men sat on over-stuffed couches around the coffee table and regarded each other with zealous gazes filled with purpose.

Ramin Kain's Head of Staff, and interim Head of the Order of Thoth, Calvin Woodstock rubbed and twirled the gold ring on his right ring finger. He was a handsome man without being striking. An even six-foot tall, he wore a classically styled dark-gray business suit and elegant Italian shoes. A light sprinkling of gray hairs dusted his neatly cut dark hair, and he quietly surveyed his colleagues with keen, dark-blue eyes.

The other three men in the room were the remaining leaders of Ramin Kain's cabal. With the deaths of Ramin Kain and Samuel Luther, there were only four men left with the intelligence, wisdom, and charisma necessary to take the Order into the future. Their mission against the vampires was too important to entrust to lesser men. The Order was in dire straits, their numbers had been in slow decline for a century and a half. The Red Empire had flourished, and the vampires had consolidated their power at the apex of human society with the ordinary people none the wiser.

But of course, the ordinary people knew nothing, they simply believed what they were told, or rejected everything and believed nothing. It didn't matter which, credulity or paranoia, both were equal marks of the irrational, the mute, and the helpless.

Fucking sheeple!

Calvin had decided in his teens that the common people were not worth defending, let alone dying for. Heroic self-sacrifice was for fools, and he was nobody's fool. He leaned forward slightly and asserted, "Luther and Kain may be dead, but Ramin Kain's legacy lives on. We will transform the Order. The force teams will know a single operational commander."

"As it should've been at the start," snapped Bill Shortman, the force leader from Seattle, and the northwest, sitting on Calvin's right. "Mirovar's failure has destroyed the Order in England and brought open war with the vampires down upon our heads."

The man to Calvin's left, Andrew Frick, force leader from New Orleans, and the southeast, snarled and said, "He's an incompetent hidebound fool."

"A dangerous bungler," added Hayden Brown in clipped tones, the heavily built force leader from Canada filled the final chair opposite Calvin.

Calvin scowled and conceded. "Mirovar's incompetence is well known, but without Justin Blake and the independent's vote to make it unanimous, it is impossible to impeach him."

"We know this Calvin, and we also know that unity will never happen," declared Bill Shortman, lifting his hands wide. He pointed his finger at Calvin, his gaze hard and flat. "But a lack of resolution has led us to this disaster. We must get rid of Mirovar, and soon. It's time for direct action against Mirovar and the young Slayne. The last thing we need is a return of the Slaynes."

Calvin raised an eyebrow and suggested, "Well, you will be pleased with my next proposal." He reached over to the coffee table, lifted back a dark cloth, revealing a pair of swords, their blades shimmering darkly in the candlelight.

Bill snorted, then grinned. "Red Empire style."

Hayden leaned back in his chair, stroking his chin thoughtfully.

After Calvin, Andrew was closest to the two-foot blades, he reached forward and lifted one from the table. The surface of the blade soaked light like a hungry shadow, and he asked with a tight frown, "What's been done to the blade."

"It's made of an alloy of titanium, tungsten, and vanadium, sheathed in a microlayer of carbon nanoshards."

Andrew flourished the blade.

Hayden lifted an eyebrow and inquired, "A ruse, are we to disguise ourselves as the Red Empire?"

Calvin's gaze locked on each of the men in turn. "I need your four best fighters. I have disguises, and more of these swords."

Andrew positioned the sword point first on the wooden coffee table and pressed down on the pommel with one finger. The blade slid effortlessly into the wood. He turned toward Calvin and demanded, "How long have you been sitting on this technology?"

"Not long," Calvin noted calmly. "I started the research over a decade ago to build a weapon capable of defeating Arthur Slayne's Black Dragon sword. These blades are the result. A timely eventuality given that Francis Mirovar and the younger Slayne now carry siblings of the Black Dragon."

Bill spat onto the floor. "What a nightmare. We must get rid of both Slaynes, starting with the youngest."

Hayden, the Canadian force leader, leaned forward in his chair, placing his heavy fists on his thick thighs. "How did you test these swords? I don't imagine that Arthur Slayne would have called by to allow you to swing them against the Black Dragon."

"We've tested them to breaking point. They're superior to anything we have been able to field."

Hayden rubbed his chin. "Not tested then?"

"Tested to your satisfaction or not," Calvin asserted. "I will need your best men."

Bill and Andrew nodded their assent. Hayden blinked and nodded as well. Bill said, "I think young Campbell West will make a perfect guide. He will be able to establish trust with the younger members of the Mirovar force team, and he can lull Mirovar and the young Slayne into a false sense of security."

Calvin nodded and instructed his fellow conspirators. "We will strike just before the conclave. Mirovar and Slayne will be no-shows, and the conclave will proceed without them. By the time we finish, we'll present those who remain, like Justin Blake who would've sided with Mirovar, with a fait accompli." He shrugged his shoulders and grinned. "There will be nothing they can do to stop the foundation of the new Order under our control."

There was a long moment of silence.

Calvin said softly, "In just over a week, the Order of Thoth will be purged of all those who hold it back, and a new Order will be born."

The eyes of all four men glistened in the candlelight. Seeds laid decades in the past were on the verge of bearing fruit. The next week would be critical; security was paramount. Everyone needed to play their part to perfection. Anything less than exemplary execution of the plan, courted the disintegration of the Order into factions that would be at each other's throats with a vehemence that would make the war with the vampires look like a kindergarten dispute.

Calvin had devoted his life to this outcome. He'd backed Ramin Kain a hundred and ten percent since his ascension to the Head of the Order. But, the news of Ramin's death had thrilled him to the core. The way was now clear. His predecessor had done the hard work. All he needed to do was act with forthright resolution, maintain a clear and decisive mind, and step forward and claim the prize. He was certain he'd managed all the risks. He'd worked out all the little details. Anticipation bordering on a famished man staring at a sumptuous meal filled his heart. In little over a week, he would be the undisputed leader of the Order, and then everyone would find out what a real leader looked like.

He was sure the Order had never seen a ruler like himself.

Oh yes, it's time for them to find out.

He would go through the Order like a wildfire, and afterward, the Order would be unrecognizable.

* * *

Anton rubbed his beard. At a week and a half old, it was becoming increasing itchy.

Damn things! But necessary in a world without a loremaster to shape the camera networks and hide them from the Panopticon. The Mirovar force team had finally arrived in Minneapolis on Sunday afternoon on the third of September. It was less than a week to the conclave, but Anton would've been happy right there and then to swap the conclave for a skilled barber. But the conclave was a certainty, and he was stuck with the beard for the foreseeable future, anything to help with hiding himself from the ever-searching eyes of the Panopticon.

His left hand slid up to his eye patch, the socket underneath still ached. Everyone was telling him that was a good sign, the eye hadn't scarred over, and was slowly regrowing under Chiara's careful ministrations. He remained hopeful that one day, he'd regain his sight in full, but if that didn't happen, he had no regrets. Marcus Drake was dead, and he'd delivered justice for Drake's part in the torture and murder of his mother, and the abduction and eternal imprisonment of his father.

Soon enough, Chloe Armitage and Cornelius Crane would meet the same fate. It would be best if he killed Crane first, let Armitage sweat in the knowledge he'd killed her boss, and was coming after her next.

Anton grinned at the thought.

Peter glanced into the rear-view mirror and asked, "What are you smiling at?"

"Ahh… life is good. Glad we've finally arrived."

"Yeah," Peter replied. "Four cars, a helicopter, and a houseboat along the great lakes, with a bonus night out in the open to cross the border. How long did it take us to get from Nova Scotia to Minneapolis?"

"Six days."

"How many fake IDs did we go through?"

"Three … each."

Li turned around from the front passenger seat, her gaze flicking between them and asserted, "You guys were like four-year-olds saying, 'are we there yet?' It was a challenge for the rest of us not to leave both of you behind."

Peter grinned broadly and declared, "C'mon, you loved every minute of it. It was an extended sightseeing tour of Canada. I mean, we saw a moose."

That was roadkill," Li remarked acidly.

"And a bear," Anton noted. "I'm sure there was a bear tooling around in those woods near the border."

"Nah, that was Peter," Chiara chimed in. "He got separated for a while, it's an easy mistake to make."

Peter cocked his right arm, muscles bulging, and suggested, "Surely you can tell the difference?"

Chiara leaned across the back seat from behind him, shook her head slightly, and said, "No, not really."

Peter feigned mock hurt, glanced to his right, and pleaded, "Ohh... I'm cut to the quick. Li, please ... come and save me."

"No one can save you," Li said, deadpan. Then a smile twitched at the edges of her lips. "You're beyond all salvation."

Peter shrugged. "Well, at least I've got some cool scars."

"Or not," Anton remarked.

"Killjoy," Peter shot back without any heat.

"Just keeping it real," Anton observed dryly, from the back seat.

Peter pulled the SUV into a parking space at a cheap motel on the outskirts of the suburbs. The team piled out of the car, stretching and stamping their feet to work out the kinks of travel.

Anton cast a long glance over the shabby exterior of the motel. It looked like it could've used a facelift – about two decades ago. There was an empty pool next to the parking lot, a rusted 'out of order,' sign hung at a lop-sided angle from a chicken-wire fence around it. At odds with the motel, an immaculate white Chevrolet Suburban was sitting three car spaces down from the team's hired SUV.

Jay and Francis had been driving another car on the last leg from the Canadian border, a small Toyota sedan loaned to them by an Order helper on the US side of the border. They'd parked on the other side of the Chevy, but there was no sign of them.

A spring-loaded wooden door swung open from the left end of the motel, and Francis and Jay emerged from the motel's reception. A lean young man, with short blond hair, casually dressed in designer blue jeans, a pale-green long-sleeved T-shirt, sneakers, and mirrored sunglasses, followed them.

Francis approached Anton and the rest. He flicked his thumb back over his shoulder, and introduced the young man behind him. "This is Campbell West, he's with the Order and will be our guide while we're in town."

The young man stepped forward, smiled warmly at everyone, and said, "Welcome to Minneapolis. We've got everything organized for you." His gaze slid over Anton and Peter and lingered on Chiara and Li. He lifted his hands wide and indicated the motel with a backward glance. "I know it's not much," he leaned in close to Li and Chiara and half whispered, "but every camera is broken." He stepped back and declared, "It's a perfect place for you until the conclave. You'll be safe here."

His head tilted down and up, his eyebrows rising behind his shades. He stuck his hand out to Chiara and said, "We're not hung up on formalities here, call me Westy."

Chiara murmured a half-hearted greeting and shook his hand coldly.

Anton decided he didn't like him there and then. One thing he'd learned from brutal experience, the idea that people knew what they were doing was highly over-rated. If someone said they were safe, it almost certainly meant the opposite. Nowhere was truly safe in a world run by vampires.

Anton and the rest introduced themselves in turn, each shaking West's hand. Anton lingered for a moment, staring through the mirror shades into West's eyes. The young man stared back, a knowing grin on his face. Anton grinned mockingly in return and released West's hand.

The instant dislike was mutual.

West looked around at everyone there, wished them well and departed in the white Chevrolet Suburban.

Francis said, "Heads up everyone," and tossed separate room keys to Anton and Li. "We have three rooms, all with twin singles. The Order booked the whole motel, and apparently, we have the best rooms – whatever that means? Peter and Anton, Li and Chiara each have a room. Jay will be with me. Keep your eyes and ears open, and your weapons close to hand. Be prepared to leave at a moment's notice. Keep an eye on our vehicles in case we need a getaway. We have no loremaster cover. Security rules apply at all times. You are in enemy territory owned by the Vampire Dominion – don't forget it."

Li asked, "Can't we get coverage from the loremasters with some of the other teams?"

Francis shook his head. "It wasn't offered, and I suspect if we asked, a reason would be found for why it couldn't be done." He frowned; his face grim. "The next week will be quite … political … which will be for Jay and me to deal with." He wagged a finger at Anton and the rest. "I want you four keeping yourselves out of trouble. Li and Anton, you'll be confirmed as members of the Order at this conclave. That will simplify things going forward, and Li, we'll make sure that ridiculous charge laid by Lamar is quashed, and struck from the record."

Li nodded.

A flash of anger passed behind Francis' eyes. "There're a few people here who still regard Kain and his beliefs as some sort of prophet with a new gospel. They're not our friends. All I can say right now, is keep your eyes open, and watch each other's backs."

There was a long pause as the team digested Francis' warning. Li caught Jay's attention with a wave of her hand. "Jay, our guide 'West,' do you know him?"

Jay nodded. "Unfortunately, yes. He was a cocky fifteen-year-old in Bill Shortman's team in Seattle when I left. I doubt much has changed."

"Why did you leave Seattle, Jay?" Anton asked, genuinely curious.

"... I thought Francis' attitude to the war against the vampires was more in line with my own."

Anton grinned knowingly. "So, what the hell does that say about Shortman?"

Jay paused again, his eyes narrowing. He shook his head once and stated, "Shortman made a lot about conserving resources, about waiting for the right moment to strike, but the bottom line is that he avoided combat. Francis offered more real opportunity to come to grips with the vampires." He looked across at Francis. "I've no regrets about changing teams."

Francis nodded, and the team fell silent. He said, "Get some rest. I'll keep you in the loop as events with the interim Order leadership progress."

Francis and Jay turned away, heading for their motel room.

Peter glanced at the key in Anton's hand, and at the dilapidated door to their motel room. "West's not slumming it with us, then, is he?"

Anton clapped him on the shoulder, and suggested, "C'mon Peter it can't be worse than a night in the open crossing the border."

"If there are bedbugs in there, it will be."

Chiara stepped up and handed Peter a throwing knife.

"What's this for?" Peter asked.

"Cockroaches."

"I've got throwing axes."

"Throw one of those at a cockroach, and it will go through the wall."

Peter flipped the dagger, caught it, and handed it back. "Maybe I'll just use a boot."

Chiara shrugged. "Have it your way."

Li and Chiara entered the motel room between Francis and Jay's, and Peter and Anton's.

Anton and Peter looked at each other, shrugged and entered their motel room. The first thing that struck them was the smell. A kind of mustiness, as if no one had used the room for a long time, or cleaned it for an even longer time. There was a pair of single beds with orange bedspreads. A garishly striped carpet straight out of the 1960s covered the floor. Faded, lime-green wallpaper covered the walls. A single framed print of a seascape hung on one wall opposite an ancient box TV sporting a rabbit-ear antenna.

Peter checked the small fridge underneath a bench. It was empty. "Damn. No minibar."

"Nope," Anton noted, looking around the room. "Definitely no minibar."

Less than a minute later a dagger slammed into the wall between them and Chiara and Li's room. Chiara exclaimed loudly, "Got him!"

Anton and Peter looked at each other, and burst out laughing, then sobered up almost immediately as they scanned their room.

Peter sighed. "Welcome to Cockroach Central."

Anton grinned. "Suck it up, princess."

Peter glanced past Anton at the bed behind him. Anton turned; a cockroach was sitting proudly on the pillow. His hand flashed forward, mashing the insect into a pale paste on the yellow pillowslip.

Peter pointed to the mess and declared with a broad grin, "That's your bed."

"Yeah, right," Anton replied, briskly brushing the wet remains of the creature from the palm of his hand. Dropping his gear on the bed, he thumbed the motel room next door. "Let's go check on the girls."

Peter dropped his backpack on the other bed and followed Anton through the doorway.

* * *

A lone combat boot propped open Li and Chiara's motel room door.

Anton walked in and asked cheerfully, "How's your room?"

Li was sitting on one of the beds, opposite Chiara who was lounging against the wall, and remarked, "One step up from the first level of hell, but we'll cope."

Anton sat down on the end of Chiara's bed and suggested, "This guy West, our," he air quoted, "'guide,' is really our keeper. He's been assigned to watch us. I'd bet my last dollar on it."

Li smiled dourly. "Yes, the guy's a sleazebag. However, we're stuck with him for the next week."

"I think we need a common strategy for this whole thing."

"Precisely what 'whole thing' do you mean?" Li asked.

Anton leaned forward, focusing on her. "The conclave, the Order, Ramin Kain's followers, our guide. Let's not forget how quick Kain was to try and kill me as soon as he found out about me. I'm under no illusions about what to expect from his followers. You heard what Francis said, there are more of them. How many of the Order are infected with Kain's beliefs? He was in charge for twenty years. That's plenty of time to establish some deep fanaticism for what he was trying to achieve. This conclave could be nothing more than a trap put in place by Kain's followers."

Li paused briefly and asserted, "Justin Blake called the conclave. There is no way that Justin is part of a Kain led conspiracy. He's a close friend of my father, and of Francis and Juliette."

Anton looked at Li for a moment. Chiara and Peter were watching them from the sidelines. "Point taken; I agree. Justin's never stood with Kain, and someone had to call the conclave, but the conclave provides a perfect opportunity for Kain's followers to take action. We're all here, they know exactly where we are, we're sitting ducks. I for one am not going to sit around and wait for them to attack us."

Li leaned forward slightly, her face tense. "Anton, you can't go off and attack other Order members on a suspicion. That's just wrong."

"I'm not talking about striking first, after all, we don't know who we're dealing with yet." He paused for a long moment to weigh his words. "After all, we haven't identified who the targets are yet. What I'm talking about is being completely prepared for any eventuality." He looked around at everyone in the room. "You three, are the most important people in my life, and I'm not going to sit around doing nothing while others threaten our lives." His sole eye glistened with intensity. He chopped his right hand up and down to emphasize his point. "I just won't have it."

The room fell into silence.

Li reached across the space between the two beds, put her hand on Anton's knee, and looked him in the eye. "I'm sure we all feel the same, Anton. But if we're going to be a team, we have to share everything we know. There can be no secrets. You have to keep us in the loop about anything you plan to do."

No secrets! Chiara was the spy. Oh my god, I can't tell her that. Not yet, but what does she suspect?

"Yeah, sure," Anton agreed, not missing a beat. "But we don't know where they're holding the conclave. We need to scout the site and its approaches. We have to identify potential escape routes. We need contingency plans for any eventuality, and we need to work this out before next Sunday. We have less than a week to understand the threats, the risks, and to establish viable options that will get us through all this shit."

"All this shit?" Li asked skeptically, "You're sure of that?"

"Absolutely. It's not paranoia when people really are trying to kill you."

Peter observed from where he sat on a chair near the door. "You gotta admit, Anton's been a target since he joined the Order. You as well Li. Kain's co-conspirators have no love for you or the legacy of your father."

Li nodded, looking pensive for a second. Then her face hardened as she came to a decision. "My father was adamant Kain was corrupt, and events proved him right. Whatever parts of Kain's organization still exist, we must eliminate them, root and branch – none can remain in power."

"So, we're united then?" Anton asked.

Li sat up straight. "On the nature of the issue, on the objective, I think yes. But what of strategy and tactics?"

Anton counted off the fingers of his left hand. "One, we find out where they're holding the conclave. Two, we scout the site and determine access and egress points to establish escape routes. Three—"

"Hang on a second Anton," Li interjected. "Do you really believe Kain's people will attack us at the conclave?"

"Not necessarily, but look what happened in Maine at the safe house. The Order showed up for one of their fancy pow wows, and then the Red Empire in league with Armitage and Drake arrived and slammed us. If that could happen, anything could happen."

Li leaned forward again, focused on Anton's face, and pointedly avoided making eye contact with either Peter or Chiara. "There was a Red Empire spy in Maine. That's a big difference from our current circumstance."

"That's an assumption, do you think the Red Empire would stop at inserting a single spy into the Order, why not two, or three, or half a dozen."

Li stared at him.

Anton stared back with his single eye and asked, "Can you rule it out?"

Li's face paled, and she conceded. "No. I can't rule it out."

"So, we find out where the conclave is being held, we scout the site, and establish two clear escape paths in case the shit hits the fan big time."

Peter asked, "What was your third point?"

"'Know your enemy,' we're flying blind, we need to find out everything we can as quickly as possible about the other members of the Order attending the conclave. And fourth we need to keep Mr. Campbell West and his nose out of our business, and without him realizing we're keeping him in the dark."

Peter noted drily. "You've still got one finger left."

Anton smiled and tapped his last finger. "And fifth, does this motel have a working bar-b-que? I'm famished."

Before anyone could answer, the unmistakable sound of Harley Davidson motorcycles arriving in the motel's parking lot filled the room.

Li stood up, her eyes sparkling, and said happily, "Justin Blake is here!"

* * *

The afternoon sun gleamed off the three Harley Davidson's pulling to a halt in front of the row of motel rooms.

Justin Blake eased his six-foot-eight-inch frame off his bike. Took off his helmet and gloves, and hung them from the handlebars. He rubbed his fingers over his scalp, mussing up his thick dark curly hair which hung down to his massive shoulders. It was mostly his mother's hair, inherited from the Maori side of his family. His African-American father had given him his height and the curls, and from both parents, he'd inherited his skin tone and legendary athletic ability.

He wore a black biker jacket over a tight black T-shirt. He shed the jacket and looked to his two companions.

They'd pulled their bikes in on his left. The nearer of the two men was Samuel Taylor, six-foot-two-inch tall, built like an Olympic decathlete, with coal-black skin and short, tight, black hair. He had doctorates in philosophy, and physics, but the other members of Blake's force team called him 'Coleridge,' because of his love of poetry.

On the far side of him was Taylor Feury, an even six-foot tall, an almost white blond, who looked like a grown-up choir boy, except when he laughed. He had a wicked laugh, and after Justin, he was the most dangerous operative in the Blake force team. A warrior specialist who didn't care to know much else. He was Samuel's partner in all things, including fighting, where they fought as a trained pair of blademasters.

Everyone in the Order knew them as 'the Two Taylors.'

The front door on the motel room to his right opened up. Francis emerged from within, Jay at his shoulder. The door on the hotel room past it stood open. Li appeared in the doorway, a big grin on her face. She reached him first and gave him a hug. He wrapped his big arms around her and held her tight.

She kissed him lightly on the cheek and said warmly, "Hi Justin, you've just made my week."

Her greeting was more subdued than the one she'd given him at the Maine safe house nearly two weeks ago. The teenage infatuation she'd formed when he'd trained with her father four years earlier, had thankfully passed. It was good to see her blossoming into a mature young woman. He felt in his heart that she would go far, perhaps as far as anyone could go. She'd always inspired within him a sense of confidence and trust; qualities that were in short supply in the world.

Francis and Jay approached, and Justin shook their hands warmly. Anton, Peter, and Chiara emerged from the other motel room, and he introduced them to the two Taylors.

Once everyone completed their greetings, Justin lifted his hands, his face momentarily perplexed. "You're not supposed to be here. Someone made a mistake." He glowered, making a mistake that troubled his friends was someone's really bad idea. "You're supposed to be close to the middle of the city, near the venue for the conclave. It took me a while to find out exactly where the Order put you." He shook his head; it wasn't an accident the Mirovar force team had ended up in a slum. His voice rumbled with an implacable threat. "Someone's playing games."

Francis nodded. "And we're going to play along for now. Let them think they have our measure, and later we'll turn their plans against them."

Justin chuckled deep in his massive chest; his dark-brown eyes twinkling. "I like it. Perhaps we could discuss it over some food, we didn't stop for lunch on our way here."

"There's been talk of a bar-b-que," Peter offered.

Jay remarked, "There's one out the back, tucked away undercover in a courtyard behind the motel."

"Excellent," Francis said. "Jay, Anton, you're on food duty. Go find us what we need, and get back here within half an hour."

"Yes, Francis," Jay replied, signaling Anton. They got into the Toyota sedan and drove off.

The rest made their way around to the back of the motel.

There was a gas-fired bar-b-que under extended cover behind the motel. Peter checked it out and pronounced it to be in working order. Justin considered that was a small miracle given the general run-down state of the motel. There were a number of plastic chairs, and long wooden trestle tables, they all sat down around one of the rectangular tables.

Samuel Taylor inquired, "Have you done a sweep for bugs?"

Peter burst out laughing.

Francis frowned at him for a moment, and then looked at Samuel. "Jay and I arrived half an hour before the rest of my team and completed a sweep. We found nothing. I don't think the Order have bugged the motel. They know we could find anything they put in. Their strategy seems to be one of keeping us separated from the rest of the Order until the conclave occurs with a," Francis glanced at the motel, "bit of petty disrespect thrown in for good measure."

"Well," Justin said. "That could work against them. I told my cousins where you are, and they'll be arriving soon with the rest of the Pacific independents."

Francis smiled.

Samuel glanced at his watch and declared, "The Prospector should be here in ninety minutes."

Francis leaned forward toward Justin. "All the swing voters are coming here?"

"Apart from Jon Thunder-Axe, he's due to arrive late Wednesday night, and Ahmad Bakhoum who couldn't make it."

Francis asserted, "I can't imagine either of them siding with Kain's followers on anything."

"Francis, I want you to be first to know, I'm proposing Samuel as the next Head of the Order. As a compromise candidate, someone who could possibly heal the rifts."

"The rifts, are more like canyons my friend."

"But still, we must try."

Francis nodded, a flash of relief passing over his face. "I'll back Samuel's nomination."

"Thanks," Justin offered. He reached over the table and clasped Francis' shoulder and requested, "Now, tell me about England."

Francis' face fell, and then he began to talk.

* * *

"I thought I could smell a barby," declared an enthusiastic voice with a classic Australian accent.

Anton turned away from the sizzling hot plates and grilling meat. Five casually dressed people walked around the corner of the motel and approached his friends. They were clearly Ramp masters, the ease of movement and coiled power was always a giveaway for anyone who knew what they were looking for.

The man in front looked like he was about sixty years old, with skin like leather, and a head of gray hair with a touch of blond sprinkled through it, but his arms rippled with the whipcord muscles of a strong man half his age. He carried a large cooler with both hands. It clinked with a load of beer bottles as he walked forward. He set it down on the ground next to the tables and looked hard at Anton. "Geez, you're the spitting image of Arthur."

He stuck his hand out and stated, "Call me Smitty, everyone else does."

Anton shook his hand; Smitty's grip was firm, powerful and warm. A dozen feet behind him a pair of hulking Maoris with full-face tattoos were greeting Justin like long lost brothers. Anton figured they were his cousins. Li had mentioned Justin had family in New Zealand, and that his mother had come from there. Two other people stepped behind Smitty and approached Anton, both young women, and he introduced them like a proud father showing of his daughters. "Mercy Kumar and Anita Chang, meet Anton Slayne." He pointed at his team members with his thumbs, and observed enthusiastically. "They terrify the local vampires. They're the best thing out of Oz in the last twenty years. But look at me, my mouth is running away with me. Operating a barby is thirsty work. I'll see you sorted out in a sec." He went back to his cooler, flipped the lid and extracted four long-necked beer bottles from a mass of crushed ice. "Here, have a real beer. I shipped it in from Northern Queensland."

"I'll try one of those," Peter said, coming over to join the conversation.

"Sure," Smitty agreed. "Help yourself, there's plenty more."

Anton twisted off the lid of the bottle, and sipped it, then took a couple of long swallows. It was an excellent beer, rich in flavor.

Smitty looked around the motel's rear courtyard, whistled and remarked, "Well, it's not the place you're at, but the people you're with that matters, isn't it?" The big Australian peered at Anton. His lips pressed into a thin line. "I heard about your parents. That's a fucking crap situation, isn't it? But nothing can be done about it now. How's your grandfather? With Kain out of the picture," he grinned broadly, "Arthur's exile will be over," he clicked his fingers with a loud snap, "just like that!"

Anton hadn't met anyone before with such a positive view of his grandfather. Smitty continued speaking like a verbal steamroller, enthusing about Anton's grandfather and about getting the old team back together.

Anton raised a quizzical eyebrow. "You were in my grandfather's team?"

"Well, actually it was teams, there were nine force leaders located at strategic points around the world. Sure, we didn't report to him, he wasn't our boss or anything like that, but we 'followed,' him, if you get my drift? He just had such fucking good ideas. He was fantastic at working things out and getting shit done." Smitty threw his empty beer bottle into a nearby bin and opened a fresh bottle from his cooler. "Barbies and talking, it's thirsty work isn't it."

Behind Anton, Jay called out, "The meat's ready."

From the corner of the motel, a gruff voice answered, "Looks like I'm just in time."

Smitty turned toward the gray-bearded, barrel-chested newcomer and half-shouted, "Prospector!" The two men approached each other, gave each other a fierce hug and fell to talking.

Anton looked to the two girls who'd come in with the Australian force leader. "He talks a lot, doesn't he?"

"Yeah, he does." Mercy Kumar noted, a slight smile twitching her full lips like she knew something Anton didn't.

Anita Chang, declared, "He just pumped you for your responses, he worked you out in the first three minutes."

"Well, that'd be a first," Peter observed. "I've been sharing a room with Anton for nearly three months, and I still haven't worked him out."

Anita looked up at Peter, cocked her head slightly, and said drily, "You guys share a room, well that explains a lot."

Anton and Peter both laughed, slapping each other on the shoulders. Peter looked around at the Australians and said, "More beer?"

Both girls nodded, and he fetched another round from the cooler.

Anton asked, "Is this your first conclave?"

Mercy and Anita glanced at each other, and Anita said, "Yeah, it is. We're both novices up for confirmation, but the main reason we're here is to get resources. The Prospector is in the same boat."

"Resources? You mean people, Ramp masters?"

"Yes," Mercy confirmed, her dark brown eyes flashing. "And a loremaster if we can get one."

"Think about it," Anita insisted. "Every surviving loremaster is associated with a North American force team. That's great for you guys, but the rest of us are fighting with our arses hanging out in the wind."

Mercy leaned forward and flicked her thumb back toward the heavily bearded Alaskan force leader. "Consider the Prospector, imagine you're working in an environment where it can be dark for days on end. Vampires have been known to descend on small towns or outposts, and depopulate them. The Prospector has a lot to deal with, and he does it alone."

Anita looked hard into Anton's face. "Smitty and the Prospector have killed more vampires between them than pretty much the rest of the Order alive today. They're old, Smitty is pushing ninety, he might even be older, and no one knows for sure how old the Prospector is."

"They're survivors," Mercy observed. "They know how to win in combat, and they keep on doing it year after year."

"But even with men like those guys, there are too few of us."

"We're spread thin, covering too much territory, and the vampires know it. It makes them bold."

"We've had people ... tourists go missing – it's vampires in the outback."

"And on the gold coast too."

"There are infestations of vampires everywhere, and deaths get blamed on everything else."

"There are rogue players out there taking vampire hunting into their own hands."

"Wild talents." Anita shrugged her shoulders. "Some people just wake up one day, and they can ramp. There's one guy in Brisbane, he's not aligned with anyone. He's a lone vigilante, but he's taking care of business."

"We've tried recruiting him, but he'll only work alone."

Peter looked at Anton knowingly, and stated soberly, "Perhaps we need to find some courageous volunteers."

"What?" Anton asked. "Do you mean using Gang's pressure point technique to switch people on?"

Peter nodded. "God knows, the Red Empire do it."

Anita said, "It's why there are about ten times as many of them as there are of us."

Li and Chiara approached, holding plates of seared, rare steak, and salmon fillets. Li suggested, "Better grab some before it disappears."

The group broke up, as everyone filled a paper plate, picked up a plastic knife and fork, and returned to a table. They fell to silence as the food disappeared from the plates.

Anton was the first to speak, and asked, "So how are you finding America?"

"I love it," Mercy offered. "I can relax here without worrying about drop bears."

"Drop bears?" Anton asked, nonplussed. "What's a drop bear?"

Anita frowned and rubbed a bit of tomato sauce from the edge of her mouth. "It's a vicious, carnivorous version of a koala. They live in the trees, often hunt in packs, and drop onto people walking in the bush."

"But," Mercy added, her eyes wide. "They're not as dangerous as a hoop snake."

"Hoop snakes?" Peter asked. "I've never heard of a hoop snake before."

"Well," Mercy said. "Let me tell you about them."

* * *

The sun was long gone.

A pair of ancient, web-encrusted fluorescent strip lights provided a wan illumination of the motel's rear courtyard. The members of the Order sat around the tables talking quietly, occasionally someone would laugh or chuckle. Francis sat with Justin, Smitty, and the Prospector at a table far enough away from the rest of their team members to hold a private conversation.

The Prospector filled shot glasses with bourbon, sat back, and said, "Let's get down to business."

Justin declared, "I'm, proposing Samuel Taylor as the new Head of the Order. He would make a great candidate. If anyone is capable of undoing the damage done by Kain and his cabal over the last twenty years, it's him. He'll focus on the internal dynamics of the Order and allow the Force Leaders to get on with the effective engagement of the vampires."

The Prospector studied Justin, then his eyes flicked over the other force leaders. "That's all good and well for you guys, but I've no one to help me in the far north."

"I'll second that motion," Smitty declared. "The situation in Australia sucks. Justin's cousins have New Zealand sown up, there are no vampires there as far as anyone can tell. While I'm counting thirty-plus in Australia based on unexplained death statistics."

"It's obvious," the Prospector noted. "We need resources. If we could get two or three of your guys rotating up to Alaska—"

"Or fucking Sydney."

"—it'd make a big difference."

"A huge difference," Smitty agreed. "As good as my girls are, and they're stellar girls that really know their stuff. We have too many vampires running loose and bold as brass they are. They don't even seem to be afraid of pissing off the Vampire Dominion. The damn parasites will snatch someone off the street and drain them in a car park."

Justin conceded the point. "Smitty, Prospector, I get what you need. Everyone is spread thin. I only have six people on my team, and I'm covering the southwest of the United States and Mexico. What about Central and South America? No one is covering those territories. There are a billion people with no one looking out for them. The only thing we have in our favor is that Crane actively limits vampire numbers because he wants to keep it all secret. If that ever changes, humanity is in for a bloodbath."

Francis asked, "What about Taylor Feury? If Samuel takes the Head of the Order role, you're going to pull one of the best warriors in the Order off the front line, or will he work with someone else."

"No, he'll have to come off with Samuel. They won't separate."

"That's a big sacrifice to make for your team," Francis noted.

"I consider it necessary."

"We should put someone up who won't be missed. Then you can send the Two Taylors to Alaska for the winter."

"Or," Francis said, "the Head of the Order could spend some time at the front line, three, or six months of the year. They could rotate through selected force teams, reinforcing wherever it's necessary to do so. That way the Order gets a sensible administrator who is also in touch with what is going on at the battlefront."

"I like this idea," Smitty said enthusiastically.

The Prospector nodded. "It works for me. I'd love to have the Two Taylor's operating out of Anchorage for a winter."

Smitty grinned. "It'd fuck those vampires right up. They wouldn't know what hit them."

Justin nodded. "Agreed. We'll put that forward as a policy position."

The table fell silent, and they drained their shot glasses.

Francis needed Justin's help. Only travelers had access to the drug Truther. And the only traveler that Francis could trust was with Justin's team. He pushed his empty shot glass away and inquired, "Justin, when can you spare Patrick Wichowski?"

"What do you need? A traveler or a loremaster?"

Patrick was the sole male loremaster within the Order and one of the four remaining alive after the recent disastrous losses in England. Francis declared, "A traveler, with Truther. I have two members of my team who I need to question."

Discipline within a force team was always a matter for the force team leader, and no one else would deign to interfere, even asking a question could deliver an insult. Smitty and the Prospector's faces froze into impassivity. Silence fell like a shroud over the force leaders' table. Justin agreed quietly. "If that is what you need, then it can be provided."

"When can Patrick arrive?"

"He's in Poland, visiting family. He's flying into New York the morning of the tenth of September. He can travel to Minneapolis later that day."

"The day of the conclave," Francis nodded once. "We'll wait here an extra couple of hours and meet up with him if that is okay?"

"Sure," Justin agreed. "I'll have him swing by Minneapolis before he heads to California."

Francis looked hard at Justin; his will as hard as glacial ice. He would discover who the spy was, and kill them. Once he'd done that, he could make the team whole again.

The conversation drifted to other topics, but it was difficult to fully engage with the other force leaders. In a little over a week's time, Francis would avenge the betrayal that led to Juliette and Yvette's deaths.

He closed his eyes for a long moment, the need to bring closure to what had happened overwhelming him.

Smitty asked, "You okay, mate?"

Francis opened his eyes and looked around at the other force leaders, and murmured, "Yes, sure ... I'm okay."

Chapter Seven

"Spare the innocent." – Francis Mirovar, senior force leader of the Order of Thoth.

* * *

Minneapolis, September 5th, 22:00

The walls of the stormwater drains were still damp from a recent downpour.

Anton adjusted the fit of his Order nightglasses, they hadn't been designed to accommodate the eye patch over his left eye. They also worked best when there was some ambient light, and the drains were almost entirely pitch black. The nightglasses now operated in a thermal imaging mode, presenting the world in sharply delineated grays and blacks. Both his hands were free, ready to draw the Blue Dragon if he needed it. The sword lay strapped in a diagonal scabbard across his back, the handle jutting up over his right shoulder.

Li stood behind his left shoulder, she was mapping the drains with her smartphone's GPS capability. The drains were close enough to the streets above to get a data link to the outside world. She'd also hacked into the local municipality's databases that morning and downloaded all their maps for the drains. The local council data was proving to be 'mostly accurate,' but there were important things missing. The escape pathway to the south was blocked by a thick, steel grill. It wasn't marked on any of the council maps. If they'd run down that pathway while trying to escape, their enemies would've trapped them for sure.

Peter walked behind them carrying a monster pair of bolt cutters, he'd used them to cut all but one strand of the steel grill. If they had to use that path, they'd be able to push the grill aside, but to casual observation, it appeared to be fully intact. He scanned the approaches behind them, looking for anyone who might be following them.

Justin Blake had provided the location of the conclave to Francis, and he'd provided it to Jay, Anton and Li. Given Francis' ongoing suspicion that either Peter or Chiara was a spy, he'd forbidden telling them about the location. Anton had chosen to ignore Francis' order. Chiara had secretly confessed to him, and Peter was in the clear. It was possible there were more Red Empire agents inserted into the Order of Thoth, but Anton was willing to bet his life that Peter was not one of them. As for Chiara, she was keeping the Order snitch, Campbell West entertained. A pair of strategically misplaced shirt buttons, an absent bra, and an offer of a couple of hours of close-in jujitsu work, and West had folded like a cheap tent in a windstorm.

Li pointed to the next bend in the drain, and stated, "The entrance into the Church's cellar should be just around that corner."

"Good," Peter declared, looking down at his right boot. "The sooner we're out of this place the better." He scraped the underside, and heel of his boot against the edge of the walkway next to the drain, and said disgustedly, "Who lets dogs loose down here?"

Anton peered forward, looking for any threats, then glanced back at Peter's boots, and declared, "It's not dog."

"How do you know?" Peter shot back.

"Probability."

Li shook her head and advised, "You two should leave math to the professionals." She glanced down at Peter's boot. "Yech, Peter, can't you tell what it is from the smell." She waved him away. "Could you follow us from a couple of yards further back."

Peter grumbled. "And to think I volunteered for this."

"C'mon, we're almost done," Li asserted, "and then we can get out of here and clean up."

Anton peered around the bend in the drain. A couple of yards in front of him an access ladder led up to a manhole cover. He declared over his shoulder, "Found it."

He climbed up the ladder and discovered a large padlock. As they'd expected, someone had closed off the external access into the chapel's cellar. He dropped back down to the walkway and waved Peter forward. "Pete, see if you can cut the padlock and test the cover to see if it can be lifted."

"Sure," Peter agreed, stepping forward with the bolt cutters. A handful of seconds later, there was a sharp snap. Peter wriggled the padlock free, and passed it, along with the cutters, back to Anton.

Peter anchored himself on the access ladder and pressed up with his free hand on the bottom of the manhole cover. It didn't budge, he ran a finger along the edge of the cover and muttered, "Ahh... it's concreted in."

He paused for a moment, testing and assessing the cover. His free hand dropped lower, and he became still. A heat plume erupted around him as he ramped, his hand blurring upward, thudding into the concrete cover.

A ring of concrete dust fell from around the cover, and Peter stated, "Almost there." He repeated the strike on the other edge of the cover, and more concrete dust spilled down.

Peter spat, and shook his head, then declared, "Third time's the charm." His hand blurred again, striking the middle of the cover with his open palm. The cover blew up and clattered away into an unlit space above the drain.

"I think we might be in," he observed drily. "Wait down here, I'll have a quick recon."

Peter rose up the ladder and vanished through the manhole.

Anton and Li approached the ladder taking up positions to either side of it, keeping watch on the approaches. Anton glanced back at the access ladder and up into the open space above it. The metal rungs on the ladder where Peter had been standing were all bowed into shallow 'U' shapes.

The ladder looked like it was old-school, constructed from solid steel and designed to last forever. It had taken a beating tonight.

Peter appeared at the manhole, peering down at Anton and Li, and affirmed, "It's all sorted." He clambered down the ladder, pausing to drag the manhole cover back into place. He dropped the rest of the short distance, landing between Anton and Li. "There's a door, and a set of stairs leading up into the main building. The door has a simple lock, which I've left locked. It won't be a problem if we need to come down here."

Anton nodded. "No one is going to trap us again like we were in Maine. We should always have at least two escape paths determined before anything else. If we lose one, it's a sure sign we need to use the other one straight away."

Li looked at Anton and observed with a note of approval. "Dropping your reckless side Anton, that's a step in the right direction."

Anton grinned in the dark. "Yeah, it's the new responsible me. Did you get a full set of maps?"

"All charted," Li replied. "We've got exit points five hundred yards north on the river, about two miles east on the riser into the alleyway we used to get in, and nearly a mile south through the disabled grill opening up onto a lake."

Peter clasped them on their shoulders and said, "And on that note, let's get out of here, clean up and get a late-night snack. I'm starved."

Anton glanced at Li, and agreed with Peter. "Sure, we're done here."

They moved away from the cellar, heading back to the eastern entry location in the alleyway. The hired SUV they would use to get back to the motel waited in the street above.

* * *

It was a perfect early autumn night, with a full moon descending to the western horizon.

It was still another two hours till the dawn of Thursday the seventh, and Anton, Li, Peter, and Chiara were making the most of the early hours of the morning with an extended stealth run through the city. They'd covered fifteen miles as the crow flies in the last two hours, but much of that was up and down the sides of buildings, and across rooftops in extreme parkour style.

They all needed the opportunity to stretch themselves. The motel offered no facilities for training, and there was almost nothing to do while they waited for the conclave to arrive.

Anton pulled to a halt on the edge of a building, his gaze catching a nondescript dark-gray van idling next to a graffiti-covered dumpster in an alleyway less than fifty yards from him. He shrank back to a nearby brick pillar to avoid providing a silhouette against the night sky. He whispered harshly, "Heads up, we've got company."

Li, Chiara, and Peter, all faded into the rooftop. Li asked in an urgent whisper, "What is it?"

Anton glanced over the edge of the building's roof, and into the alleyway. Two operatives man-handled a black body bag into the back of a Shadowstone OPSEC van. He whispered over his shoulder, "Shadowstone, taking out the vampire trash. It burns me up, but we can't touch them. We can't alert Shadowstone to the fact that we're here."

"There's a vampire nearby?" Li asked, going still for a moment, before slowly scanning the nearby cityscape.

"Probably long gone," Anton suggested. "If I were a vampire, I wouldn't be spending my nights waiting to see if the lackeys were doing their job. That would be boring. That vamp won't be hanging around."

"Can we track it?" Chiara asked. "It would be good to take it out."

Li shook her head. "There's too little to go on. Especially now that Shadowstone are involved. They'll erase all traces of vampire activity."

Peter asked incredulously, "How can they not understand who they're working for or what they're really doing?"

Anton asked rhetorically, "Who says they don't understand? Perhaps they do. I'm not surprised anymore by the ability of people to align themselves with whoever is in power and call it 'working for the greater good.'"

"That's a bit cynical Anton," Li said.

Anton's eyes hardened as he looked back down at the van. It pulled away from the curb and accelerated down the alleyway. "Well, I've had to grow up fast." He looked across at Li. "I didn't know that naïveté was a virtue."

"It's not, but neither is cynicism."

Anton stared at her for half a second and inquired, "You have a third alternative?"

Li suggested quietly, "That would be wisdom."

Anton snorted and shook his head. "We're holding this conclave under the noses of the vampires. How can that be wise? Frankly, I'm expecting a shit-show, something will go drastically wrong. Surely, Ramin Kain was backed by some sort of cabal of fellow conspirators, and I'm certain, whoever they are, they'll take action against us."

Chiara said, "We'll need to be on our guard, perhaps we should take weapons."

Li said, "We're supposed to be unarmed, it's normal conclave protocol."

"This is not a normal conclave," Anton asserted quietly.

Peter remarked soberly, "Remember Maine."

"We need to be prepared," Chiara added.

Anton stepped away from the pillar, and declared, "We should be fully armed and ready for anything."

"I, agree," Peter said.

"Me, too," Chiara added.

Li frowned in the moonlight, then shook her head once, and shrugged her shoulders. "Well, if you're all agreed … I'm in too."

The team fell silent, there was nothing they could do about the vampire feeding in Minneapolis or the Shadowstone operatives that had cleaned up the evidence of its bloodlust. The conclave was too close, and they had to maintain operational security. The vampire would get to live and kill for a while longer until they or another team could safely destroy it.

Anton's hands hardened into fists, and he clenched his teeth. There were too many restrictions. There had to be a better way to bring the war to the vampires and do them real damage, damage they would never recover from.

Peter suggested from behind him, "Let's head back to the cafe we passed near our motel, and grab breakfast."

Anton turned to face him, letting his fists relax, and agreed. "An excellent idea. There is still time for a shower and change before they open."

Li and Chiara nodded; they turned away from the alleyway and headed back. Anton let the others lead the way to the motel, he was having trouble letting go of the idea of a vampire running rampant through this city.

Something like a thousand vampires lived in the world. They had to kill to feed about every second day. That meant about five hundred people died for their blood every day. Five hundred people with hopes, dreams, and expectations of a future. Five hundred people with families, friends and loved ones, all slaughtered like cattle for the benefit of a ruling caste of parasitic predators.

Every day the Vampire Dominion persisted sickened him. He would put an end to it. He would put an end to all of them, even if it took his last breath to do it.

Anton looked up at the full moon and the broad city gleaming brightly beneath its pale light, and his purpose sang in his veins with every beat of his heart.

He was a vampire killer — he would kill all the vampires — every last one of them.

He could do nothing less.

* * *

The cafe had a lovely courtyard dominated by an enormous St. Croix elm tree.

The morning was crisp and clear, and the aromas drifting through the air were making Anton's mouth water. They'd scouted the place in the early hours of the morning while running the cityscape. Three nearby street cameras had encountered some 'very bad luck,' and were no longer operational. Li had insisted on full hoods and sunglasses and was running hacking software of her own design against personal mobile phones from her laptop. She was able to create a bubble fifty yards across centered on her computer, where phone cameras and microphones appeared to be working, but silently failed to record anything.

"Time for a decent breakfast," Peter declared, as he studied a menu.

A young waitress walked up to their table and took their orders. When she finished listing Peter's request, she asked, "Do you want those dishes all at once, or separated."

"Just bring them out as soon as they're ready," Peter said with a grin.

The waitress walked away, and Li remarked, "I don't know where you put it all. I get the enhanced metabolism, but you just ordered four thousand calories in one meal."

Peter rubbed his hands. "And I'm going to enjoy every last one of them."

Anton leaned onto the table, tilted his head, looked hard at Peter, and said in mock seriousness, "You need to fuel up for the mission."

"Ahh … yes, the mission." Peter looked across the table at Anton and said deadpan, "I've got a bad feeling about this mission."

Anton looked back at him, a grin tickling the corners of his mouth. "Yeah, it'll probably be a SNAFU."

"If you're leading it again," Peter frowned. "It's bound to be FUBAR."

Anton sat back, raised an eyebrow, rubbed his chin, then pointed his finger at Peter. "When the bad guys show up, we should conduct a frontal assault on their strongest position."

Peter glanced upward. "Or we could draw them into a position of over-confidence—"

"By letting them surround us first."

"That would do it."

"SOP," Anton declared.

"SOP," Peter replied.

Li nudged Anton. Indicating the front of the cafe with a flick of her head, she said quietly, "Heads up, another Ramp master just arrived."

Anton glanced sideways at Li. She had an uncanny ability to pick out those who had Ramp capability from the rest of the population. He looked to the front of the cafe and spotted a middle-aged man, dressed in an open dark-gray jacket, blue jeans, and well-worn work boots. He was of medium height and build, his hair was mostly gray mixed with black, long, straight and pulled back into a neat ponytail, and matched with a circle beard shot with gray. He glanced across at Anton's table, caught his gaze, and nodded an acknowledgment. He faced back, smiled warmly at the girl behind the counter and paid for his order.

Li whispered, "Do you know him?"

Anton shrugged his shoulders, perplexed. "No. But, he seems to know me."

The gentleman approached their table, stood next to the lone empty chair and asked in a warm, Texan drawl, "Do you all mind if I sit here?"

Everyone at the table nodded, and he sat down. "Thank you, my name is Jonathan Thunder-Axe. My friends call me Jon."

"Do we know each other?" Anton asked.

Jon looked at Anton for half a second, his heavy-lidded, dark-brown eyes missing nothing. "When I last saw you, you were still in diapers. I knew Anna and William quite well, and I'm a close friend of your grandfather." He looked past Anton at Li, and said, "My condolences for your losses, Gang, and Tatsu were much loved. I regret that I didn't get to know your brother Qiang better. Too many good people have died recently." He sighed quietly and quelled a shiver. "Our world is on a knife edge, and it won't take much to tip it over."

"What do you mean?" Li asked.

The waitress approached with an espresso coffee for Jon and a tray of breakfast dishes for the table. The conversation lapsed until she left.

Li caught Jon's gaze and asked, "What do you mean about 'knife edge,' and 'tipping over?'"

Jon sipped his espresso, frowned for a moment and observed quietly. "There's a lot happening in the world at the moment. Chaos is growing and breaking out. If it continues, then our current civilization will collapse, and many will die."

Anton leaned forward and asked, "If the chaos leads to the destruction of Crane's Vampire Dominion, isn't that a good thing?"

"That depends entirely on what replaces it."

Li asked incredulously, "It could be worse?"

"It could be worse?" Jon asked rhetorically, then asserted, "It could be a lot worse."

"What's the worst-case scenario?" Anton inquired.

"What's the worst thing you can imagine, and then multiply it by a thousand?" Jon sighed. "My number one fear is that Crane will be backed into a corner and use the Key of Ahknaton to modify the Metaframe. Any change he introduces will most likely be catastrophic."

Chiara asked, "And that could happen anytime?"

"Yes," Jon answered. "Crane and the Key are a wildcard for the world."

Anton cocked his head and asked, "While I'm sure Crane intends nothing good, Catastrophic is a strong term, is it really warranted?"

Jon looked at Anton carefully as if weighing up his ability to appreciate what he was about to say, and instructed them. "The Metaframe doesn't like being 'touched.' It doesn't like people tampering with reality. No one gets what they really want from it."

"You talk about it as if it's alive," Anton observed.

"What makes you think it isn't?"

The table fell silent, the noisy clamor of the busy cafe washing over them. They were discussing some of the deepest subjects in the universe, and the other patrons ignored them, obsessed with the personally important minutiae of their lives.

"What are you suggesting?" Li asked.

"Just what I said," Jon asserted. "The Metaframe doesn't like people changing reality. We're already off course, reality isn't supposed to have vampires in it."

"It's alive?" Anton asked, his lip curled into a sardonic grin caught halfway between belief and skepticism. "It has an agenda of its own?"

"The divine presence in the Metaframe always shapes the response to any change, and it's unforgiving of requests."

Anton frowned. *What the hell? Who is this guy?*

"How do you know this?" Peter asked.

Jon paused for a long moment and said, "I'm sure you'll all find out soon enough. I'm a man of tricks – I have partial access to the Metaframe."

Everyone at the table stopped what they were doing and stared at Jon. A genuine sorcerous ability to access the Metaframe, and create local or specific shifts in reality, what was commonly known as real magic, or miracles, was extremely rare. Whole generations of people could be born, live and die without a single person able to access the Metaframe in even a partial way being present.

Anton's eyes narrowed, and he stroked the two-week-old beard on his chin. "And luckily, you're on our side, what can you do?"

A smile tickled the edges of Jon's mouth. "I don't normally talk about it."

Anton arched an eyebrow and declared, "Well, it's too late to stop now. We're probably risking our lives by the end of this weekend, and you want to be coy about an important tactical ability?"

Jon's smile broadened. "You're just like Arthur. He would've said the same thing."

"My grandfather isn't here. He's not a factor. We're the ones who'll have to face whatever is coming. Honestly, what can you do?"

Jon frowned and then nodded. "Okay, I can create a mist over a large area that renders my opponents lost. They can't tell where they are. They can't tell friend from foe. They're beset by strong feelings of abandonment, loss, and regret. It completely messes them up."

Anton looked hard at Jon. "How fast can you do it."

"Fast, the raising of the 'mist,' is almost instantaneous once I access the Metaframe."

"And how long does that take?"

"About thirty seconds. The Ramp state for accessing the Metaframe is extreme."

Li leaned forward over her plate of breakfast, and asserted, "This is a game changer."

"Wait a second," Anton said, "Does it work on vampires?"

"Absolutely," Jon replied. "With full effect, just the same as anyone else."

"What the hell," Anton swore, "If we ever find out where Crane's citadel is, we need you inside it. You're a one-man army, we could use your power to kill all the vampires in Crane's citadel."

Jon smiled gently. "Yes, we just need to know where it is."

Anton asked, "What about area of effect and duration?"

Jon's eyes twinkled. "You really are just like Arthur, always looking for a tactical or strategic edge … a small space like this cafe, I could cover for a couple of days. I can cover an area ten miles across for an hour."

"Any side-effects?"

"Only on me. If I use the power, I can't ramp for weeks afterward, and I can't use the power again until I recover."

Anton leaned forward and said with quiet intensity, "This is like having a nuclear weapon, why haven't you made a difference with this power before?"

Jon looked hard at Anton and offered quietly. "You're still alive. There were people who wanted your family dead for over twenty years. There was a mission nearly twenty years ago to put your family in hiding and another mission to keep them hidden when the Panopticon came online. Your grandfather, some other force leaders, myself, we all played a role in keeping your family alive."

"Was it Kain?"

Jon nodded. "Yes. Kain and his fanatics have always wanted the Slaynes dead."

"Fanatics who are still around," Li remarked.

Jon nodded.

Chiara asked, "What do you mean by a divine presence, are you suggesting God is within the Metaframe?"

Jon looked at Chiara. "There is a genuine divine presence within the Metaframe, a god captured within the machine. As to what it means beyond that fact, I don't know. How the Metaframe came to be is a mystery, but I'm certain it is alive, intelligent, aware, and actively pursuing its own purposes. And furthermore, it's not happy with the existence of vampires. Ahknaton's request to save Mekra tore this reality into existence. It wasn't meant to happen."

Anton's eye tightened. "You talk of a captured God, captured by who? And where are those captors now?"

"Thoth is one of many, I don't know more than that."

"So, it's Thoth that is trapped in the Metaframe?" Li asked. "Thoth's engine is literally his prison?"

Jon lifted his hands and declared, "Hold your horses young lady. I don't know that for sure."

"What do you know?" Li asked.

Jon sighed; his dark brown eyes half-lidded. "Not enough?"

Anton inquired, "If the Metaframe is a god, Thoth or whoever it is, could it communicate?"

"What do you mean, communicate?"

"With visions or anything like that," Anton answered quietly. Was Thoth the source of the visions he'd had since the murder of his mother and the abduction of his father?

Jon stared at him for a long moment. Before he could answer, Campbell West entered the cafe, strode to the table and snapped at Anton and his friends, "What are you doing here?" he pointed at Jon, "and what are you doing here Thunder-Axe, you should be with the other force leaders." He looked around the cafe. "This place is completely unsecured, what were you thinking?"

Li stared at West and affirmed, "The situation is under control, I've got it handled."

"Don't pretend you're a loremaster Wu," West snarled. "'cause you're not."

"Really," Li shot back. "I'm not pretending to be a loremaster, that would be obvious to anyone with an ounce of common sense."

West opened his mouth to interrupt and Li shut him down with a hard look and a jutting finger. "Let's be crystal clear, I'm only doing what's necessary to protect our team, if you have a complaint, I suggest you take it up with Francis Mirovar, and if you don't have the balls to do that, then shut up and fuck off."

West's mouth shifted into a derisive sneer. "You presume everything Wu, and know nothing."

Anton and Peter leaped to their feet and Anton warned in a hard voice, "Back off West, you're not welcome here."

West stared at Anton and Peter, looked back at Li, then flicked his gaze around the wall of hostility at the table. "Okay," he raised his hands and took a step backward. "I spoke hastily, what the hell, I'm young, what do I know. You guys have a great day." He grinned like nothing had just happened. Turned and headed off.

"What a prick," Peter declared, and sat back down.

Jon remarked, "Truer words have not been spoken."

Anton snorted softly, then looked at Chiara and asked, "How did it go with your jujitsu training session?"

Chiara laughed. "Every time he attempted to cop a feel, he got an extra bruise. He limped home with his tail between his legs."

Anton smiled at her. "Perfect."

Chapter Eight

"Anyone who thinks politics equals power has no understanding of either politics or power. The games of politics are sponsored by the powerful, and are designed to deliver a single end – to secure their power." – Cornelius Crane, King of the Vampire Dominion

* * *

Minneapolis, September 10th, Sunday morning

The target building was an old chapel recently converted into an events venue.

Louise sat in her command chair in the middle of her Mobile Command Center. The MCC lay hidden within a long shipping container mounted on the back of a semi-trailer and parked eight miles from the chapel. She studied the feeds from two high-flying drones. The well-maintained gardens and parking lots around the chapel covered off a broad area to the north, south, and west of the building. Although the east side of the building had a thick screen of trees, the chapel had an open-topped sixty-foot-tall tower that provided an excellent location to observe all of the surrounding approaches. The Order had chosen the building well, it would be impossible to surprise them. However, she could cut off any avenue of escape, and with the effective staging of her forces, she could ensure the Order had the least amount of time available to react.

She glanced at a timer display on one of the many monitors in her mobile command center, it read 07:30. Her team leaders and squad commanders would begin final positioning at 09:55, five minutes before the conclave was due to start, and twenty minutes before the scheduled attack.

The main monitor in front of her flagged an incoming video conference call. General Clayton Maze, the vampire in charge of Shadowstone and the Day Guard appeared on the screen.

Maze looked at her as if he was about to talk to a piece of raw meat and said, "Wesson, I have additional instructions for you to pass onto your men."

He paused for a moment, seemingly waiting for her to respond.

"Yes, Sir?" Louise asked, staring with a veneer of rapt attention at Maze's face on the screen.

Maze stared back and declared, "Your men must limit the use of weapons to gunfire only, no explosives. It is essential they leave the Order bodies intact. Ensure your men bag and tag all the bodies for pickup. I will have a specialized team on site for the purpose of clearing the Order dead. Is that clear?"

"Yes, Sir. But, what if the Order use explosives, may my men respond in kind?"

"They will not use explosives under any circumstances." His eyes tightened. "These troops are expendable, never forget that."

Louise considered her next words carefully. This change in orders made no sense, she was missing essential information. Information that could get her men killed or worse disrupt her own secret mission against the vampires. "Sir, may I know why these orders have been issued?"

Maze's lip curled derisively. "You most certainly may not. Now follow your orders, Wesson."

Maze cut the video call, and the screen returned to a sequence of Panopticon camera feeds of the target site.

Such a winning personality, Louise thought, her face a veneer of dedicated respect for the benefit of the cameras in the command center. Shadowstone was recording all her words and actions, and could replay the videos at will. Crane and Maze would assess and judge her performance, and they would hold her accountable for today's results. Regardless of her private objectives and her mission to destroy the vampires, in this battle, she needed to demonstrate loyalty and effectiveness.

She planned on displaying both qualities to the best of her ability.

On the previous Thursday evening, Louise had scouted the stormwater drains beneath the old chapel. She'd discovered a disabled steel grate hanging from the ceiling of a drain junction leading directly to an external access point at a lakeside south of the chapel. Someone had cut all but one strand of the grate. The metal cuts were fresh, lacking any trace of rust and slime. Someone had cased the drains within the last two days, most likely some member of the Order. It was possible, even probable that it was a member of the Mirovar force team, and specifically Anton Slayne.

Louise had studied all the available video from the recent attacks in the United Kingdom. Anton had been the one who'd commandeered a commander tank and smashed the Shadowstone base in South Lincolnshire. He'd been first onto the mobile rendition unit and had driven it into a transport aircraft, providing cover for the rest of the team to escape the RAF airbase at Coningsby. Then he'd captured a nightfalcon, taking out Major Quiver and his phase IV day guards.

Some of his tactics didn't necessarily make a lot of sense on first examination, but he typically caused so much mayhem to his opponents that he'd get away with whatever he attempted. And while his methods weren't elegant or schooled, they were effective, and he'd continued to survive while those who opposed him died.

And survival was the name of the game. Anton Slayne was a natural survivor, and survivors managed risk and established escape paths. She was willing to bet that it was Anton and some of his friends who'd scouted the stormwater drains and cut a path through the steel grill.

Louise had discovered three distinct escape paths, to the north, south, and east. She'd assigned three squads of four men each to guard each escape route, and worked with her squad leaders to establish the optimal positions for their men. She'd equipped each squad with a 7.62mm minigun sentry weapon in addition to their augmented close-quarter carbines, and established a set of tactics for the drains, using small autonomous flying drones to funnel any Order escapees into the path of the sentry weapons.

She could also flood the drains with a non-lethal anti-personnel gas. She kept a supply of gas grenades and launchers mounted on a pair of crawlers with her reserve Day Guard squads. Her Day Guard's new tactical helmets would filter out the gas, but most likely, the Order would not be carrying a defense against it.

If they attempted to escape via the stormwater drains, they'd need to be quick and smart, or else they'd die down there. It was a risk she had to take, she had to demonstrate effective use of her men and specialized equipment regardless of the result of the coming battle. At all times, the Panopticon watched her actions and choices, and the discovery of her secret objective by the vampires was not a part of her plan.

She could provide a single window of opportunity for the Order and they needed to take it, or all would be lost. The discovery of an Order conclave was a once in a lifetime opportunity. For her mission to progress, she needed enough of the Order to survive the initial assault, escape into the stormwater drains, encounter the Day Guard squads, win past them, acquire one of the tactical helmets, use the GPS signals to discover the location of the Panopticon in Utah, and then destroy it.

A sequence of events that seemed more far-fetched the longer she thought about it, but it was all she had, and it was what she was going with. Everything was at risk, and it all depended on the Order of Thoth, and more precisely, Anton Slayne, Li Wu, and their companions. She allowed herself a long sigh, a visible reaction she could pass off as pre-battle anticipation. All the parts were now in place; all she could do was wait, and adapt her plans as the battle unfolded, but the slightest misstep would invite utter failure.

Anton Slayne and his companions needed to win through and target the Panopticon. Louise would then be free to execute the second phase of her plan, the co-option of the second Panopticon under construction at the East Coast Hub. With the new Panopticon 2.0 under her control, she could wait for the Day Guard numbers to grow, and then launch a devastating surprise attack at Crane and his generals.

She would destroy the vampires, and restore the republic of the United States.

Louise slid her chair along its rail covering the distance from one end of the command center to the other, scanning all the data and video feeds available from the Panopticon.

"Everything is in place for victory," she declared, her face filled with determination.

Hear my words, vampires, your time is coming to an end.

* * *

Francis and Anton watched as Jay and the others departed for the conclave in the hired SUV.

They retained the Toyota sedan to make their way to the Order meeting. Francis had sent the rest of the team ahead. He was certain that if the remaining members of the Kain cabal chose to attack, it would be before the conclave started, and that only Anton and himself would be the targets. He'd explained that an attack would occur in one of three places, at the motel, on the road to the conclave, or outside the conclave itself. Jay, Peter, Li, and Chiara had all protested the idea of leaving them behind, but Francis had insisted, and in the end, they'd obeyed.

The last of the three options was the riskiest for the conspirators as it allowed the members of the conclave to intervene against them, but perhaps the conspirators expected the conclave attendees to remain unarmed in accordance with normal conclave protocol. A rule everyone aligned with Francis had broken. All the Order members Anton had met this last week, the Australians, Justin Blake's cousins, the two Taylors, Jon Thunder-Axe, the Prospector, and all the members of the Mirovar force team, were carrying every single weapon to the conclave they could hide about their person.

Long coats had suddenly become stylish amongst his friends and allies.

The SUV with Jay, Peter, Li, and Chiara disappeared from view. Francis and Anton sat down on a pair of faded white plastic chairs in front of what had been Li and Chiara's motel room. It was just after nine am, in less than an hour the conclave was due to start, and it would take thirty minutes to get there from the motel. Francis had decided that if there was to be a fight, he preferred it here with plenty of open space in which to maneuver, rather than in a car half way to the venue.

"I suppose now we wait?" Anton asked.

"Yes, Anton. We wait."

"I won't be surprised if they try to kill us here."

Francis frowned. "We should expect them to try … even though it would be a severe departure from protocol."

"No kidding," Anton observed, dryly.

Francis sighed, his fingers brushing lightly over the scabbard of the White Dragon resting across his thighs. "This may all seem an imposition to you Anton, but the Order was once something noble and pure."

Anton glanced at Francis. "Honestly, Francis, I think those days are past."

Anger flared behind Francis' eyes. "While there is a single member who holds a commitment to the defense of the innocent then the Order still exists."

"I hold to that principle," Anton asserted. "However, I think we could do a lot more."

Francis looked out across the nearly empty parking lot. His eyes glazed over as if he was looking at something Anton couldn't see. "A lot more? It may surprise you Anton, but I agree with you. We must do more." He paused for a moment, rubbing the inside of his orbit, just to the left of his nose. He looked sidelong at Anton. "What are you willing to sacrifice to reach your goals?" Francis focused into the distance again. "This war can claim everything you're willing to give and more, and I suspect your biggest sacrifices are still in front of you."

Anton fell quiet, letting Francis' words rest between them. Yes, they'd already made sacrifices, and they'd make more in the future. If called upon, he'd willingly lead any of his friends into battle, but the last thing he wanted was for any of them to die.

He'd make their enemies die first.

Tension had been growing within him since the flight from Reykjavík. They'd encountered vampires, but something else had killed them. The thing that had hidden in the drains had stolen a vampire kill from him, and he'd resented it. He let the feeling pass, it receded into the background but didn't disappear. A hot desire rises quickly and is easily satisfied. A cold desire grows slowly and finds no satisfaction.

Anton affirmed with deadly softness, "We need to bring the war to the vampires."

"Agreed. The question is how? We need information, we need targets."

"Crane's citadel?"

"Somewhere in the North East, no one knows for sure where it is."

"The Panopticon?"

"Apparently, it's better hidden than Crane's citadel."

"They would be the two best targets. What about other means of attack, could we destroy the financial basis of the Dominion?"

"Not without destroying the world economy at the same time. Lots of collateral damage with that one."

Anton rubbed his face.

Francis leaned back in his chair. "It's frustrating, isn't it? Even if we took a straight cold calculus to this problem, any proposed solution that killed more than five hundred people a day is worse than the vampires. The Red Empire experimented with a bio-warfare weapon. It was a set of viral DNA spliced with influenza, that modified human blood making it undrinkable to a vampire. The flu side of the virus had a ninety percent kill rate, but the survivors would be immune to a vampire attack." He held up his right hand, his finger half an inch away from his thumb. "We came this close to billions dying, but the vampires would've died out."

"What happened?"

"The Red Ghost decided the price was too high to pay, even for a group as ruthless about human life as they are."

"How do you know this?"

"Sometimes the Order and the Red Empire don't fight when they meet. After all is said and done, we have a common enemy."

Anton snorted and shook his head ruefully. "This whole situation keeps getting more complex."

Francis hummed softly, his eyes scanning the streets visible from the edge of the motel's parking lot. Silence fell like a shroud between them, the minutes ticking away. Anton spent his time scanning possible attack sites. A short ramp to extend his senses, then look hard for signs of snipers. Francis was better at spotting the tell-tale signs, he had two eyes. There was no evidence of a long-range attack. No, the enemy would come in close, go hand to hand, or they'd wait for them to leave the motel, and attack them in the car.

The time approached for them to leave, Francis said, "I note that you have still not mastered water. You will have to do that one day if your mastery of the blade is to be complete."

Anton pursed his lips and stroked his beard. "Are you really sure about that?"

Francis nodded sagely. "Yes. There is a gap in your technique that mastery of water will fill."

Anton sighed; his gaze wandered onto the empty parking lot. "With a bit of luck, they'll attack us here. Anything would beat this waiting."

Francis sat quietly for a long moment. "It's your lack of patience that defeats your mastery of water."

Anton snorted.

An engine revved hard, and tires squealed outside the entrance to the motel's parking lot. A black van turned off the street, charging across the open concrete space. It was darker than a moonless night. The windows were heavily tinted, making it all but impossible to see into the interior of the cabin.

So, the Order is into vampire chic these days, Anton thought. A dire grin flashing briefly across his face.

The van screeched to a halt twenty paces short of where Francis and Anton were sitting.

Francis declared, "I'm going right."

"Left it is then," Anton observed, the Blue Dragon coming free of its scabbard with a sibilant hiss.

The van's doors burst open. Five fighters, dressed in black and tan Red Empire body armor, and flowing blood-red capes, hoods, and veils, blurred from the van. Each of them wielded a pair of two-foot short swords, the blades drinking the morning light like hungry shadows.

"'Ware the blades," Francis called as he rushed forward, the White Dragon held above his right shoulder.

Anton screamed in defiance, the Blue Dragon gleaming naked in the bright morning light.

He blurred to attack.

* * *

Campbell West leaped from the left-hand side of the van.

He grinned behind his red veil. Five hours earlier, he'd installed three hidden cameras around the motel's parking lot. They would capture the coming victory, and provide cast-iron evidence of the involvement of the Red Empire in the 'assassination,' of Francis Mirovar and Anton Slayne.

His heart sang with joyful anticipation. Assisting with the deaths of Mirovar and Slayne was everything he could hope for. They must purge the Order of traditionalists, of those who believed in protecting the innocent. There were no innocents in the world. If someone was too willfully stupid and ignorant to understand what was happening, then they were complicit in the predation of the vampires. Ignorance was no excuse, and there was no way to help those who couldn't or wouldn't help themselves.

As for people who couldn't ramp, what use were they to the great cause? Calvin Woodstock had explained the correct place of those without the ability to ramp was to serve the natural elite of those who could.

It made perfect sense.

Ramin Kain was the next best thing to a Messiah the world had seen. Calvin Woodstock and the other core force leaders like Bill Shortman were the astute few with the capability to fulfill Kain's legacy, and today would see Kain's legacy made real. Today would mark the final conclave, they wouldn't be necessary in the future. With the wise counsel of the best force leaders, Calvin Woodstock would rule, and the rest would follow.

In time, Campbell would follow in Calvin's footsteps. He'd be loyal to Calvin's rule, and one day Calvin would retire. He would step forward into the role of rulership of the Order of Thoth. A role he was uniquely suited for.

Campbell's boots struck the concrete, and he ramped hard. Johnson and Rodriguez appeared from the rear of the van and rushed forward, their nanoshard swords whistling faintly as they snapped into attack positions.

Slayne had gone to the right, the rest of the team would deal with him.

Mirovar blurred toward him. Campbell leaped in a high arc over his head, flipping mid-air. The battle started before he landed, silvery sparks laced with dark flickers flying as Johnson and Rodriguez's swords came in contact with Mirovar's blade.

Mirovar was committing suicide by fighting them. Johnson and Rodriguez were the best fighters in the Shortman force team. The fight would be over in moments. Campbell was certain he wouldn't even get a chance to wet his blades in Mirovar's blood.

He landed. The battle was evolving in front of his eyes, still ramped, he leaped back to land next to the van. He wanted to make sure no one got behind him.

Mirovar blurred between Johnson and Rodriguez, trading attack and counter-attack. One of Rodriguez's blades made it through Mirovar's defenses, a thin line of blood appearing on his left shoulder. Mirovar blurred again, his sword snapping left and right.

Johnson rushed to Campbell's left, half a dozen feet away, trapping Mirovar in a triangle between the three of them.

His heart leaped, Campbell grinned, his eyes ablaze with triumph.

Mirovar was about to die.

* * *

The first Order operative leaped from the passenger side of the van, blurring across Anton's line, before pivoting hard to attack his blindside on the left flank.

The second operative rushed forward on a line between Anton and the van, setting up an attack on Anton's right.

It was a classic blademaster team maneuver. The two Order operatives in 'clown suits' were a fighting pair. They were the same height and athletic build and could have been identical twins for all Anton knew.

Anton's head swiveled, he had to work harder now he only had a single eye. He dived into silence, blurring forward and dropping low between the two Order operatives. He slid between them, their dark blades whistling, clashing against the Blue Dragon in guard position above his head. He planted his right foot, halting the slide as they recovered to strike again. He whirled while crouched, his left foot lashing out and up into the solar plexus of the operative on the right side. He collapsed around Anton's boot, his blades falling away from nerveless fingers as he flew backward into the side of the van with a reverberating crash.

The van rocked, skidding half a dozen feet across the parking lot. The operative crumpled to the ground, leaving a man-shaped dent in the side of the vehicle.

The second operative attacked furiously, his dark blades arcing forward, seeking purchase in Anton's flesh.

Anton was on his feet, blurring to the left and pivoting hard. Words whispered from the depths of his mind, threatening to rob him of silence and the Ramp, *betrayer, traitor, enemy*. A red mist descended through his soul, and cold fury flared, a bright blue flame excoriating all that it touched.

The operative attacked, matching Anton's pivot, his dark blades racing in. The first a high feint to draw Anton's defenses, while the second blade came in low, destined to rise, and penetrate from beneath Anton's ribs before slicing through his heart.

White lightning coruscated deep within Anton's limbs, the Blue Dragon snapping forward in a deep thrust, punching through the body armor over the operative's chest. Anton pivoted to the right, the low blade catching the edge of his jacket. He twisted his right wrist, turning the Blue Dragon a quarter turn. The operative grunted, his eyes wide above the red veil.

Anton ripped his blade clear. He dropped out of Ramp, the Order operative falling away to his left. A look of disgust twisted its way across Anton's face as he watched the man strike the ground and lie still in a pool of spreading blood.

The other operative groaned and started lifting himself off the concrete.

Anton strode forward, the Blue Dragon arced down, slicing into the back of the man's skull, pinning his head to the pale concrete. He quivered, his arms and legs spasmed, blood gushing from beneath his face. Anton pulled his blade clear, and the man fell limply to the concrete.

Anton flicked the Blue Dragon, the blood flying from the blade.

He was in no mood to take prisoners today.

* * *

A loud bang shattered the morning air.

The van skidded across the concrete knocking the youngest operative forward. He put a hand out to steady himself, fouling the operative to his left.

Francis' blade licked forward, flashing in the morning light, slicing through the fouled operative's throat. Arterial blood sprayed, painting a red line along the side of the van. The stricken man staggered to his left and crumpled to the ground.

The other operative snarled at the younger one, who visibly quailed, then promised desperately, "You'll pay for that Mirovar."

"Right…" Francis observed, sardonically, stepping sideways to put himself directly opposite his two remaining opponents. "Now, you're only going to try and kill me." He took a sudden step forward. The senior operative's blades blurred into guard position, the younger operative's responses were slower, less confident, he was sweating under his hood.

Francis looked hard at him and inquired, "It's West, isn't it?"

The sweating operative's eyes darted left and right.

Francis' gaze flicked between the two men, and he affirmed. "You will not escape."

The operatives glanced at each other and rushed toward Francis.

Francis blurred to the right, positioning the senior operative between himself and West. The White Dragon arced down. The operative's left hand blurred upward, his dark blade rising to meet Francis' katana.

The two blades struck; bright sparks littered with glittering shadows flying away.

Francis whirled. The silver blade he kept hidden in a holster under his left sleeve flew forward, piercing the middle of the operative's throat before exiting the other side, coming to rest in the side of the van. The stricken operative gurgled, blood sluicing from his gaping mouth. He dropped to his knees clutching the open wounds on the sides of his neck.

The White Dragon flashed in a horizontal arc. The operatives head, and hands, separated from the rest of his body, making a dismembered mess at Francis' feet. He stepped over the body, angling toward West, the White Dragon snapped into position over his right shoulder.

He stared hard at West.

The young man hesitated for the briefest of moments, then threw his dark-bladed swords down and blurred toward the parking lot exit.

"Damn," Francis shouted. "I want him alive."

West was halfway across the parking lot when Anton appeared from the other side of the van. He caught up with West at the gate and slammed him into the sidewalk with a hard tackle.

"Bring him here," Francis called.

There was an accounting to be made.

* * *

Anton lifted West by the scruff of the neck, dragging him stumbling and wailing back to the van.

He snarled, and declared, "You're coming with us."

Francis indicated the back of the van with a flick of his head.

Anton slammed West's face into the rear of the van, leaving a blood-smeared dent in the panel. Then threw him bodily into the rear of the cabin, where he sprawled in a limp tangle of limbs.

Francis looked at the unmoving West, then glanced at Anton, and asked, "How hard did you hit him?"

"Not hard enough."

Francis shrugged his shoulders then slammed the rear door shut and said, "Let's get to the conclave. Looks like we'll be late, but with this little fish dressed up as a Red Empire assassin, there's going to be some explaining to do." His eyes narrowed. "This should be a very interesting morning."

"Yep," Anton agreed. "I'm sure it will."

The van's engine was still running. Anton and Francis got into the drivers and passenger's seats respectively, turned it around, and left the motel.

My first conclave, what a joke, Anton thought.

* * *

The clock ticked over to 10:00, and a bell rang three times.

Calvin Woodstock stood before a lectern on a raised wooden dais in what had once been a chapel, and addressed the assembled members of the Order of Thoth, "I call the conclave to order." He surveyed the room. Mirovar and Slayne had not yet arrived, but there hadn't been a text message confirming their deaths. Something had gone wrong. "All are here in good faith, for the good of the Order of Thoth and the vanquishing of our enemies. All will be bound by the decisions of the conclave."

Bill Shortman stood and shouted, "Assent."

The assembled full members of the order followed with a collective shout, "Assent."

The novices, Li, and the two Australians remained silent.

The first order of business was a roll call of the dead. He would name every Order member who'd died on active duty since the previous conclave, and detail their most significant exploit. With the recent losses in the United Kingdom, the process of remembering the dead would take about ten minutes.

Calvin glanced at the video prompt in front of him and began speaking.

* * *

Calvin Woodstock looked around the assembly and declared, "There ends the recital of the dead. There will now be a brief period of quiet contemplation to remember those who have given their lives for the great cause."

Justin Blake nudged Li in the right side with his elbow, and whispered out the side of his mouth, "Where's Francis and Anton?"

Li blinked, then whispered back, "I don't know. They were expecting an attack by Kain's followers."

Justin tilted his head slightly. "I know, he mentioned it. I thought you might have heard something. He hasn't contacted you?"

Li shook her head once, her lips pressing into a thin line. "I don't like it. It's nearly quarter past ten. Something should have happened by now. I don't know where they are." Her eyes widened. "I'm getting worried."

"You worry too much. They're big boys, they can look after themselves."

Li glanced at him.

"You always care too much Li. You can't save everyone." Justin paused for a moment. "There's something I would like you to consider."

"What?"

"If they don't show."

"They will."

"But if they don't."

"What is it?"

"I'll offer you confirmation."

"Join your team?"

Justin nodded with a single slight tilt of his head.

Li's heart jumped. What if Francis and Anton were lying dead in a street somewhere. Could she leave Jay, Peter, and Chiara to whatever fate would befall a force team of three? Four was the minimum size for a force team in North America, without her, the Order would disband the Mirovar force team and spread them around the other teams.

She glanced up at Justin's face. He was a warm, powerful man. A true leader, if he led his team into hell, every last one of them would follow willingly. She'd had a teenage crush on him, but her feelings had matured since then – into what? Love? Of a sort. Respect, admiration, friendship, all of those flowed between them. She'd be a good fit for his team, and he'd be a great mentor.

She could also receive training from his loremaster, Patrick Wichowski. She could fulfill Juliette's legacy.

She glanced to her left, Jay, Peter, and Chiara sat in a line next to her. Recent horrors swarmed through her memory. She couldn't abandon them, there was too much unfinished business between them. "No, Justin. I'm sorry, but no."

He nodded. He studied her for a moment, then whispered, "Our door is always open."

A single bell resounded a sad note. The mourning for the dead was over.

She would have to find another way to fulfill the promise made to Juliette's secret flame.

* * *

Anton pulled the van to a halt directly outside the front entrance to the converted chapel. The Sunday traffic in Minneapolis had been worse than expected and they were running late.

Francis had gone into the back of the van and held West in an arm lock. The operative had woken up five minutes before, stopped sniveling, and then flipped to the opposite, a loud, boastful belligerence. If everything West asserted was true, then Anton and Francis should already be dead.

Anton leaped from the van, circled around to the back and opened the rear doors.

Francis clambered out, dragging a struggling West with him. He cuffed the young man across the ear, and West shut up long enough for the three of them to ascend a handful of gray-stone steps to the front doors into the main hall.

A pair of Order guards, wearing suits and katanas stood to either side of the closed doors. The one on the left observed with a half-grin. "The conclave is already in session Mirovar, you're barred from entering."

Francis pushed West into Anton's hands and surged forward. His right fist lashed out in a vicious right cross. The man's jaw shattered and sagged, and he dropped to the floor like an empty sack. The other guard took a step back and froze.

Francis stepped past him as if he wasn't there, pushing the doors open with a crash of splintering wood.

Anton glanced at the other Order guard as he followed Francis into the hall, and noted in passing. "I think he just said, 'Fuck you.'"

An indignant voice shouted within the hall, "Order! Order! Mirovar, you can't bring weapons to a conclave—"

"Merde!" Francis thundered. "Woodstock, you're a traitor, a conspirator, and an attempted murderer."

Anton dragged West forward until they stood next to Francis. Everyone in the room shifted their gaze from Francis, to West and Anton. West remained dressed in black and tan Red Empire body armor with a flowing blood-red cape and hood. His veil had been torn away and lost in the motel's parking lot.

Woodstock's face flushed red. His knuckles whitened as he tightened his grip on the lectern. He raged at Francis and Anton, "What is the meaning of this?"

Francis leveled the tip of the White Dragon at Woodstock and declared in a low, intense voice, "Treason."

The chamber fell to silence.

Woodstock tapped the earbud in his right ear. A look of incomprehension seized his face, his eyes widened, and he uttered hoarsely, "Impossible!"

Chapter Nine

"When your life depends upon secrecy, you must always be ready for the day when your secrets are revealed to your opponents." – Louise Wesson, Head of Shadowstone (North America), and Director of the Day Guard program.

* * *

Minneapolis, September 10th, 10:14:45

Louise rolled her slide chair down the length of the mobile command center, scanning her monitors as she went from one end to the other.

Everyone was in position; the attack would begin in fifteen seconds. Just over a minute before, a black van had pulled up in front of the main entrance, and Anton Slayne and two other people she didn't recognize had entered the hall. There had been a brief altercation at the front doors, and Slayne's companion had felled one of the Order operatives guarding the entrance. His fellow door guard stooped over him, checking out his colleague's still form.

The disruption of the two Order operatives guarding the front door was a useful distraction.

The four guards of Bravo squad were already in free fall above the chapel's tower. They would open their parachutes three hundred yards above the ground. The rest of her forces were advancing to attack at the same time as Bravo squad made contact with the two Order operatives on top of the tower.

Alpha squad was on the move and would hit the front doors in ten seconds. The guards of Charlie squad were sprinting across the parking lot to breach the west-side door. Delta, Echo, Foxtrot and Golf squads were rushing through the screen of trees toward the windows on the east side of the main hall. Hotel, India and Juliette squads were pacing Charlie squad across the parking lots and would hit the west-side windows in five seconds.

Bravo squad opened their combat-drop parachutes with three seconds to go.

The Order operatives on top of the tower started firing up at the descending guards of Bravo squad. One of her guard's life signs flatlined on a report monitor, the rest of his squad mates firing back at the operatives beneath them.

Alpha squad opened fire, the lone Order operative at the front door reared up, before falling in a hail of bullets. The other squads hit their entrances a moment later. Alpha squad hit the front doors of the chapel a second after the rest of the squads hit the walls.

The three surviving members of Bravo squad landed on the top of the tower. They dropped their chutes, stepped past the two dead Order operatives, proceeding down a spiraling staircase within the tower toward the main building.

The battle of the Order conclave had begun.

* * *

Gunfire erupted above the chapel's tower. Sustained submachine gun fire, interspersed with the short rips of assault rifle bursts.

Automatic fire burst into life behind Anton, several stray bullets splintering the front doors, and whizzing a yard to his right. He dove deep into silence and ramped hard, time slowing around him. He still had Campbell West in the iron grip of his left hand. His right hand flashed to the handle of the Blue Dragon jutting above his right shoulder, and it flew free from its scabbard like a hungry beast.

Anton blurred hard to his left out of the line of fire from whoever was coming through the front doors. Barely slowed by West's one hundred and eighty pounds, he accelerated toward the left side of the hall, and the members of the Mirovar faction.

Francis was on the move, whirling and blurring toward his team.

A 9mm Uzi submachine gun and a glimmering katana appeared in Justin Blake's hands. The two Taylors stood armed with pairs of the same weapons. All three were ramped, either standing perfectly still or moving in a blur. Li, Peter, Chiara, and Jay, carried their edged weapons and a 9mm Uzi each. The Australians and New Zealanders carried the same weapons.

Justin Blake was the only one in position to get a hold of weapons in a hurry and must have delivered for today. The only ones not holding one of the ubiquitous Uzi submachine guns were the Prospector and Jon Thunder-Axe. The Prospector pulled a sawn-off automatic shotgun from beneath his coat, his eyes scanning the approaches into the hall. Jon Thunder-Axe had stepped away from the rest, pushed his back up against the nearest wall, and stood completely still.

Peter glanced toward the back of the chapel. That would be the path leading toward the entrance into the cellars, and from there, the stormwater drains.

Anton moved hard and fast, lining up with the rest of the Mirovar faction on that side of the hall. He was closest to the front and had the greatest distance to travel to reach the back of the hall.

The old stained-glass windows shattered along both sides of the hall, shards of razor-sharp glass blooming in deadly clouds. Troopers clad in black and gray armor, and wielding carbines, streamed through the breached walls. They started firing before they landed, rapid-fire gunshots reverberating throughout the room.

Everyone in the Mirovar faction blurred into action. Separating, leaping, dodging violently aside from the first fusillade. The Uzis went berserk. Carbine and submachine gun fire filled the hall, muzzle flashes were everywhere, the reek of burned propellant was inescapable, spent 9mm shell casings flying in wild arcs.

Blood splashed backward into the middle of the hall, the young Australian Mercy Kumar twisting away, a row of bullet holes across her chest. One of Justin's cousins, a burly Maori took a bullet through his left arm, then blurred forward with his brother, taking two of the troopers off their feet, and driving them head first into the brick wall. Spine shattering snaps resounding above the gunfire.

The Prospector's automatic shotgun boomed and thundered. The first three troopers into the hall all died in the first second, but more troopers streamed through the broken windows into the ranks of the Mirovar allies. On the other side of the hall, the force teams aligned with Calvin Woodstock and the legacy of Ramin Kain faced four smashed windows. A dozen or more troopers were through the windows and amongst them. Unarmed, Calvin's teams fought hand to hand. They were faster and stronger than the men they confronted, but the carbines were proving to be a decisive advantage. Savage bursts of gunfire erupted, and puffs of pink mist bloomed wherever the rounds hit flesh and bone.

Four more troopers appeared at the entrance to the hall, firing immediately at a single Order operative on the right-hand side of the hall. Four bursts hit him in the back, shredding his torso and sending gouts of blood over those fighting in front of him.

Anton moved into the melee amongst the Mirovar allies on the left-hand side of the hall.

The two nearest troopers were coming to their feet. Anton threw West at them with all his might. West hit them hard, bowling them both over before ricocheting another twenty feet over the melee. Anton blurred forward, the Blue Dragon slashing left and right, blood followed the arc of his blade in wet ropes, leaving both men dismembered on the floor behind him.

More troopers leaped through the smashed windows.

How many of these guys are there?

* * *

Calvin Woodstock's world descended into chaos.

Dozens of black and gray armored soldiers were blurring into the conclave hall, firing their short-barreled assault rifles with deadly effect. His men and women were fighting without weapons and dying before his eyes. A woman shrieked, and then fell silent, the Canadian loremaster was down.

Mirovar and Slayne had blurred to the right, that side of the hall was alight with guns firing at point blank range.

Calvin's mind raced with outrage. *Mirovar cheated. Those bastards brought weapons to a conc-*

Something punched him hard in the chest. It was like being hit with a sledgehammer. He staggered backward; one hand frozen in a death-grip on the lectern tipping it onto him as he fell to the floor. The heavy lectern crashed down on his pelvis. He stiffened from the agonizing jolt running up from his crushed hips. He gasped, nothing seemed to be working, his arms splayed left and right twitching spasmodically.

People were shouting and screaming amongst the wild gunfire. His mouth was suddenly dry, while his back was warm and wet.

He lifted his head up. It was like trying to lift a boulder in a dream. There was blood all over his chest, several of the many holes littering his body spurted like mini fountains.

That's my—

His last breath gurgled out of his throat, and his head flopped back to the wooden floor with a thud, darkness crushing his world into oblivion.

* * *

Like a diver sinking into an oceanic abyss, Li plumbed the depths of silence.

Time slowed precipitously. The Green Dragon rested in her left hand, one of Justin Blake's 9mm Uzi submachine-guns in her right, blazing away at a trooper she could almost reach out and touch with her sword. The 9mm bullets bounced off his nano-ceramic armor. He rushed forward, the barrel of his carbine rising toward her chest. She whirled, moving a step in, the Green Dragon slamming through his chest plate. His visor darkened as blood rushed out of his mouth. She reversed, drawing her katana clear, a thin ribbon of blood trailing her blade. The trooper slumped forward to the floor.

She dropped the Uzi, grasped the Green Dragon with a two-handed grip, spinning in a circle to assess what was happening.

The new Shadowstone troopers were moving with stunning speed compared with anyone who wasn't a Ramp master or a vampire. Their speed was bad enough, but what made it worse was the accuracy of their weapons.

A squad of troopers was cutting the Order to pieces with concentrated fire. Four of them at the front of the hall killed another man who was blurring toward them. Their carbines concentrating a hail of bullets into his chest. A moment later they targeted the Prospector, he staggered backward, bullets ripping into his big chest. He fell to one knee, his automatic shotgun fired a final two rounds, taking the lower leg off of one of the troopers before clicking on empty. He rolled forward to the floor, his sightless eyes staring at the ceiling.

How were they doing it? She had to know. The troopers who had landed amongst the Mirovar allies were getting slaughtered, although they were doing damage, and Mercy Kumar was certainly dead. They had to close with all the troopers, or the squad at the front door would pick them off one at a time – there were no other options, except—

Li blurred in close to Jon Thunder-Axe, guarding his left-hand side. He was doing his 'thing.' She wanted to make sure no one disturbed him while he summoned the Metaframe. He was their only hope of escaping this hellhole alive.

* * *

The action exploded on twenty screens.

Everyone was moving three to five times faster than normal. Louise sat back stunned, it was impossible to follow. It was one thing to witness training events, it was another to witness a pitched battle between enhanced forces.

The Order operatives were firing back at her men, but apart from that obvious fact, it was impossible to process what was happening in real time.

Her eyes widened; the evolution of warfare had outclassed her.

How can I lead these men?

She contacted her squad leaders in the stormwater drains, and instructed them. "The battle has commenced. Be prepared for Order operatives to enter the drains at any time. Fliers will be active, and will target any hostiles in your area of operations."

Her squad leaders acknowledged her directions, they were as ready as she could make them.

She started tapping a touchscreen attached to the right arm of her sliding chair. The flying drones could fit into the palm of her hand, and each carried a single deadly shaped charge that would detonate on contact. They waited in swarms in the stormwater drain network, programmed to attack anyone who wasn't a member of the Day Guard or Shadowstone.

In moments they would be flying the drains beneath the chapel.

* * *

The world righted itself.

Campbell West had landed and slid up against the wall, he picked himself up from the floor. A massive chaotic melee filled the hall. To his immediate right, one of the armored soldiers slammed back against the wall, a foot-long knife jutting out of his chest, pinning him to the wall. The man's carbine fell from his nerveless fingers.

Campbell blurred, plucking the short-barreled assault rifle out of mid-air. He whirled a hundred and eighty degrees and accelerated away from the battle. He'd landed on the edge of the melee, and the way was clear in front of him. He dashed forward past the toppled lectern and Calvin Woodstock's blood-soaked corpse to a large chamber at the back of the hall. He'd been a junior member of the team that had selected and prepped the site for the conclave. There was a door at the back of the second chamber that led to a stairwell descending to a level of cellars beneath the chapel.

New soldiers burst through two doors at the left and right rear corners of the hall. The doors led to the west entrance, and the tower, respectively. The lead soldier on Campbell's left raised his assault carbine.

Campbell fired his captured carbine, near panic racing through his veins. The gun spat fire, and he flashed it to his right at the three soldiers streaming into the hall from the base of the tower and fired a second burst. He kept blurring forward, not waiting to see if any of his bullets hit their targets.

A moment later he was past the threshold of the second chamber and out of the direct line of return fire from the soldiers. He dashed through the door and flew down the stairs to the lower level.

No one chased him. The deathmatch in the main hall must have absorbed the soldiers he'd just ran into. If he was quick and careful, he could sneak away. There was no point in dying in a stupid battle. He could hide in the cellars and wait the battle out, or better yet, find an exit point and escape the site completely.

The stormwater drains? Yes, that would do it. There was an entrance to the drains in one of the cellars. He could get away from the madness in the hall. He could live to fight another day. No need for any sacrifices on his part. *After all*, he thought to himself, *discretion is the better part of valor.*

Yes, he was too clever to die today, too clever by half.

Dying was for stupid people to do, and Campbell West was certain he wasn't stupid.

He dashed into the lowest cellar, the one with a manhole cover in the floor.

* * *

The Blue Dragon blurred down, cutting a carbine in half, and taking the trooper's hand with it.

Anton slammed into the man's chest with his shoulder, pushing him a dozen feet through the air to crash into the chapel wall. He caught up with Li, Peter, and Chiara, who were guarding Jon, and shouted, "Go! Now!"

Magazines on both sides began hitting empty, creating pockets of reduced threat as fighters reloaded their weapons or went hand to hand. Two troopers drew long knives and attacked Jay. He spun between them, his katana blurring through a pair of graceful, horizontal arcs. Their heads followed their bodies down to the floor before jarring loose on impact and rolling away.

It created a gap between Anton, his friends, Smitty the Australian force leader, and four troopers recovering from evasive action. The troopers fanned out, bringing their weapons to bear on the Australian.

Peter dropped his empty gun, blurred, retrieving one of the dead troopers at his feet. He whirled, throwing the dead trooper's limp body at the four troopers at the back of the hall. They were close to another three troopers on the far right of the hall, which were methodically picking off Order members on that side of the hall.

Smitty threw a twelve-inch hunting knife toward them. The troopers began firing back. The knife sunk to the hilt in the throat of one, the force of the strike taking the man off his feet, blood spraying in a corona around his head. The other three filled Smitty's chest with lead, and the Australian force leader whirled away in a pink cloud.

Anton's ramp deepened, going wild. Time slowed to a crawl. The trooper's armored body sailed through the air, halfway between Peter's outstretched hands and the four troopers at the back of the hall.

Bullets pummeled the flying body, striking wild sparks from the dead trooper's combat armor, some penetrated, sending thin strings of blood into the air.

To Anton's left, Jon Thunder-Axe trembled, his eyes unfocused as he murmured words in an ancient tongue, a stray bullet from the far side of the hall struck ocher brick dust from the wall a handspan above Jon's head.

Rainbow lights flickered throughout the hall.

Hard white light blazed in Anton's skull. He dropped to one knee, the Blue Dragon falling from his grasp as his hands flew to his head. An inarticulate scream of utter agony erupted from his lips.

* * *

Deeply ramped, Jon Thunder-Axe called upon the powers of the Metaframe in the ancient unwritten language of his tribe.

He always used his native language to interact with the Metaframe, it was easier to speak precisely with his native language, than with English. The Metaframe resisted use, and the slightest mistake in phrasing would invite disaster.

He'd spontaneously accessed the Metaframe the first time as a nineteen-year-old kid mastering the ramp. He'd dropped out of that ramp with the power to access the Metaframe at will, and create a defensive mist. There were hints that he could do more but another forty years had passed without achieving any other powers.

Rainbows emanated from a golf-ball-sized sphere of white light, strobing in slow motion throughout the hall. The acuity of every sense expanded; the world became hyper-real. Fully ramped members of the Order were moving in slow motion, the troopers were moving even slower. The hall was a bloodbath, all the members of Kain's cabal on the opposite side of the hall were dead. There were casualties on the Mirovar side of the hall as well, but there was no time to make an accounting. He couldn't have helped even if he wanted to, the extreme ramp state he'd entered froze him to the spot.

The ball of white light spun, expanding to the size of a basketball, becoming an uncountable host of tiny points of colored light orbiting an unseen axis. Jon concentrated his mind to a single outcome and summoned all his will and physical energy to utter one powerful word. The Metaframe vanished, reality snapping back into motion with an energy-sapping wave.

He staggered forward a half step. A thick gray mist filled the hall, visibility dropping to a couple of yards. All the nearby troopers were dead or bleeding out. The guns fell silent.

On his left, Li asked urgently, "Anton, Anton, are you okay?"

Anton was panting noisily, Jon moved toward him. Peter, Chiara, and Li were assisting Anton to his feet. Li called out, "Everyone, follow my voice."

She moved off toward the rear of the chapel, counting out loud as she went.

Jon slipped into line behind them, the other survivors following behind him. He stepped past an armored trooper curled into the fetal position on the floor. It was a common enough reaction to the mist.

In moments, they came to a staircase and descended down it.

Chapter Ten

"Under no circumstances should anyone attempt the first activation of a loremaster implant without expert guidance. The risk to the mental health of the novice loremaster is too great." – Juliette Mirovar, loremaster of the Order of Thoth.

* * *

Minneapolis, September 10th, 10:15:34

A thick gray fog appeared in a cloud around the chapel.

Louise Wesson did a double take, then shouted on broadcast. "Abort mission. All squad leaders in the chapel, abort mission. Immediate exfil to recovery sites."

There was no response from anyone in the chapel. What the hell was it? The fog, or gas, or whatever it was, had appeared from nowhere. One second there was nothing, the next there was a circular cloud of gray mist a hundred and fifty yards across centered on the chapel.

Louise shifted her comms link to the three squads in the drains, and commanded, "Mike, November, Oscar squad leaders: Sitrep!"

The Mike squad leader responded from his position in the stormwater drains, "Operational, no hostiles, all systems green." The November and Oscar squad leaders responded with the same words.

"Hold your positions," she ordered. "Hostiles in your area are imminent. Fire at will."

She looked across her monitors, ten squads had entered the chapel. Hotel, India, and Juliette had hit the west side of the hall through the windows and were all dead. Their life signs flatlined on the displays. Delta, Echo, Foxtrot, and Golf squads had hit the east side of the hall. Of the sixteen men, seven were dead, but the other nine were still in the green.

Alpha, Bravo, and Charlie squads were mostly intact, bar the man lost from Bravo as they descended upon the tower at the beginning of the battle, and one of the Charlie squad guards who'd just flatlined. One of the Alpha squad's life signs remained compromised, he was bleeding out, and without assistance, he was a certain casualty.

Twenty-two men were dead or as good as, and eighteen were still alive from the forty who'd assaulted the Order conclave. She shook her head, over half her forces were dead after first contact with the enemy, and there was no way to tell what the fog was doing to the survivors.

She called up the Kilo and Lima squad leaders. She needed to position her reserves to support the guards in the stormwater drains.

Her men had lifted a manhole cover at the edge of a parking lot outside the reach of the gray fog allowing direct access into the stormwater drains. The two reserve squads were in MRAPs and were approaching the parking lot from a staging area off-site. They would take a pair of crawlers with them into the drains. The tracked ground drones were the size of a large dog and could carry a heavy load. These ones carried belt-fed grenade launchers armed with anti-personnel gas grenades. A sniff of the gas produced instant nausea, rendering anyone struck by it incapable of combat for minutes afterward.

Louise ordered Lima squad down the manhole with their crawler. Their mission was simple, block the west drain with anti-personnel gas. She ordered Kilo squad to reinforce November squad at the north exit point facing onto the Mississippi River. They would use their gas to create another wall. Her strategy would push any escapees toward Mike squad and their sentry gun covering a one-hundred-and-forty-foot corridor that provided access to the eastern exit.

Mike squad was covering the longest stretch in the drain network near the chapel. There was nowhere to hide in front of their sentry gun, it would be a shooting gallery for anyone foolish enough to approach it.

She checked her flier drones. They were hovering in a swarm at an intersection southwest of the chapel cellar entrance, ready to push anyone entering the drains from the cellar toward the kill zone in front of Mike squad's sentry gun.

Kilo and Lima squads would be in the drains with their crawlers in under two minutes. Louise glowered at her screens for a brief moment, a lot could happen in two minutes.

A heartfelt sob came over the tactical link. There was a burst of crying, and then a third voice whimpered, and cried softly, "Mommy!"

Louise's hand flew to her mouth, her eyes widened, what on Earth was in that mist?

One of the Alpha squad members staggered out of the fog south of the chapel. He'd already pulled off his tactical helmet and was rubbing his eyes. He shook his head, straightened, and backed away from the mist. He put his tactical helmet back on.

Louise made a direct call over her tactical comms link, "Harrison. What the hell happened?"

The man stood in the parking lot, staring into the fog, a pair of MRAPs with the reserve squads pulling into position forty yards back from him. His voice came over the comms link, low and steady, "It's the mist, Ma'am … it's … it's hell in there."

"What do you mean?" Louise asked. How was she going to get the rest of her men out of there? Dark memories of the warehouse on the Boston docks flooded her mind.

Not again.

An alarm trilled. The fliers had discovered a target in the stormwater drains.

A second alarm buzzed. General Maze was opening another video call.

She flipped screens, damn this battle was evolving fast.

* * *

Campbell West pulled the manhole cover back into place above him and dropped to the concrete maintenance walkway in the stormwater drain.

A perfect rendition of pitch-black darkness filled the drains. Campbell lifted his smartphone and flicked on the lamp facility. A cone of pale light lit up the drains to his left, he swung his phone to the right, the drains looked the same in either direction. He wished he was packing a pair of Order nightglasses, but why on Earth would he have needed them today?

"Where's the nearest freaking exit?" he whispered to himself.

He shook his head, why wasn't there signage down here? How much would it cost for the city to put a few helpful signs in the stormwater system to help anyone lost in it? The city was obviously staffed with a crowd of penny-pinching assholes who couldn't see past their morning cafe lattes to discover what really needed doing.

Campbell sniffed, at least no one was chasing him. He would treat the drains like a maze, just keep one wall to his left at all time, and sooner or later he'd discover a manhole or a stormwater outlet, and he'd be free.

He set off to his left, westward from the cellar entrance, it was as good a choice as any.

The conclave had turned to shit. Calvin Woodstock was dead, and it looked like most of the loyal force leaders, their best warriors, and the loremasters had died too.

It was a complete disaster.

Mirovar's followers had come armed and had fared much better, perhaps most of them would survive. Would they come hunting him? They would judge him as someone who would thwart their traditionalist ways. He would have to spend the rest of his life looking over his shoulder for an attack from the Mirovar faction.

Fighting the vampires was a lost cause. With Calvin Woodstock dead, the legacy of Ramin Kain was kaput. The traditionalists had won, and the Order was finished as an effective fighting force. Oh, Campbell could rebuild it, but it would take time, and it would be laborious finding people with the right skills, and the capability to appreciate his natural flair for leadership.

He shook his head. No, events had gone too far, there was no coming back from what had just happened. Perhaps the smartest thing to do was find a vampire and throw in the towel, share some blood and join the winning side. It was certainly better than dying as part of a lost cause. His nose twitched in disgust, what was the sense in belonging to a group of losers anyway?

It was finally time to start looking out for number one.

A hum came from the darkness in front of him. Campbell paused, lifted his smartphone higher, extracting another yard of illumination along the drain. The hum grew into a high-pitched whine and split. It sounded like a hive of wasps was coming right for him. He prepared to ramp, stilling his mind. A quad-copter micro-drone emerged from the darkness.

Behind it was a swarm.

Campbell dropped into silence, ramped, and whirled around.

An ear-splitting whine filled his ears, the swarm was almost upon him.

He blurred forward, rounded the first corner, he took a second, then a third.

A 7.62mm mini-gun opened up thirty feet in front of him. It was too late to change his forward momentum. The heavy slugs plowed into him. In a fraction of a second, the burst of fire ripped him in half.

He fell face first into the water filling the bottom quarter of the drain.

Campbell West, self-styled future leader of the Order of Thoth, bled out before he could drown.

* * *

The last of the surviving Order dropped to the concrete pathway beneath the cellar entrance.

The electric rip of a mini-gun firing faded away in front of them.

"Damn it – the east exit is guarded," Anton whispered to Li. "They're covering the drains."

Li frowned and whispered over her shoulder. "Begs the question of who they just took out."

"Wasn't one of us," Anton observed, fitting his nightglasses. The pitch dark vanished, the drains appearing in stark outlines of grays and blacks. The survivors were in bad shape. Only Anita Chang remained of the Australians. The Prospector was gone. One of the Maoris was supporting his brother who'd taken a round in the hip and was trailing blood, a bright line of white fire running down the back of his left leg. Everyone was standing close behind Li, Anton, Peter, and Chiara, as they were the only ones who were wearing nightglasses.

"Oh, well. It doesn't matter," Li observed. "We've got to get past them. Are you fully recovered from whatever happened when Jon accessed the Metaframe?"

The agonizing torment had evaporated as quickly as it had arrived. The presence of the Metaframe for a second or two had been debilitating. It was not lost on Anton that the Metaframe hadn't affected anyone else, but he had no explanation for what had happened. The pain was just an unpleasant memory now, he was ready for whatever might come next. He'd followed Li into the drains. He glanced back at the other survivors, then whispered, "Sure, good to go, but what about the other escape routes?"

Li glanced back at him. "If they're covering the east exit, they will be covering all of them." She shook her head. "This is a huge mess. They knew about the conclave, they've had time to position forces to cover off escape paths, they even sent in some newly enhanced troopers that are nearly as fast as we are, and how did they shoot? They were incredibly accurate."

"It will be new tech," Anton noted.

"Certainly, and we need to find out what it is."

"Agreed, but not now. Now, we have got to get out of here."

"And then what? The Panopticon will pick us up as soon as we hit the streets."

Francis, Justin, and the two Taylors came up behind them. Francis whispered urgently, "What's the holdup? Sounded like a mini-gun going off."

"There's one covering the east exit," Anton stated. "That's our preferred way out, as it's the farthest from the chapel."

"Preferred?" Francis asked. "You had this scouted. When were you going to tell us about it?"

Anton shrugged. "Well—"

"Wait," Li warned, putting her hand on his arm. A hum emerged out of the gloom in front of them, it increased in pitch. "Drones. Fliers. Lots of—"

"Francis, give me the White Dragon," Anton snapped.

Francis hesitated.

"You can't see."

Francis thrust the handle of the sword forward. Anton took it in his left hand, his right shot to his shoulder, grasped the Blue Dragon and drew it free. He whirled, dived deep into silence, blurring forward into the twilight world within the drain.

The hum flared into a hard whine.

It remained unspoken, if any of the drones got past Anton, then Li, Chiara, and Peter were the final line of defense. The rest of the Mirovar allies were blind without nightglasses. Fighting against human fighters while blindfolded was a common Order training technique for coping with a dark environment, but against a swarm of drones – you had to be able to see to survive.

Anton's friends were in danger, a fell alloy of sadness and rage surged like a dark fire through him. His chest tightened, he wanted to scream, but that was beyond his power as the Ramp took him. He wouldn't let another one of them die. He wasn't going to lose anyone, not today, not ever.

Not while he was still breathing.

Anton stood in the middle of the drain, the water lapping at his ankles, the two magnificent blades swirled, accelerated, and vanished.

* * *

Michael Michaelson was the squad leader for the Mike squad guarding the eastern exit.

One of the terrorists from the chapel had conveniently committed suicide by running into the sentry gun's kill zone. He lay in two halves at the bottom of the stormwater drain. The water was not quite deep enough to cover his body. Michaelson scanned a readout on the heads-up-display on the edge of his visor. The sentry gun had dropped from five hundred rounds to four hundred and sixty. There was still plenty of ammo left to deal with anyone else coming through the drains. He flicked the tactical comms link to his team's channel and inquired, "Status?"

Mortimer and Maguire were guarding the team's rear. They stood thirty yards deeper into the drain network, and could easily rush forward to reinforce Sander, and himself at the sentry gun.

"All quiet back here boss," Mortimer replied.

"Wait a second … no, we've got company," Maguire said, his voice was surprised, but not alarmed."

Michaelson asked, "Who is—"

A voice cut across the tactical link, "Be calm guards. General Maze has assigned us to reinforce your position."

Four figures in matt-black armor, armed with M249 light machine guns and a variety of edged weapons emerged from the gloom. Mortimer and Maguire followed them. It was the team they'd trained with all week. The super-enhanced special forces who reported directly to general Maze. The general and Ms. Wesson had called them praetorians. It seemed a strange name, archaic, but it had caught on within the guards.

The closest tilted his head at Michaelson and instructed him. "You will report directly to me for the remainder of the mission. Please, contact your commanding officer for confirmation."

Michaelson flicked his comms link to the command network and stated, "Ma'am, a squad of general Maze's praetorians have arrived, and are requesting tactical command."

There was the briefest of hesitations, then Wesson replied, "It's confirmed, your men and yourself will report to general Maze's forces for the duration of the battle."

"Yes, Ma'am," Michaelson replied and looked hard at the praetorian. "Sir, we're at your disposal."

The praetorian nodded and said, "Hold your position. We'll see how this situation develops."

Michaelson turned away; things were getting weird.

* * *

Anton emerged from his ramp.

The detritus of the drone swarm littered the drain. One was nearly intact; its propellers twitching in fits and starts. Anton crushed it beneath his boot as he stepped out of the drain, and returned to the team. He handed the White Dragon back to Francis and slid the Blue Dragon back into its scabbard.

He whispered, "Does anyone have an idea for getting past the sentry gun?"

"Could you use a grenade?" Peter asked.

"You've got a grenade?" Anton asked, shocked. "You never said."

Peter looked nonplussed for a moment, then shrugged his shoulders, and observed quietly. "I've always got a grenade somewhere nearby." He pulled a pale-green anti-personnel grenade from his jacket pocket. "I picked up this little beauty at the safe house in Reykjavík. You never know when you might need one."

"How long is the fuse?" Anton asked.

"Four seconds," Peter replied, handing the grenade to Anton.

"Anton," Li warned. "The sentry gun will fire at you."

"That's what I'm counting on," he called out quietly to the rest. "Follow me, but stay back. I'll need some room."

Chiara broke away from the group, caught up with Anton and said urgently, "Don't attempt this, there must be another way."

He shook his head.

"Why are you taking all the risks?" she asked angrily.

Anton half turned, putting his right hand on her shoulder. "I'm on point here. The team needs Li to lead them out of these drains, she's the one who knows the way. Do you think I'm going to ask Peter or yourself to do a job I can do? Forget about it … hey, if it doesn't work out, you can toss a coin with Peter, 'cause you're next in line."

Anton increased the pressure on Chiara's shoulder pushing her back toward the rest of the team. He let her go, pulled the pin on the grenade, and blurred away. The drain zigged left, then right, coming up on a 'T' intersection. The sentry gun would be either left or right down the other drain. There was no way to surprise a piece of machinery that was simply waiting for the next target to show up. He would have to rely on speed and moving in a way the sentry gun couldn't handle.

If that was possible?

The entrance to the intersection was another thirty feet in front of Anton. He reached deep, power flooding through him, hitting top speed as he entered the intersection.

The opposite wall loomed before him. Light flashed to his right. His hand flicked the grenade at the light source. Bullets whipped just behind him. He rotated mid-air, hit the far wall, the shock of impact rippling through his bones. He squatted deep into a crouch, his forward momentum washing away. A stream of bullets swung toward him. He launched himself over them, flying back into the drain, and out of the line of fire.

The gun swiveled back, the stream of bullets chasing the space he'd just vacated.

Anton hit the bottom of the drain, stormwater splashing wildly as he rolled to his feet.

* * *

It may be bright daylight above, but it was cool and dark in the drains.

Tamsah al Ramil, aka 'the Sand Crocodile,' had rested in the shadows listening to the battle above. There were many heartbeats, but fewer than before. The truth speaker was amongst the survivors, he'd know the beat of her heart anywhere, but for how much longer would she survive? There were many of the strange new Shadowstone troopers closing in, as well as machines, crawlers and fliers, and worst of all – vampires.

She needed his assistance.

Four of Crane's praetorians had reinforced the squad in front of him. He'd picked up their trail within the stormwater drains and shadowed them. They were oblivious to his presence. The alloy forged from vampire blood and Red Empire Ninjitsu of the second rank was a strong one.

The information he'd torn from Rose, the Shadowstone operative in New Jersey, had led him to this place and time. It was a sign of Providence, a power greater than himself had brought him here – a power who'd designed a single purpose for his strange half-life as a vampire.

He must protect the truth speaker.

Clad in close-fitting dark clothes, he stepped away from the wall, a blackened twelve-inch tri-bladed knife in each hand. The weapons seemed simple enough, but the twisted blades would gouge a wound that was near impossible to suture closed. In the hands of a Ramp master vampire trained to the second rank of the Red Empire – they were dire weapons of mass destruction.

There were four of the new troopers and the four praetorians between the truth speaker and safety. He would test the strength of their faith and introduce them to the full meaning of justice.

Tamsah emerged from the shadows, his feet padding silently along the concrete pathway. Two of the troopers were on the edge of the group, the outermost one turned toward the drain. Tamsah was sure no one had heard him, no, the man was simply checking behind him for a threat.

It was a perfectly reasonable thing to do, and completely useless.

Tamsah's left hand blurred forward and up. The point of his tri-bladed knife entered the man's throat just above his Adam's apple and exited out through his brain stem. Death was instantaneous, and the trooper started to wobble at the knees.

Tamsah was already beyond him, his second strike running through the back of the next trooper, taking out his aorta where it connected with the heart. A rope of blood followed his blade out of the man's body as his right hand flashed back.

The first man was still standing, dead on his feet. The second swayed forward an inch, blood rushing from his heart into his chest cavity.

The sentry gun began firing, a moment later, a grenade exploded next to it. The ammunition in the drum magazine started cooking off, then detonated all at once. The blast threw the last two troopers through the air into the knot of praetorians. The two men and the four vampires became starkly outlined silhouettes against the blinding glare.

Tamsah hissed, the sudden light searing his eyes. He squeezed them shut, they'd heal soon enough, and he didn't need the light to fight.

Four hot pieces of metal had lodged in his left shoulder, left chest, and left thigh. The pain was nothing before the fire of Tamsah's faith. He blurred forward into the midst of the flailing vampires, his dark tri-bladed knives striking deep and true.

The echoes of the ammunition explosion faded away as the bodies slumped around him. Tamsah emerged from the silence of a deep ramp, the gushing of blood from death wounds and the lapping of the disturbed stormwater in the drain the only sounds nearby.

Her path is clear.

He leaped to the nearest walkway and vanished into the dark.

* * *

"I think we can afford some light," Li suggested, switching on the lamp function of her smartphone.

Her nightglasses automatically adapted to the increase in illumination, the world snapping out of thermal blacks and grays into full color. The sentry gun lay scattered over a thirty-foot wide area. Beyond the blast were bodies lying in pools of dark blood. More smartphones switched on, and in a handful of seconds, the drain was well lit.

Francis ordered, "Chiara, Peter, guard our rear approaches. Anton slip forward and see if there is anything coming from the east. Li what do you see here?"

"Bodies. Shadowstone troopers killed by the blast, wait … there's more. Praetorians! Four vampires, and another two guards killed with an edged weapon of some sort."

Peter whispered harshly as he moved to cover their rear, "I found West, he's over here."

"And over there too," Chiara said quietly, pointing behind where Peter stood.

"Someone else is here," Justin murmured, his towering frame moving in close beside Li. "Those strikes are expert Red Empire technique."

"The Red Empire here?" Francis asked, incredulously. "What's the chance of that happening? How could they know to be here today?"

Justin shook his head, his mane of thick, curly hair a dark halo around his face. "I can't explain it, but someone who trained with the Red Empire killed these vamps and the Shadowstone troopers."

Li moved forward, one of the troopers was slumped against the wall. He'd taken a knife through the upper chest. It had cut his aorta free from his heart. Death would have been mercifully quick. She reached for his tactical helmet. It had the look of brand-new equipment straight off the factory floor. There was something about the helmet that drew her. Here was the secret of Shadowstone's new accuracy in the chapel hall, and their capacity to have a squad target the same opponent at the same time. Such coordination couldn't be human, there was a system involved, and everything she knew about computers and networks screamed it was the Panopticon.

Somehow, the trooper's assault rifles, no, these were shorter barreled, they were carbines. A brief smile flitted across Li's face. Peter's skill set was rubbing off on her. The carbines connected wirelessly with the tactical helmet, and from there to the Panopticon. GPS would be in the mix; super-accurate ground-penetrating GPS, the very latest in satellite technology would pinpoint the target, gun, and squad. All the trooper had to do was point and pull the trigger, the system would do the rest.

It all made sense. Why? Because it was precisely how she would have designed a system to connect a shooter with the Panopticon. A wave of disappointment welled through her; she should have anticipated this advance. She sighed and let it go. Spilled milk as her father would say.

But still? Li lifted the tactical helmet carefully, ensuring she deactivated all recording devices. She frowned, her eyes widened, and she declared with sudden urgency, "We need to hack this and hack it now."

Francis and Justin nodded, and Francis said, "We're flying blind here. We need to get out, and we have no situational awareness of Shadowstone's forces, or if there are more praetorians down here. If you can do something, do it."

Li pulled her backpack off and lifted her laptop out of it. Her laptop fired up in seconds, and she ran a set of programs. Several seconds ticked by, then she said quietly, "It's no good. No protocols are matching, I need something stronger than my laptop to breach the defenses on this helmet." She looked hard at Francis. "I need Joan Lewis' implant."

Francis' eyes widened. "No, Juliette was adamant. It's too dangerous without proper guidance."

Li shrugged her shoulders and lifted her hands wide. "Are there any other loremasters left?"

Justin looked up from his smartphone and said, "Patrick Wichowski has landed at JFK airport. He can assist with Panopticon cover, but he can only provide a fifteen-minute window of opportunity to escape, he asked if any of the other loremasters survived, as the loremaster network was silent. If he had another loremaster at this end, he can double the window duration and broaden the effect to the whole of Minneapolis."

"Thirty minutes of cover," Li declared, her eyes flashing. "The whole city. We could split up; our chances of escape will go way up."

Francis looked hard at her and noted. "I'm not happy with this Li. You're risking madness. Are you sure there's no other way?"

"Yes. This is the only way," Li affirmed, glancing back and forth between Justin and Francis. "I'm the only one here who could attempt it. No one else has a hope in hell of making this work."

Justin put one of his big hands on her shoulder and cautioned her. "This is too risky."

Li shook her head. "No, what's too risky is not seizing this opportunity. We may never get another one like it. The way those troopers were shooting at us, it was too accurate. They had help, the simplest way would be to hook their rifle up to the Panopticon somehow, and I'm sure these new tactical helmets are part of a system to do just that. There is a real chance we can find out where the Panopticon is by hacking one of them right now and tracking the GPS data."

Francis looked at her, blinked and sighed.

"We get to escape, and we find out where the Panopticon is," Li asserted.

Francis pressed his lips into a thin line for a moment, then said in a voice filled with reserve, "Okay. Do it."

Li pulled Joan Lewis's laptop out of her backpack. The implant remained taped to the laptop lid. She peeled the implant away from the top of the laptop and fired the computer up. The only way to log into the computer was to insert the implant into her right forearm. The implant's nanotechnology would do the rest.

The laptop came online. Li rolled up her right sleeve and hesitated briefly, *Will this send me insane?*

Li blinked slowly, she had to do it. She was the only one who could. The implant resembled a small-bore rifle bullet, but slimmer and longer. She pressed it against the inside of her right forearm, exactly where Juliette had instructed her to place it. Gleaming tendrils emerged from the tip of the implant and dived into her flesh, dragging the implant after them. She gasped suddenly, no one had mentioned how much it would hurt.

The implant burrowed deep into her arm, attaching itself to the largest nerve it could find. It activated in full, the laptop pinged, automatically logging her in. Every program was available, silent tendrils of connectivity reaching out to every device within a mile of the loremaster laptop.

The technology was pervasive, comprehensive, every link to another device providing a potential conduit to a broader set of networks. In moments, she'd reached the loremaster quantum encrypted cloud and the full reach of all the available networks it touched upon.

The Panopticon hove into view, a vast non-localized web of hundreds of millions of devices. No wonder no one knew where it was in the real world. Its network presence was thoroughly decentralized, impossible to track back from the loremaster cloud to its source.

Li reached with her mind toward the tactical helmet sitting on the concrete pathway next to her. A beam of light emanated from her laptop, caressing the side of the tactical helmet. Nothing happened, she didn't have the right key, at least, not yet. She pushed harder, the laptop pulled in more resources, sending the cryptography of the tactical helmet into the loremaster cloud, recruiting hundreds, then thousands, then tens of thousands of servers worldwide into the effort of cracking the key.

A heartbeat later, the helmet gave up its secrets, and her attacks penetrated its outer defenses. But, where was the information? Where was the situational awareness? Where was the true location of the Panopticon?

She had to wear it, she had to experience it.

"Damn it, I need to put it on," Li whispered, lifting the tactical helmet and placing it on her head. The impact was immediate. In her enhanced state, the information flowed at rates a normal human could never process, images, maps, disposition of forces, all flowed across her visor. Her eyes flicked left and right a dozen times in a second.

She dragged the helmet from her head and threw it with all her strength at the nearest wall. It shattered into a dozen pieces. "The Panopticon is in

Utah, and we're almost surrounded. There's a new general, Clayton Maze in charge of Shadowstone, and the new troopers, they're enhanced with a serum – they're called the Day Guard." She pointed to the concrete floor. "They know we're here. The helmet activated a beacon when I put it on. We have to leave now. The exit is east."

Francis waved his hand high. "The eastern exit, follow Li, she knows the way."

Li picked up both laptops, put them into her backpack, and headed down the maintenance path next to the drain. A moment later, she caught up with Anton, who was guarding the forward perimeter. He fell in beside her, and they led the rest of the Order forward through the stormwater drains, Chiara and Peter forming a rearguard.

Li kept her eyes forward, watching the gloom evaporate beneath the power of her nightglasses. There were voices, dark, seductive voices, whispering at the shadowed edges of her mind. She took a deep breath and let it out slowly. What price would she pay for this power?

Power always extracted payment, and nothing came for free.

She ran on, they were over a mile from the exit into the alleyway.

* * *

Sam Mortimer's tactical helmet registered a life sign.

Mortimer's life signs had flatlined about two minutes before. Louise would be very surprised if Mortimer had suddenly come back from the dead. The fact that Mortimer's resting heart rate was normally in the mid-forties, and whoever was wearing his helmet had a heart rate of thirty beats per minute convinced her that Mortimer was, without a doubt, still dead.

She quickly observed for the benefit of the command center's recording systems. "Looks like Mortimer is still alive."

Louise scanned the other readouts. The helmet's forward-facing camera displayed a blank picture, deactivated by whoever had picked the helmet up. The new life signs flatlined after four heartbeats, and the helmet's transponder cut out half a second later.

"No, false alarm."

Their location was clear, the survivors from the conclave hall were right on top of Mike squad's sentry gun position. General Maze's four praetorians were casualties. They'd reinforced the squad less than a minute before they were all killed, and they'd died quickly. The whole position went from alive to dead in less than two seconds.

There had to be another player in the mix. Someone had conducted a surprise attack from the eastern drains. No video had captured the assailant, and whoever it was remained a mystery.

Louise put the question of who'd killed Mike squad and the praetorians aside. Adding Mike squad to the casualty list from the chapel hall, she'd lost twenty-six men from her total force of sixty. From the helmet camera footage, it appeared the Order had lost more than twenty-six personnel. Achieving a better than one for one casualty rate against the Order of Thoth was unprecedented.

With the loss of much of the leadership cadre of the Order, the vampires would deem the battle a victory. A victory that had seeded their eventual defeat. One of the Order operatives had compromised the helmet for just under ten seconds. Plenty of time for someone smart to comprehend the location of the Panopticon. Li Wu had lived up to her reputation and seized the opportunity Louise had provided.

Now her strategy was in motion.

Louise would have to write a report on the battle, it would need to align with all the available physical evidence, but she could shape the interpretation of what had happened. She scanned the helmet camera video logs. Three of the Alpha squad had survived the battle, their life signs were still in the green. They'd fought at the front of the hall, just inside the front doors. She slowed the replay of the squad leader's helmet camera. His team had finished the destruction of the Order on the right side of the hall and were swinging their weapons to fresh targets on the left side.

She zoomed in on the video and froze it, four figures were barely visible near the back of the melee. Even from the rear, it was easy to pick out Peter Lamb and Li Wu, Anton Slayne was just behind them, wearing a gray hooded jacket, plus another young woman with a long plait of dark hair.

On Anton's left was another man; middle-aged, who looked like he was an indigenous American. He was remarkable for not having a weapon. He stood frozen beside the wall. Was he immobilized by terror or was it something else? She stepped the video forward, frame by frame. A bullet ricocheted off the wall a couple of inches above the man's head, and he didn't even flinch – it wasn't terror holding him still. His lips were moving, rainbows emanating from a source outside the frame strobed through the hall, and then suddenly – the mist was everywhere. Alpha team's squad leader dropped to the floor, the camera feed following him down in a dizzying arc.

What on Earth were the rainbow lights in the hall just before the mist appeared? Clearly, the colored lights and the mist were somehow linked, but how were they associated with the native American. He was the only one not fighting and assuming the mist had a cause, he was the only person in the room who could be a candidate for causing it. She would have to study all the other helmet cams to see if any had recorded the light source from a better angle.

A chill slipped up Louise's spine. Was this something she was never meant to know about, another secret like the existence of vampires? She would have to mention the rainbows and the mist within her report, but she'd be careful not to draw any conclusions. It would be a case of 'something strange happened,' cause 'unknown.' It would be best to suppress any expression of curiosity in the report.

It was time to close out the battle. The Mirovar force team still needed to escape, but there was nothing Louise could do to assist them. She'd prosecute the battle to the full extent of her force's capabilities. Anything less would risk exposing her to the vampires.

She'd reinforced the other squads in the drains with her reserves, ground drones, and two squads of four praetorians. They were all pushing to the east. They were her hammer, now she needed an anvil at the exit she'd scouted.

General Maze had forbidden the use of explosives. That order was still in effect. No nightfalcons or blackwidows had been released for this mission. She did have two full swarms of anti-personnel micro-drones. A hundred units in each, all under Panopticon control. She tapped a screen; the drones were on their way. The Order survivors would have to fight their way clear if they were going to escape. Given the loss of the swarm in the drains, it was clear the Order could defend themselves from micro-drones, but they were the only weapon she could position in time to have an effect.

General Maze's prohibition against explosives and the withholding of helicopter attack gunships was materially impacting the course of the mission. She wondered for a moment if he would admit to that. Of course, he wouldn't, but the general's order had assisted her own strategy.

Her attention returned to the chapel. The lone member of Alpha Squad to emerge from the mist stood twenty yards back from it. He'd managed to extract himself from the mist, perhaps he could assist others to do the same. Louise called him, "Harrison, re-enter the mist and effect retrieval of our casualties."

"Negatory, Ma'am."

She frowned briefly. "Did you misunderstand my order?"

"No, Ma'am. No can do – I'll just become another casualty once I enter the mist."

Louise paused briefly, then nodded. "Understood. Watch the perimeter of the mist. Report any changes, and assist anyone else who emerges."

"Copy that."

The gray mist continued to envelop the old chapel. She wondered how long it would last. How long it would be before she could extract her surviving troops from whatever was trapping them inside the mist?

A series of alarms blared. A dozen screens crashed, the displays vanishing to white points, before winking out altogether.

"Oh, shit!" Louise whispered.

Someone was attacking the Panopticon network.

* * *

Francis pulled himself through the manhole into bright sunlight and crisp autumn air.

He'd insisted on making sure the rest of the survivors exited the drains first. Peter returned the manhole cover back into position and stamped it down with his boots.

Li looked up from her loremaster laptop and assessed the situation. They were in an alleyway between a pair of factories in a light industrial area two miles east of the old chapel. The wounded were resting beside a dumpster. Chiara and Samuel Taylor were tending bullet wounds with wads and strips of torn cloth. Fortunately, no one needed immediate surgery, and they would be able to make good their escape.

Justin Blake's loremaster, Patrick Wichowski, was running a Panopticon cover campaign from a lounge cubical at JFK airport. His international flight had landed less than ninety minutes before. Li didn't want to think what the consequences might have been if his flight had run late. Patrick had started coverage for their escape two minutes earlier.

Malfunctioning micro-drones cutoff from the Panopticon by Patrick's attack littered the alleyway.

Francis slapped his forehead and swore, "C'est un foutu bordel! The other loremasters, their bodies are in the hall. We'll have to go back."

Li shook her head. "We'd have to fight our way in versus an unknown number of Day Guard troopers and praetorians."

"Their loremaster implants and laptops, there are three of them back in the hall. The vampires will seize them tonight."

Li frowned. "Those laptops are quantum encrypted, it would take millennia to break into them, and besides which only a Ramp master could use the implants."

"Crane and Armitage are both Ramp masters, what if they used the implants?"

"Would the implants even work in a vampire?" Anton asked, stepping forward to join the conversation.

"I don't know, but I don't like giving them the opportunity to try. Imagine if Crane or Armitage had a precognitive ability, it'd be a nightmare."

"Nightmare or not," Anton observed, his eyes narrowing. "Why didn't they blow us up with a five-hundred-pound bomb dropped from a shadowstar drone? They wanted the loremasters all along. That's why they just used troopers. Did you see the under-barrel grenade launchers they had on their guns? They never used them, no grenades, no explosives, and no bombs."

Francis' face fell and he shook his head. "It's a catastrophe."

"Oh? I don't know about that," Anton offered, a grim smile curling the edges of his mouth. "Shadowstone smashed Kain's cabal, and we know where the Panopticon is. Now we have a real target, and what's the bet we can find Crane's citadel from within the Panopticon?"

Peter answered from behind Li's shoulder, "I'd put money on that."

Francis shook his head again – the loss of the loremaster technology to the vampires was a foregone conclusion.

Anton proposed, "What looks like a defeat now has laid the groundwork for victory."

"That remains to be seen Anton," Francis asserted disconsolately, "and we lost good people today."

Anton caught Francis' gaze with a knowing look. "Yes, we did, but no one ever promised there wouldn't be sacrifices on this journey."

Francis' eyes went flat and hard for a moment, then he blew through his lips, and shrugged. "So, be it."

Li stated, "I'm initiating the combined assault on the Panopticon network. We'll have about twenty-five minutes of city-wide coverage."

Justin approached and affirmed, "I'll make sure everyone else gets home, my cousins are both wounded, and Jon is defenseless. He won't be able to ramp for weeks."

Francis nodded and shook Justin's hand. "I understand. Good luck with your journey."

Justin held Francis' hand for a moment longer, and said, "Good luck with your mission, if you need help, my team will be south of you."

"I hope you don't regret that offer."

"Never."

Anita Chang walked over; her face drawn with grief. "I'll leave with Justin, and make my way back to Australia. There's no one left back home, except a couple of wild talents who imagine themselves to be vigilantes." Her eyes hardened. "I'll have to get them organized."

Luck was wished, and goodbyes said, half a minute later the Mirovar force team stood alone in the alleyway.

Francis looked hard at his team, his gaze lingering briefly on Peter and Chiara before moving on. "Our mission is to destroy the Panopticon. We have to act quickly before the vampires realize we've discovered the secret of its location. Are you with me?"

Peter grinned. "Hell yes, Boss."

Jay nodded; his eyes fierce.

Anton said, "Count me in Francis."

"And me too," Chiara said, firmly.

Li paused, looked up from her laptop, glanced briefly at Chiara, and said, "Let's do it."

Francis nodded and said, "Then let's find some transport." He strode forward down the alleyway, the rest of the team fanning out behind him.

Li closed her laptop; it would keep running as she moved with the team. Her eyes unfocused as uncountable network nodes stretched into infinity within her heightened awareness. She stumbled on a fallen drone. A strong arm flashed around her waist, and a deep voice said, "Do you need some help?"

"Yes, thanks – I'm going to be distracted for the next half hour."

"Then lean on me as we go, and I'll watch out for you."

She did, and Peter did, but on the edges of her mind, in the gloom and shadows at the far edges of the light, an insistent voice murmured and waited for her.

A voice filled with dreadful intent.

Chapter Eleven

"We have the skins of vampires and the minds of men." – Cornelius Crane, King of the Vampires

* * *

Matahat al Diydan, The Caucasus Mountains, September 11th, 05:45

The Red Empire citadel had returned to Matahat al Diydan.

Dalien Morte, aka the Red Ghost, supreme leader of the Red Empire stood at the edge of an observation deck, peering into 'The Neck,' a sandy pit ninety feet below him. The pit was a deadly location within the maze of worms for which the citadel was named.

An adult Olgoi Khorkhoi was lying on the pale-yellow sand beneath the observation deck. Dalien rubbed a momentary itch on the side of his nose. The beast reared up, its thin rust-colored cowl expanding around its gaping maw. The creature's throat widened, the inward pointing teeth, the size of daggers and twice as sharp, gleamed wetly in the overhead lights. Its tail rose, the foot-long barb at the end glistening with venom and quivering with threat. The worms were sightless but possessed with an ability to sense movement bordering on the supernatural.

Dalien regarded the beast. The worms were things of urban myth, but the Red Empire had owned them for more than two thousand years. They were cunning and treacherous hunters originating from the Gobi Desert. Their native intelligence, utterly inhuman, alien, remote, geared to the sole purpose of assuaging their hunger and penchant for lethal violence made them perfect for testing the warriors of the Red Empire, only the quick and clever could survive the presence of a single worm in the maze.

In the thirty-eighth year of his life, to reach the third rank, Dalien had bested three adult worms. Like his daughter, Chiara Morte, a prodigious talent who'd conquered three worms in the maze four days after her ninth birthday. A week later, he'd sent her on her first, and so far, only mission – to take over the Order of Thoth from the inside.

A mission obsoleted by events, the Order had been all but destroyed less than twenty-four hours earlier. Only a fool would underestimate the Red Empire's ability to infiltrate the information systems of the world, and much of Shadowstone was an open book to the Red Empire. Dalien had sufficient information at his fingertips to understand the Order had largely ceased to exist as an operational organization.

There would be some good people left. Willing fighters, the odd loremaster or traveler, but their lack of faith in the one true way had long led them astray. Now, there was naught but destruction awaiting them. The Red Empire would fill the vacuum of their demise, and confront the Vampire Dominion in a final struggle to the death.

His only concern lay with his daughter. She'd gone dark, her communication systems had been offline for the last seventeen days. He'd first tried to contact her hours after the destruction of the Jerusalem citadel. The attempt had ended in failure, a failure repeated with every attempt since then. Dalien trusted she was still alive, but for some unknown reason, she'd turned her back on her family, on her heritage, and on the Red Empire.

She was a lost sheep, he must return to the fold.

Dalien turned away from the maze. There was little he could do about his wayward daughter; he would have to wait for her to come to her senses and contact him. She belonged at his side, where he would complete her training. There was every reason to believe she would one day lead the Ramp masters.

Should he fail in his quest to gather the Metaframe artifacts together, she would be his final hope for victory.

He made his way toward the newly commissioned control center at the heart of the fortress. He wondered how Taipan and his team were progressing. Perhaps he'd been precipitous in his actions enforcing communications silence, but perhaps it was better he didn't know what was happening. It was one less distraction for Taipan and his team.

Dalien strode forward into the heart of his citadel, his footfalls little more than scuffles within the stone-walled chambers and halls of the ancient fortress.

* * *

Giant floodlights lit the busy Mediterranean seaport. The morning sun remaining a pale hint on the eastern horizon.

Taipan's eyes narrowed. Six of his elite Red Empire team carried the Special Atomic Demolition Munitions, SADMs, up the gangplank and into the freighter's hold. He watched them closely from the ship's bridge. It was essential there were no errors, there could be no mistakes. This mission was the most important he'd conducted within the fifty-four years of his life.

The weapons were Russian designed and manufactured; stolen from a Russian submarine several months earlier. They had an explosive yield of twenty kilotons, equivalent to the weapons used against Japan in the second world war. When he triggered the SADMs at the end of the mission, they would obliterate Manhattan Island with nuclear fire, and reduce New York city to a radioactive wasteland.

It was a necessary price to pay to seize the missing Metaframe artifacts and rip the heart from the Vampire Dominion. Worthy goals that sat well with Taipan's conscience. What if a couple of million people died, if their deaths cleared the way to eliminate the vampires forever? The success of this mission would save millions of future lives. The calculus of benefit was irrefutable. He would pull the trigger on the SADMs with a clear mind and heart, knowing what he did was for the greater good of humanity.

Taipan's men reached the deck of the ship, strode along the edge between the guardrails and container stacks, entering the lower decks of the aftcastle. He turned to the ship's captain and asked, "When can we leave?"

"Within the hour, Sir." The captain, an overweight, balding man, with a ream of broken blood vessels on his bulbous nose, was nearing retirement. The ten million US dollars Taipan had placed into a secret Swiss bank account would ensure it was a sweet retirement indeed. One filled with sun, beaches, copious alcohol, and willing brown-skinned young women to indulge his every appetite. The captain was oblivious to the true nature of the mission, he only knew that he had some extra passengers to take to the port of Newark in New Jersey, and he'd indicated this would be his last voyage before he disappeared from the world.

Taipan was sure the captain would never get to his island, nor would he ever spend the money in the Swiss bank account. The captain was in the last month of his life, he just didn't know it. Taipan turned away from the man and stared out at the docks and the rows of ships surrounding the freighter. The Red Empire had paid more than fifty million dollars in bribes. The money sourced from recent Red Empire embezzlement operations of several Italian, French and German banks. Of course, those officials bribed to look the other way had no idea what he was smuggling across the United States border. Every man bribed would end up dead, there would be no loose ends. The bribes were real, but the recipients would never live long enough to enjoy their betrayal of their homeland.

Taipan had seen the illusory news reports regarding the gas explosion beneath the Mount Scopus Museum. The Red Empire had lost its new citadel in Jerusalem. In accordance with standard protocol, the Red Ghost would've evacuated once the Vampire Dominion compromised the citadel's location. But where would he have taken the seat of command of the Red Empire? Most likely he would move back to the Red Empire's most secret base of operations – Matahat al Diydan. The maze of worms remained hidden deep within the eastern boundaries of the Caucasus mountains, near the Caspian Sea. Once the mission was complete, and Taipan was free to initiate communication, he would find out what had happened in detail.

A six-man fist team was already in the United States, paving the way for his arrival with the rest of his force. In three weeks' time, his men would combine into one team on the soil of the United States of America.

Shortly thereafter, they would infiltrate Crane's citadel, breach his inner sanctum, return the Metaframe artifacts to their rightful owners, and then – unleash hell upon the city of New York.

It would be as it should be unless the vampire general Chloe Armitage conducted an intervention. Was his team marching to the beat of her drum? Was this all a trap of her design? Did she stand on the periphery of events, like an eagle waiting to swoop in and claim the prize of the Key of Ahknaton?

Taipan's eyes went hard as dark river stones. He would wait and watch for her certain appearance. The premier warrior of the Red Empire promised to himself, he would be ready for the moment when Armitage made her inevitable move against his mission to recover the Metaframe artifacts and destroy the Vampire Dominion.

His eyes would be open, he'd take every precaution, he'd be ready for her.

* * *

It was late on Sunday night.

Chloe relaxed in a comfortable chair opposite James Haley. He was sitting behind his desk at Shadowstone HQ in New York City. Chloe was wearing a top-end dark-gray pants suit, offset with a scarlet chiffon blouse. James was wearing a suit and tie, with the jacket hanging on a coat rack next to his office door.

She directed the full strength of her regard on him, and asked, "What results do you have for me?"

James nodded seriously and replied, "Medical Control Systems in Tokyo looks like the primary site for Crane's research into vampire suitable implants. Their CEO and Head of Research apparently died in a murder/suicide on the twenty-third of August. That's the cover story provided by Shadowstone. It looks like Crane killed them. I have no evidence on what his motive may have been. The current Head of Research is a woman named Hana Tanaka. She will be the key person to assist with disabling your implant."

"Make contact with her and find out what she wants."

"Yes, Chloe."

"Price is no object."

James nodded once. "Understood."

"This must be done with the utmost discretion; Crane must not find out that I'm attempting to disable this implant."

James frowned slightly and remarked, "Of course, Chloe. I always operate with discretion."

Chloe tilted her head and paused for a moment. "True. My words were ... pedantic, which is not my usual style. Forgive me, James, I did not intend to imply any lack of competence on your part. To determine the source of one of Crane's more secret research facilities in under three weeks is quite an achievement."

James smiled quietly. "It's no problem, Chloe, we're a team. I share your goals."

Chloe smiled; her blue eyes bright. "Yes, we're a team." She leaned forward tapping her thumb with her finger. "We're on track with the implant issue." She tapped her forefinger. "Next, we have to deal with the chameleons. I've made contact with three of them, and they've agreed to ally with our cause. I'll need fast and effective ground and air-transport sufficient to move them from New York to anywhere in North America within twelve hours."

"That can be done, any special requirements or advice on how to handle them?"

Chloe pushed a data stick across James' desk. "Everything you need to know is in here. Just don't open the stick up on any device reachable by the Panopticon. This has to be off the network."

"Everything will be secret," James promised.

Chloe tapped her middle finger. "Uprating the defenses of the citadel and New York. What's the status?"

"I've been meeting with general Maze. He has allocated twenty day guards from the first one hundred and twenty, and another twenty-four from the rest of the force. The first five squads were deployed to Citadel defense today. Shadowstone has been stretched to the limit. Everyone is working double shifts, and all leave has been canceled. The available resources have been focused on New York and the northeast of the United States."

"Excellent," Chloe affirmed, and tapped her ring finger. "And the battle at the Order Conclave this morning. I've seen a preliminary report from Louise Wesson. What are the highlights from your perspective?"

James looked at her for a second, his fingers flashed over the keyboard in front of him, and he glanced up at a display on the wall of his office. Chloe followed his gaze.

"Watch this helmet cam video, someone we thought was dead is still alive – Li Wu."

Chloe's world spun. "She's not dead? Tamsah al Ramil cheated me." She turned back to James, tapping her lips with her finger, and staring into space. "... I never saw his body. Tell me, James, what was the report on how Maze's praetorians died?"

"Stabbed to death. Multiple strikes with an unusual spiral edged blade. They bled out faster than they could heal. Looks like an advanced practitioner of Red Empire Ninjitsu."

Chloe's full lips curled into a sardonic grin. "Well, he's still alive." She laughed. "Now there really is a Red Empire vampire on the loose."

"Excuse me?" James asked. "We're talking the same guy I dropped off with the rest of his fist team in the UK?"

Chloe shook her head once. "Don't worry about him. The Sand Crocodile's survival may be something I can use."

James looked at her silently. Chloe met his gaze and smiled softly. She knew he didn't like secrets between them. "I'll tell you about Tamsah al Ramil another time, anything else unusual to report?"

"There was a strange weather effect, a circular mist about a hundred and fifty yards across appeared around the old chapel where the conclave was held. It had a debilitating psychological effect on all of our soldiers. It vanished about eight hours later and we recovered all the day guards who survived combat without undue harm."

Chloe's lip curled, her eyes flashing with insight. "The Order has a Metaframe sorcerer. I wonder what else he can do besides call up a defensive mist? Was there anything else?"

"General Maze ordered no explosives were to be used during the battle and then descended on the site with a specialized vampire team. He collected all the Order dead and any equipment they had with them, and departed by nightfalcons back to New York."

"Crane's citadel?"

"No. Another location. A warehouse in Queens. It's a front for another research facility."

Chloe frowned for a moment and then grinned. "He's after the loremasters."

James tilted his head quizzically.

Chloe ignored James' implied question. Crane was after the loremaster technology; he'd mastered the capability to put an implant in a vampire, but only a Ramp master could utilize the loremaster technology. That meant Crane was aiming to use either Haras, or Chloe, or himself as the recipient.

Unless he had someone else.

"James," Chloe said, "I want you to keep an eye on this research facility in Queens. I need to know what Crane is doing with the Loremaster technology and how far he's progressed with it."

"Yes, Chloe."

Chloe nodded. James was an able operator. He'd earned his place in the future world she would bring into being. She would reward him for his loyalty.

It was always appropriate to reward loyalty.

She glanced at a switched off display opposite her chair. It reflected the room, and she caught her reflection. Yes, reward the loyal and punish those who betray. *But Crane will have to catch us first.*

Her plans were still alive.

* * *

White tiled floors, cream-colored walls, and forty stainless steel tables marked the large chamber as an autopsy room.

Thirty-five naked corpses lay neatly arrayed on the metal tables. Three, all women, lay flagged with black sashes draped over their chests. At the end of the room stood a long bench, covered in computer terminals and laboratory equipment. Cornelius stood at one end of the bench with his hands clasped behind his back. He leaned forward slightly, examining three laptops and a stainless-steel kidney dish holding three slim implants.

Cornelius remarked to the assembled staff, "Let's see what can be recovered from these laptops and precisely how these implants work."

"Yes, my liege," replied the lead scientist. His two staff stood quietly behind him; their pale faces impassive. All the staff in this facility were vampires, the work performed in research facility number one was of such high secrecy that he never allowed humans to enter it — at least not live ones.

There had been another massive attack on the Panopticon the previous morning, creating an outage that covered Minneapolis for just under thirty minutes. The Order's method of attack relied on disrupting the Panopticon's access to a myriad of devices ranging from mobile phones to military satellites. The Panopticon was unharmed but blinded within an area for a time.

Time enough to allow Anton Slayne and a solid cohort of the Order to escape. An Order sorcerer had appeared at the conclave, allowing some of the Order to flee the Day Guard attack on the conclave hall. Cornelius didn't need to access his precognitive powers to know Anton Slayne was still alive. The absence of his body amongst the dead was enough evidence of that. Sorcery had ensured Slayne's escape from the hall, and the surviving loremasters had enabled enough of the Order to escape Minneapolis to ensure the Order survived as a functioning, albeit small, organization.

Crane looked up from the laptops and surveyed the bodies. Most were gunshot fifteen or twenty times in the chest. The Day Guard technology had worked, his new force would tip the balance of power in his favor. More than half the Order was gone, their loremaster capabilities greatly degraded. He glanced back down at the three implants, slim, sleek, silvery metallic in appearance, but not silver. His staff would reverse engineer the technology. He would find a suitable recipient – someone hidden and utterly under his control.

There was only one person who matched that description. He would need to visit them soon and confirm they were still a suitable subject for this technology.

Cornelius said quietly, "The time of the loremasters is coming to an end."

"It is certain, my liege," remarked the lead researcher, a leer seizing his face.

Cornelius glanced at him and turned away, dismissing the man with a wave of his hand. He left the autopsy room, walking down the stark and silent halls of research facility number one. His gaze was distant, his mind preoccupied with the lack of progress in Northern China. Shen Zhen, Haras Mosule, and a combined force of twenty praetorians aided by the Chinese arm of Shadowstone had still not found the final Obsidian Claw ninja vampire.

They were tracking his kills, but he was zig-zagging over a territory more than two hundred miles across, doubling back and moving forward at will, the only constant was the overall progress to the west.

The vampire was born of Mekra's blood and was heading toward her like a summer night's moth flying toward a lantern. But how did he know where Mekra was? The location of Mekra's donjon, even her very existence, were Cornelius' most closely guarded secrets, and yet, the ninja vampire continued to progress toward her. It was deeply unsettling, but it also meant that Cornelius could narrow his search the closer the ninja vampire got to Mekra's donjon.

The only question was, would Cornelius catch him and destroy him before he reached Mekra's donjon, or would he reach Mekra's donjon and free her before Cornelius caught him?

Cornelius reached the elevators, tapping the up button. The elevator doors swished aside, and he stepped forward into the elevator chamber. He turned, the doors closing in front of him, and whispered to himself, "These new vampires will be the death of me."

The elevator rose a dozen floors to street level.

* * *

Silvery moonlight doused the night sky with a fey luminescence.

Akimitsu, the last ninja of the Obsidian Claw clan stood at a crossroads, a vast tree marking the edge of the intersection of paths. The tree was ancient, its gnarled trunk rising into the night sky, its crooked limbs reaching out like enormous fingers clutching at eternity. The crossroads lay surrounded by a plain covered in low grasses and little else. To the west loomed mountains and the heart of his destination.

A woman emerged from the base of the tree, walking gracefully toward Akimitsu. She was nearly naked, wearing only a net of fine silver chains, her eyes were pools the color of night, her skin was dark and luminous with health, her face was exquisite, a blend of innocence, wisdom, and terrifying perfection. Scimitar fangs curled down over her bottom lip, and she spoke with a voice of soft seduction, "Remain hidden, avoid those who hunt you, do not reveal your powers."

"Yes, my queen," Akimitsu answered.

"There are others you will convert to our cause, great fighters with skills such as yours. Their home is in the mountains in front of you. You will capture four, a 'Red Empire Fist,' team they are known as. They will obey my will as all will obey my will."

"Yes, my queen," Akimitsu answered a second time.

"You will continue west beyond the first mountains, there is a village near my prison, you will convert half the people there and consume the rest as food. You will bring an army to the door of my prison, and you will tear it down."

She took a step closer, laying gentle fingers on his cheek, her gaze locked with his own. "You will be my first consort, together we will bring this world into the night."

"Yes, my queen," Akimitsu answered a third time.

The woman faded away like a ghost.

But she wasn't a ghost.

Every day she visited his dreams. He could feel her in his mind, her will growing stronger as he approached her. A part of him remembered his humanity and would flee if he could, but that part of him was dying, growing cold and silent, rotting like a corpse in its grave.

Mekra was his goddess now. A bright star in an endless night. She was his one true guide. He would do as she willed – whatever she willed. With obedience had come limitless freedom.

The final shred of his humanity collapsed. Akimitsu clawed his way to the surface of the field he'd buried himself in the previous night. There was a farmhouse nearby; he would feed, and then travel far before word could spread of the deaths of the farmer and his family.

The humans smelled delicious, Akimitsu was famished, his throat dry with thirst. He stood silently in the field. Humans moved past the windows of the farmhouse, silhouetted by lamps within. He grinned, his fangs descending into attack position.

It was time to feed.

The End

The story will continue with the next instalment of The Metaframe War.

"The Crane War."

ON THE EDGE OF ANNIHILATION!

The Order of Thoth is on the verge of destruction. Arthur Slayne has returned from exile. The foremost foe of the Vampire Dominion seeks the aid of the Mirovar force team.

The secret location of the Panopticon has been revealed within a Vampire Dominion fortress of terrifying defenses. Only someone bereft of sanity would attempt to infiltrate it, or a Slayne.

Anton Slayne and his friends must defeat the might of the Vampire Dominion, but will Anton's grandfather prove to be his strongest ally, or a foe with a dark agenda more dangerous than Anton's arch-nemesis, general Chloe Armitage?